The Great Substitution

Human Effort or Jesus
to Heal and Restore the Soul?

Dedication

To my wife, Ellen, and my daughter, Karissa.

Other Books by Dieter Mulitze

The Great Omission: Resolving Critical Issues for the Ministry of Healing and Deliverance, 2001, Essence Publishing

Planned Publications

The Great Reduction: From Healing Souls to Fixing Brains
by Dieter Mulitze
Into the Heart of Deeper Love by Carsten Pellmann

Deeper Love Ministries Books are written by the Spiritual Directors of Deeper Love Ministries, Winnipeg, Manitoba, to help advance spiritual wholeness, healing, and growth in individuals based on the model and ministry of Jesus Christ. The ministry Web site is **www.deeperlove.ca**.

DIETER MULITZE, PH.D.

The Great Substitution

Human Effort or Jesus
to Heal and Restore the Soul?

Forewords by Dr. Carl E. Armerding and Dr. Brian F. Stelck

Essence

PUBLISHING

Belleville, Ontario, Canada

The Great Substitution
Copyright © 2003, Dieter K. Mulitze, Ph.D.

National Library of Canada Cataloguing in Publication

Mulitze, Dieter Konrad, 1953-
        The great substitution : human effort or Jesus to heal and restore the soul? / Dieter K. Mulitze.

Includes bibliographical references and index.
ISBN 1-55306-655-3.--ISBN 1-55306-658-8 (LSI ed.)

        1. Spiritual healing. 2. Prayer--Christianity. I. Title.

BT732.5.M84 2003   234'.131   C2003-904817-9

Essence Publishing is a Christian Book Publisher dedicated to furthering the work of Christ through the written word. For more information, contact: 20 Hanna Crt, Belleville, Ontario, Canada K8P 5J2.
                Phone: 1-800-238-6376. Fax: (613) 962-3055.
                        E-mail: info@essencegroup.com
                        Internet: www.essencegroup.com

About the Author

Dieter K. Mulitze, Ph.D., completed graduate theological studies at Regent College, Vancouver, BC, and a doctorate in quantitative genetics from the University of Saskatchewan. Dieter worked as a scientist at an international agricultural research center (ICARDA) in Syria and then was an assistant/associate professor of agronomy with the University of Nebraska while working in Morocco. Upon returning to Canada, Dieter founded a computer software company.

Responding to God's call, Dieter has become increasingly involved in the ministry of healing prayer and deliverance. He serves on several healing prayer teams in the local church and has conducted training courses and seminars on healing prayer and deliverance. In 1998 Dieter co-founded Deeper Love Ministries, Inc., a ministry for advancing spiritual wholeness, healing and growth in individuals based on the model and ministry of Jesus Christ. Dieter and his wife, Ellen, are the Spiritual Directors of Ministry Development for Deeper Love Ministries. Deeper Love Ministries conducts healing prayer conferences in the local church. Dieter is available as a speaker at churches, conferences, and other venues. Dieter has also served as adjunct faculty for Carey Theological College, Vancouver, BC. Dieter and Ellen live in Winnipeg, Manitoba. They have one daughter, Karissa.

To contact the author, e-mail: dieter@deeperlove.ca, or visit the ministry Web site at www.deeperlove.ca.

Table of Contents

Acknowledgements

Foremost, I wish to acknowledge Ellen, my faithful wife over the years and now also a partner in the ministry of healing prayer. Without Ellen's support and encouragement, this book could not have been written.

To Rev. Carsten and Rev. Linda Pellmann for much encouragement, friendship and mutual vision for the ministry of healing prayer. Additional thanks to Carsten for many hours of theological discussion and deepened understanding of the healing presence of Jesus among His people.

Special thanks to all the precious brothers and sisters in Christ who have shared their lives and their pain with me in experiencing the healing presence of Jesus.

The stories of people as recounted in this book have been written to safeguard the identity of the individuals involved. Names have been changed, along with some of the details.

To God be the glory!

Forewords

There are a couple of basic questions we are forced to answer as we walk our journey of faith. Is God unchanging, that is, do we really believe God is the same yesterday, today and tomorrow? Is the God who healed Naaman of leprosy in Elisha's time and who healed the ten lepers in Jesus' time actually unchanging? Is the work of the Spirit of God still accomplished in our day? I read the Gospel accounts of Jesus' work of bringing health to *"a man in their synagogue who was possessed by an evil (unclean) spirit"* (Mark 1:23), and I read of the man asking Jesus, *"If you can do anything, take pity on us and help us."* To which Jesus replied, *"If you can? Everything is possible for him who believes"* (Mark 9:22-23). There is great significance to the prayer of the boy's father, *"I do believe; help me overcome my unbelief!"* (Mark 9:24). That is the prayer we need for the Church today. Sadly, we have substituted our great human knowledge in place of faith, our structured learning for belief and our definitions of reality for God's revelation. God is not dead, nor has the Holy Spirit ceased to act in the same fashion as was poured out at Pentecost, or on Cornelius' household, or on the believers in Ephesus. Our God reigns and Jesus is alive; the Holy Spirit was not the one who was chained.

Having worked in East Africa over a number of years, both resident as missionary and more recently working in leadership development with African church leaders, I have seen, witnessed and experienced the gifts of the Holy Spirit being manifest in my day. Whether one describes them as apostolic gifts or just the regular gifts of the Spirit it matters not; the presence of the living God is still evident. I find it somewhat incredible that the Western Church would choose to do it all in our own strength and wisdom. Why did we make that "great substitution" and cut God out of the picture? The arrogance of the Western Church is that we can know it all and so perhaps think we can control it all—that is, of course, the secular way.

I was present one day in a conversation between a Baptist denominational leader of mine and the Bishop of the Africa Brotherhood Church, the Rev. Dr. Nathan Ngala, the leader of an independent church of some 650 congregations representing perhaps half a million people on a Sunday morning. Dr. Ngala was asked, "To what do you attribute the growth of your denomination from fourteen people in one local gathering to the size it is today?" Dr. Ngala was quiet for a moment, picked up his Bible, opened it and said, "We read God's Word and we do what it says." Who do we think we are in the West to substitute our word for the Word of God?

One of my African colleagues said to me, "The difference between you from the West and the African Christian is this: when you are sick, you go to the doctor and if you don't get well then you pray. We Africans, when we get sick, first we pray, then if we don't get well we go to the doctor." How true! We have substituted God's desire to walk with us and teach us with the science of the last few centuries. However, the evidence is in. Science is not able to give all the answers to the issues humans face. We have sold our souls for the Enlightenment view of reality, and we are into the era we call post-modernism. Not to be mistaken, I do seek appropriate medical attention where it is warranted. I also am a strong believer that God has given us brains to use for the glory of God, and medical science has brought great relief to the human condition and improved our lives. I spent years in advanced education gleaning the works of B.F. Skinner, Jung, Maslow, Freud, Rogers and was still never able to see the human mind freed from the effects of sin by any of the therapies or interventions science had developed. The secular humanists make assumptions about life that are mythical and based on a faith in the scientific method. However, when we always substitute human interventions for God's place in our lives rather than adding them as a complement, we cross over onto the path of excluding God from acting, and the Church becomes a social club. Dieter's text calls us through sound theology and practice to allow God's ways to be part of our care for souls.

We live in a dynamically changing world where the cultures of the ages are thrust together by immigration, by population shift and hence the world views in our communities are now much broader and more diverse than ever before. How do we approach the individual or community that knows for certain it is the spirit world that has caused the disruption in the physical, social or spiritual components of life? Science and great learning would substitute the limited knowledge gained by the five senses for the experience, wisdom and revelation of the ages. We allow our world views to be reshaped by CNN or Hollywood and reduce the scriptural, revealed knowledge accounts of the spiritual, or demonic or mystical to cartoon or fable. What grave danger there is in assuming that because we cannot measure a phenomenon it does not exist! How many of our scientific realities were "impossible" before they were "discovered"?

Dieter makes the point in this text of calling us to revisit the secular techniques for making people whole. Rather than buying the consumerism of faith practices that are sold to us by the world, he knowingly suggests we can actually experience the presence of the living God in our lives. In good balance he does not dismiss the need for medical attention, nor does he dismiss the positive aspects of counseling and psychiatric work. He affirms the need for spiritual discernment to hear not only the Lord speaking but also to be able to distinguish the enemy in the midst.

The text also graciously takes to task the formulaic techniques that Christian "self-help" and "how-to" books tend to place in front of the reader. Many begin to resemble magic arts texts rather than the practice of the presence of God or the waiting upon the Lord that Scripture encourages for us. Healing prayer is indeed the work of the Spirit of the Lord when we call upon Jesus to be present with us. I appreciate Dieter's clarification and critique of Theophostic ministry and his bringing of a calming approach to this somewhat controversial method. When we return our focus of healing prayer to the work and presence of Jesus, we re-establish not only a theologically appropriate base, we also turn the human method back to the Lord. I am pleased to affirm Dieter's concern that people in need and the care-giver not create a co-dependency. Part of our role in counseling and healing is to introduce the person to Jesus but not have them become dependent upon us.

This text has as one of its structural pieces a delightful way of introducing each chapter; however, this also becomes a weakness. Each chapter begins with a relevant case or illustration where the power of God has been present in this era to bring healing to various types of hurt, injury, trauma and abuse. I know God's works; I know our Lord is the great physician and I know the Spirit empowers today. However, I also know that sometimes we are left with a limp, or a thorn in the flesh or a scar, and I also wonder why some of the Christian folk I know were not healed at all. The Scriptures

14

show us a balance, and the Church also needs to wrestle with the theological questions that arise when emotional and psychological wellness do not occur. Perhaps that will become the next volume.

Today's Church does need to regain the knowledge and practice that was part of the Scripture's story. That is, we need to reclaim the dependence upon the living God to care for souls, to touch broken lives and to restore and rescue the perishing. We are called *"to proclaim freedom for the prisoners and recovery of sight for the blind, to release the oppressed, to proclaim the year of the Lord's favour"* (Luke 4:18-19). This call has never been repealed, rather, we are sent in the power of the Spirit to set the captive free in all the literal and figurative ways this implies. Dieter's text calls us back to Jesus to heal and restore the soul.

BRIAN F. STELCK, PH.D.
President, Carey Theological College
Director, Kenya Leadership Project
Vancouver, Canada

Dieter Mulitze has once again provided us with a provocative, yet practical, challenge to fill out the content of the Gospel. His first book, *The Great Omission*, exposed the absence of healing ministry as a major lack in the Church's faithfulness to a New Testament mission. The latest volume examines the nature of the biblical divine healing mission and finds a mélange of bad practices in the contemporary Church. The bad examples are the 'Great Substitution'.

The Great Substitution is explained in the sub-title, and this is really what the book is all about. As it turns out, there may be less of an omission than was thought. Although divine healing, in the sense Jesus did it, is often missing from Christian vocabulary and practice, various other forms of healing ministries abound, the more psychological of which are one particular target of Mulitze's treatise. Of course, mainstream Christians from Dr. Luke onward have always employed the physician's art, but recent decades have seen a profusion of 'Christian' psychological science and practice. As Mulitze points out, much of this seems little more than a quick baptism of the latest psychological fad, subject to many of the same limitations and partial successes experienced by non-Christian users of the same method. *The Great Substitution* examines this history and finds it wanting, both in terms of effectiveness in healing and faithfulness to gospel models.

Dieter Mulitze is well acquainted with psychological arts, and the literature that supports them, whether generated by Christians or secularists. Further, he is committed to full use of the best of medical techniques as part of a holistic healing ministry. By 'substitution' Mulitze clearly does not intend a rejection of legitimate psychological and physical healing arts, but a recognition of their limitations, together with recovery of a biblical emphasis on Jesus as Healer.

Central both to the book and to the author's understanding of its teaching about healing is the person of Jesus. But far from creating a 'how-to' handbook that reduces Jesus to yet another method, this book calls its readers to a fuller and more complete relationship with Jesus himself as the source of healing. Jesus is Good News both for the sinner seeking forgiveness and the wounded seeking healing.

The question still must be asked, "Is yet another book on divine healing needed?" The literature in the field is extensive, and various perspectives are not wanting. But *The Great Substitution* should gain a hearing precisely because so many of the available books fail at the very point that Mulitze considers fundamental, i.e., the healing presence of Jesus. If Jesus is indeed the divine Healer, surely finding a way to bring him into our pain and disease should be pivotal, but sadly it often is not. That is the point this book addresses, and why it is needed.

The book is a delight to the reader and an encouragement to the seeker. Dieter Mulitze writes well, blending information and instruction with encouragement. As he demonstrated in his first book, Mulitze mixes the art of the skilled biblical exegete with the rigorous logic of the scientific thinker. As a practitioner as well as a theoretician, Dieter has a passion not only to 'get it right' but to see people come to wholeness and health. The book is full of apt illustrations, and the illustrations bear out the central thesis.

In short, *The Great Substitution* is a timely book, representing a worthy sequel to *The Great Omission*. In the first book we learned what was missing; in this book we learn what the missing ingredient looks like. Strange as it may seem, in a world constantly seeking novelty, the answer Dieter gives is as old as the Gospel itself. When all else fails, try Jesus.

CARL E. ARMERDING, PH.D.
Director, Schloss Mittersill Study Centre
Mittersill, Austria
Former President, Regent College
Vancouver, Canada

 Introduction

Carla's Story

My first experience with counseling began almost ten years ago when my marriage began to crumble. My husband and I had been married eight years, and we were spending more and more time fighting. My husband refused to go for counseling, believing it was me who needed to be fixed. I decided to go by myself. Since we didn't have a pastor at the time, I asked if a fellow I knew, who was a counselor, would see me. He was a Christian who went to our church but who worked as a counselor for a provincial agency. I explained my situation to him, and one of the areas we were having trouble was in our sex life. He asked if I had ever been sexually abused and suggested that my father may have molested me and that was why I didn't want to make love to my husband. As much as I tried to make myself remember, I couldn't think of anything ever happening to me in the way of sexual abuse. I was frustrated and sensed I wasn't making any headway, so I stopped going. I believed there must not be anything wrong with me; it must be my husband who needed changing.

Several months later our new pastor invited my husband out for coffee. They spent time talking and praying and dealing with some issues in my husband's life. When he came home, he was like a new person—happy and at peace with himself. I refused to believe that simply praying to God could change someone. Refusing to believe it was a permanent change, I waited for the old "Fred" to show up again. Weeks went by, and as much as I hated to admit it, I was slowly beginning to accept that God had performed a miracle in his life. I was angry and felt cheated. How could he get "fixed" in a couple of hours when I didn't get anywhere over several months of counseling? I felt like I was really messed up. Fred told me to go for healing prayer. I wanted to believe God could change me too, but it seemed too simple.

I finally got up the courage to talk to our pastor. After I told him my situation, the Holy Spirit directed us to pray for God to reveal the lies in my life. The first lie I remember believing was that I was unlovable. My earthly father had never told me he loved me. I suddenly remembered running downstairs when I was about five years old and asking my dad for a bedtime hug and kiss. I told him I wanted to do this every day. He brushed me away and said, "Why would you want to do that?" Rejected, I made my way upstairs feeling foolish and hurt. As I was led through healing prayer the Holy Spirit took me through the scene again in my mind, but this time as I went up the stairs, I looked up and there was Jesus standing with His arms open wide. I ran to Him, and He held me and told me He loved me. It was such a complete and deep healing—I felt completely loved. Through more prayer I was able to forgive my father for his rejection by understanding he had never received love and therefore didn't know how to respond to me.

The second lie God exposed was that I believed I had married the wrong man. My husband and I had engaged in premarital sex, and since I knew it was wrong, I felt dirty and ashamed but unworthy to marry anyone else. Even though I loved him, I felt obligated to marry him because I thought no one else would have me. Through healing prayer I was able to forgive my husband for taking this gift from me and see that, although God was displeased with me, He had forgiven and promised to bless me which He has.

Other lies that were dealt with were ones I had heard my mom say, like, "All men want is sex." I was withholding sex from my husband because I believed he didn't love me, he was just using me. Through prayer I was able to see that sex is an act designed by God to be pleasurable to both men and women, and it is an expression of love. God did amazing things through prayer that day. I was able to recognize that my negative behaviour toward my husband was based on lies I had believed.

Wounded Hearts, Minds and Spirits

Many Christians have abundant life in Christ (John 10:10) with much joy and fullness in the Holy Spirit that comes only from knowing Christ and the hope of eternal life in one's heart. Many Christians can enter into worship fully and have a strong and vital prayer life. Many others can faithfully fulfill their ministry in the Church and the world and confidently use their spiritual gifts. But as all in the body of Christ who are truly honest will admit, that this is not the entire picture.

There are a significant number of Christians who have never really experienced the fullness of life Jesus intended for them, or maybe they did once and now do not. There are others who have at least one area in their life which is causing deep emotional pain or bondage that might even be hidden from everyone else. Carla's true story, as recounted above, is an example of the pain some people carry. I know of Christian women (and some men) who have experienced sexual abuse as children, often, sadly enough, by their very own fathers. What is even worse, in some cases the family is

21

outwardly very Christian and totally denies any problem and will accuse and shame the abused person if the issue is ever raised. Worse still for some such precious sisters in Christ, the very deep wounds of pain and shame remain in their hearts and spirits for years, crying for release. Other believers have painful recurring memories and do not know what they really mean or how to process them. Then there are believers with sexual problems— pornography, sexual dysfunction in marriage, defilement, gender confusion, aftermath from abortion or rape, personal sexual sins for which there appears to be no release or victory and more. Others cope with addictions of which there are many. Sadly there are Christian marriages that, on the outside, appear as if they have it all together and yet have deep issues and heartaches for either or both spouses. Some Christians cannot forgive themselves or feel accepted by others, including many who have been divorced. Others, in spite of their theology and strong grasp of the Scriptures, do not really know in their hearts that God loves and accepts them. It's as if the gospel has not yet evangelized their whole being. Yet others suffer from fear, anxiety, depression, suicidal tendencies, mood swings, apparent disorders and dysfunctions—to name a very few of the many psychiatric diagnoses—and are on psychiatric medication. Many such Christians have told me they were reluctant to take the medication and yet finally consented. Then there are Christians who hear voices or have had very disturbing spiritual experiences and suspect, even if their theology will not really allow it, the presence of evil spirits. I have encountered all of the above in ministering to fellow Christians, and this is but a small sample of the multitude of issues and pain in the body of Christ.

Some Christians and even entire churches are unwilling to admit the reality of such problems and issues in their midst. After all, Christians are not supposed to have such problems since all Christians are expected to live the "victorious" Christian life wherein, upon conversion, the past is "under the blood" and "the past is past at last." I heard of a church where a Christian couple unfortunately had serious marriage problems that led to a separation. The response in the church was total denial and avoidance wherein the husband was treated as if he no longer existed. In fact he eventually lost his entire business because all his former Christian clients wanted nothing to do with him. In another church a man coping with depression was told several times that his problem was sin and if he would just confess the sin in his life he would be healed. He was also told, in no uncertain terms, that if he just "walked right" with God, he would never be depressed. I wonder if such responses reveal the insecurity and inability of some churches to help the deeply wounded and hurting in their midst. Denial and avoidance, with their masks and proverbial fig leaves, prevent healing and restoration for people in such churches.

Confusion Just About Everywhere

Where and how do Christians experience help, restoration, healing or release from such deep needs and very real pain in the body of Christ? Certainly caring friends and fellow believers can show much love and comfort, bear one another's burdens and more. But beyond this the issue appears very complex and confusing.

There are not a few "self-help" books written by Christian authors, some well-known, that point to formulae or steps to more or less guarantee release and healing of even very deep emotional and spiritual issues. Yet if we are truly honest, we'll admit that many Christians have followed the steps and are no better off. I know because I have encountered many who have experienced this. One lady I had the immense privilege of ministering to through

very deep depression and suicidal tendencies had, some years earlier, read a Christian book on depression. She told me that she was
so depressed she could not realize any of the steps and thus was
even more depressed and discouraged. She had even become angry
over the book which, of course, did not help. If not self-help, then
perhaps counseling or therapy?

Some Christian scholars and writers will argue that psychology
and psychotherapy provide helpful insights and can be integrated
to some degree with Christian counseling and the care of souls. As
a result a seemingly endless number of books are written on how
this integration might be accomplished to truly help Christians.
The debate between Christian faith and psychology storms back
and forth with the latter apparently impacting the former more
than the reverse. An intense and complex dialogue about Freudian
psychoanalysis, Jungian therapy, cognitive-behavior therapy, rational emotive therapy, Adlerian and reality therapies, logos therapies,
existential therapy, Gestalt therapy, family therapy—to name a very
few—rages on. Then there are numerous discussions on techniques
and methods in psychology and psychotherapy and the knowledge
and skill to apply them.

But not everyone is helped by counseling, psychology or psychotherapy even when offered by believing and trained Christians.
In fact some world-renowned scholars point to numerous studies
which show that the efficacy of all this effort is much less than
often claimed.

Meanwhile other Christian writers with equal commitment
and seemingly convincing arguments strongly maintain that integration is not possible at all. Many such writers maintain that the
Scriptures are all we need, so why go elsewhere? In fact to go elsewhere is understood as compromise and faithlessness. While I
expect the vast majority of Christians will approve of biblical or

Christian counseling and have no doubt been helped via able counselors in the Church, some will argue that what is offered even there is actually not very Christian or biblical at all. In fact some Christian "integrationists" and scholars themselves state quite openly that Christian counseling and therapy is not essentially and fundamentally different from that of the world. Confusing indeed.

Not many will argue against the use of psychiatric drugs for Christians. In fact the Church is more or less accepting of psychiatry. Some major Christian authors maintain that more Christians than is often realized have malfunctioning brains and will need psychiatric medication for the rest of their lives. In fact they need to learn to "live victoriously" with lifelong psychiatric "meds." After all, they write, psychiatry is very scientific, and we should be thankful for the relief of psychiatric drugs and how amazingly complex God has made our neurons and brain chemistry. Who dare argue with scientific fact? Not the average pastor and lay person and not many Christian theologians. Yet in spite of the arguments, not a few Christians are very uneasy about taking psychiatric drugs. The side effects and withdrawal symptoms, only now becoming apparent from long-term use of even the "newer and safer" drugs, is causing a huge debate and second thoughts.

But there are some equally committed Christian writers, including fully certified psychiatrists completely competent in their field, who will argue with considerable scientific evidence on their side that, except for a few cases of truly "organic" mental illness, Christians should not take psychiatric drugs. Such writers view the Church's acceptance of psychiatry as an unfortunate and costly surrender, almost "madness" in itself. They tend to deplore an apparent shift from the care of souls to the care of brains. There is, in fact, an entire anti-psychiatry movement that challenges many of the major assumptions and practices of modern neuropsychiatry. Most Christians are unaware of the fact that, while there is a philosophy of science, there is also a philosophy of psychiatry. Among secular scholars there are some world-renowned writers and scientists who totally challenge the critical assumptions of so-called mental illness and the use of psychiatric drugs. For example some prominent writers view the theory of chemical imbalance in the brain, a scientific mantra in many places, as "junk science" and more myth than anything else. This is often a startling revelation to many Christians who have simply believed the popular notions about psychiatry. Some writers look to a history of psychiatry, among other things, to make this a very compelling argument. The result is that the supposed scientific basis upon which some Christian authors justify the use of psychiatric drugs becomes shaky, like feet of clay. More confusion still.

More and more Christians, it seems, are turning to alternative medicine which often includes "energy medicine" and the management of "energy fields" in the body. Such an approach to reality can reportedly bring even emotional healing. A number of Christian writers, some with growing ministries, are supportive of these practices. Attractive as this may seem even with glowing testimonials, a number of other Christian writers have offered an exhaustive analysis, arguing that the science behind this is dubious to say the least, and the theology is even worse, basically undercutting the cross of Christ and violating the very character and nature of God.

But what about prayer which, after all, was taught by Jesus? Well, as some claim, if your brain is malfunctioning or you have an organic illness, you will need medical help in addition to any prayer. Then there are those times when prayer seems not to work, as if God is asleep at the proverbial switch. Okay, but what about "healing prayer"? Surely healing prayer must be a main avenue of experiencing God's healing and restoration. After all, "healing" and "prayer" are two very deeply entrenched concepts and themes in the

Scriptures. Surely healing prayer is even safer than apple pie and Mother's Day. Unfortunately there is much confusion here as well.

Many have associated healing prayer and prayer ministry with the charismatic movement in the Church. Not everyone in the Church has taken healing prayer seriously or favorably. After all, it involves untrained and unprofessional people rather than professional counselors and mental health professionals. Apparent excesses and questionable practices have not endeared everyone to this type of ministry. The controversy over the spiritual gifts has not helped either. There are Christian authors who are deeply critical of anything that looks like "inner healing" or "healing of memories" and take exception to such practices. They criticize anything in healing prayer that appears even remotely to be psychoanalytic technique or New Age visualization. Other authors claim that such healing prayer has New Age roots and must not be allowed in the Church at all. Then there is the issue of evil spirits and "deliverance ministry" which has caused a whole other debate and is often associated with healing prayer. So, sadly and surprising for some, even healing prayer in the Church is not without its critics and detractors. Confusing, if not downright depressing.

Getting Lost in a Therapeutic Jungle

Why are so many people "lost in a therapeutic jungle" with a maze of methods and seemingly endless rabbit trails? Why is this whole issue so complex? Must one really plumb the depths of transaction analysis, psychodynamic theory, cognitive-behavior therapy, rational-emotive therapy, family therapy, selective serotonin reuptake inhibitors (SSRI) and more? Let's stand back for a moment and look at the forest and not the trees. If becoming a Christian were so complex, few people would come to Christ. The gospel itself is quite simple. Even a child with Down's Syndrome can know Jesus and the hope of eternal salvation. Even little children can understand the basics of the kingdom of God and the simple, direct love of Jesus. God has made His plan of salvation and the gospel accessible to all people. It revolves around a personal relationship with Jesus Himself. Since God the Father desires all people and nations to come to know Him, His message is simple and accessible to all people. The call to salvation is simple: repent and be saved and believe in the name of the Lord Jesus.

Whenever I watch a Billy Graham crusade, I am always encouraged by the clear, simple, straightforward appeal for people to commit their lives to Jesus and be adopted into the Kingdom. No techniques or complex methods operate there. In fact when anyone suggests that techniques could be used to "convert" more people, justifiable criticism and alarm is voiced by many. The basic, simple core reality is a *personal encounter* with the living Lord Jesus Christ.

Why does it then get so complex in the transformation of the human soul? I fully realize that a life of discipleship and sanctification is more involved than the initial conversion. The point is, why does the *how* of transformation, or restoration, or healing seem so complex? If salvation is by grace, why is the restoration and care of the human soul by technique, method, or human skill and analysis? If salvation is centered on a personal relationship with Jesus, why is our healing not also fully centered on Jesus? Having begun by grace, do we effectively continue by human effort (Gal. 3:3)?

The Great Substitution

The basic thesis of this book is that the complexity and confusion outlined above is mostly a consequence of the substitution of the authentic, incarnational healing presence of Jesus by all sorts of methods, analyses, theories and techniques. Whenever the Church ceases to practice the presence of Jesus, other things fill the void. In addition, the anointing of the Holy Spirit has been substituted by professionalism, and the gifts of the Spirit have been substituted by ministry skill or learned competence.

As a trained research scientist I do not devalue the life of the intellect, or learning, or professional training. Yet I contend that we must first fully value the scriptural categories and realities and most fundamentally, the presence of Jesus. We must learn how to minister firsthand from His example. Who would ever pretend to improve upon Jesus? In this book I will present a theology of healing prayer as the basis for the care of souls, historically a mandate of the Church.

In the following pages and building upon my first book, *The Great Omission: Resolving Critical Issues for the Ministry of Healing and Deliverance*, I have endeavored to show that the complexity and confusion of all the issues outlined above can be resolved by challenging their critical assumptions and, most importantly, looking to the teachings of Jesus. If we dwell enough in His presence and more deeply comprehend the profound depth of what appear to be His "simple" teachings, the whole issue becomes clearer. The Gospels present, among other things, "ultimate psychology." Jesus Himself is, among other roles, the Ultimate Psychotherapist.

An obvious implication of the Great Substitution is that significant numbers of Christians have not been sufficiently helped in their desire for healing and wholeness. While I do not question the integrity and commitment of Christian counselors and therapists to bring healing to fellow Christians, or that believers are experiencing some measure of help, it's not enough for all Christians. I have met Christians at healing prayer conferences that have looked in many places and not been deeply or sufficiently helped. *It's as if people with broken hearts are being led to broken cisterns.*

Over the years, I, and others involved in healing prayer ministry which requires the presence of Jesus and His Spirit, have seen people deeply healed and transformed in a matter of hours rather than not at all or only to some degree after months or even years of therapy, counseling or psychiatry.

The true stories of healing as recounted in this book revolve around the presence of Jesus. The names of the people involved and a few details have been changed to safeguard their identity. In some cases, a story is actually a composite from several other stories.

This is not a self-help book. This book is about personally encountering Jesus and His Spirit in the healing and restoring of one's soul and inner being. It is about experiencing more of the love of Jesus. If you are looking for steps, or programs, or a "package," you will be disappointed. But if steps or programs or therapies for your own healing and wholeness have disillusioned you, I expect you will be blessed and encouraged by this book.

A Mother and Daughter in Need of Healing

Dana had been deeply concerned for years about discord and disharmony between herself and her young daughter who was about eight years old. Like any mother, she desired healing of the relationship, but she did not know what was the source of the problem. She sought the Lord in prayer, and finally He revealed the root cause. Elsie, her daughter, required surgery at age three. The Lord brought back the vivid memory of that entire event. She could clearly remember Elsie being wheeled down to the elevator that would take her to the operating room. She wrote:

> I could still see that wee one sitting on the cart with her finger in her mouth and holding tightly onto her pink blanket. When the nurses moved the cart onto the elevator, they said, "Say goodbye to Mama." She suddenly looked at me and realized I wasn't going with her and out

came a wee bleat, "Mama!" Then the doors shut. We
moved through the surgery/recovery time with a strong
sense of God's presence. But, as the months progressed,
they were not easy for her or us. She had regular check-ups
under anaesthesia and was fitted for a prosthesis that she
fought and fought. It took five to hold her down so they
could get a mould. We had to bribe her with the promise
of a surprise when she went to get her new prosthesis put
in. Wow, did she fight that—no physical pain involved,
but she trusted no medical person to touch her!

The Lord revealed to Dana that Elsie, from her viewpoint,
began to feel rejection and abandonment when the doors shut
because she believed, understandably at age three, that her mother
had decided not to come with her. That was, of course, a painful
false realization at a fearful time with so many unknowns and
strangers around her. The negative feelings and emotions for Elsie
surrounding that time of surgery must have been strong given the
resistance to the medical procedures.

Dana began to pray over her daughter when she was asleep,
now having more compassion in understanding the root of the
problem. That did help, although it required sorting out the usual
issues of mother and daughter relationships with a young, growing
daughter. As might be expected, this whole part of Elsie's life deeply
affected Dana. She wrote:

> It was such an emotional time. When the elevator doors
> closed, I leaned against a wall and sobbed and sobbed until
> a nurse came along and offered a cup of coffee. I probably
> needed someone to pray for me, eh? I began to suffer
> depression. I would awaken in the a.m. crying, had very
> little energy and I didn't cope with life very well. We

couldn't figure out what was going on. But later, after being delivered at a healing prayer conference—which I didn't want to attend!—I realized that I had absorbed her pain over the six months from diagnosis to the conference. I wonder if it actually began when I had to let her go to surgery? Interesting thought. When I was prayed for at the conference, I "felt" something leave my body, and I knew I was free. The best part of that encounter was that, as I processed it before the Lord, He said, "I love you so much. If I knew about that hurt down inside you and could heal you, there's *much* more I long to do if you'll just let me."

It was then that I began my two-hour morning time with the Lord five days a week. That went on for almost two years. How did I get free time? Elsie was in pre-school, I refused to answer the phone or the door for those two hours—much to my family's chagrin though we can laugh about it now—and I stayed in my bedroom. One of those five days Elsie was at home, and she sat in my bedroom and coloured, drew and read books while I met with the Lord. Those were difficult, precious times. I've never wept so much in my life as the Lord met me, tenderizing me towards His desires in my life. I'm all teary just writing this.

In the final analysis, it's all about Jesus.

Chapter One

Healing and Restoring the Soul: Drinking from Which Cistern?

My people have committed two sins: They have forsaken me, the spring of living water, and have dug their own cisterns, broken cisterns that cannot hold water (Jer. 2:13).

On the last and greatest day of the Feast, Jesus stood and said in a loud voice, "If a man is thirsty, let him come to me and drink. Whoever believes in me, as the Scripture has said, streams of living water will flow from within him" (John 7:37-38).

Roberta's Restoration from Sexual Abuse

The following true story from Roberta (not her real name) reveals how the Lord healed, restored and directed her through the deepest pain in her life. She had attended one of our healing prayer conferences where she encountered Jesus and received part of her healing. She wrote:

I just had to write to tell you what God is doing in my life since that weekend and just before. Two weeks prior, I was going through anxiety attacks. This only happens to me when physical abuse memories are about to surface. I have very few childhood memories. Most of those years are a blank. Because I was so young when the abuse began, the mind compensated by erasing those painful memories. Or so one thinks. With me, the memories started to resurface about five years ago. They began with nightmares and then manifested themselves physically through my body in vomiting, stomach cramps, nervousness, unexplainable fear of being touched, sleeplessness and a host of other symptoms. Just a smell or a certain touch would trigger fits of vomiting. I would build a wall of pillows between my husband and myself so that his skin wouldn't touch mine when we went to bed at night. I thought I was going crazy, so I sought a Christian counselor to help me. This had happened on three other separate occasions, and each time I went to a counselor. The Friday we were driving to the conference was the day I decided to seek another counselor. This was the fourth time in my life that these things started happening to me, so I was in bad shape by the time we got there.

You can imagine my relief when I found out it wasn't a marriage enrichment seminar! By the end of the Friday evening session, I wasn't any better, but I knew I wanted a prayer of blessing. That's when I came to the ministry team. I was so scared while walking towards them because I thought God had already told them everything about me and they knew what a mess I was. I just about fell over when I was asked if I had anyone to forgive before being blessed. And yet, I could only think of two people. I prayed and blurted out something silly like, "God has a plan for my life and I don't know what it is, but I'm sure He has one." Then I asked you to bless my ministry I have with children. I think I walked away feeling like I was off the hook.

I didn't sleep at all that night. In fact I was in worse shape than the day before. We arrived at the conference Saturday morning; I had a hard time keeping breakfast down. During the worship time, I lost it (not my breakfast!) as we sang "Faithful One." My husband took my right hand and a friend of mine took my left. I didn't think I was going to make it. Fortunately God gave me the strength and the courage to stay for all the sessions. Then I came again, but this time for healing prayer. You know what happened! But what you don't know is that some physical healing also took place. While the ministry team prayed, I felt a warmth in my left heel and in my stomach. I didn't really pay much attention to it until I got home that night. When I took off my shoes and started walking I suddenly realized that my left foot didn't hurt. I sat down on my bed, took off my sock and started pinching my foot. The heel spur I'd had was gone, and so was the pain. Then I remembered the warmth in my foot during prayer and realized that my stomach had felt warm too. I hadn't been able to eat toast for breakfast or drink coffee in years without eating at least ten or more antacids during the day. Yesterday I had four cups of coffee, and I went to bed with no problem! Isn't God wonderful?

The following week I thought I was in heaven. I told everyone and anyone who wanted to listen about what God did for me. I talked with God like I had never done before, and I saw how God was working in every situation. I was so filled with His love that I thought I would burst. I was crying tears of real joy all the time because of what God did for me.

My husband was working a night shift on Saturday, so I was sitting alone in my bed praying. I was praising God for this amazing week when I started to feel that unmistakable, overwhelming feeling again. It had never happened while I was praying, so it really surprised me. I started crying as memory pictures began to unfold in my mind. This time, they were the most painful ones I had ever experienced. I didn't think I was going to make it, I was crying so hard. The memory was of my dad coming into my room at night. My sister and I shared a bed. My dad was trying to wake her up, and I woke up hearing him whisper to her. I told him to leave her alone, but he kept insisting. Finally I told him to take me instead, and he did. I had always tried to resist him. I thought I had always said no. But when I said yes, I felt like I was no longer innocent. This is where Satan planted the lie. He told me I deserved this abuse because "I asked for it." This is where the root of self-hatred began. I blamed myself all these years for the things that happened to me without ever knowing why. It took a lot of work to forgive all those people who hurt me, but I did forgive every one of them. Except the person I needed to forgive most—me!

During the conference I stood up and shared that God told me I needed "me to be me." Now I know what He meant. God wanted me to see the place where the lie was planted. He wanted me to find the truth, stop hating myself and start loving myself the way He loves me. That's why He brought the memories a week later. He wanted me to experience His true peace and joy first. Then, as the painful memories came back, I had the hope of joy and healing that was still to come. I was afraid of facing those memories that helped me to find the root of Satan's lies and fill them with the truth of God's Word. The truth has set me free, and the pain is gone!

The Demise of the Pastoral Care of Souls

The care of souls has historically been the responsibility of the Church. For centuries there has been a tradition of pastoral care, spiritual direction and healing within the Church. The ministry of healing prayer was vital to the healing and restoration of the human soul. This tradition was anchored in Christ's command to love one another as He has loved us (John 13:34; 1 Pet. 1:22; 1 John 3:11) and Paul's exhortations to bear one another's burdens, comfort one another, be tender hearted and compassionate and to mourn with those who mourn and rejoice with those who rejoice (Rom. 12:15; Eph. 4:2). It was certainly built on the teaching and model of Jesus' ministry of healing and deliverance.

Hurding, a medical practitioner and lecturer in pastoral counseling at Trinity College, Bristol, defined the nature and role of pastoral care around four essential functions: "healing, sustaining, guiding and reconciling of troubled persons whose troubles arise in the context of ultimate meanings and concerns."[1] This definition underscores the spiritual issues of life and fully recognizes the need for healing of troubled people. Healing in the care of souls involves bringing people towards wholeness, both physical and spiritual and is always focused on the whole person.[2] Sustaining involves helping a "hurting person endure or transcend a circumstance in which restoration or recuperation is either impossible or improbable."[3] Reconciling involves restoration of broken relationships wherever possible, built upon forgiveness as one of Christ's commands. Guiding involves growth in maturity and wisdom with wise choices in life. Indeed the overall goal of Christian soul care is spiritual and "character formation—the formation of the character of Christ within His people."[4] Roberta needed physical healing, emotional healing from anxiety, relational healing in her marriage and towards her father as well as reconciliation with herself and release from the pain of the past.

With the coming of the Enlightenment in the eighteenth century, new ideas about human nature and the issues of the heart, mind and spirit began to challenge pastoral care. Pastoral care was influenced by new ideologies and began to borrow ideas from them.[5] In time, pastoral care was challenged by behaviorism, psychoanalysis, personalism and transpersonalism originating from developments in seventeenth and eighteenth centuries using early

Greek philosophies of human nature.[6] These new views of human nature threatened to overcome and weaken traditional Christian pastoral care.[7] *Unfortunately, during the Enlightenment, pastoral healing was essentially discarded and has still not fully recovered.*[8]

A critical turning point came in 1905 in America. Some in the Church, starting with Episcopalians, were increasingly impressed with the new "science" of psychotherapy. It was decided to no longer allow the tradition of pastoral care to guide the care of souls; that role was given to psychotherapy.[9] In time, soul care shifted from the Church to the realm of psychotherapy and psychology, due mostly to the growth of science from the seventeenth and eighteenth centuries and the parallel decline of religion.[10] *Psychotherapists began to take the place of meeting human needs formerly undertaken by clergy, but they emphasized self-realization and self-actualization instead of salvation and sanctification.*

The Appearance and Rise of Counseling

Into the early 1900s, psychology became increasingly hostile to faith, and more Christians desired professional help in addition to, or in place of, soul care in the Church. A new movement called Christian or biblical counseling eventually arose from the thinking of some Christian psychologists in the 1970s and 1980s.[11] As well as appearing in reaction to the secularizing influence of psychology and psychotherapy, this new movement also sought to integrate psychology with conservative biblical theology.[12]

The core goals of Christian counseling are the stimulation of personality growth and development, helping people cope more effectively with the problems of life including inner conflict and crippling emotions, providing encouragement and guidance for those who are facing losses or disappointments and helping people with self-defeating life patterns that cause unhappiness.[13] This definition is beyond a more strict biblical definition of counseling as offering advice, wise counsel and help in plans and direction (Prov. 12:15; Isa. 9:6; 2 Sam. 16-17).[14]

The difference between counseling and psychotherapy has been debated often, with some scholars viewing psychotherapy as more focused on "significant personality change rather than adjustment to situational and life problems."[15] It is now more common to view counseling and psychotherapy as very similar since they utilize similar theories and techniques.[16]

Baptizing the World's Thinking

Like most Christians, I thought that if I were to seek help for my troubled soul through pastoral and Christian counselors and therapists, I would experience a uniquely Christian therapy or at least a therapy primarily rooted in the Christian faith. I was shocked to find out that this is not the case.

So where did pastoral care and the growing biblical counseling movement get much of its content and methods? Certainly some came from the Scriptures themselves, and no doubt many Christian authors and scholars endeavored to remain faithful to Christ. But a considerable amount of the world's thinking has been incorporated into Christian counseling and therapy.

Pastoral care has basically conformed to the world. Dan Blazer is an evangelical Christian, former medical missionary, author and dean of medical education and professor of psychiatry at the Duke University School of Medicine.[17] Blazer noted how Rogerian therapy has dominated much of pastoral care in recent history.[18] Blazer summed up the current (1998) state of affairs:

> Pastoral care in large part became indistinguishable from secular therapies popular during the later twentieth century.

Despite the separate training programs, pastoral care today is defined more by its distinctive role rather than by a unique approach to caring for those suffering emotionally. In other words, the pastoral counselor is a pastor who counsels using methods, for the most part, indistinguishable from those of the secular psychologist.[19]

Oates, professor of psychiatry and behavioral sciences and former professor of psychology of religion at Southern Baptist Theological Seminary, outlined the history of modern pastoral care by its "center." The center has been shifting sometimes in response to transient fads not unlike the Athenians and foreigners who "spent their time doing nothing but talking about and listening to the latest ideas."[20] Initially, as Oates outlined, preaching from the pulpit was the central focus for modern counseling and pastoral care. Then, under the influence of Anton Boisen and others, came visitation as the central focus. Then, within clinical pastoral education, came the influence of Frederick Kuether who advocated analytic psychotherapy resulting in a very Americanized form of Freudian therapy which became the core and center of pastoral counseling. Another result of Kuether's influence was the shift from bedside visitation to the professional counseling office. Then the center shifted from a Freudian or Sullivanian type of psychoanalysis to the "client-centered therapy" of Carl Rogers. Then came a "pop-psychology cafeteria" where transaction analysis, Gestalt psychology, "bipolar" approaches, psychosynthesis and many more became the center for numerous pastoral counselors.

The next shift appears to be towards family therapy and also Heinz Kohut with his theory on the development of the self derived from Freudian psychoanalysis.[21] The center of pastoral care appears to be built on shifting sand and not on the solid Rock (Matt. 7:24-27). For the Christian seeking help, this means that help will be determined by *whatever is the fad of the day*. The Christian counseling movement has not fared much better. In fact much of the content of Christian counseling has been "Christianized" and drawn from the secular psychotherapies as learned by the Christian psychologists who helped create the movement.[22] A careful analysis of Christian counseling and therapy as commonly practiced today reveals a "strong underlying reliance on the psychotherapies even though the terminology at times has been 'Christianized.'"[23] Similarly McMinn, professor of psychology at Wheaton College, wrote:

> Most contemporary forms of Christian counseling are religious adaptations of mainstream counseling techniques. For example, many Christian writers and therapists have adapted techniques from Albert Ellis' Rational-Emotive Therapy (RET) to Christian counseling. Though Ellis is an outspoken atheist, many Christians have adapted his techniques as legitimate.[24]

Blazer identified the roots of the evangelical counseling movement as follows:

> The roots of evangelical Christian counseling in the common-sense therapies of Adolf Meyer, Aaron Beck and others are clear. Yet these roots also extend back to practical guidebooks earlier in the twentieth century, such as Norman Vincent Peale's *The Power of Positive Thinking.*[25]

As an example of such roots affecting many Christians through popular books, Blazer critiques LaHaye's book *How To Win Over Depression,* with its formula for guaranteed success over depression:

> Tim LaHaye bases his formula on the work of Aaron Beck, proposing a spiritual version of cognitive therapy for

depression. LaHaye appeals to evangelical Christians by sprinkling biblical quotes liberally throughout his writing.... LaHaye intermixes the inspirational message of the evangelical minister with the practical message of the cognitive therapist. ...after grounding his steps to victory over depression in acceptance of Jesus and dependence on him, his formula encourages the power-of-positive-thinking, mind-over-matter approach of cognitive therapies, along with a scattering of the imagery therapy used by behavioral therapists such as the psychiatrist Joseph Wolpe.[26]

Blazer also critiqued Bruce Larson's book, *Living on the Growing Edge*. Blazer noted how Larson drew on the work of Viktor Frankl and most significantly in overcoming fear, the psychological technique of desensitizing oneself as practiced in behavioral and cognitive therapies.[27]

Blazer maintains that Christians have, as a whole, not really developed anything unique or different in terms of counseling or therapy:

Despite best-selling popular Christian counseling books, despite well-attended Christian counseling seminars, despite the influx of evangelical Christians into psychiatry and other mental health professions, Christian counseling has not established a distinctive niche in mental health services. **Popular self-help books are mostly applied secular psychiatry and psychology adapted to an evangelical orientation...** the Christian counseling industry has incorporated neuropsychiatry and cognitive therapy. Christian counseling and Christian psychiatry have failed to establish a clearly unique or superior package of mental health services (emphasis mine).[28]

Ed Smith, founder of Theophostic Ministries, after many years of counseling people who experienced sexual abuse, wrote:

> We have bought into the secular psychological model which is medical and humanistic. If you take the spiritual robes off much of what we call Christian counseling, you will find basically the same foundation as is holding up the secular world of psychology. [29]

> Much of what we Christians do that we call victorious Christian living and spiritual maturity is simply human effort and nothing more than what any non-believer could do with a little personal discipline and self effort.[30]

David Benner is a respected authority in clinical psychology, author and co-editor of the 1273-page *Baker Encyclopedia of Psychology and Counseling*. He wrote about the rise of psychology and psychotherapy with their powerful techniques and very real potential for seduction:

> In spite of the fact that the major authors in pastoral counseling have repeatedly called for the primacy of theology and the pastoral tradition in shaping pastoral counseling, the actual practice of counseling has often merely mimicked current psychological fads. Thus North American pastoral care has gone through phases during which it was dominated by Rogerian client-centered therapy, Freudian psychoanalysis, the growth and group therapies of the human potential movement and the interpersonal therapies having their origins in the work of Harry Stack Sullivan, family systems therapy and object relations theory.[31]

In his book, *The Healing of Fears*, Wright provided considerable scriptural understanding and insight plus an emphasis on one's relationship with God. To actually overcome fears and worry and to control one's thoughts, he referred to a number of mental and cognitive techniques. Those techniques included thought stopping, thought substitution, thought interruption, thought switching, relaxation therapy, visualization, mental imaging and positive reinforcement.[32] The technique of positive reinforcement, which involves repeatedly imaging a positive situation to overcome a negative situation and therefore desensitizing the emotions, takes from two weeks to a month to realize the maximum benefits.[33] Wright referred to the works of Peale.[34] Such techniques are not unlike similar techniques found in books by other Christian authors.

Cloud, in his book, *Changes that Heal*, offers many helpful insights into human nature and behavior and considerable biblical wisdom. Instead of focusing on methods and techniques, Cloud focuses on a developmental approach to human personality and the skills required to complete one's development.[35] The overwhelming emphasis of the book is one's own understanding, acquiring skills, hard work in therapy and on-going effort required to develop oneself.[36] While Christians can profit from life skills, and establishing boundaries is helpful and necessary at times, healing comes more from union with Jesus and experiencing His presence and His Spirit than from the changes we make or our behavior modification. Roberta's healing, for example, was simply centered in the presence of Jesus and did not involve any new skills or hard work in therapy.

The above is, in part, a reflection of the fact that the real work of developing a careful theological foundation for Christian counseling and therapy has hardly begun.[37] Predictably most Christian counselors have learned counseling techniques in the materialistic and Western humanist perspective.[38] Archibald Hart, former dean of the Fuller Seminary School of Psychology, assessed much of Christian psychology as "theologically bankrupt."[39]

The obvious consequence of reliance on the methods, theories and techniques of the world is the inability to go farther than the world. *If we use the methods of the world, we will fare no better.* There will be disappointments among believers in finding that the methods or techniques do not really help as is all-too-true in the case of "self-help" books.

Imagine going to a medical clinic because of an unknown illness. After a series of tests, X-rays and consultations with specialists, your illness is finally diagnosed. What would you think if you were then told simply to go home and given some direction on "trying to get well"? That can happen with counseling or therapy—much analysis and effort yet little actual healing. At times your emotions and inner being are "opened up for surgery" and then just "sewn back together." More pain, no gain?

Dallas Willard contends that there is a very low level of spiritual life in our current form of Christianity which "has not been imparting effectual answers to the vital questions of human existence."[40] As a result there are currently many psychologies and other spiritualities competing with Christianity.[41] The transformation of the human soul, or the renovation of the human heart, "is an inescapable human problem with no human solution."[42] This low level of spiritual life comes from not living sufficiently out of the power and presence of Jesus and from then adopting the methods and techniques of the world. People will be saved by grace but then "maintained" by the wisdom of man. *Remember, if we use the methods of the world, we will fare no better.*

Burnout as a Symptom of a Larger Problem

Burnout is a well-known problem in the counseling and therapy professions. Not unlike many other counselors, Smith became defeated and burned out after years of traditional counseling primarily with sexual abuse victims.[43] Meeting many deeply wounded and hurting people, not always seeing much change and ministering out of one's own resources can be draining. As Collins, professor of psychology at Trinity Evangelical Divinity School, wrote:

> Graduate students in counseling often assume that the act of helping will provide a lifetime of satisfaction and vocational fulfillment. At some time after graduation, however, most counselors discover that counseling is hard work, that many counselees do not get better and that constant involvement with the problems and miseries of others is psychologically and physically draining.[44]

In a survey of 100 counselors asked what they would do if they had the means to do anything they wanted with their lives, only three said they would spend their lives counseling.[45] This does not appear very encouraging.

Is burnout an almost inevitable result of commitment and dedication on the part of Christian counselors and therapists? Partly. I see it more as a symptom of a larger problem—of using the methods and techniques of the world with a reliance on the counselor or therapist as the "change agent." Analysis, knowledge, will-power, self-discipline, self-determination and more mean hard work for counselor and counselee. Even Christian authors use terms such as "hard work" and "long road of therapy." *Remember, if we use the methods of the world, we will get burned out.* But if we come into Jesus' presence, there is much healing as Rosalind joyfully discovered and wrote as below.

Rosalind's Struggles

There always seemed to be a storm brewing inside of me with short periods of peace and rest in between. Though I had accepted Jesus

Christ as my Saviour and determined to live for Him, I couldn't quite let go of all the fears and bondages of my past. I lived in fear and insecurity. These things kept me from being the person God created me to be. After suffering through a miscarriage, which was one of the loneliest times in my life (not too many people understand or sympathize with the loss of someone who has not yet been born), I was not allowed to grieve. The anger and rage built up inside me, spilling over to those around. A couple years later, I discovered that one of my children had been sexually abused as a child. I never told anyone and suffered for years feeling responsible and guilty.

I decided to see a professional counselor and deal with this so that my children wouldn't have to suffer as I had. I saw two different counselors but soon realized that they had really no help to offer. I actually came away with more luggage than before because, in the process of counseling, one counselor wounded my one son and myself. I felt these counselors were struggling with unresolved issues of their own and, in counseling others, were desperately seeking relief from their own pain. So it was back to "square one."

I really wanted to live for God, but instead I lived in constant fear of failure and depression with suicidal thoughts as my constant companion. I hated myself and would hit myself repeatedly as hard as I could, trying to punish myself for some hidden guilt I didn't quite understand. Finally my pastor suggested I go for healing prayer. They didn't counsel me. Instead they prayed, asking God to reveal to me the things that were keeping me in bondage to fear and hatred. They let me talk and they listened and then prayed. God's healing came into the areas of my life where I had been wounded.

I had a lot of issues with my mom which I could never understand. But as we prayed, I was able to forgive her for not protecting me and for not protecting herself. I loved my dad, but I knew at a young age that he didn't love Mom. It's not that he was unfaithful to her, he just married out of convenience. That alone really affected how I felt about myself as a woman and how I was able to respond to love. It also affected how I felt about my mom. God began to heal me from the inside out, one issue at a time.

I have more confidence than I have ever had in my life. I know it's because God has worked a healing in my life. He is continuing that work, giving me boldness and wisdom to be the person He created me to be. Each time I recognize a bondage in my life, I surrender it to God's healing, and He sets me free. God is great!

Two Simple Facts from the Gospels

One day I was getting ready to leave home on an important errand. I could not find my glasses which I needed to drive my car. I looked everywhere in the house for about twenty minutes, trying not be become frustrated. At last I found them; I had been wearing my glasses all along! Sometimes things are so close to us we overlook them.

A few years ago I was preparing a teaching series on the healing ministry of Jesus. I was praying at some length to understand what was common to all the healing encounters in the Gospels. A day later I had a strong realization that all the healing encounters revolved around Jesus. This fact kept coming to my mind for some time. This may seem very simple, basic and obvious. We all know that this is an incredibly basic fact of the Gospels. But sometimes a thing can be so familiar we don't see it. Sometimes things are so close to us we overlook them. *The healings and deliverances in the Gospels revolved around Jesus.*

A second simple, obvious fact from the Gospels is that there were no techniques or methods by which people were healed or delivered. The means varied—word of command, touch, word and touch, saliva, mud, a call to simple obedience or a combination thereof. Kydd, in his book, *Healing Through The Centuries: Models For Understanding*, put it this way:

> Reviewing the ministry of Jesus makes it obvious that He did not follow any patterns or use any formulas. **The only feature that appears in all of His healings is Jesus Himself.** Healing has its source in the grace of God (emphasis mine).[46]

Jesus purposely used simple means to heal and transform people so that the healing would center on Him and not any method.[47] The presence of Jesus through His Spirit, instead of any technique, is central and faithful to the healing of people.[48] From Jesus' healing ministry we see that "no two healings are ever the same and therefore prayers for healing can never be reduced to mere formulas or methods."[49] Faith must be in Jesus and not any method or technique.

Crabb emphasized the need for a central core or unity for counseling, like a framework to develop the theory and practice of counseling.[50] I contend that the core or central unity of Christian counseling should be the presence of Jesus and our relationship with Him. That realization should determine the theory and practice of counseling and most directly the ministry of healing prayer.

From One Jesus to 260 Methods and 10,000 Techniques

Why am I laboring such seemingly simple points? Because most of modern Christian counseling, therapy and even pastoral care typically focus on methodologies and techniques borrowed from the world and "Christianized" but not on the healing presence of Jesus. **It's like practising the non-presence of Jesus.** There are about 260 different schools of psychotherapy[51] and about 10,000 different techniques[52] used by therapists. The focus on method and technique is well known and acknowledged since there have been many meetings by Christian professionals to discuss techniques and methods in counseling.[53] Counseling and psychotherapy have been defined in terms of the application of techniques.[54] With the preoccupation with theory, method and technique in Christian counseling and therapy, it is no surprise that graduates of such programs from Christian schools are rarely trained in the Christian spiritual disciplines,[55] receive only little attention to prayer or even its possible use in counseling[56] and are rarely taught anything about the transforming power of Christ.[57] Advanced competence of counselors is typically focused on psychological theory and technique and not on theology or spiritual formation.[58]

The mere fact that there are so many methods and techniques should tell us that there is a basic problem. After decades of comparing one theory or method to another and developing still more, it is obvious that each of those theories or methods must be deficient. Each has a weakness and is incomplete or blind to some part of reality. Even if you knew each method perfectly, which do you "apply" to a person and how do you "apply" it correctly? What if the fundamental premise—that of developing and using any method or technique—is wrong in the first place?

The obvious non-presence of Jesus should not be a great surprise when you consider that the secular world of counseling and therapy is attempting to reconstruct and change people without any involvement with Jesus. So if Jesus is not the center, theories and methods must be constructed in His place to "do the job." The world of psychiatry, for example, did not want any involvement with an "imaginary God."[59] *The assumption is that man can transform himself by his own efforts without God and most specifically without Jesus.*

This is all entirely opposite from the Gospels where the heal-ing presence of Jesus is central and methods and techniques are inconsequential. Roberta received little help from counseling. Granted, the particular counselors she saw may not have been very capable, or perhaps she was not ready to benefit from them. In her life example, though, her real healing came from encountering Jesus and not through any method or technique whatsoever. She was healed and restored by simply being in His presence, hearing His voice as uniquely suited to her and experiencing the direction and communication of the Holy Spirit. That is similar to the heal-ing encounters in the Gospels.

One Jesus and no methods in the Gospels; over 260 methods with 10,000 techniques and virtually no presence of Jesus today. This is a Great Substitution, a curious reversal. Has there been such a great focus on method and technique for the care of souls because of a limited or deficient understanding of the presence of Jesus?

I used to read the Gospels as models or examples of people meeting Jesus almost two thousand years ago. I used to believe, with many others, that since we are all born centuries later, we can-not have such "direct" experiences because, as we know, Jesus has ascended to heaven and is seated at the right hand of the Father. I used to believe that I could not hear Jesus' voice or experience His presence as did people in the Gospels. As I will explain throughout this book, I now know this is not true and many others find this repeatedly untrue in the ministry of healing prayer.

Christians are called to be disciples of Jesus. By using methods and techniques in the transformation of the human soul, one unwittingly becomes a disciple of Ellis, Adler, Beck, Meyer, Jung, Freud, Wolpe, or Rogers—among many others. To a large degree, the Church has not been following Jesus and has instead been drinking at other cisterns. Michael Green, for one, wrote:

51

It is acknowledged on all sides that He (Jesus) is the greatest psychiatrist of all time and yet even Christians tend to look everywhere else for insight into counselling, than to Jesus Himself. Counselling is a major industry in many industrial societies in the world, not least in the U.S.A., yet how few of the insights and methods used owe anything to Jesus Christ? It is one of the many ways in which the church has surrendered to the spirit of the age that, when she does at length get round to counselling, she sits at the feet of mentors other than her Master.[60]

If we use the techniques and methods of the world to transform the human soul, then logically we go no farther and do no better than the world. Furthermore, the world will not come to the Church since everyone knows that the Church has nothing much else to offer. If we do not put into practice the model and teaching of Jesus in the care of souls first above anything the world would offer, then we build everything on sand (Matt. 7:26).

Counseling and Healing Prayer: Establishing a Context

Strictly speaking, Jesus did not command His disciples to "go and counsel," but He did command them to "go and heal and deliver." My concern is not about counsel in the stricter sense of giving people advice and wise counsel about career decisions, who to marry, how to counsel an engaged couple on communication in marriage, issues in parenting, how to cope with an alcoholic family member, wisdom in finances, identifying and understanding co-dependency, the possibility and implications of getting a restraining order in an abusive marriage, practical ways of coping with stress, how to establish and maintain boundaries in relationships, legal issues and implications about wills and inheritance, advice on secular agencies, placing someone in a nursing home and much more. In such cases, which occur frequently in life, the need is for counselors who offer true Godly wisdom, discernment and the overall sense of the involvement of the Spirit who remains the ultimate counselor. In the majority of such cases, people do not need healing and thus will seek counselors.

The burden of this book is for the healing and restoration of the human soul which is beyond counsel and direction. A partial list of the needs that healing prayer can address would include depression, anxiety, all forms of emotional pain commonly diagnosed as supposed psychiatric "disorders," infertility, the inability to receive love or give love, spiritual oppression, emptiness in one's heart and the need for love, gender confusion, self-acceptance or rejection, addictions, chronic and physical illness, painful or recurring memories, all types of fear, sexual abuse, ritual abuse, misogyny (hatred of women), hatred of men, spiritual abuse and indeed much, much more.

A person suffering from chronic back pain or asthma might seek healing prayer but probably not counseling. A person coping with depression could be helped through wise counsel, for example, but there is often the need for spiritual, relational and emotional healing and thus healing prayer. Counseling, as defined in the Scriptures, has as a profession been stretched beyond its boundaries to bring healing and restoration to people's souls. As noted earlier, counseling and psychotherapy are seen as quite similar.[61] This creates a problem since counseling is now required to do that for which it is inherently inadequate. When you stretch an elastic too far, it will break. Collins echoes the concerns of those who wonder about the effectiveness of counseling:

> Even well-trained, experienced counselors who keep abreast of the professional literature and apply the latest

techniques find nevertheless that their counselees do not always improve. Sometimes individuals even get worse as a result of counseling. It is hardly surprising, therefore, that some people give up and conclude that counseling really is a waste of time.[62]

The above observation is a result in part of the use of techniques in the first place, as well as going beyond the intention and nature of counseling.

Counseling and healing prayer ministry should be seen in a complementary role and not in opposition or mutually exclusive. The ministry of healing prayer is not about giving advice or counsel except for what is traditionally referred to as spiritual direction. The confusion comes when counseling attempts to do what is more clearly understood as healing and realizing wholeness.

Janine came for healing prayer for painful memories and repeated verbal and some physical abuse by her husband. Her husband's sexual demands amounted to rape even though they were a married couple. She received significant healing such that her emotional being was restored and she was able to make some decisions. She concurrently saw a counselor who was able to advise on the legalities and implications of restraining orders and separation as well as future issues of custody for the children. That involved professional counseling which was complementary to the healing prayer.

Counseling can offer a complementary role when Christians are not open to healing prayer or prayer ministry of any description although they know they need help. They may be inclined to see a counselor since that might be more in their "comfort zone." Sometimes as needs are expressed and issues become clearer, they will be open to healing prayer. Both counseling and healing prayer then operate together in a person's spiritual pilgrimage.

Healing prayer is but one main avenue for restoring the soul. Loving and caring relationships are key to healing and wholeness. For some people, recovery from sexual or spiritual abuse will involve not only healing prayer but also fellowship with truly caring Christians of integrity; this is vital for restoring trust and hope. Healing can also come through worship as one is focused on the Lord and away from unhealthy introspection, narcissism or idolatries of the self. Modern medicine must not be overlooked as a valid means of healing, having its origin in Jesus as creator, healer and author of all truth lest one fall into "spiritual schizophrenia" with an artificial division between medicine and spiritual healing.[63] But in the final analysis, Jesus is the ultimate model and example in the healing, spiritual direction and restoration of the human soul and body.

Endnotes ————————

[1] Roger F. Hurding, *Roots And Shoots: A Guide To Counselling And Psychotherapy* (London: Hodder and Stoughton, 1985) p. 16.

[2] David G. Benner, *Care of Souls. Revisioning Christian Nurture and Counsel* (Grand Rapids: Baker Books, 1998) p. 31.

[3] Ibid.

[4] Benner, p. 32.

[5] Hurding, p. 17.

[6] Ibid.

[7] Ibid.

[8] Ibid.

[9] Benner, p. 37.

[10] Benner, p. 38.

[11] Carol Deinhardt, ed., *Foundational Issues In Christian Counselling* (Otterburne: ProvPress, 1997) p. 9.

[12] Hurding, p. 276.

[13] Gary R. Collins, *Christian Counseling: A Comprehensive Guide* (Waco: Word Books Publisher, 1980) p. 14.

[14] Deinhardt, pp. 22-24.

[15] Stanton L. Jones and Richard E. Butman, *Modern Psychotherapies. A Comprehensive Christian Appraisal* (Downers Grove: InterVarsity Press, 1991) p. 12.

[16] Jones and Butman, p. 14.

[17] Dan Blazer, *Freud vs. God: How Psychiatry Lost Its Soul & Christianity Lost Its Mind* (Downers Grove: InterVarsity Press, 1998) pp. 17-23.

[18] Blazer, p. 22.

[19] Blazer, p. 83.

[20] Wayne E. Oates, *The Presence of God in Pastoral Counseling* (Waco: Word Books, 1986) pp. 27-31.

[21] Robert C. Roberts, *Taking the Word to Heart: Self and Other in an Age of Therapies* (Grand Rapids: Eerdmans Publishing Co., 1993) pp. 133-150.

[22] Deinhardt, p. 9.

[23] Ibid.

[24] Mark R. McMinn, *Psychology, Theology and Spirituality in Christian Counseling. AACC Counseling Library.* (Wheaton: Tyndale House Publisher, 1996) p. 16.

[25] Blazer, pp. 153-154.

[26] Blazer, pp. 157-158.

[27] Blazer, pp. 155-157.

[28] Blazer, p. 174.

[29] Ed M. Smith, *Beyond Tolerable Recovery* (Campbellsville: Alathia Publishing, 1996, 4th ed. 2000) p. 23.

[30] Smith, 2000, p. 157.

[31] Benner, p. 39.

[32] H. Norman Wright, *The Healing of Fears* (Eugene: Harvest House Publishers, 1982) pp. 53, 93-104, 131, 142-143.

[33] Wright, pp. 131-132.

[34] Wright, pp. 142-143.

[35] Henry Cloud, *Changes That Heal: How to Understand Your Past to Ensure a Healthier Future* (Grand Rapids: Zondervan Publishing House, 1992) pp. xiv-xv, 77.

[36] Cloud, pp. 29, 94, 334.

[37] Deinhardt, p. 5.

[38] Neil T. Anderson, Terry E. Zuehlke and Julianne S. Zuehlke, *Christ Centered Therapy: The Practical Integration of Theology and Psychology* (Grand Rapids: Zondervan Publishing House, 2000) p. 60.

[39] Deinhardt, p. 5.

[40] Dallas Willard, *Renovation of the Heart: Putting on the Character of Christ* (Colorado Springs: NavPress, 2002) pp. 20-21.

[41] Willard, p. 20.

[42] Ibid.

[43] Edward M. Smith, *Healing Life's Hurts: Let the Light of Christ Dispel the Darkness in Your Soul* (Ann Arbor: Vine Books, 2002) p. 16.

[44] Collins, 1980, pp. 44-45.

[45] Collins, p. 46.

[46] Ronald A.N. Kydd, *Healing Through the Centuries: Models for Understanding* (Peabody: Hendrickson Publishers, Inc., 1998) p. xxiii.

[47] Mark A. Pearson, *Christian Healing: A Practical and Comprehensive Guide* (Grand Rapids: Chosen Books, 1995) p. 56.

[48] Brad Long and Cindy Strickler, *Let Jesus Heal Your Hidden Wounds: Cooperating With the Holy Spirit in Healing Ministry* (Grand Rapids: Chosen Books, 2001) p. 9.

[49] Leanne Payne, *The Broken Image: Restoring Personal Wholeness Through Healing Prayer* (Wheaton: Crossway Books, 1981) p. 66.

[50] Lawrence J. Crabb Jr., *Basic Principles of Biblical Counseling* (Grand Rapids: Zondervan Publishing House, 1975) pp. 22-24.

[51] Jones and Butman, p. 11.

[52] Gary Collins, *The Rebuilding of Psychology: An Integration of Psychol-*

ogy and Christianity (Wheaton: Tyndale House Publishers, 1977) p. 44.

[53] McMinn, p. 8.

[54] Clyde M. Narramore, *The Psychology of Counseling* (Grand Rapids: Zondervan Publishing House, 1960) pp. 277, 292.

[55] McMinn, p. 15.

[56] McMinn, pp. 86-89.

[57] McMinn, p. 58.

[58] McMinn, p. 85.

[59] Benner, p. 38.

[60] Michael Green, editor's preface, in Duncan Buchanan, *The Counselling of Jesus* (Downers Grove: InterVarsity Press, 1985) p. 5.

[61] Jones and Butman, p. 14.

[62] Collins, 1980, p. 14.

[63] Dieter Mulitze, *The Great Omission: Resolving Critical Issues for the Ministry of Healing and Deliverance* (Belleville: Essence Publishers, 2001) pp. 92-98.

Chapter Two

Understanding the Presence of Jesus

Whoever has my commands and obeys them, he is the one who loves me. He who loves me will be loved by my Father, and I too will love him and show myself to him (John 14:21).

The following night **the Lord stood near Paul** *and said, "Take courage! As you have testified about me in Jerusalem, so you must also testify about me in Rome"* (Acts 23:11; emphasis mine).

Cindy and Her Abortion

Thirty-one years ago, in December, I had an abortion. For the secular world, that is "the end of the story." Get "it" done, forget "it" and "go on with your life." But an abortion leaves its aftermath in any woman's life, and for me it was physical problems from a damaged cervix causing future miscarriages, plus emotional problems from nightmares and depression as post-abortion syndrome. Fortunately the doctors discovered the cervical damage and were able to perform surgery during subsequent pregnancies so that I could deliver two healthy babies although I miscarried two as well.

I remember trying to get help after the abortion. I went to some spiritual counseling sessions and ended up more confused and feeling abused emotionally because the root issues weren't dealt with. I went to a secular psychologist with Gestalt therapy and "primal therapy" and I hit pillows and yelled, but felt no relief. Abortion was not seen as wrong, just as a removal of unwanted tissue, so there was no post-abortion therapy. I carried the shame of the abortion for years because I was told, "Just get over it." Inside I was feeling terrible shame and guilt that no one addressed in the secular world. I had all the symptoms of post-abortion syndrome (sleeplessness, night terrors and anxiety attacks), all of which I tried to drown with alcohol. Covering up the pain did not help; only when it was exposed and Jesus Himself appeared and brought healing did the pain leave. I had repressed the feelings through alcohol and ended up an alcoholic until Jesus met me and set me free. The pain was still repressed even after I met Jesus. I didn't know who to go to and talk about the pain because I didn't think anyone could understand or even cared. The lie of the evil one was "*No one* will understand, and *no one* even cares."

Finally in December during a healing prayer session in which I was receiving prayer because of my fear of making decisions, the Lord revealed a memory about the decision I had made, very unwillingly, to abort my first baby. Dieter led me through each memory of the decision-making process leading up to the abortion. In the first part I had gone to a pastor to ask his opinion, and he had said, "Oh sure, go ahead." I left that session disappointed that "God" would say such a thing and felt totally hopeless. I wandered aimlessly and hopelessly through the streets. In the healing prayer session, I chose to forgive my pastor. Then Dieter prayed, and the Lord came and walked on the street beside me. He took the pain out of my heart, washed my heart and gave me a clean, pure heart.

In the next memory brought by the Holy Spirit, I was in the hospital and the nurses had started the procedure. I wanted to run out of there. They yelled at me and told me to co-operate. I hid under the covers of my bed. Through healing prayer, I chose to forgive those nurses. Then Dieter prayed, and the Lord came and pulled back the covers and took me out of there. In the next memory I was in the operating room and the doctors were continuing the procedure. The pain of the procedure was so intense it felt as if a hundred knives were piercing my body. I screamed. The doctors told me to "shut up!" I felt terrorized and traumatized. In healing prayer, I forgave the doctors, and the Lord appeared and picked me up, bleeding and limp. He held me close and He was weeping. I could see *He understood.* He had felt my pain and much more on the cross. A wonderful sense of relief and peace came over me. The lie of the enemy was broken and the truth Jesus spoke was that *He understood, He cared and He loves me.*

Then for the final step, we looked to see what Jesus would do about the baby. He picked it up gently, and I could see He was weeping. He took the baby's spirit with Him to heaven. I had not thought this was possible, but Dieter asked if I would like to know the baby's gender and so I asked Jesus. The words "twins—a boy and a girl," came instantly to me. Dieter then asked if I would like to name the babies. I hesitated a bit, not really sure if I could do that. But the names "Andrew and Sarah" came to me, and I then named the babies and released them to Jesus.

Concerning after-effects from this healing prayer session, I felt drained but very peaceful. There was closure to that trauma of the abortion so long ago. That night through a nightmare the enemy tried to re-instate the fear and terror I had felt about the abortion. When I awoke, I recognized the lie of the enemy that "I had to live in fear," and I released the feelings to Jesus and again received His peace.

Concerning my feelings now, I know that Jesus understands the pain and trauma of abortion. He has felt our pain and grieves over us and over our babies. I pray this testimony will encourage many women to let Jesus come and heal their wounds from abortion. For those contemplating abortion, I pray that they will see and understand that abortion is a tragic and traumatic solution that should not be even considered. Jesus will help you through whatever situation you are in, no matter how hopeless it seems at the time.

The Centrality of His True Presence

Cindy had not fully recovered from an abortion many years earlier. She came seeking a complete healing from all the personal pain and trauma, as well as closure. As she has testified, Jesus met her need and healed the deepest places of her being.

The healing and restoration she experienced came from intentionally calling upon Jesus and His Spirit and believing in their actual presence to direct the ministry, recall past events and their memories, expose lies, bring understanding and truth and heal the deepest wounds and places in her heart.

The incarnational presence of Jesus is fundamental to the ministry of healing prayer and the restoration of the human soul. The true stories in this book—like Cindy's abortion—of how Christians have encountered the Living Word in healing prayer will help to develop an understanding of His presence. Healing prayer ministry sessions can be quite different from one person to the next, even for the same type of need and even from one session to the next for the same person. Thus the stories recounted in this book do not give a full account of the range of experiences people have in healing prayer ministry.

Towards a Theology of the Presence: A Critical Assumption

What of His presence today to heal and restore the deepest places of the human soul? Is Jesus more or less confined to the throne of heaven, largely absent from the world? If Jesus and certainly His Spirit are much more present than we realize, this will profoundly impact the ministry of healing prayer and any Christian therapy.

When Jesus said where two or three are gathered in His name He would be there in their midst (Matt. 18:20), did He mean that He would be there but invisible and silent, as a number of theological traditions seem to imply? Or might He on occasion manifest His supernatural presence and at times speak audibly or inaudibly? An answer to this question reveals some theological assumptions, especially unstated ones.

A theology of the presence is a critical, major assumption upon which all else rests. Do we acknowledge His presence but in practice rely on our ability to analyze and assess people for their healing, or do we come into His presence and expect Him to actually initiate and direct along with His Spirit? It makes all the difference in the world.

A biblical foundation for the ministry of healing prayer requires a theology of the presence. To this we now turn our attention, both to the Old and New Testaments.

The Presence in the Old Testament

Although God is ever-present or omnipresent throughout all of time and all of creation, the Old Testament distinguishes between the ways in which God was present among His people. The theology of God's presence (or *theophany* as theologians call it) in the Old Testament deals with both His general and "more localized" presence. When considering the theology of Leviticus, for example, the "enduring presence of God is one of the theological presuppositions running throughout the whole book."[1] God was of course always present with His people by virtue of His omnipresence in all of creation. But the book of Leviticus also reveals His "more direct presence" with His people (*"My Presence will go with you and I will give you rest"* [Exod. 33:14ff; 40:36-38]) in cloud and fire, in talking directly to Moses, in the temple and in worship.[2] Concerning God's presence as shown in Leviticus, Wenham wrote:

> Leviticus distinguishes between the permanent presence of God with His people, a presence which is to regulate their whole way of life and His visible presence within the camp of Israel and His localized presence above the ark within the tent of meeting... according to Exod. 29:43-45, God's real and visible presence in the tabernacle was the heart of the covenant. "There I will meet with the people of Israel and it shall be sanctified by my glory.... And I will dwell among the people of Israel and will be their God."[3]

Since the whole of life is lived out before God who is everywhere and holy, and these were God's people, they had to be holy because God is holy.

Jesus in the Old Testament

The preincarnate presence of Jesus in the Old Testament provides more concrete examples of the *localized* presence of God. Ron Rhodes, in his book, *Christ Before the Manger: The Life and Times of the Preincarnate Christ*, presents compelling evidence for the preincarnate presence or manifestations of Jesus as recorded in the Old Testament. God the Father appointed Jesus as the visible manifestation of God in both the Old and New Testaments.[4] All the Old Testament references to the Angel of the Lord were actually Jesus appearing in bodily form before the incarnation.[5] This is based on the Angel of the Lord identified in the Old Testament as being God or Yahweh yet distinct from the person of Yahweh or God and the Angel of Yahweh being Jesus when one weighs all the biblical evidence about the nature and function of each person of the Trinity.[6]

Although Christ is the second person of the Trinity and is fully divine and present everywhere, or omnipresent (Jer. 23:24, 1 Kings 8:27), that does not contradict or preclude His specific local presence anywhere at any time.[7] Just as Jesus comforted, commissioned, saved, preserved, directed and revealed God's truth in the New Testament among His people, He also did so in the Old Testament at times in bodily preincarnate form. The Hebraic idea of "Angel" is that of a messenger or envoy.[8]

Sarai abused Hagar after which she left and wandered in the desert, pregnant and deeply discouraged. It was Jesus who appeared as the Angel of the Lord to comfort her and bring a promise for her child, Ishmael (Gen. 16:11-13).

> It is highly revealing of Christ's nature that His first appearance as the Angel of the Lord in the Old Testament times was to bring comfort to a downcast soul. Because of a brutal confrontation Hagar had with Sarah (Abraham's wife) over the issue of childbearing, Hagar fled into the desert. She was emotionally devastated and spiritually wasted. After she stopped at a well of water, Christ appeared to her as the Angel of the Lord to bring her comfort and physical sustenance (Gen. 16:7-14). He had heard her cry from the *eternal realm*, felt compassion for her and came *in person* to minister to her needs in the *earthly realm*.[9]

Jesus, as the Angel of the Lord, called from heaven to Abraham and, as an equal to God, directly made the promise of his descendants and blessing to all nations (Gen. 22:15-19).[10] Jesus appeared as the Angel of the Lord to Jacob in a dream at Bethel (Gen. 28:10-15; 31:13) and also in a dream during the breeding season involving male goats (Gen. 31:10-13).[11]

Jesus, as the Angel of Lord, appeared to Moses in flames of fire in the burning bush (Exod. 3:1-6) in order to commission Moses, not unlike commissioning the disciples.[12] Jesus disclosed Himself as the "I Am" (Exod. 3:14) just as He referred to Himself as the "I Am" to the Pharisees (Matt. 22:32; John 8:58). Jesus, as the Angel of the Lord, appeared as God to Moses (Exod. 3:16; 4:1). Moses saw the *form of God* because of his humility and faithfulness (Num. 12:3, 8). During the exodus, Jesus accompanied the nation of Israel and was the spiritual rock from which they drank (1 Cor. 10:1-4). Just as Jesus came down from heaven in response to His people's suffering in Egypt (Exod. 3:8), He is the one who came down from heaven (John 6:33, 38, 51) and is the only one who has gone into heaven (John 3:13). Did Moses and others see the preincarnate Christ with an apparent pavement of sapphire underneath His feet (Exod. 24:10)? Could it have been the preincarnate Christ who came down in a pillar of cloud to Miriam, Aaron and Moses and stood at the entrance of the tent (Num. 12:5), or is that just a Hebraism?

Jesus appeared as a man of God, awesome and looking like an angel, to the sterile wife of Manoah to inform her of the birth of Samson and what would be required of them (Judg. 13:1-22). Manoah prayed thereafter and Jesus appeared again, like a man, as the Angel of the Lord, to his wife while she was in the field (Judg. 13:9-11). When asked of His name, Jesus replied that it was "beyond understanding" (Judges 13:18), which is the same word for "wonderful" as Isaiah used of the Messiah (Isa. 9:6).[13] Jesus then left by ascending into heaven in the flame that blazed heavenward from the altar with a burnt offering (Judg. 13:21) upon which Manoah and his wife fully realized that the angel was divine—God Himself.

When the Lord first began to speak to Samuel, it was Jesus who appeared to him in preincarnate form—*"The Lord came and stood there, calling as at other times..."* (1 Sam. 3:10)—in a vision (1 Sam. 3:15). Although it does not refer here to the Angel of the Lord, it seems perfectly consistent with the other accounts in the Old Testament to acknowledge this as another bodily presence of Jesus.

Just as Jesus appeared to Hagar to comfort and encourage her, Jesus appeared as the Angel of the Lord to the depressed Elijah by gently awakening him from his sleep, giving him food and encouraging him on his way (1 Kings 19:5-7).[14] Just as Jesus is the intercessor in the New Testament (John 17; Heb. 7:25), He physically appeared and interceded to the Father on behalf of the Israelites under oppression (Zech. 1:12-13; 3:1-2).[15] When the Angel of the Lord encamps around those that fear Him, it is actually Jesus (Ps. 34:7) although at times ministering angels are sent to believers (Heb. 1:14).[16]

Isaiah encountered Jesus in a vision, seated on a throne (Isa. 6:1-4). This is clear from John who wrote that Isaiah *"saw Jesus' glory and spoke about him"* (John 12:41).[17] Ezekiel saw a *"figure like that of a man"* with a waist (Ezek. 1:26-27) in an incredible vision of Jesus' majestic glory (Ezek. 1:4-28). It was actually Jesus who spoke to him (Ezek. 2:1-3:10), commissioning him as He did with Isaiah. When Daniel and his two friends were thrown into the fiery furnace, Nebuchadnezzar saw four men walking in the fire and the fourth looked like a son of the gods (Dan. 3:25). That fourth person was most likely the preincarnate glorified Christ.[18]

The above accounts were probably part of what Jesus explained to the believers on the road to Emmaus concerning Himself in the Scriptures from Moses and the Prophets (Luke 24:27).

Christ After the Resurrection and Before the Ascension

Jesus, in His incarnation, is the final fulfillment of God's presence among His people (Col. 2:9). This is especially clear in the passage, *"The Word became flesh and lived for a while among us. We have seen His glory, the glory of the one and only..."* (John 1:14). The Greek word for "made His dwelling," *skenoo*, can be translated "pitched His tent" or "tabernacled" and is an intentional reference to the Old Testament with the Tent of Meeting, the Tabernacle and hence God's presence among His people.[19] John's immediate reference to "glory" in the same verse recalls the glory of God's presence in the tabernacle in the wilderness, from the moment when "the glory of the Lord" first filled the tabernacle (Exod. 40:34).[20] Christ referred to Himself as the temple (John 2:21). Christians are the temple of the Holy Spirit, signifying His dwelling within us (1 Cor. 6:19).

After the resurrection, Jesus appeared in some very miraculous ways to His people. He appeared in "a different form" to two believers as they were walking in the country (Mark 16:12). He appeared to two believers, Cleopas and another, on the way to Emmaus, but they were kept from recognizing Him (Luke 24:13-16). Jesus spent a good part of the day with them (Luke 24:17-29), and it was not until the evening that their eyes were "opened" and they recognized Him (Luke 24:30-31). Although they had not clearly recognized Him that day, His presence and teaching nonetheless convicted their hearts (Luke 24:32). Jesus then suddenly miraculously disappeared (Luke 24:31) and later suddenly appeared (Luke 24:36) to the disciples when they were discussing the report from Cleopas and the other believer. Seeing they were startled and somewhat disbelieving, Jesus showed them His hands and feet with the marks of the crucifixion, ate some fish, invited them to touch Him and declared He was not a ghost since He had flesh and bones in His resurrection body (Luke 24:37-43).

After the resurrection Jesus appeared to Mary Magdalene, but she also did not recognize Him and actually thought He was the gardener (John 20:14-17). But when He spoke her name, she recognized Him. With the doors locked Jesus suddenly appeared to the disciples on the first day and a week later (John 20:19-20; 20:26). Jesus appeared a third time while they were fishing and again, it took a while for them to recognize Him (John 21:1-14).

After Jesus had spoken to the apostles, He was taken up into heaven and sat at the right hand of God (Mark 16:19; Luke 24:51; Acts 1:9; Eph. 1:20). This is also clear in the passage, *"But when this priest had offered for all time one sacrifice for sins, he sat down at the right hand of God"* (Heb. 10:12). Similarly, *"The Lord says to my Lord: 'Sit at my right hand until I make your enemies a footstool for your feet"* (Ps. 110:1). One might be tempted to simply believe that after His incarnation, ministry and ascension to heaven, Jesus was no longer present to touch and heal people in any "direct" way as shown in the Gospels. Is Jesus effectively "tied" to the throne of heaven?

Jesus After the Ascension

While it is true that Jesus is seated at the right hand of the Father, it does not logically follow that He is *only there*. A simple reading of the book of Acts informs us otherwise. Consider the following. Jesus appeared to Saul in a bright light and spoke from it: *"Saul, Saul, why do you persecute me?"* (Acts 9:4). Jesus then spoke directly to Ananias about Paul and his need for healing (Acts 9:10-18). Jesus called Paul in a vision (Acts 9:10-15). There was a vision of a man of Macedonia, not of Jesus, yet nevertheless a vision that gave direction to Paul (Acts 16:9). One night, the Lord spoke to Paul in a vision, telling him not to be afraid and promising His protection

(Acts 18:9). While praying at the temple, Paul fell into a trance and saw the Lord telling him to leave Jerusalem immediately (Acts 22:17). The most pivotal verse is, *"The following night the Lord stood near Paul and said, 'Take courage! As you have testified about me in Jerusalem, so you must also testify in Rome'"* (Acts 23:11; emphasis mine; cf. 2 Tim. 4:17). Jesus did say He was going back to the Father where He can be seen no longer (John 16:10, 28; 17:11; 20:17), yet since He appeared directly to Paul after the ascension, He must have meant He would not be seen publicly and continually any longer.

Clearly after the ascension Jesus spoke directly to Paul, appeared in a bright light or a vision or a trance-like state and even appeared in person in resurrected bodily form. That is similar to the Old Testament accounts as seen above where, for example, Jesus spoke in dreams to Jacob, appeared in a burning bush, disappeared in a flame of fire and appeared in visions. But notice most importantly, Jesus as Lord decided how and when He would appear and even if He would appear. No one visualized, conjured or imagined Him. There was no power of the mind in any way operating here. He might be present but not recognized (Luke 24:16), and even that depends on God's grace and God's opening up one's eyes (Luke 24:31).

The appearances of Jesus underscore His redemptive love and purposes to direct, encourage, empower and give hope to His people at typically crucial moments in their lives. Jesus is divine; we must not limit His presence by our theology. This gives more meaning to the promise that He will always be with us to the end of the ages (Matt. 28:20), and that where two or three are gathered in His name, He is surely in their midst (Matt. 18:20). The question really is: how might Jesus manifest His presence with us and in our midst? The theology of some would only allow that He is always completely invisible and totally silent but of course doctrinally present. Considering all of the Scriptures, the manifestations of His presence may at times be beyond what we expect or anticipate. The belief that Jesus cannot appear after the ascension is an example of reading something into Scripture (*eisegesis*: He is only at the throne) and not using all of Scripture to interpret Scripture, a basic principle of biblical interpretation.

We must be careful not to limit God's presence and working in our lives to a limited personal theology or belief system. But at the same time we should not ever open ourselves up to the numerous and seductive occult, New Age, human potential or transpersonal humanistic techniques.

Could Jesus Appear Today?

Someone might then argue that such appearances of Jesus were just for the apostles and the immediate Church and do not apply to us today. But nowhere do the Scriptures support such an idea. The appearances of Jesus and His ways of speaking to His people as recorded in the Scriptures must be understood as a *model* of how Jesus reveals Himself to His people in addition—and never in contradiction—to His written Word. He did not appear to everyone, nor did He speak directly to everyone, since there are many accounts in Acts of people praying to the Lord, waiting on the Lord, being prompted by the Spirit and so forth, all without His more "direct" appearance. We have every reason to believe that those believers were just as spiritual and loved by Jesus as those who had a more direct encounter with Him. Yet Jesus did at times appear more directly and speak more directly. If He did so out of His love and grace at critical times, as the Scriptures show in both the Old and New Testament, then why not today out of equally critical or difficult moments? Does Jesus love His people today any less than those in the early Church? His appearances depend on

His character, grace and purposes and not on when (as in a "dispensation"), where or to whom.

Acts presents, among other things, a model of how Jesus and His Spirit interact and communicate with the Church. If we reject any part of that model, why not also reject house groups, fasting and much more from the life of the early Church? On what basis does one reject or claim as inapplicable any of the life of the Church in the first century? On what basis would one claim the communication model is invalid for today but everything else is valid? Objections to the presence of Jesus today and His speaking to believers today often come from a cessationist mindset which holds that some of the spiritual gifts ceased soon after the early Church was established and all the Scriptures were written. Cessationism, however, is both unbiblical and untenable.[21] All the spiritual gifts are active today.

Obeying and loving Jesus is linked to the revelation of Himself. Consider John 14:21: *"Whoever has my commands and obeys them, he is the one who loves me. He who loves me will be loved by my Father, and I too will love him and show myself to him."* This verse applies to all Christians since it is based on obeying Jesus' commands which leads to God the Father loving the person and He and Jesus "making their home" with that person (John 14:23). If one argues that this applies only to the believers in Jesus' day, only those believers can expect His peace (John 14:27)—not a terribly comforting thought—and His Spirit (John 14:26) which we know is for all believers (Rom. 8:9; 1 Cor. 3:16). This disclosure of Jesus cannot refer to the second coming when He will reveal Himself to the world, since in response to Judas' question Jesus says this "showing" of Himself is not public but only for those who obey and love Him (John 14:19, 22-24). This verse refers then to Jesus' showing Himself to believers on this earth before the second coming. But exactly how will He appear or "show Himself" to believers? This is not indicated, but "in some undefined way he will reveal himself to those who love him."[22] John used the Greek word *emphanizo* instead of the usual word for "manifest" (*phaneroo*).[23] *Emphanizo* in John 14:21 "is used of the spiritual presence of Christ with the one who keeps Christ's commandments. It thus connotes here a manifestation to the *spiritual* faculties rather than to the senses."[24] Considering a theology of the presence overall from Scripture, this verse would support the manifestation of Christ's supernatural presence to those receiving healing prayer—those who love and obey Him—including prayer for past painful events. Jesus' promise of His presence in John 14:21 could apply to healing prayer but of course is not restricted just to the ministry of healing prayer.

There is a similar theme in *"Blessed are the pure in heart, for they will see God"* (Matt. 5:8), wherein those devoted to Jesus will have a revelation of Him. This verse refers to spiritual vision as in John 14:21, since one day all people—including those *impure in heart*—will see Jesus in the second coming and of course on the day of judgment (Matt. 24:30; 2 Thess. 1:7-10; Rev. 20:11-15). To insist otherwise, like only a revelation with the natural eyes, would nullify the meaning of the verse.

Theophostic ministry relies on the presence of Christ to expose lies and reveal truth and thus bring instant, lasting healing.[25] However, apparently Jesus does not actually appear in a memory but only a "visual representation" of Jesus.[26] This understanding is based on 1 Tim. 6:16 where Jesus is understood to be the one who is immortal and dwells in unapproachable light and whom no man has seen or can see.[27] But that verse refers to God the Father who will arrange Jesus' return (1 Tim. 6:15; Matt. 24:36) and cannot refer to Jesus since He obviously *has been seen* before and after the incarnation. It is the Father who is invisible (1 Tim. 1:17; Col. 1:15) and who is Spirit and has been seen only by the Son (John 6:46). If the next time anyone truly sees Jesus is "in the clouds,"[28] did Paul just see a visual representation of Christ (Acts 23:11)? A theology of the presence would indicate that Paul truly saw Jesus and that Jesus can truly and supernaturally manifest Himself to someone in a memory, vision or dream.

Jesus still does appear even today in whatever sovereign way He chooses. This is especially true of the ministry of healing prayer which is based on the absolutely necessary presence of Jesus and His Spirit. The late Dr. John White, former professor of psychiatry, medical missionary and author, wrote about the three occasions the Lord appeared to Him personally.[29] He did not seek those encounters with the risen Lord, nor did He visualize Jesus in any way. But the Lord appeared nonetheless.

Does God Speak Today Apart from the Scriptures?

In healing prayer, Jesus or the Holy Spirit or God the Father may well speak to a person to expose lies, bring truth, reassure the heart and so forth. *Jesus communicated directly* to Cindy during her healing from the effects of abortion, also telling her the genders of her two aborted babies as recounted at the beginning of this chapter. Those were precious moments, and it was a great joy and privilege for me to be a part of her healing. There are many other examples in this book of healings where Jesus, the Spirit or God the Father spoke in various ways to His children.

But some evangelical theologians would argue that this is no longer possible since God does not speak today to any of His children apart from the Scriptures. Some evangelical theologians maintain that the Bible "gives us no reason to expect that God will speak to His children apart from the Scriptures."[30] This idea is based largely on the fact that the Church now has the completed and written Scriptures (final "canon"), and thus with the "completion of salvation in Christ comes the cessation of revelation."[31] But this is cessationist thinking which is unbiblical and untenable.[32] While purporting to defend the authority and sufficiency of the Scriptures, this idea actually causes more problems than it attempts to solve.

Let us suppose for a moment that this view is true and say that in 200 AD the Scriptures were "completed" so that, with the final books of the Bible thus decided, the canon was closed. At that time there would have been a whole generation of Christians accustomed to Jesus and the Spirit speaking through visions, dreams, prophecies and all the ways recorded in the whole Bible and certainly the book of Acts. Suddenly one day, as the ink dried on a parchment when the Scriptures were "completed," God ceased all direct communication. Would not those Christians wonder what had happened and be alarmed as to why Jesus and His Spirit were suddenly totally silent? Wouldn't you? Does this not appear rather strange?

How would a woman feel if one day, after years of marriage, her husband said he would no longer talk to her because he had given her several books on marriage and communication and insists she could deduce all decisions and feelings and directions in the marriage from studying them? Oh yes, thankfully she could talk to Him, but He would never talk with her. Would that not change their relationship? Remember, we are the bride of Christ.

On a very practical level, what about illiterate Christians, or those who belong to a tribe that has no written language, or those who simply cannot afford a copy of the Bible? This has been the reality for millions of Christians down the centuries and is still true today. Do we want to believe that unfortunately those fellow believers cannot hear anything directly from God in any way? Of course having a copy of the Scriptures is a great joy and eternal benefit to every single Christian. But this view means that God has basically tied His own hands in communicating with His own beloved people.

A further problem is that part of the Bible has no relevance for believers today except for clearly telling them what they will *not experience*. All the examples of God speaking to people through dreams, visions, directly via audible or inaudible words and more, are now detailed examples of what suddenly ceased centuries ago. As Deere wrote, "Where would we find a New Testament text that teaches that New Testament experience is no longer valid?"[33] There is none. In essence, it actually undermines the authority of part of the Scriptures for believers today by declaring it irrelevant for today. The authority has actually has been shifted from the Scriptures to a teaching based on a historical event (closing of the canon) outside the Scriptures and now superimposed onto the Scriptures. This reminds me of God's warning to never add or subtract from His commands (Deut. 4:2, 12:32).

A glaring weakness of this view is that no verse directly and clearly supports it. But there are verses which directly challenge the view. Did not Jesus say that we, as His sheep, *will hear and recognize His voice* (John 10:4, 16, 27)? That applies to every single believer today, unless one is willing to argue that only believers who lived before the completion of the canon had eternal life and would not be snatched out of Jesus' hand (John 10:28). Who is prepared to argue that? Not me! Some argue that hearing a voice from heaven will cause pastoral problems since they may not know where the voice is coming from or whose voice it is. But Jesus said they will know His voice because He is *in relationship with them* (John 10:3, 5, 14, 16). For example when my wife or daughter phone me, I know exactly who it is after one word because I know them and they know me. Likewise we will know the voice of Jesus when we need to because we belong to Him and He lives in us (John 6:56, 14:20, 23). Everyone who comes to Jesus listens to and learns from the Father (John 6:45). Did not Jesus say that He will give us words and wisdom when we are persecuted and interrogated (Luke 21:15; 12:12)? Or does that promise of Jesus no longer apply to us today because the canon is closed? Does not listening to the Father and being taught by Him (John 6:44-45), for believers as a whole, involve more than the study of the Scriptures? Why would the writer of Hebrews warn us to not harden our hearts should we hear the voice of God (Heb. 3:7, 15, 4:8) if God no longer speaks to His people? Are Christians after the closing of the canon no longer in danger of hardening their hearts? If we need to be rebuked and disciplined, Jesus may well speak to us in addition to the conviction of the Holy Spirit and through the Scriptures. Jesus might knock on the door of our hearts, urging repentance and a restored relationship, and we may hear His voice in the process (Rev. 3:20).

Those who hold this view generally do not doubt that Satan or evil spirits can talk to Christians or put thoughts in their minds (Luke 4:1-13, 33; Acts 5:3) even though the canon is closed.[34] Is it not strange, then, that although Satan and his evil spirits can speak to believers apart from what is written, Jesus and the Father have ceased doing so centuries ago? Oddly enough, this implies that we could have clearer communication with evil spirits than with Jesus. Has God also ceased speaking to us through angels who are sent to minister to Christians (Heb. 1:14; Luke 1:19, 2:9; Acts 5:19-29, 27:23-24; Ps. 91:10)? If He has, does this mean that all ministering angels are now mute whenever they may appear in our presence? If not, then why may angels speak to us but not God Himself? If angels do not speak to Christians today in their ministry to

Christians, it is even stranger that only the devil and evil spirits can speak to us. If God so silenced Himself, why did He not silence the devil and evil spirits as well?

Another main argument against this view is the simple fact that believers today *are* experiencing dreams, visions, the audible and inaudible voice of God and more. This also happens in healing prayer as I have witnessed many times. But there are counterfeits out there, and that is precisely why we need discernment, must test the spirits and read the Scriptures carefully regarding how God communicates with His people. All the Scriptures are relevant today and provide a sure model of how God communicates with His beloved children.

Some believers say things like, "So who do you think you are that God would talk to you?" Such a statement appears to come from envy. God speaking to anyone has everything to do with His grace and sovereign will. Otherwise we might as well say, "So who do you think you are that God would save you?" Rather, should we not rejoice and be glad that the Father still speaks to His children?

This view, as supported by some evangelical theologians, will *create* a crisis in the Church since many thousands of Christians will not have learned or experienced these forms of communication or suppressed and denied them and have practiced very little discernment. That puts the Church at a grave tactical disadvantage when encountering the New Age movement and people who have actual spirit guides, for example.

The most unsettling and alarming thing about this whole debate is the implications on one's relationship with Jesus. Christ is in us (John 6:56, 14:20), we are to know Christ and the power of His resurrection (Phil. 3:10), Christ is to be formed in us (Gal. 4:19), we must abide in Him (John 15:1-5), and yet we are told that He is silent and will never speak to us directly and personally except through the Scriptures. We can pray and speak to Jesus all we want, but apparently He will never speak directly and personally back to us. This effectively limits an intimate, personal relationship with Jesus. Ultimately, this whole debate is about defending a system of biblical thinking at the expense of one's relationship with Jesus. I do not think it is worth the cost. This whole debate is so unfortunate because one part of the body of Christ is busily constructing and defending arguments from the Scriptures as to why the rest of the body of Christ cannot have as close a relationship with Jesus as they claim.

The idea that God does not speak today apart from the Scriptures is thus untenable and unbiblical. It is not the Scriptures but an interpretation of the Scriptures that is behind this view and the supposed defense for biblical authority. This is another example of the traditions of men (Mark 7:8-9). It has a lot more to do with biblical deism, supporting unbelief through theology, confidence in theology over relationship, fear of losing control and fear of relationship with Jesus.[35]

Concerning whether God speaks today, Dallas Willard concluded:

> ... there is nothing in Scripture to indicate that the biblical modes of God's communication with humans have been superseded or abolished by either the presence of the church or the close of the scriptural canon. This is simply a fact, just as it is simply a fact that God's children have continued up to the present age to find themselves addressed by God in most of the ways He commonly addressed biblical characters.[36]

Most assuredly, Jesus did speak to Cindy as He does today to many others of His precious children who long to simply experience His love and get to know Him better. *In the final analysis, it is all about relationship.*

Christ Within Us: The Incarnational Presence

In understanding the presence of Christ around us, we now consider the presence of Christ within us. This is crucial for the ministry and theology of healing prayer. Christ is in us and we are indwelt by Jesus and His Spirit. Christ is in the Father, we are in Christ and Christ is in us (John 14:20; 2 Cor. 13:5). Jesus dwells in us (John 6:56; 14:20) and we must abide in Him (John 15:5). As we obey Him and the Father, they will dwell within each of us (John 14:23; 17:23). Indeed, the heart of the great mystery of the Christian faith is Christ being in us (Col. 1:27). In order to be Christians, the Spirit of Christ must live in us (Rom. 8:9,11; Ezek. 37:13) and thereby Christ is in us (Rom. 8:10). Logically, then, our bodies are members of Christ (1 Cor. 6:15), and in the corporate sense we are the body of Christ (1 Cor. 12:27).

As God dwelt in the temple in the Old Testament, God's people now are the temple of the Holy Spirit (1 Cor. 3:16-17) and of the living God (2 Cor. 6:16). The "indwelling" terminology of Paul relates to the indwelling of the Spirit both in the individual and in the Church, and it is the ultimate fulfillment of the imagery of God's presence begun and lost in the Garden, restored in the tabernacle in Exodus 40 and in the temple in 1 Kings 8.[37] Paul prayed for the Ephesians that the Spirit would strengthen them in their inner being and that Christ would dwell in their hearts through faith (Eph. 3:16-17). The new life in Christ, being "crucified with Christ," means that Christ lives in the believer (Gal. 2:20). The life of Christ must be manifested in Christians (2 Cor. 4:10).

While we can fully appreciate the sovereignty (transcendence) of God, we do not always fully appreciate the nearness (immanence) of God. Historically in the Church, this has not always been the case.

For the first four centuries the Church understood the incarnational presence of Christ and saw itself as a holy people indwelt by God, but then increasingly the focus turned to holy things.[38] With the rise of science and the "modern" era, which shifted from a God-centered universe to a man-centered universe, there came increasingly the "practice of the non-presence of God."[39] From the time of Descartes onwards, man was in the center making observations, perceiving and consciously knowing the world. Descartes' famous dictum, "I think, therefore I am" (*Cogito ergo sum*), epitomized a humanistic understanding of truth and knowledge. Yet this is far different from the Christian way to truth which comes from relationship and not the power of intellect or analysis. As Leanne Payne, founder of Pastoral Care Ministries, wrote:

Christianity is incarnational. We are linked to ultimate Reality by His Presence within. Christian epistemology is unique in that our way of knowing is rooted in Christ's incarnational Presence.[40]

Our way of knowing (epistemology) is rooted in union and communion, not analysis. This does not devalue or discredit analysis and thought. Rather, it gives the wider and complete context for knowledge. This understanding of truth is totally different from the world's; in fact it is a stumbling block and foolishness to the world (1 Cor. 1:20-25). Apart from our union with Christ and remaining in Him (John 15:1-5), we can do nothing and will have no lasting fruit. Nothing is not very much. All effort comes out of union and relationship, never the reverse. In total contrast to Greek thought, truth is relational, not technical or analytical. Our way of knowing is relational and depends on the grace of God. Jesus' statement, "*I am the way and the truth and the life*" (John 14:6) defies much of the world's thinking. No one can know God the Father until they first know God the Son (John 14:7). No one can see or know or understand or truly comprehend the kingdom of God until they are born again, which only comes from a relationship with Jesus and no other (John 3:3-8; Acts 4:12).

This understanding of the incarnational presence of Jesus was crucially fundamental to all the thinking of none other than C.S. Lewis himself who fully believed that "to know God was to be indwelt by Him. The creature is linked to the Creator by the Spirit of the risen Christ."[41] The world's religions offer all sorts of spiritual techniques and methods to ascend up and into "God," yet Christianity is about God by His Spirit descending into people so they might receive His life and know Him. Unfortunately, since much of modern Christendom does not have such an experience and knowledge of the supernatural from the real presence of Christ within, many Christians are "...no longer free to 'listen' to God, to receive His guidance, or to collaborate actively with the Holy Spirit...."[42]

It is certainly true that when we love and bless others, when we speak a word of truth or counsel, when we encourage others, when we give someone a cup of cold water, when we visit someone in prison, it is also Christ who is ministering to others through us. That is also part of incarnational theology, since all believers are the body of Christ. Thus, in one sense, we are the hands, feet and arms of Christ to others. As Thomas put it concerning the importance of an incarnational presence in the ministry of healing prayer:

> Our eyes are the eyes that God uses to weep for the pain of the world. Our emotions are the emotions God uses to have compassion upon his people. Our hands are the hands God uses to bestow his blessing upon those in need. If we do not weep, some people will never know God cares. If we

do not lay our hands on others in a gesture of acceptance, some will never experience healing in this world.[43]

A theology of healing prayer requires a more robust and comprehensive theology of the incarnational presence of Jesus. With His Spirit, Jesus works through us, but He also may come alongside us or around us as seen from Acts and the Old Testament. If we do not fully grasp this, we will unwittingly adopt a non-incarnational model with intercessory prayer as the only means of healing prayer ministry.[44] A fuller appreciation for the incarnational presence of Jesus is pivotal in order to even begin to comprehend the appearance of Jesus, who is the Lord of time in our past when the Holy Spirit recalls memories for our healing.

Some years ago I was experiencing anxiety which I could feel in my whole body as I was about to leave on a long business trip to the Republic of South Africa. I resolved to practice the presence of Jesus by sitting down for a few moments and consciously asking Jesus to fill me with His peace and remove the anxiety. I had received some healing prayer for anxiety months earlier, so I sensed this was not an issue of healing *per se* but of being more consciously in His presence. I prayed quietly and repeatedly, expecting His presence to come over me. After about five minutes of intense prayer, His peace came and it was so solid and real that the anxiety totally disappeared and my body was totally relaxed. It was a peace beyond all understanding and came because I was intentionally looking to the presence of He who is in me by His Spirit. This was not a relaxation or meditative technique of any kind—it was simply coming intentionally into His presence.

Some years ago I was in Cairo, Egypt, on business. On that last night, I needed to wake up at 4:30 in the morning to catch my ride to the airport for my flight to Frankfurt and back home to Canada. I had been away from home for two weeks and was anxious about

83

sleeping through the alarm and missing my flight home to be reunited with my family. I submitted this to prayer. That morning I woke up suddenly in the middle of a relaxing dream, fully awake at precisely 4:29 a.m. Coincidence? No—another example of the presence of God. A year later exactly the same thing happened for a 5 a.m. wakeup when I was unexpectedly stranded in Detroit due to a snowstorm. I woke up exactly at 4:59 a.m. I'm not sure if the dream was equally relaxing.

Gilberte and Alex: Transformed by the Presence of Jesus

Tournier wrote about Gilberte, a lady who experienced much pain, disappointment and instability early in life, plus an engagement broken by an unfaithful fiancé. Her woundedness was largely responsible for marital discord. He wrote what happened when she encountered Jesus:

> ...on Easter Day Gilberte had an important religious experience. She suddenly had a vivid feeling of the presence of Christ and an inward conviction that He alone could deliver her from the whole of her past and all her rancor and bitterness. When she came back we prayed together. When she got to her feet she told me that she felt as if all her bitterness was falling away from her like a chain. She felt free and lighthearted. She completely forgave, not only her husband, but also her fiancé.... Her face shone.[45]

Alex, who was wondering about the Christian faith, was at an evangelistic meeting at the invitation of some faithful Christian friends. As the evangelist spoke, his heart was warmed to the gospel, and he was increasingly convicted of his sin. In fact as the evangelist spoke, he suddenly remembered a number of sinful and shameful things that he had done over the years. When an invitation to come forward and repent of his sins and call upon Jesus so that he might be saved was given, he responded. He followed through the sinner's prayer at the front and, as he did so, an amazing peace came over him. In addition, he knew deep down that his sins had been forgiven and he just felt "clean" inside as he said later to his friends. In his heart for the first time in his life, he felt truly loved and accepted as if he had finally come home. It was such a deep and powerful experience that he will never forget it. The joy of his friends, now his brothers and sisters in Christ, added to the blessings of the moment.

Alex's story is completely hypothetical, but a story that many Christians can relate to. Sometimes addictions are completely overcome at conversion and regeneration or there might even be physical healing. What's the point? Few will argue that salvation involves coming to Christ; in fact, we often talk about "leading people to Christ." The core of salvation involves encountering the living Lord Jesus. Few would disagree and insist that it's just a matter of logical agreement and being connected to Jesus is not that important. Many Christians would cringe (I hope!) at the idea that we need to employ all kinds of techniques to "make salvation happen." Hopefully we can agree that the core of salvation is encountering Jesus, experiencing His presence, as different as that is for each person.

Then why should it suddenly be different when it comes to the care of our souls? Why start with His presence and then continue with methods, techniques and human analysis? Why not be consistent and continue with His presence in the transformation of the human soul? Why not rely as much on His presence in the care and cure of souls as in coming to Him in the first place? Would you not think it strange if a couple told you that they have a "technical marriage"? Then why do we so easily accept "technical healing" of the soul? Having begun in the Spirit, do we now continue by human effort (Gal. 3:3)? Why switch gears all of a sudden?

Gilberte simply had another encounter with Jesus for the healing of her soul. What if Alex had been a Christian for several years and had come forward for prayer and, in once again encountering Jesus, experienced a release from depression and recurring panic attacks? Why could that not be as normal in the Christian life as coming to Christ in the first place?

Asking the Right Questions

There are multitudes of debates on how to make various methods or techniques of counseling or therapy more Christian or how to integrate them into the healing of the soul. It is not so much a matter of making our methods more Christian, but becoming more Christian ourselves. We have to first know who we truly are and who is truly in us before we do anything. Similarly Payne wrote the following concerning educational systems: "...*our hope is not in calling for our systems to be Christian, but in becoming truly Christian ourselves.*"[46] Could it be that the whole debate is being argued in the wrong dimension?

A theology of the presence of Jesus, or lack of it, is effectively a major fork in the road and determines much of what follows. I suspect that many Christians have worked in counseling, therapy and psychology in a Christian context yet are largely oblivious to the fork that others have unwittingly chosen for them. I know of a number of Christians who never completed their studies in counseling at seminary because they were disillusioned with their studies, convinced that upon graduation they would not be really equipped to help anyone. Before we adopt or believe something, we should check out the assumptions.

Oates, after many years of experience in pastoral counseling and searching for a lasting and true center for his ministry, concluded that the presence of God should be the center.

> In this the fortieth year of my career as a pastoral counselor, I have found my concern for the Presence of God in a trialogue with counselees to be the living heart of my work.... Over the years, my most significant memories in pastoral counseling have been in those spiritual breakthroughs when the Presence of God became intensely evident without contrivance or technique on my part and much to the awe-struck amazement on both the counselee's and my part. ...to me, only an explicit and articulate concern for the appearing of the Presence of God in the pastoral counseling relationship is an adequate center of pastoral counseling.[47]

When Moses came down from Mount Sinai with the stone tablets, his face was radiant since he had been in the presence of the Lord (Exod. 34:29, 35). Concerning Gilberte above, Tournier noticed that "her face shone." I have seen this many times, and often friends who have come with the person seeking healing prayer will comment how the person looks radiant or glows upon experiencing the healing presence of Jesus. In my experience this is most often true for those who in a session or two are healed from deep pain like clinical depression, suicidal tendencies, sexual abuse or deep bondages that have imprisoned them for years. I see this all as a sign of His presence in the ministry of healing prayer when people have encountered the Lord Jesus.

After Israel's apostasy with the golden calf, Moses was about to continue leading the people but only with the assurance and promise of God's presence. The Lord assured Moses that *"My Pres-*

ence will go with you" (Exod. 33:14). Moses replied that without His presence, he would not continue. He also said of God's presence, *"What else will distinguish me and your people from all the other people on the face of the earth?"* (Exod. 33:15b).

Similarly it is the intentional presence of Jesus that will distinguish Christian healing prayer from therapies and counseling with their methods and techniques. Invoking the presence of Jesus also brings us deliberately and more consciously into the kingdom of God (Matt. 10:7) wherein we live.[48] That being the case, one must learn to listen to He who is present with His Spirit. Since Jesus is present, how might He and His Spirit speak to us? Do we fully understand the language of the Holy Spirit? Since Jesus now becomes the therapist and we facilitate in His presence, we must learn to collaborate with Him and listen to Him.

Endnotes

[1] Gordon Wenham, *The Book of Leviticus: The New International Commentary on the Old Testament* (Grand Rapids: Eerdmans Publishing Co., 1979) p. 16.

[2] Wenham, pp. 16-17.

[3] Wenham, pp. 17-18.

[4] Ron Rhodes, *Christ Before the Manger: The Life and Times of the Preincarnate Christ* (Grand Rapids: Baker Books, 1993) p. 15.

[5] Ibid.

[6] Rhodes, p. 80.

[7] Rhodes, p. 45.

[8] Rhodes, p. 80.

[9] Rhodes, pp. 94-95.

[10] Rhodes, p. 83

[11] Rhodes, pp. 81-82.

[12] Rhodes, pp. 80-81.

[13] Rhodes, p. 82.

[14] Rhodes, p. 95.

[15] Rhodes, p. 94.

[16] Rhodes, p. 97.

[17] Rhodes, p. 214.

[18] Rhodes, p. 76.

[19] Leon Morris, *The Gospel According to John Revised: The New International Commentary on the New Testament* (Grand Rapids: Eerdmans Publishing Co., 1995) p. 91.

[20] Ibid.

[21] Dieter K. Mulitze, *The Great Omission: Resolving Critical Issues for the Ministry of Healing and Deliverance* (Belleville: Essence Publishing, 2001) pp. 115-185.

[22] Morris, p. 580.

[23] Ibid.

[24] T. McComiskey, article on *emphanizo* in Colin Brown, ed., *Dictionary of New Testament Theology*, Vol. 2 (Grand Rapids: Zondervan, 1976) pp. 488-490.

[25] Edward M. Smith, *Healing Life's Hurts: Let the Light of Christ Dispel the Darkness in Your Soul* (Ann Arbor: Vine Books, 2002) pp. 14-18.

[26] Smith, p. 154.

[27] Ibid.

[28] Ibid.

[29] John White, *When the Spirit Comes With Power: Signs & Wonders Among God's People* (Downers Grove: InterVarsity Press, 1988) p. 24.

[30] R. Fowler White, "Does God speak today apart from the Bible?," in John. H. Armstrong, ed., *The Coming Evangelical Crisis: Current Challenges to the Authority of Scripture and the Gospel* (Chicago: Moody Press, 1996) p. 87.

[31] Ibid.

32 Mulitze, pp. 170-173.

33 Jack Deere, *Surprised by the Voice of God: How God Speaks Today Through Prophecies, Dreams and Visions* (Grand Rapids: Zondervan Publishing House, 1996) p. 285.

34 Deere, p. 251.

35 Deere, pp. 235-306.

36 Dallas Willard. *Hearing God. Developing A Conversational Relationship With God* (Downers Grove: InterVarsity Press, 1999) p.103.

37 Gordon D. Fee, *God's Empowering Presence: The Holy Spirit in the Letters of Paul* (Peabody: Hendrickson Publishers, Inc., 1994) pp. 689-690.

38 Leanne Payne, *The Healing Presence: How God's Grace Can Work in You to Bring Healing in Your Broken Places and the Joy of Living in His Love* (Wheaton: Crossway Books, 1989) p. 80.

39 Payne, 1989, p. 82.

40 Payne, 1989, p. 84.

41 Leanne Payne, *Real Presence: The Christian Worldview of C.S. Lewis as Incarnational Reality* (Wheaton: Crossway Books, 1988) p. 14.

42 Payne, 1988, p. 49.

43 Leo Thomas, O.P., with Jan Alkire, *Healing Ministry: A Practical Guide* (Kansas: Sheed & Ward, 1994) p. 12.

44 Thomas, p. 14.

45 Paul Tournier, *The Healing of Persons* (New York: Harper & Row, 1965) p. 255.

46 Payne, 1988, p. 51.

47 Wayne E. Oates, *The Presence of God in Pastoral Counseling* (Waco: Word Books, 1986) pp. 32-33.

48 Leanne Payne, *Crisis in Masculinity* (Wheaton: Crossway Books, 1985) p. 21.

Chapter Three

Listening
in His Presence

When she reached the man of God at the mountain, she took hold of his feet. Gehazi came over to push her away, but the man of God said, "Leave her alone! She is in bitter distress, but the Lord has hidden it from me and has not told me why" (2 Kings 4:27).

And afterward, I will pour out my Spirit on all people. Your sons and daughters will prophesy, your old men will dream dreams, your young men will see visions. Even on my servants, both men and women, I will pour out my Spirit in those days (Joel 2:28-29).

Lynn's Severe Headaches and Pain

At a healing conference I prayed for Lynn who had a history of severe headaches with much pain and tension around her forehead. It had been so severe that years ago she had spent some months in a hospital. She was still not cured in spite of medication and therapy. Not being tempted to rely on my analytical skill, I simply anointed her with oil and asked the Holy Spirit to reveal the source of this problem. I could think of several reasons as to what may have caused her condition, but I did not say anything since I wanted the mind of Christ on the matter. The Lord brought to her mind no less than six memories of specific instances of fear involving an evil presence, all in chronological order and starting from when she was a small child. Each experience built on the others, was progressively more intense and the fears compounded throughout her life. She had totally forgotten three of the memories. The Lord made it clear by word of wisdom that the tension in her head was caused by the continual emotional stress from fear, most of it long forgotten but not at all inactive. As I prayed for healing she told me that all the fear from the memories totally vanished, and all the tension and pain caused by it left her as well. I could give numerous such examples where the leading of the Spirit and the gifts of the Spirit bring quick and precise understanding.

Uncovering the True Issues of the Heart and Soul

Counseling, therapy and healing prayer typically attempt to understand the real issue(s) in a person's life, the real needs of the soul, the causes and roots of the problem(s) and so forth. This logically requires that the understanding be based upon true and correct information. Unless one trivializes the heart, soul and life, one must agree that this is not always that simple. There are a number of logical and critical requirements in this part of the counseling or healing process.

A basic requirement is that all the relevant and true information is uncovered since much that follows depends on this. That in turn assumes no repressed or forgotten memories or details, that the relevant information from years or decades of life experiences with many thousands of memories is selected and recalled correctly and that no false or distorted memory or information has been presented.

Another requirement or assumption is that the person receiving prayer is not withholding, repressing, distorting, or denying any of the information. Defense mechanisms might be operating, as well as deception. Perhaps the "family name" is at stake and there is a real hesitation to share something or there is something personally embarrassing and so forth. There are also drug-induced complications when praying or counseling with a person on psychiatric drugs.

Further, even given that the above two major assumptions are met, one also assumes that the counselor or therapist will process the information correctly. This requires much understanding and experience. One cannot make assessments too quickly. For example for two different people with a very similar painful experience, the true problem or need and then healing may be quite different.

Due to the mystery and complexity of the human soul, the above requirements are not quickly satisfied. This is partly why counseling or therapy typically involves many hours of sessions when relying on human analytical skill. How is this information reliably arrived at? How do we "know that we know"? It is not terribly difficult to spend four years or more studying theories and methods of counseling or therapy. It is quite another matter to know exactly what may apply from what has been studied, if anything at all, to an actual person in front of you.

Jonathan had come to others and myself for healing prayer. His testimony below is an example of someone receiving and understanding healing from the Lord as well as comprehending the role of images and pictures in healing prayer as part of the Spirit's way of communicating truth. Part of knowing the true issues pertaining to a persons' healing often involves visual forms of communication from the Holy Spirit.

Jonathan's Testimony: Healing, Images and Pictures

For many years something in life just didn't seem right. Zeal for the Lord and a sense of His presence were often lacking. I wondered why the Lord seemed far away, why I rarely heard Him speak. Physically I often felt lethargic and not mentally alert. I knew that the so-called "victorious Christian life" was not my experience, but amazingly I never considered that there might be wounds and lies from my childhood operating in my present life. It was actually through a long-term, painful physical condition for which I sought healing many times, that Jesus began to reveal other areas that first needed healing. Over a one-year period Jesus revealed and healed many areas of bondage in my life that ranged from generational sins to a transference of evil rooted in witchcraft from a childhood friend. Jesus did not heal everything at once; rather it was a process so that I would receive a full understanding of what He was doing.

He is not finished yet, but He has given other individuals prophetic insight through pictures for me as an encouragement that there is more healing to come. He specifically revealed that the timing for my full physical healing is not yet but will come. Words cannot describe the hope that gives me after living in almost con-stant pain for ten years. It is so obvious that the people God has brought into our lives to be His mouthpiece and agents of healing are not coincidental but brought by divine leading for which I am so grateful.

God could have healed me physically many years ago, and I always wondered why He didn't. Now I know. If He had, I would never have seen the need for healing of the inner man. I would have gone on my way healthy in body but sick and wounded in spirit. There are countless benefits one receives when Jesus reveals our pain and then brings His healing touch. Our relationships improve. No longer is it the "norm" to lash out because of my woundedness; rather there is a sense of perspective, peace and healthy balance with immediate family and others.

I began receiving words, impressions and pictures from the Holy Spirit for the benefit of others with whom I came in contact. For example last week, as I was praying for a man who was working in our building, Jesus revealed to me that this man grew up in an abusive and alcoholic home. Being so new to hearing God speak like this I struggled with how to ask a complete stranger such an up-front question. For fear of appearing foolish—what if I had heard wrong?—I almost talked myself out of approaching this man. Finally I struck up a conversation and asked a safer question: "I was praying for you, and God showed me that you've had a very hard life. Is that true?" His tone of voice and facial expression indicated that he had. "You got that right. I sure have," he said, and then he changed the subject. I continue to pray for him. I wonder what the outcome would have been if I had been a little braver and asked him about the specific impression the Lord gave me?

The Visual Language of the Holy Spirit

Images or "pictures" in people's minds are not uncommon in the ministry of healing prayer. At a healing prayer training conference where I was teaching, two of the trainees were pastors. They were both quite comfortable with hearing and communicating scriptural truth as words or thoughts. They were beginning to learn the basics of healing prayer, and both were surprised to spontaneously receive images in their mind during the practicum. For one pastor, it was so new and different that for a while he did not share what he had received. It did not "fit his theology" and prior Christian experience. Then later, as the prayer time unfolded, he shared what he had received because it fit exactly with the core issue of the person receiving prayer. Only then did he have confidence that it was not his "vain imagination" or overactive analysis. The other pastor had experienced this before and was more willing to share but still cautious as to how significant or relevant the images might be. Every time it happened he still felt some amazement.

Randy came to me for healing prayer concerning difficulties in relationships, including being close emotionally to his loving wife who truly cared for him. After I had anointed him and invited Jesus and His Spirit to come, we just waited in the Lord's presence to see what He would do. I asked Randy if anything was happening, and he said that he saw an image in his mind. He was surprised since this was a "new thing" for him. The image was very clear. He saw a heart made out of stone surrounded by a fence with some barbed wire. As the prayer time progressed it was evident that this image or "vision" was God's communication about the status of his heart.

At a healing conference Long prayed for a woman with feelings of abandonment and deep insecurity that had significantly and negatively impacted her life and relationships.[1] As they waited upon the Holy Spirit for direction, Long received an image:

> ...an image spontaneously intruded itself into my mind. The image was of a little girl in a very pretty dress with lace trim, running from room to room in a big house crying, "Mommy, Mommy!" I told the woman about the image and asked, "Does this mean anything to you? Does it remind you of anything, or is this all my imagination?" As I spoke, the woman suddenly broke down sobbing. She said, "The Lord has just given you a picture of the most terrible day of my life... that was the day I was ten years old and my parents had a horrible argument. My father hit my mother very hard and she ran into another room

screaming. My father stormed out of the house. I went running after him and crying....[2]

Long recounted a similar situation in praying with an elderly Reformed pastor who suffered from depression and feeling abandoned by God.

> Suddenly, as we waited on the Lord for guidance, there came into my mind the picture of a boy sitting on the bank of a wide river holding a fishing pole. Beside him lying on the ground was another fishing pole. The boy's face was engulfed in sadness and his eyes had a lonely, far-away look. When I shared this image the man looked up in amazement. Then he started to cry and shake all over. When we finally could get him to talk he said, "That boy is me! That lonely boy is me!" Then out poured the tragic story that moved the whole prayer team to tears.[3]

The images Long received were totally accurate, depicting the woman's and the man's most painful memories. Since the images fit what had actually happened many years earlier, it was not Long's imagination at all. The Lord brought the images to mind as a form of spiritual communication in order to begin the process of healing for those two people. I have served on a number of healing prayer teams where a similar phenomenon has occurred—a completely accurate recall of a memory as a picture or image that was later confirmed by the person receiving prayer. This initiates or continues the healing process wherein the Lord indicates where the healing should be focused. The Lord seems to do this at times because the person receiving prayer may recall the memory but believe it is their overactive memory, or they did not expect that memory, or they felt the memory was not significant, or they have long forgotten the memory.

Gregg wrote about a prayer session with a man named Dennis. As they were waiting on Jesus, he had a "picture of Jesus standing by a park bench while Dennis went running by him at top speed—so fast that he was a blur."[4] The image or picture was profoundly accurate since he was so anxious and emotionally "wound up," he did not take time to be with Jesus and settle in His presence.

Tapscott wrote about how the Holy Spirit gave her a mental image of "a snarling dog, a fence and a little girl" when she was praying for a friend. That image described exactly a fearful encounter with a dog when her friend was very young.[5]

Often an image will symbolize a person's need or issue like the image Randy received. Other times an image will reveal the healing that is taking place. A man that I prayed with for cleansing from pornography and lust had an image of a large waterfall coming over him. That image was the Lord's way of reassuring him that he was, in fact, being cleansed.

Janice came to me for healing prayer at a conference. Upon receiving final deliverance from a spirit of witchcraft, she could clearly see a huge cross of Christ come down from heaven upon her as she lay face down on the floor of the church sanctuary. The presence of the cross and the acknowledgment of the blood of Jesus to cleanse her and nullify evil forces at work in her life were provided by the Lord to deal the "final blow" to several evil spirits.

Marnie was healed from the effects of sexual abuse as a little girl. At the end of an hour's prayer session, she could clearly see herself with a crown of jewels on her head. Another member of the prayer team was prompted earlier by the Spirit to share Isaiah 61:3: *"...to bestow on them a crown of beauty instead of ashes."* It was clear to us that the image was Jesus' way of symbolizing her healing and restoration. Before that point there were many tears and a deep release from a huge load of guilt, sadness and shame.

I have also witnessed healing prayer sessions where the person receiving prayer and one or more of the team members saw the same picture of Jesus bringing healing. For example two people see an identical image of the Lord putting His arms around the person in a past event to console and comfort, or standing between an abuser and the person being sexually abused.

Laura came for prayer concerning a number of fears in her life. The Lord was gracious to reveal the roots of those fears. As she was about to leave, a prayer team member received an image of a bright white flower, apparently a lily. Not being sure what this had to do with the prayer time, the image was shared. Laura released more tears and explained that this same image has been given to a number of different healing prayer people over the last few months. The people involved did not in any way know one another and always prayed in confidence. She explained that this was God's reminder of His love to her as a sign from the times of healing prayer. The lily in fact related to her middle name. While this may not seem significant as the theological intricacies of infralapsarianism or transubstantiation, it was profoundly meaningful to Laura.

Images, Pictures and Visions: From God or Delusion?

But some authors claim that images and pictures as experienced in the ministry of healing prayer, or hearing from God in general, cannot be from the Lord. Some would argue that this is occultic, or New Age, or at least one's own imagination. They insist that whatever it really is, it's not from God. After all, it is claimed, we now have the complete Scriptures and that is the final authority for belief and practice. God does not reveal truth beyond His Scriptures, and today God only speaks through the Scriptures. Hence,

God does not communicate directly by words let alone pictures or images. I disagree totally.

First, as in biblical times, the Holy Spirit today gives practical instructions. The Holy Spirit does more than reveal biblical truth and inspire Scripture. The Spirit told Philip to go to a chariot and remain near it, to meet the Ethiopian eunuch (Acts 8:29) and instructed Ananias to go and pray for Saul (Acts 9:10-18). After Peter saw a vision the Spirit instructed Peter to go downstairs and meet three men (Acts 10:19, 11:12). The Spirit instructed the church at Antioch to set aside Paul and Barnabas for ministry (Acts 13:2) and told Paul not to preach the gospel in Asia and then led Paul in a vision to go to Macedonia (Acts 16:6-10). The Spirit warned Paul in every city that prison and hardship awaited him (Acts 20:23). These examples have nothing to do with revealing doctrine. As Long and Strickler put it:

> This type of day-to-day, active guidance of the Holy Spirit does not reveal new doctrine; instead, it has to do with the details of how we work with Jesus. This is the type of revelation that we are speaking of in this process of working with Jesus in inner healing. If we exclude it because we believe that the Holy Spirit speaks to us only through the literal words of the Bible, then we will cut ourselves out of the dynamic workings of Jesus Christ in the lives of people today.[6]

The images or pictures given by the Lord are to communicate truth, give direction and facilitate healing for a specific person. Since the Spirit gives practical guidance as shown in the Scriptures, we can fully expect Him to give practical guidance in the ministry of healing prayer. A person may believe in his mind and know theologically that God loves him, for example, yet in his heart not really embrace this truth. God may thus use a picture or image to convey this truth and what the person truly and actually believes in his heart. The spiritual communication serves to apply biblical truth specifically to that person. It is an appropriation of divine revelation already received (Jude 1:3). Communication by the Living Word never contrasts with the written Word. Of course one must always discern and test the spirits since there can be false visions and false divinations (Ezek. 13:2-7).

Flying Scrolls, Horns, Baskets and Boiling Pots

The second most compelling argument for the validity of visual communication of the Spirit in the ministry of healing prayer is the Spirit's examples as recorded in the Scriptures. One might reluctantly agree that, although the Holy Spirit does speak today, it is through words and Scripture verses only and not through any images or pictures. But the Scriptures clearly teach that God Himself communicates with images or visions.

Consider the prophet Zechariah. On the night of the twenty-fourth day of the eleventh month of Shebat, in the second year of Darius, Zechariah had a vision (Zech. 1:7-8). He saw a man riding a red horse, standing among the myrtle trees in a ravine and behind him were red, brown and white horses. The Angel of the Lord was standing among the myrtle trees and, as shown in the previous chapter, Zechariah actually saw Jesus in the vision. Zechariah talked with the Lord, asking what the vision meant, and the angel who was with him also talked with him about the vision. This is not at all unlike seeing a vision in healing prayer and asking for the significance of it from the Lord and seeing how the Lord reveals more of the vision. I have witnessed this numerous times in healing prayer.

101

Zechariah then looked up and saw another vision—four horns—which symbolized the nations that scattered Judah, Israel and Jerusalem (Zech. 1:18-19). Then he saw four craftsmen which symbolized four nations that will bring justice to God's people (Zech. 1:20). The four horns and four craftsmen were not in Zechariah's room at all; they suddenly appeared in a vision. He then looked up and saw a man with a measuring line in his hand to measure Jerusalem (Zech. 2:1-2).

Zechariah had still more visions. He saw a solid gold lamp stand with a bowl at the top and seven lights on it, also with seven channels to the lights (Zech. 4:2-3). There were also two olive trees, on each side of the bowl. The lamp stand symbolized God's strength, glory and watching over the earth (Zech. 4:5-10) and the olive trees symbolized two anointed servants of the Lord (Zech. 4:12-14). Then he saw a flying scroll, thirty feet long and fifteen feet wide (Zech. 5:1-2) which symbolized a curse going out upon the whole land (Zech. 5:3-4). Then the angel instructed Zechariah to look again and see what was appearing and it was a measuring basket that symbolized the iniquity in full measure of the people throughout the land (Zech. 5:5-7). He then saw in the vision the cover of the basket being raised and there was a woman who symbolized wickedness (Zech. 5:7-8). Then he saw two women with wind in their wings that were like stork wings, who lifted up the basket between heaven and earth to take it to Babylonia (Zech. 5:9-11). Then Zechariah saw four chariots with horses coming out from between two mountains of bronze, which symbolized God's spirits of heaven going out upon the earth (Zech. 6:1-8).

God gave Jeremiah some pictures or images when He called him to ministry. The Lord told Jeremiah to look, and he saw the branch of an almond tree that symbolized His watching to see that His word is fulfilled (Jer. 1:11-12). The Lord then instructed him to look again, and he saw a boiling pot tilting away from the north, symbolizing disaster coming from the north (Jer. 1:13-16). Jeremiah also denounced false visions or delusions that come from people's sinful hearts and minds (Jer. 14:14; 23:16).

Ezekiel experienced a major and emotionally overpowering vision while among the exiles by the Kebar River. He saw a windstorm with flashing light and what appeared like glowing metal and four living creatures with wheels and wings and more (Ezek. 1:1-28). This was more than just a small image or picture; it was a major revelation from an overwhelming vision. While sitting in his house with elders, he looked and had a vision of a man with fire from his waist down and glowing from waist up (Ezek. 8:1-2).

Daniel had many visions, including a man dressed in linen with a body like chrysolite while he was standing on the Tigris River (Dan. 10:4-6). He was the only one who saw the vision, yet others who did not see the vision knew there was a presence since they were overwhelmed by terror and fled (Dan. 10:7). This is not unlike healing prayer where usually only one or two people will see a vision. Daniel saw a vision with himself in it, in the citadel beside the Ulai Canal (Dan. 8:1-2). This can also happen in healing prayer where the person receiving prayer is seen in an image or picture.

Amos saw a vision of locusts that the Lord was preparing to bring in judgment (Amos 7:1-4). Then Amos saw the Lord standing by a wall that was built true to plumb and the Lord had a plumb line in His hand (Amos 7:7). The plumb line represented what Israel should have been like given all that the Lord had graciously done for her. Amos saw an image or picture of a basket of ripe fruit which represented the "ripeness" of their sin and the time for impending judgment (Amos 8:1-2).

Peter fell into a trance while he was hungry and waiting for a meal (Acts 10:9-10). He had a vision of a large sheet with all kinds of four-footed animals, including reptiles and birds of the air (Acts 10:11-12). He heard a voice telling him to rise up and eat, and he said he could not because some of the animals were unclean (Acts 10:12-13). This happened three times, and the Lord thus used an image to communicate the biblical truth to him that Gentiles will also be saved. Peter should have known this from his knowledge of the Old Testament, but the Lord used a rather direct image to make His point.

From the Scriptures we see that God has used images or pictures to symbolize a certain truth, as well as images with a voice from which He speaks or an image almost like a short movie drama with events taking place. Images or visions of horns, craftsmen, baskets, myrtle trees, lamp stands, flying scrolls, chariots, horses, locusts, mountains of bronze, plumb lines, a branch of an almond tree, a boiling pot, a sheet with animals—to list a few from Scripture—are not any more unusual or foreign than the images received in healing prayer. These are models and examples of how God has communicated with His people, especially the prophets, in addition to the written Word or an audible voice or impression of truth. The Lord or an angel often asked the prophet to declare what he saw and then was invited to understand the meaning of the image or picture. Like in healing prayer, either a symbol or an event or a mixture was involved to communicate truth.

The Scriptures as a whole use pictures and images repeatedly to convey spiritual truth. The Lord is our shepherd (Ps. 23), the person who trusts in the Lord will be like an eagle (Isa. 40:31) and the righteous person is like a tree planted by good water (Ps. 1:3).[7] Jude refers to false teachers as clouds without rain, autumn trees without fruit and uprooted, wild waves of the sea foaming up their shame and wandering stars (Jude 12-13). This is all vivid and highly descriptive imagery, powerful metaphors of speech meant to convey truth. Jesus Himself used pictures in parables repeatedly in His own teaching.

Images, Pictures and Visions Today

But Christians are not prophets of the Old Testament, so does this apply today? Joel 2:28-29 was fulfilled in Acts 2:17-19 onwards in the early Church when believers by definition were filled by the Holy Spirit. Thus Christians as a whole can prophesy, have visions and have dreams that are part of God's communication to His people today. This is what we see in healing prayer like the examples given above.

The images and pictures must be accepted as valid communication from God because they follow the biblical model and examples. They come spontaneously to those who did not ask or expect the images, so there is no fabrication. The particular truth applied to a person does not contradict biblical truth. Kraft, professor of anthropology and intercultural communication at Fuller Theological Seminary, acknowledged the role of images or pictures as one of God's ways of communicating and revealing truth about a person receiving healing prayer:

> …God can lead through pictures. Frequently, he puts a picture in our minds to show us what he wants us to know. Sometimes this will be a picture of the person in a difficult situation, such as an abusive event. Sometimes it will be a picture of some event or situation in the future—for example the person walking in newfound freedom. Sometimes it will be a picture with symbolic meaning.[8]

An important safeguard is to begin every prayer session asking for the presence of Jesus and His Spirit to reveal and heal. God must initiate everything lest it be a vain or false imagination or a "flattering divination" (Ezek. 12:24). One must use discernment since the enemy might try to distract or deceive. Not everyone receives images or pictures in the ministry of healing prayer, and the Lord does not always lead or reveal His truth about a person with images or pictures. Not all the prophets had an image or vision either; some like Zephaniah had only words and truth from the Spirit. This might be due to some people being more visually oriented than others. Some people will receive Scripture verses in addition to images or only Scripture verses.

The Epistemology of Jesus

Some years ago I went for my regular dental checkup. There was a new dental hygienist, a younger, somewhat petite lady. I started a conversation with her, hampered by the usual dental equipment in my mouth. When I mentioned that I had lived in the Middle East, the conversation deepened. Judging by appearances I assumed she had traveled there as a tourist or maybe she was an exchange student. I was completely wrong. It turns out that she had actually served in the Israeli military and trained soldiers to operate their tanks for combat. Appearances were not reality! I then made sure I obeyed her completely during my dental checkup (I would have anyways).

For the reader who has a fear of big words, please take a deep breath, count to two and relax. "Epistemology" is simply the study of the theory of knowledge, or how we know things. It turns out that the epistemology of Jesus far outstrips anything in the world.

Jesus did not rely only on the five senses; He was not restricted by empiricism. Jesus did not judge only by what He saw with His eyes and heard with His ears (Isa. 11:3). Although Isaiah 11 applies in context to justice, it implies that Jesus was able to look beyond appearances and comprehend the reality of any situation as He admonished others to do (John 7:24). Jesus was filled with the Spirit of wisdom, counsel and power (Isa. 11:2) and used the spiritual gifts of word of knowledge, message of wisdom (1 Cor. 12:8) and discernment of spirits (1 Cor. 12:10).[9] He knew Nathaniel's true inner state before ever having met him (John 1:47-48). He knew that the woman at the well had five husbands (John 4:17). He actually knew "in His spirit" what the Pharisees were thinking without any word having been spoken (Mark 2:8; Luke 5:21-23; 6:8). While Jesus certainly took into account what He saw, heard, touched, tasted and smelled, His ways of knowing were beyond empiricism.

At times in healing prayer one can actually see into the spiritual realm. For example when Elisha was surrounded by King Aram's many horses and chariots in Dothan, his servant was afraid. Then Elisha prayed that his servant's eyes would be *opened* (2 Kings 6:17) so that he could see into the supernatural realm and the Lord's horses and chariots of fire. His eyes were already open to see physically; now his spiritual eyes must be opened to see into the spiritual realm. Similarly, as explained above, Daniel was the only one standing on the banks of the Tigris to have his spiritual eyes opened to see an awesome heavenly being while everyone else only felt the terror of the being's presence (Dan. 10:7). Paul wrote about a man in Christ who was caught up in the "third heaven" and heard "inexpressible things" (2 Cor. 12:1-4). The epistemology of God then includes knowing and experiencing the supernatural realm as revelation which comes by grace and utterly transcends modern empiricism. As Christians indwelt by the Spirit (Joel 2:18-19; Acts 2:17-18) of Jesus (Luke 4:1), we must follow His ways of knowing. But this all involves intuitive and experiential knowledge which is difficult for many Christians because of the "Cartesian-Kantian split between thought and experience" since the Enlightenment.[10] We must forsake the Enlightenment's major axiom wherein "...the modern scientific world-view provides the only reliable account of how things really are and that the Bible has to be understood only in terms of that account."[11]

This is all the more crucial when we consider the mystery and complexity of the human heart and soul. We live under an illusion if we believe that we can rely on anyone's ability to analyze or "figure out" the soul. Psychological attempts to unravel the mysteries of the heart are insufficient. "Insight-oriented" therapy has real limitations and often takes numerous hours and sessions to understand a person's situation—which may not happen at all. God alone knows the secrets of the heart (Ps. 44:21), searches a man's spirit and inner being (Prov. 20:27), weighs motives of the heart (Prov. 16:2), tests the heart (Prov. 17:3) and examines the heart and mind (Ps. 26:2). The Lord looks at the heart and not at appearances (1 Sam. 16:7). The heart can be deceived and is beyond anyone's understanding (Jer. 17:9), thus the Lord examines and probes the heart and mind (Jer. 17:10, 20:12). The Holy Spirit will lead us into all truth, including the truth of our personal past (John 14:26, 16:13). Wisdom, power, counsel and understanding belong to the Lord (Job 12:13). The Lord reveals mysteries, reveals the deep and hidden things and gives wisdom and knowledge to the discerning (Dan. 2:19-22).

We must always rely on God and His ways of knowing. The spiritual gifts must be exercised in the ministry of healing prayer along with the complete language of the Spirit and listening to Jesus. This does not negate wisdom and understanding that one can bring to the prayer time, but that is always subject to the wisdom of Jesus. Revelation from God is always above any human analysis.

Many people involved in the ministry of healing prayer—which relies on the leading of the Spirit—exhibit these gifts. For example a person might have the word "abandoned" or "rejection" or "father" suddenly appear in one's mind, or the Spirit might prompt to ask a specific question. It is often the case that a verse from Scripture will come into a person's mind, or the Lord will impress a biblical truth that applies to a given situation. One might also receive impressions from the Lord, like Nehemiah did where God put it into his heart to assemble the nobles, the officials and the common people (Neh. 7:5). He did not hear an audible voice but had the discernment to recognize it was from God.[12]

One of my team members knew that there was a lady with cancer who had come to the evening healing prayer service. As it turned out, the first lady who came for prayer did have cancer and my team member knew correctly the exact type of cancer and that it had been diagnosed recently. This was a word of knowledge from the Spirit meant as an immense encouragement to the lady and helped initiate a deep time of healing.

Tapscott wrote about a word of knowledge she received from the Lord regarding a nun who was resting in the Spirit. The Lord revealed that the nun had a fear of death and choking which started at birth. Tapscott was led to pray for the nun's healing while the nun was still not fully conscious. During the prayer time the nun grabbed her head with her hands as if in pain.[13] When the nun got up, she felt better, confirmed the complete accuracy of the word of knowledge and a few weeks later it was fully evident that she had been deeply healed by that prayer time. Tapscott wrote:

> ...we absolutely must trust the Holy Spirit in ministry. The nun had not shared with me her problem. *I trusted the voice of the Holy Spirit and not my own understanding and He revealed to me the root cause of her problems* (emphasis mine).[47]

A number of times people have come to me for healing prayer, but they had no idea why they came. They did know, however, that the Lord told them to come for healing prayer. Thus there was no presenting problem at all. What does one do then? Ask questions and start probing? Begin to basically invent problems for them? In every case, as I simply waited on the Spirit to lead, the Spirit soon revealed deep and significant issues. Usually the person was quite surprised but could soon see what the Lord was doing. In most cases there was deep healing in one short session. No method or analytical skill can do this.

Jesus' ways of knowing do not diminish wise counsel, spiritual insight from mature counselors, thinking and using the minds God gave us and the application of biblical truth. Our minds and our thinking must be submitted to Jesus, redeemed for His purposes and transformed by His Spirit (Rom. 12:2). Everything must submit to the Lord's leading and be exercised in His presence under His direction.

Jesus' ways of knowing are fuller, deeper, more comprehensive, incredibly efficient and richer than anything the world offers. One must learn to listen and hear from the Spirit and Jesus who are there and learn to collaborate with them in ministry as pictures, words, impressions, memories, verses and such come. We are then spared the temptation of relying on our wisdom or a method:

> When we wait upon the Lord for His mind on the task or the difficulty, then we are spared from substituting our own limited vision and unaided wisdom for the mighty work He would do.... We must never allow some preconceived idea of what is wrong or of what is the usual remedy to get in the way of what God wants to do.[15]

We must be like Elisha when approached by the Shunammite woman in great distress. He looked to the Lord to reveal the cause: *She is in bitter distress, but the Lord has hidden it from me and has not told me why* (2 Kings 4:27).[16] When we refuse to believe in, or practice, Jesus' ways of knowing, we are more like disciples of Descartes than of Jesus.

Endnotes ───────

[1] Brad Long and Cindy Strickler, *Let Jesus Heal Your Hidden Wounds: Cooperating With the Holy Spirit in Healing Ministry* (Grand Rapids: Chosen Books, 2001) p. 98.

[2] Long and Strickler, p. 99.

[3] Long and Strickler, p. 114.

[4] Mike Flynn and Doug Gregg, *Inner Healing: A Handbook for Helping Yourself & Others* (Downers Grove: InterVarsity Press, 1993) p. 76.

[5] Betty Tapscott, *Inner Healing Through Healing of Memories* (Kingwood: Hunter Publishing, 1975) p. 20.

[6] Long and Strickler, p. 84.

[7] Charles H. Kraft, *Deep Wounds, Deep Healing: Discovering the Vital Link Between Spiritual Warfare and Inner Healing* (Ann Arbor: Servant Publications, 1993) p. 118.

[8] Kraft, p. 106.

[9] Dieter Mulitze, *The Great Omission: Resolving Critical Issues for the Ministry of Healing and Deliverance* (Belleville: Essence Publishers, 2001) pp. 33-34.

[10] Leanne Payne, *Listening Prayer* (Grand Rapids: Hamewith Books, 1994) pp. 133-134.

[11] Lesslie Newbigin, *Foolishness to the Greeks: The Gospel and Western Culture* (Grand Rapids: Eerdmans Publishing Co., 1986) p. 45.

[12] Jack Deere, *Surprised by the Voice of the Spirit* (Grand Rapids: Zondervan Publishing House, 1996) p. 154.

[13] Tapscott, pp. 46-47.

[14] Tapscott, p. 47.

[15] Leanne Payne, *The Healing Presence: How God's Grace Can Work in*

You to Bring Healing in Your Broken Places and the Joy of Living in His Love
(Wheaton: Crossway Books, 1989) pp. 37-38.

16 Payne, 1989, p. 38.

 Chapter Four

Letting Jesus into the Pain of the Past: A Theology of Memories

Peace I leave with you; my peace I give you. I do not give to you as the world gives. Do not let your hearts be troubled and do not be afraid (John 14:27).

He asked them, "What are you discussing together as you walk along?" They stood still, their faces downcast (Luke 24:17).

Frank's Healing from Painful Memories

My experience has been that healing prayer comes in many forms. It cannot be confined to methods, situations or people. In fact one of my most profound healing events happened as I prayed alone! After having experienced healing prayer at a number of Deeper Love Ministry conferences, I was so moved by the power of the presence of Jesus, I felt I needed to learn more about healing prayer. I signed up for an introductory training session led by the Deeper Love Ministries team.

During the second day of teaching Pastor Carsten Pellman shared his personal testimony. As he spoke, it was as if each word spoke directly to an unidentified pain in my heart, and it was all I could do to refrain from weeping throughout the session. As we broke for lunch I stayed behind in the church and, once alone, fell to the floor and wept. I cried out to the Lord to show me where this pain came from, and almost immediately it was as if He started peeling away onion-like layers of my childhood memories. One at a time He brought memories of childhood pain forward. With each memory, I asked Him if it was indeed the root cause of the pain and each time He said no until I came to one that brought a fresh round of tears.

As a child I was (as many children are) quite a self-centered individual, seldom taking other's feelings and desires into account. My parents often responded by telling me, "The world doesn't revolve around you; you are not the center of the universe!" Over time I misinterpreted this to mean that I was unimportant to them, unloved and, in fact, not worthy of anyone's love and attention. This may seem trivial to some, but I have come to realize that the feeling of being unloved is one of the most powerful negative influences in existence.

As the Lord brought this memory to the forefront I completely broke down and sobbed. I realized that this belief had become a core part of my being. As my sobbing subsided I prayed and asked Jesus to reveal to me the truth of how He saw me. Immediately, and in a soft and gentle whisper, He stated, "You are the center of my universe." Again I wept as I realized just how much my God loved me.

Somehow in that moment when I experienced His healing love for me, my life completely changed. My priorities changed, my lifestyle changed and my relationships to my family changed. Suddenly things that had seemed so important to me were no longer relevant. I had a real desire to know the Lord more intimately. My appetite for spiritual things experienced an unprecedented growth. I was hungry for the things of God. Over two years later I am still in love with the Lord. I am still experiencing the healing presence of Jesus, and I look forward to what He will do next.

The Gospels and Healing the "Inner Person"

Some Christians have the impression that Jesus did only physical healing as recorded in the Gospels. Some writers contend that Jesus healed organic disease and not invisible ailments like lower back pain, heart palpitations or headaches.[1] In following Jesus' example, it is argued, the apostles also healed only organic disease and "did not deal in functional, symptomatic, or psychosomatic problems."[2] But why not believe that Jesus' love, healing and restoration applies to the whole person? Is any part of us exempt from His salvation? Would we want to limit His grace? Is the Good Shepherd limiting His concern for any of His sheep?

Scanlan thought it strange to "...contend that Jesus healed all forms of physical diseases but did not heal the very real diseases of the inner man."[3] He defined inner healing as:

> ...the healing of the inner man. By inner man we mean the intellectual, volitional and affective areas commonly referred to as mind, will and heart but including such other areas as related to emotions, psyche, soul and spirit. Inner healing is distinguished from outer healing commonly called physical healing.[4]

Tapscott, well known in the inner healing ministry in the 1970s, described inner healing as follows:

> ...the healing of the inner man: the mind, the emotions, the painful memories, the dreams. It is the process through which prayer whereby we are set free from feelings of resentment, rejection, self-pity, depression, guilt, fear, sorrow, hatred, inferiority, condemnation, or worthlessness, etc.[5]

115

Inner healing is not just going into the past and digging up sordid details. It is not seeing how much garbage we can remember; it is throwing away all the garbage that is there. It's having Jesus shine His divine light in all those dark places where Satan has hidden those hurts and painful memories. It's having Jesus walk hand-in-hand through every second of our lives, being right there with us during those unpleasant situations.[6]

Jesus taught a lot about the "inner person." His teaching covered anxiety, worry, lust, adultery, idolatry, forgiveness, anger, meaninglessness, love, peace, joy, hope, judging others, sin, guilt, salvation, meaning and purpose in life, truth, lies, deception, spiritual abuse, legalism, jealousy, demonic oppression, pride, humility, rejection, acceptance, reconciliation, deception, hardness of heart, connecting to God and others, prayer, purity, mercy, righteousness, fear, eternal life and much more. Does that not sound like the "inner person"? Those are all intensely spiritual issues.

Jesus truly ministered to the "inner person." He met the deepest needs of love and spiritual fulfillment—living water—for the woman at the well (John 4:4-29). He forgave sin and released from guilt the woman who anointed Him (Luke 7:36-50). Zacchaeus was healed from rejection and transformed by Jesus' acceptance of him (Luke 19:1-10). Jesus visited Mary at the tomb in the midst of her trauma and grief (John 20:10-18). Jesus comforted the troubled hearts of His disciples and promised His unique peace (John 14:1-27). God wants to comfort us in all of our troubles (2 Cor. 1:3-4), comfort the downcast (2 Cor. 7:6) and strengthen our hearts so that we will be blameless and holy in His presence (1 Thess. 3:13). Jesus, as the perfect High Priest who experienced all our temptations, can Himself fully identify with our weaknesses (Heb. 4:14-16, 5:7-9).[7]

For examples of Jesus ministering emotional and psychological healing, consider Jesus' appearance to the two depressed disciples on the road to Emmaus and His reinstatement of Peter.

The Depressed Disciples on the Road to Emmaus

Two disciples from Jesus' wider circle of disciples were on their way to Emmaus (Luke 24:13-35). Like many people at the time, their hearts were heavy with the events of the last few days—the arrest, crucifixion and burial of Jesus. The One they loved and had placed all their hopes in was now dead for a few days. These two disciples were discussing all these things on the way to Emmaus, when suddenly Jesus Himself came up to them and walked along with them (Luke 24:15). Why did Jesus appear to them, uninvited? Because He knew their deep sorrow and discouragement and came to heal them emotionally and spiritually which we see as the story unfolds. Why were they kept from recognizing Jesus (Luke 24:16)? Maybe they did not expect Him to appear or did not know He had arisen or that His body was not recognizable due to its heavenly nature.[8] I'm not convinced those are the reasons and certainly not because of Jesus' body having a different nature because they saw Him as just another visitor to Jerusalem and thus nothing noticeably different (Luke 24:18). Rather, Jesus divinely arranged this so that He could first enter into their pain and sorrow by bringing truth and hope, thus healing them. If He had revealed Himself at the beginning, the steps to their healing would be jeopardized. Later, when the time was right, Jesus opened their eyes so they could see Him for who He really was, so we know it was a divine initiative on Jesus' part to withhold His identity at first (Luke 24:31).

Jesus proceeded to ask questions to open their hearts and share their deepest pain. His first question was simply, "What are you discussing?" Jesus knew how to approach depressed people—sense their pain and help them talk out their feelings.[9] To show how deep and real their emotional pain was, Luke records that they stood still with their faces downcast (Luke 24:17). Surprised, Cleopas asked why He did not know what had happened in Jerusalem in the last days, as if everyone knew. Then, coming deeper to the issue, Jesus asked "what things?" (Luke 24:19). They shared the recent events which were memories of Jesus' accomplishments, their hope in Him, the crucifixion and the story about an angelic visitation and that His body was now missing. Effectively they had poured out their hearts. Their love for Jesus was evident but so was their deep emotional pain.

Jesus then chided them for their not believing *all* that the prophets had spoken about Him and specifically saying that He had to suffer crucifixion but then would rise again and enter into His glory (Luke 24:25-26). Jesus then instructed them concerning what the Scriptures—from Moses and the Prophets—taught about Him (Luke 24:27). Jesus re-framed or re-interpreted the past events for them. He knew that the first part of their "healing of memories" would be to expose lies and reveal the truth from these painful events. These two disciples were downcast, "depressed" because they believed that the crucifixion was the end, all hope had died on the cross and they would then never again see Jesus whom they loved. That belief was causing the emotional pain. Jesus' first step here was to expose the lie and declare the truth from the Scriptures. The logic of Jesus is simply this: if a lie from a past event, as believed in a memory, is causing emotional pain, expose the lie and reveal the truth for release from the emotional pain. We know this was happening deep in their hearts because they said later that their hearts were burning within them as Jesus was teaching them (Luke 24:32).

But the healing was not complete, for Jesus knew that a revelation of His risen presence would bring the final healing. He was not going to force an invitation to their home, so He pretended He was going on further, but they then invited Him home (Luke 24:28-29). Jesus "pretended" so that they would have an opportunity for more healing, for closure with complete joy by the revelation of His presence. At the evening meal, Jesus broke the bread and gave thanks and gave the bread to them (Luke 24:30). It was at that point that their eyes were opened and they recognized Him (Luke 24:31). These two disciples, not being part of the inner circle, would not have had Communion or the Last Supper with Jesus, but they would most likely have seen Him break the bread and give thanks several times publicly (Matt. 14:19; Mark 8:6; Luke 9:16).[10] Why didn't Jesus just "open their eyes" after teaching them? I think it is because the healing impact would be stronger to see Jesus in a setting they had seen Him in before. On a purely human level, it would help the recall of memory in recognizing Him. Memories and recognition usually come back faster when more of the elements of a memory—taste, touch, sight, sound and feeling—are involved. But in the final analysis, it was Jesus' opening their eyes that allowed them to recognize Him. There was the final closure in healing. They knew that Jesus had risen from the dead, and their hopes were totally and undeniably restored. Their sadness was replaced with such joy that they returned at once to Jerusalem, even though it was late in the day. Two downcast disciples were now joyful, exuberant disciples because they had encountered the healing presence of Jesus who had fully removed the pain from past events. The events did not change, but their reactions did. This is a genuine example of the "healing of memories:"

> The Emmaus road encounter (Luke 24) can be seen (among other things) as a form of "memory healing." The

119

risen Christ met two of his despondent disciples and engaged them in conversation, putting their recent memories of failure and frustration in a new and positive light. As he expounded the Scriptures, Jesus reinterpreted their negative recollections and turned them around so that they became fundamentally meaningful—a source of power and hope. In a very concrete and practical way, we can say that Christ was healing their memories.[11]

Peter's Reinstatement

As Jesus had prophesied, Peter denied Jesus by saying three times that he did not know Jesus (John 18:15-27; 21:15-17). This was in a courtyard area around a fire where Peter was keeping himself warm. It was no small thing to deny Jesus, for in the end he called curses down upon himself and swore to those present that he did not know Him (Matt. 26:74; Mark 14:71-72). When the rooster crowed, he remembered Jesus' words and went outside and wept bitterly (Matt. 26:75; Luke 22:62). Jesus looked straight at Peter when it happened (Luke 22:61). That denial obviously had a deep, negative emotional impact on Peter. Would he ever forgive himself? Would Jesus forgive him? Could he ever live with himself again? We can only begin to imagine if we can recall having deeply disappointed or betrayed someone we really loved.

Peter met Jesus who appeared to him and others while fishing. Jesus prepared breakfast and invited them to the bread and fish that He had prepared (John 21:12-13). After the meal, Jesus addressed Peter as "Simon son of John" in the more formal sense to signify that there would be a serious discussion. Jesus did not ask Peter why he denied Him nor directly confronted him. He already knew that Peter was deeply hurt and sorry for what he had done. Nevertheless, Jesus knew that the sin of denying his

Lord had to be dealt with as part of Peter's reinstatement.

Jesus asked Peter whether he truly loved Him "more than these." Of the three logical meanings of "these," I agree with most commentators that Jesus was asking Peter whether his love for Jesus was greater than the love the other disciples had for Jesus.[12] This is really the pivotal question behind the whole denial in the first place. Peter expressed this "greater devotion" to Jesus by claiming that others may well fall away, but not him (Matt. 26:33; Mark 14:29). When Jesus told Peter that no one could follow Jesus where He was going, Peter contested that and said that he would even lay down his life to go where Jesus was going (John 13:36-37). In effect Peter was boasting about his commitment to Jesus and comparing his love to the other disciples as well as almost judging Jesus' words. While the other disciples would not go where Jesus went, Peter apparently would. But Jesus immediately disputed the level of Peter's commitment to Him (John 13:38) and asked if he really would lay his life down for Him. He knew that Peter was afraid his denial showed he did not love Jesus at all, for who would deny someone they really loved? Thus Jesus questioned Peter on the core issue of whether Peter himself knew that he loved Jesus given all that had happened. Peter replied simply that Jesus knew he loved Him with no comparison to others at all.

Further healing for Peter came through Jesus' prophetic word. In the past denial it was clear that Peter was not ready to lay his life down for Jesus. But by indicating the *"kind of death by which Peter would glorify God"* (John 21:19), it was now clear that Peter would not in the future deny Jesus but would, in fact, lay his life down for Jesus. It appears that Jesus was addressing any fear of failure in the future in this area of Peter's life and ministry.

The occasion with a warm fire, other people and asking the same question three times was a direct reference back to Peter denying Jesus three times by a warm fire and in response to the same question. The healing for Peter came by reversing the past event in which he could now state his loyalty and love for Jesus three times. Peter was hurt by Jesus asking the question the third time because it was if Jesus still did not believe he really loved Him, and perhaps it brought back the pain of denying Jesus the third time. When Jesus reinstated Peter by telling him to feed His sheep and follow Him, the healing was complete; Peter knew Jesus accepted him and forgave him. We also see that a basic and indispensable qualification for Christian ministry is a love for Jesus above all else.

Peter's reinstatement is an encouragement to all believers when they feel they have failed the Lord or made decisions for which they have many regrets. The power to transform people from the past is certainly seen in the life of the apostle Paul who once was a persecutor of the Church, a blasphemer and a violent man. He would have had a lot of regrets (1 Tim. 1:13), yet he was changed by the grace of God (1 Tim. 1:14-16).

The Role of Memory in the Scriptures

People can have problems remembering and are prone to forget. In fact that is why the Lord repeatedly told His people to remember the Lord and not forget what they had seen (Deut. 4:9), or the covenant (Deut. 4:23) or the Lord Himself (Deut. 6:12). Once in the promised land they might be so pre-occupied with being blessed, they could forget the Lord (Deut. 8:11) and the real reasons He brought them there (Deut. 9:4-7). Their appalling short-term memory was such that they forgot the kindnesses of God and His miracles (Ps. 106:7; Neh. 9:17). Though a maiden does not forget her jewelry or a bride her wedding ornaments, God's people can forget God (Jer. 2:32; 18:15; 50:6). In spite of all the admonitions and commands to remember, the children of Israel forgot and forsook their God (Judg. 3:7; Ps. 106:13; Jer. 23;27; Ezek. 23:35; Hos. 2:13, 8:14, 13:6). No wonder the continual commands and exhortations to remember! To remember the covenant meant to obey and to act; it was more than just a mental recollection.

Changes in life can cause one to forget the memory of previous events.[13] Famine caused the abundance of grain to be forgotten (Gen. 41:30). Suffering might cause one to forget to eat (Ps. 102:4). Rebekah hoped that in time Esau would forget Jacob's deception (Gen. 27:45). Enough alcohol might cause one to forget poverty and misery (Prov. 31:7). A current crisis could be so emotionally strong that one could essentially forget better times (Lam. 3:17). Changes in life can "stir up memories of relief or nostalgia" like Zophar assuring Job that if he would just repent, he would be released from the pain of past troubles (Job 11:16).[14]

How deep can memory loss be in people? An incredible example is from the book of Isaiah. Although it appeared as if the Lord had truly forgotten and forsaken His people (Isa. 49:14), this was not the case at all. *"Can a mother forget the baby at her breast and have no compassion on the child she has borne? Though she may forget, I will not forget you!"* (Isa. 49:15). One would think it impossible and unthinkable that any woman could forget her child, but the Scriptures declare it is possible. People may have major memory loss and forgetfulness, essentially buried or repressed memories.

Past memories can directly effect present emotions. The author of Lamentations wrote how past afflictions and negative emotions caused his soul to be downcast or deeply discouraged (Lam. 3:19-20). Yet bringing to mind God's great love began to restore his soul (Lam. 3:21). The Psalmist, when his heart was downcast and he poured out his soul to God, was encouraged when he remembered how he used to worship the Lord in joy with others (Ps. 42:4). *"My soul is downcast within me; therefore I will remember you from the land of the Jordan* (Ps. 42:6; cf. Ps. 77:3-11). Similarly, *"So my spirit grows faint within me; my heart within me is dismayed. I remember the days of long ago..."* (Ps. 143:4-5). Remembering God's laws brings comfort (Ps. 119:52). Remembering the Lord and His power is a way to overcome fear (Neh. 4:4,14; Deut. 7:18). We see how good memories of the past bring healing and hope into the present. In the Psalms this is often part of God's healing and restoration in the present. The opposite happens when the remembrance of past sins brings humiliation and shame into the present (Ezek. 16:60-61).

Joseph's story has an example of memory recall by association. Joseph had a dream where his brothers essentially bowed down before him (Gen. 37:7). The memory of that dream came right back when he first saw his brothers bowed down before him. *"Then he remembered his dreams about them"* (Gen. 42:9). The Lord was with Joseph through all his painful events (Gen. 39:2,21), ministered to him and finally healing him so that those memories were no longer painful. In other words God released him from the pain of the past. The facts of the past had not changed, but their effect on his spirit had. We see this quite clearly in Genesis 41:51 where Joseph named his firstborn son Manasseh and said, *"It is because God has made me forget all my trouble and all my father's household."* It wasn't that Joseph resolved to just forget or "get over it" or that time eventually healed him. It was the Lord who made him forget so that there was no more pain from the harmful events in Egypt and the very real hurt from his family.[15]

The Lord brought healing of memories for His people as a whole. Even though Israel had abandoned the Lord and had been unfaithful in spiritual adultery and idolatry, His people will one day be able to forget the shame of their youth and will no longer remember their reproach (Isa. 54:4) because of His deep redemption, grace and love. Their shame and disgrace will be replaced with everlasting joy (Isa. 61:7), their spirit of despair with a garment of praise (Isa. 61:3). Similarly Ezekiel declared that when the Lord brings back His people from captivity and shows His compassion to them, *"they will forget their shame and all the unfaithfulness they showed toward me"* (Ezek. 39:26). How God's people felt about themselves and their emotional well-being was important to Him. If God removed feelings of shame and reproach from His people due to past events, I see no reason at all why He would not want to do the same for Christians today who, for example, have suffered sexual abuse or have failed or sinned in the past.

God is vitally concerned about our personal past because in His Son there is atonement for our past sins. What we did in the past matters to God. As far as the east is from the west, He removes the effects of our sins from us (Ps. 103:12). It is blessed to have one's sins covered (Ps. 32:1; Rom. 4:7). God is concerned with our past sins and also our past hurts and pain. To know that a specific sin committed in the past, maybe many long years ago, is totally and completely forgiven upon our confession and reliance upon the work of Christ (1 John 1:9) on the cross is in itself freedom, healing, release and restoration for one's soul. To experience release from shame, fear, false guilt, regret, sadness, rejection and more from the past is also part of God's redemptive and restorative work in our lives.

Memory involves more than sight and sound. Some people can remember taste, touch and smell. I think Jesus knew about the power and depth of memory by instituting the Lord's Supper with actual bread and wine (1 Cor. 11:24-25). This is much more memorable than just recalling the event or having it declared cognitively from the pulpit. One remembers by participating, hearing, touching the elements and eating. All those sensory dimensions help to reinforce the vital truth about Jesus' death for us.

The Scriptures therefore teach us much about memories and their importance and relevance in our lives. Painful memories from the past can negatively effect our emotions and inner being in the present. Conversely, good memories from the past may bring healing and hope to the present. Life situations, crises, time and more, may well cause us to forget things of the past, including those events which have not yet been "processed." God is concerned about our memories and how past events affect us in the present and is not above bringing healing, reconciliation and release from their effects. God has ways of bringing healing and release where needed from the pain of our personal past, no matter what it is. "Memory is one of the most potent means of opening up the areas of hurt feelings."[16]

The Significance of Our Personal Past

The Scriptures and many psychologists, although often with different assumptions, agree that our past history matters. Each of us has a personal history that cannot be overlooked. As Storkey wrote:

> ...our past experiences, our memories and often those events which lie now beyond the recall of memory can deeply affect both the kinds of persons we are and the ways in which we relate to other people.[17]

Past events and how one reacts to them is part of who one is today. In the Scriptures the development of people is seen in the acknowledgment that young children do not know good from bad (Deut. 1:39; Isa. 7:15-16) and that fathers should not exasperate their children lest there be problems later in life (Eph. 6:4). Parents are admonished to bring up children so that they will not depart from the way they should go later in life. If one generation is not brought up in holiness and righteousness, it will effect the next generation (Exod. 20:5). Adulthood involves putting behind or growing out of childish talk, thought and reasoning (1 Cor. 13:11).[18] Timothy's timidity may have come from the lack of a strong male spiritual role model since only his mother and grandmother are mentioned as examples of faith (2 Tim. 1:5-7). Our past and our upbringing will affect our sense of self, ability to relate, trust, level of intimacy, sex and much more. This is not determinism but reality. Storkey explained further:

> Each of us has thousands of hours of memory tape recorded from years back which often lie dormant in our memories. Some lie even deeper than that, in fact beyond the recall of memory, yet they still influence us with attitudes, fears or anxieties that we carry around with us.[19]

The challenge, then, is to live under the power of Jesus and by His Spirit in the present and not under the power of the past in any area in our life. When Paul wrote about forgetting what is behind (Phil. 3:13), he was writing about his past accomplishments as a Hebrew, a Pharisee, the lineage of the tribe of Benjamin and his "qualifications." Those mattered no longer; his status and identity were now in Christ alone and what Christ had done for him. The reason for the healing of memories is precisely to understand what issues and events of the past keep us from spiritual maturity (Phil. 3:14-15). As we press ahead in Christ, there are times when we need to know what keeps us back.

The Healing of Memories: Avoiding Confusion

Agnes Sanford first used the term "healing of memories" when the Church was so bound by abstract and rational thinking that very little healing was practiced.[20] Sanford applied the term to healing of deep wounds that are not uncovered by one's own self-searching, prayers or normal awareness.[21] In psychological terms those would be "unconscious" or "subconscious" wounds that require the Spirit's illumination in healing prayer.[22] The Holy Spirit then points to Jesus who was there in the past event (seen or unseen), and the individual then receives Jesus' healing word, embrace or glance.[23] This is what happened to Peter, the disciples on the road to Emmaus, Joseph, Frank and others as shown by their stories in this book. The term is somewhat misleading since past events do not change; it really involves the healing of one's heart and soul from the effects of what happened in the past as well as one's reactions to the events. Thus one would be better to say "healing from the pain of the past."

Many writers have criticized this type of healing. Some have written that this ministry appears to be an easy road to sanctification as if people are declared victims of the past and their own sin is bypassed. But Sanford wrote clearly from the very beginning that the "healing of memories" could also be called "the forgiveness of sins" because of the importance of recognizing past sin from past events and the great need of forgiveness in one's emotional and spiritual healing.[24] The ministry of healing prayer, when it involves the "healing of memories," never bypasses the cross and one's personal responsibility for sin. Forgiveness and repentance also bring healing and restoration to the soul. But there are many times when one has been sinned against and suffered at the hands of others, even one's own earthly family. When this happens to a small child, for example, the pain runs deep. I have heard countless stories of deep emotional pain that are unbelievable to most people. The ministry of healing prayer is never about fabricating victims. But it most certainly brings deep and substantial healing to those who were truly victimized, those who have ashes and despair and yearn for gladness and praise (Isa. 61:3).

The healing of memories does not negate personal responsibility, issues in discipleship, the spiritual disciplines, obedience to Jesus, connection to a local church and more. As we grow in Christ and encounter difficulties or "get stuck," we attempt to understand what is holding us back. Under the direction of the Holy Spirit, if it is an issue from the past (and that is not always the case), prayer for the healing of memories is offered. Our eyes must be firmly fixed on Jesus with the right posture of faith (Heb. 12:2). We should not be looking backwards and digging around in our past, or looking sideways and comparing ourselves to others and circumstances, or looking downwards and "practicing the presence of our problems," or looking inwards and analyzing ourselves to pieces or looking straight ahead with fear and worry about the future. Instead we should be looking upwards to Jesus and so run the race with perseverance (Heb. 12:1-2). That is our true posture of faith.

Many have criticized the healing of memories because it seems to involve the unconscious and appears Freudian. But that is simplistic logic known as "guilt by association" when an idea is rejected simply because it is held or originates from a heretical group or person.[25] Doctrines or ideas must be assessed on their own intrinsic merits or error by the Scriptures and not by who happens to hold them. Because the Jehovah's Witnesses and the Children of God are premillenialists, does that mean writers such as Dave Hunt or David Wilkerson or premillenialists in general are seduced by error or supportive of the Jehovah's Witnesses or the Children of God?[26] Since Dave Hunt quotes the secular psychiatrist Thomas Szsasz,[27] does that mean he endorses humanistic psychology?[28] Every time anyone uses the term "introvert" or "extrovert" which are Jungian terms for personality types,[29] does that mean all of Jung's teaching is endorsed or that that person is a follower of Jung? Certainly not! We must get beyond "spiritual third party liability."

The goal in prayer is to bring truth to the inner being (Eph. 3:16; Rom. 7:22; Ps. 103:1), the inner parts (Ps. 51:10) and search the heart (Ps. 139:23-24). As seen above some memories are forgotten or even repressed, and the Spirit may well bring them back as part of one's healing. While this seems to involve the "unconscious," it does not support Freudian thinking as whole. Rather, it only means that in spite of the major and serious errors in Freud's thinking, by the common grace of God Freud may have been partially correct. It is not just a question of whether a practice or terminology appears in the Scriptures or not. Rather, it is a question of whether it is contradictory or inconsistent with the Scriptures.[30] If we reject the concept of "unconscious" or "subconscious" just because they do not appear in the Scriptures, what do we do with "Trinity"? Or pews, pipe organs, the altar call and so forth? We need a Christian mind to think in the categories and truth of Jesus and His Word and apply them to the issues of the day, intellectual and otherwise.

Others maintain that the memories that come back are often false, especially concerning sexual abuse. A battle has been raging between the Recovered Memory Therapy Movement and the later False Memory Syndrome Movement as well as its role in Christian counseling.[31] I don't doubt that there are therapies and techniques which may have fabricated or falsified past memories. However, one cannot discount the role of the Spirit as the counselor and one who reveals truth plus the visual language and the gifts of the Spirit. I have seen numerous times how the Spirit and His gifts have revealed past events that were found to be totally accurate, as seen, for example, in the chapter "Listening in His Presence."

The Objectives of Healing Prayer

The ministry of healing prayer, including the healing of memories and inner healing, has a number of objectives. These include the following.

Restoring the broken image of man as created originally.[32] We are all "broken images" in need of repair and restoration so that we can again walk in a correct relationship with God and have true spiritual vision. This involves healing deep wounds, uncovering lies, cleansing the heart, renewing the mind (Rom. 12:2), learning to walk in the light (1 John 1:7), redeeming the emotions, breaking bondages, rebuking Satan and his evil spirits and much more.

Receiving abundant life. Healing prayer involves receiving more of the abundant life of Jesus (John 10:10) by His resurrection power. Since redemption also involves the *impartation of His life* into every Christian,[33] this involves uncovering hindrances and blockages that restrict the flow of His life into every Christian.

Renouncing idols. Idols of the heart and mind appear when we look to the world for meaning, significance, identity or fulfillment instead of from Jesus. This is often behind addictions and compulsions. This "bentness" of soul occurs when we listen to the world and others or our past instead of to Jesus when centered in His presence.[34]

Growing in sanctification. Christians *are* positionally sanctified, justified, have the righteousness of Christ and have been raised with Christ (Col. 3:1). But in experience we are also being sanctified. We grow up into Christ (Eph. 4:15), work out or apply our salvation (Phil. 2:12) and grow up in our salvation (1 Pet. 2:2) while His power (not techniques) is at work in us (Eph. 3:20). We are being transformed into the likeness of Jesus with ever-increasing glory by His Spirit (2 Cor. 3:18; Rom. 8:29) and being renewed daily (2 Cor. 4:16). We are to put on the character of Christ and have Christ "formed in us" (Gal. 5:19). We must live in Christ as we received Him, rooted up and built in Him (Col. 2:6). We are no longer in sin but in Christ. Since we are in Christ and filled by His Spirit, we are a new creation (2 Cor. 5:17) and need to learn how to live out of that new reality. Since we are born again, we must learn to live again and move beyond being infants (*nepios*) in Christ (1 Cor. 3:1). We must walk in the light as Jesus is in the light (1 John 1:7). Healing prayer involves mind renewal (Rom. 12:2; Eph. 4:23).

Healing prayer, as part of sanctification along with our active involvement and growth in discipleship, then involves putting on the new self (Col. 3:10; Rom. 6:4; Eph. 4:24, 5:8) which reflects the character of Christ and the fruits of the Spirit and also putting off the old self (Eph. 4:22).[35] We must cooperate with Jesus under the direction of His Spirit in no longer living out of the old self which was crucified in Christ and to which we are reckoned dead (Rom. 6:11). We must decide to not walk according to the flesh (Rom. 8:12-13) which includes ingrained patterns, behaviors and responses learned from the past. The old self, or the flesh, is characterized by envy, anger, rage, greed, impurity, lust, sensuality, idolatry, conceit, pride and more (Eph. 4:29-31; Col. 3:5-11; Jas. 4:1-2; 1 Pet. 2:1). Fear, shame, false or real guilt, bitterness, unforgiveness, hatred, condemnation, lies and more can be tied to the past and must be dealt with to more fully put on the new self.

Paul's psychology revolves around one's failure to put on the new self which was created by Christ.[36] This is accomplished by study of the Word, fellowship, prayer, worship, obedience, repentance and all the other means of grace, but most centrally by our direct union and communion with Christ who is in us by His Spirit. This "mystical union" between the Christian and God is "the reality that empowers us to be transformed from the inside out."[37] That is precisely the basis of the ministry of healing prayer directed by His Spirit. And that is also precisely where much of Christian theology and therapy goes wrong due to a missing theology of the presence. Methods or techniques simply cannot achieve this transformation. *We need more of the new self instead of more self-help.*

Healing prayer is a part of one's spiritual journey, a major step at times in spiritual formation. It is not an "instant fix"[38] but more like a major turning point or a removal of a major blockage so the person can continue in their life. One healing prayer session can make all the difference in terms of the person's spiritual growth for years to come. Progressive sanctification means that the results of healing prayer are appropriated over time, and there may be need for more prayer in the future. Marshall put it well:

> In strict terms, you cannot be healed of immaturity or delivered from it: you can only grow out of it. Therefore, while the removal of the blockage or dealing with the inhibiting experience may take place in a moment, there is a time factor involved in the completion of the process.[39]

Healing prayer can help to realize the Great Commandment, to love the Lord our God with all our heart, soul, strength and mind (Mark 12:30; Matt. 22:37). You cannot fully obey this commandment if you believe or feel that God does not really love you, or you are not able to receive His love, or God cannot be fully trusted, or God cannot be your heavenly Father and so forth.

Jesus, Time and Healing

With an understanding of the presence of Jesus from the chapter "Understanding the Presence," one must also realize that as co-creator of the universe and the Lord of time, Jesus may well reveal Himself to

133

our memories as we come for healing prayer. Philosophers and theologians have debated concepts of time and eternity for centuries. Time can be measured by the clock or experienced as time by personal human consciousness.[40] Our experience is always in the present even though God may show us something from the past or into the future. Our memories are present phenomena and they "enable us to compare that *which is* to that *which was*."[41] Our memories are reconstructions of the past in our consciousness, whether we are fully aware of them at any time or not. From the time of Augustine it has been understood that "God knows things 'timelessly' all at once. For Him the past, present and future of the world are known instantly."[42]

There is a new dimension of healing beyond the Old Testament due to the coming and incarnation of Jesus and His Spirit being in all believers. Payne described the healing of memories as follows:

> In prayer for the healing of memories, the power of the memory to make the past present to us in a very real way is extraordinary. The reason for this, of course, is that Jesus, the infinite One who is outside of time and to whom all times are present, enters into what for us is a past occurrence, one known only in retrospect, though we experience its consequences in the present. Here the past-present-future time sequence in which we experience existence comes together in a particularly meaningful way with the eternal.[43]

In the ministry of healing prayer, we invoke the presence of Jesus and wait to see what He will do. The Holy Spirit, as counselor, will bring back any memories as needed if the healing involves a memory of a past event. Since Jesus is the Lord of all time, He can reveal anything that must be known about any past event, and He can even reveal how He was present in the past event. Just as Jesus appeared in a dream, or vision or flashing light, Jesus can show His presence to us while we see a memory and then bring healing. With His healing presence, the pain and power of a memory and hence its impact in the present is diminished. The facts of the past do not change; the effect of the past into the present does change.

Since the core of healing prayer is listening to Jesus and His Spirit, who are truly there, Jesus will determine what will happen. Memories do not always come since it is not always an issue of past hurts and pain. When they do come, Jesus does not always appear in them either. But then again, He might appear and one must have a theology which can allow for this.

Consider Solomon's dream while he was at Gibeon (1 Kings 3:5-15). In the dream, the Lord appeared to him and asked him what he wanted. Solomon replied that he wanted the ability to govern his people with discernment and wisdom. The Lord then gave him more and suddenly he awoke and realized it was a dream. Even though it was a dream, Solomon was involved in a conversation with the Lord in the dream and that affected his future. Consider also Jacob's dream where he saw angels ascending a ladder and heard the Lord speak directly to him (Gen. 28:10-17). The Lord's presence was no less real because those encounters involved dreams or because Solomon or Jacob were not awake at the time. Likewise to have the Lord appear in a memory while one is awake and speak about the past is not much different and no less real or possible.

Frank's healing, as recorded in the beginning of this chapter, was real and substantial and was directed by Jesus Himself. Similarly Marshall wrote about how he began to relive feelings of anger, shame and embarrassment from poverty as a schoolboy in the Depression.[44] Suddenly the Lord spoke to him directly and clearly: "I know how you feel, I was poor too." In an instant he was healed because he knew the Lord could identify with his feelings and cared enough to speak to him. The present hurt and all its influences on his life were removed. Similarly the Lord healed Greg from rejection and loneliness, thereby strengthening his marriage.

Greg's Rejection and Loneliness

Ever since Martha and I married, I carried a fear that I would lose her shortly into our marriage. For this reason my mind was constantly working out a "backup plan" should anything happen to her. As a result I developed a very unhealthy pattern of "wife shopping." Every woman in my acquaintance was evaluated on the basis of whether or not she would make a good partner for me. Naturally this pattern of thought led to some very unhealthy and sinful fantasies that were not beneficial to our marriage. I realized that this thought pattern was wrong, and I wanted to be committed to my wife, but I felt that I was powerless to change. In retrospect I realize that, in time, I would have been a prime candidate for an affair.

As God brought this situation to the forefront of my mind during a healing prayer conference, I realized that I needed to go for prayer. I wrestled for some time before I finally acquiesced. A lady on one of the prayer teams prayed with me. As I confessed my sinful habit to her, she asked me if I was able to summarize in a word what the root of this sin was. I wasn't. Jesus then spoke through her and she asked if it was loneliness. As she spoke it, my heart broke, and I wept.

I had experienced a lot of rejection and loneliness as a teenager. Although I had recovered somewhat from those injuries as an adult, I was never able to fully accept the fact that someone else could truly love me. In the two years just prior to this conference, my best friend of twenty years had turned his back on his family, his church and our friendship. Once again I felt deeply wounded, rejected and alone.

As she prayed I continued to weep and was finally able to ask

Jesus to come into this pain and show me His presence in my pain. Almost immediately I saw an image of Him on the cross. Despite the pain He was feeling, He looked at me with His compassionate eyes and said, "Loneliness is not for you to bear. That is why I am here." Again I wept and as I wept I felt Him absorb the loneliness into His body. I was drawn up to Him on the cross, and as I laid my head on His sweaty, bloody shoulder, He healed me. The loneliness was gone. I felt loved.

My wife received similar healing at the conference, and on the journey home, we knelt together in our motel room, confessed our sin to each other, forgave each other and recommitted ourselves to each other in marriage. Since that time our marriage has grown immensely in every way. I still experience temptation, but it no longer overwhelms me. Satan has lost his foothold.

Endnotes

[1] John F. MacArthur, Jr., *Charismatic Chaos* (Grand Rapids: Zondervan, 1992) p. 259.

[2] MacArthur, p. 263.

[3] Michael Scanlan, *Inner Healing: Ministering to the Human Spirit Through the Power of Prayer* (New York: Paulist Press, 1974) p. 11.

[4] Scanlan, p. 9.

[5] Betty Tapscott. *Inner Healing Through Healing of Memories* (Kingwood: Hunter Publishing, 1975) p. 13.

[6] Betty Tapscott, p. 15.

[7] David A. Seamands, *Healing for Damaged Emotions: Recovering from the Memories that Cause Our Pain* (Wheaton: Victor Books, 1981) pp. 38-46.

[8] Norval Geldenhuys, *The Gospel of Luke: The New International Commentary on the New Testament* (Grand Rapids: Eerdmans Publishing Co., 1951) p. 632.

9 Rita Bennett, *Emotionally Free* (Old Tappan: Fleming H. Revell Co., 1982) p. 148.

10 Geldenhuys, p. 634.

11 Steve Scott and Brooks Alexander, "Inner Healing," *SCP Journal*, Vol. 4/1, April 1980, Spiritual Counterfeits Project, Berkeley, California. p. 13.

12 Leon Morris, *The Gospel According to John Revised: The New International Commentary on the New Testament* (Grand Rapids: Eerdmans Publishing Co., 1995) p. 768.

13 Willem A. VanGemeren, *New International Dictionary of Old Testament Theology & Exegesis*, Vol. 4 (Grand Rapids: Zondervan, 1997) p. 104

14 VanGemeren, Vol. 1, p. 1101.

15 Dennis and Matthew Linn, *Healing of Memories* (Ramsey: Paulist Press, 1974) p. 12.

16 Tom Marshall, *Free Indeed!* (Kent: Sovereign World Ltd, 1975) p. 54.

17 Elaine Storkey, *The Search for Intimacy* (London: Hodder and Stoughton, 1995) p. 93.

18 David A. Seamands, *Healing of Memories* (Wheaton: Victor Books, 1985) p. 62.

19 Storkey, p. 95.

20 Leanne Payne, *Crisis in Masculinity* (Wheaton: Crossway Books, 1985) p. 34.

21 Agnes Sanford, *The Healing Gifts of the Spirit* (Philadelphia: Trumpet Books, A.J. Holman Co., 1976) p. 110.

22 Sanford, p. 115.

23 Payne, 1985, p. 37.

24 Sanford, p. 110.

25 Gary DeMar and Peter J. Leithart, *The Reduction of Christianity: A Biblical Response to Dave Hunt* (Fort Worth: Dominion Press, 1988) p. 142.

26 DeMar and Leithart, p. 144.

27 DeMar and Leithart, p. 146.

[28] DeMar and Leithart, pp. 145-147.

[29] Stanton L. Jones and Richard E. Butman, *Modern Psychotherapies: A Comprehensive Christian Appraisal* (Downers Grove: InterVarsity Press, 1991) p. 124.

[30] Seamands, 1985, pp. 61-62.

[31] Gary Almy, *How Christian is Christian Counseling?* (Wheaton: Crossway Books, 2000) pp. 239-281.

[32] Brad Long and Cindy Strickler, *Let Jesus Heal Your Hidden Wounds: Cooperating With the Holy Spirit in Healing Ministry* (Grand Rapids: Chosen Books, 2001) pp. 18-32.

[33] Dallas Willard, *The Spirit of the Disciplines* (New York: Harper-Collins, 1991) pp. 36-38.

[34] Leanne Payne, *The Healing Presence: How God's Grace Can Work in You to Bring Healing in Your Broken Places and the Joy of Living in His Love* (Wheaton: Crossway Books, 1989) pp. 52-53.

[35] Robert C. Roberts, "Outline of Pauline Psychotherapy," in Mark R. McMinn and Timothy R. Phillips, *Care for the Soul: Exploring the Intersection of Psychology & Theology* (Downers Grove: InterVarsity Press, 2001) pp. 137-144.

[36] Roberts, p. 149.

[37] Mario Bergner, *Setting Love in Order: Hope and Healing for the Homosexual* (Grand Rapids: Hamewith Books, 1995) p. 98.

[38] Payne, 1989, p. 55.

[39] Tom Marshall, *Free Indeed!* (Kent: Sovereign World Ltd, 1975) p. 57.

[40] Karl M. Busen, "Eternity and the Personal God," *Journal of the American Scientific Affiliation*, 49(1):40-49, 1997, p. 42.

[41] Ibid.

[42] Ibid.

[43] Leanne Payne, *The Broken Image: Restoring Personal Wholeness Through Healing Prayer* (Wheaton: Crossway Books, 1981) p. 27.

[44] Marshall, p. 53.

 Chapter Five

Healing the Whole Person: Understanding the Heart-Mind-Body Connection

Do not be wise in your own eyes; fear the Lord and shun evil. This will bring health to your body and nourishment to your bones (Prov. 3:7).

My son, pay attention to what I say; listen closely to my words. Do not let them out of your sight, keep them within your heart; for they are life to those who find them and health to a man's whole body (Prov. 4:20-22).

Kristin's Migraines and Fibromyalgia

It has been five years since I re-dedicated my life to Christ. In those five years God has graced me with deep healing that flows from His love for me and His promise to bring me into wholeness in the perfect plan He has for my life. As God healed layer after layer of past wounds, I found an ever-increasing freedom, a deep peace within and an abundance of joy! Through the revelations given to me by God and by praying into these revelations, what was once pain, despair and brokenness became filled with the joy, love and peace that can only come from the healing power of Jesus Christ.

As a therapist in the psychology profession I knew all of the various theories of well-being and healing and how to apply them. And while this promoted an intellectual understanding of my pain and some degree of healing and increased coping, the application of theory and counseling did not heal the deep inner needs of my heart. But Jesus did.

I believe that wounds of the soul can crush the spirit, burden the body and cause illness to arise. While I was rejoicing in my newfound freedoms and my increasing intimacy with God, I began to experience intense headaches. Although I have fibromyalgia and am no stranger to chronic pain, these headaches were different. They became more and more debilitating and soon they were diagnosed as atypical migraines. Along with the intense pain came an aura that included vomiting, momentary paralysis of the left side of my body and seizure activity which required brief hospitalization. The intervals of these attacks became more frequent and the pain more chronic. A CAT scan was clear, but I was then scheduled for an MRI to rule out possible brain tumors.

Without several Tylenol #3 per day I was unable to carry out my daily activities. There were countless days and nights when I could only lie in the dark and cry out to Jesus. As always He was faithful and I would find a reprieve, not always from the pain but in the incredible peace of the Holy Spirit. I felt buoyed up as if floating on a vast sea of the softest pillows. I would feel His perfect love envelop me, and I could rest assured that He knew my needs.

In the middle of a nine-day bout of migraine activity I sensed that God was going to deliver me from this condition. The morning that my healing prayer was scheduled God quickened some verses of Scripture to my thoughts. In Psalm 41 I read, *"The Lord will sustain him on his sickbed and restore him from his bed of illness"* (v.3). As I read further, verse 9 said, *"Even my close friend, whom I trusted, he who shared my bread, has lifted up his heel against me."* I saw a vision of the family member who had sexually abused me and those who had betrayed me by denying the abuse. I felt a very strong sense that my migraines were rooted in the betrayal I had experienced from family members.

Though confronted with the abuse many years ago, the offender and other members of my family either denied the abuse, or were unaware of its occurrence. As part of my healing a few years ago God had led me through a process of breaking the secret, bringing it from darkness into light. Despite my terror and my desire to protect my family, I disclosed the secret to all the members. Despite a mixed reaction the Lord was with me and I experienced a release in my spirit. With this newfound freedom God brought a deep healing into many areas of my life. Yet I also knew at a deeper level that I feared to delve any further into the pain of my family's responses. It was no coincidence that within three months of disclosing the family secret and facing betrayal all over again, my migraines began.

In healing prayer God revealed to me my broken heart from this betrayal. God knew, better than I ever could, that my spirit had been crushed by the weight of this burden. God took me to the depths of the feelings I had tried to bury deep, the pain I had tried to numb. I was so very tired of carrying this burden. In those moments of healing prayer God revealed feelings I had long ago lost connection with. And as I wept, all of those feelings, thoughts and desires came tumbling out. God showed me that I wanted to be released emotionally from the burden my family had become. And that is exactly the gift God gave me.

My healing prayer partners prayed for deliverance and healing from those roots of betrayal. And I did my part of repenting for any sins of unforgiveness towards those who had so deeply hurt me. We asked God's blessings upon the Godly family ties that I may experience more love from those bonds that were strong, healthy and loving. We then prayed for the physical healing of the migraines and all other illnesses caused by this root. I suddenly felt the burden lift off me as if a heavy pressing yoke had been removed from my neck and shoulders and an anvil lifted off my heart. Suddenly what was once the burden was far removed *"as far as the east is from the west"* (Ps. 103:12) and in its place was a sense of indescribable lightness. My feet, my soul, my heart, my spirit were leaping with joyful abandonment, yet I had never left my sitting position of prayer. I was dancing with Jesus! And I knew with absolute certainty, with every fiber of my being, that God released me from the chains that had bound me emotionally to that betrayal. And with the breaking of those chains I was set free from every illness that came with them!

I have been migraine free for going on five months. I have also experienced significantly less pain from my fibromyalgia. Its affects on my everyday life have been dramatically reduced. As each day passes I am aware of less and less pain. I also have His perfect peace that I will be healed one day of this condition as well, in His perfect timing. It also became clear with that same healing prayer that the tightness in my chest and the frequent inability to catch my breath also left me that day. I was diagnosed with asthma four years ago and used a Ventalin inhaler. I have not needed that inhaler, and since that day I no longer carry it with me. In fact at this moment, I don't even know where it is! God really does bring freedom from illness and its burdens! Jesus is the ultimate healer!

The Healing and Restoration of Whole Persons

A theology of healing prayer must clearly and intentionally understand the whole person in the context of one's whole being, whole life and all relationships including one's relationship with God. People are integrated beings with mind, heart, conscience, wills and emotions all interrelated with body, soul and spirit. While we readily think of health as a biological concept, the Scriptures clearly teach that it is fundamentally a relational concept involving our relationship with God (salvation, forgiveness, obedience, faith, righteousness, reconciliation and trust), others (forgiveness, reconciliation and harmony), ourself (forgiveness and self-acceptance), even creation (ecology, toxicology, environmental issues, etc.) resulting in *shalom* when all is truly well with one's soul.[1] The quality of our relationships will often determine the quality of our health and well being. While we can be thankful for all the medical advances of modern science, the biological reductionism that has come with it has been hazardous to our health. The huge interest in "holistic" medicine testifies to the need to look beyond the physical and consider the other dimensions of people's lives.

The dynamic connection between body, soul and spirit is clearly taught in the book of Proverbs. *"Do not be wise in your own eyes; fear the Lord and shun evil. This will bring health to your body and nourishment to your bones"* (Prov. 3:7). So unforgiveness, bitterness, anger—among other evil things—will undermine your health. The words of wisdom in Proverbs concerning life and relationships are: *"life to those who find them and health to a man's whole body"* (Prov. 4:22). How we live our life and the degree to which we cultivate the wisdom of God will impact our health. Fearing God, or obeying Him from a committed heart, will add *"length to life,*

but the years of the wicked are cut short" (Prov. 10:27). *"Hope deferred
makes the heart sick, but a longing fulfilled is a tree of life"* (Prov.
13:12). *"A heart at peace gives life to the body, but envy rots the bones"*
(Prov. 14:30). *"A happy heart makes the face cheerful, but heartache
crushes the spirit"* (Prov. 15:13). *"Pleasant words are a honeycomb,
sweet to the soul and healing to the bones"* (Prov. 16:24). *"A man's
spirit sustains him in sickness, but a crushed spirit who can bear?"*
(Prov. 18:14). Personal sin that leads to God's judgment and discipline may also affect our health (Ps. 38:3, 5-8; Ps. 32:3-5).

New Testament examples include the paralytic whose sins were
forgiven as part of his healing (Mark 2:5) and the invalid at the pool
of Bethesda whom Jesus admonished to stop sinning *"or something
worse may happen"* (John 5:14). Unconfessed sin can lead to weakness, sickness and even death among believers (1 Cor. 11:27-30). In
contrast, no sin was responsible for a man born blind (John 9:1-3).

The truths we live by, how we react to the world and people
around us, the inner disposition and strength of our spirit—all
such things will affect our health to different degrees. The spiritual
and relational dimensions of our life must be considered along with
the physical. Any other view of personhood leads to either biological reductionism (the body alone) or spiritual reductionism where
medical research is despised or the body is devalued or sickness is
treated as an illusion.

"Whole-person medicine" had been known and practiced for
centuries. A Hittite king many centuries ago noted how feelings
could relate to illness when he developed paralysis and speech loss
after a traumatic thunderstorm.[2] Hippocrates, five centuries
before Christ, believed that curing an illness required that doctors
"have a knowledge of the whole of things."[3] "During the Middle
Ages both physical and mental illnesses were treated by ministering to the whole person, through that part of him that theology

called his soul."[4] The belief that all disease had a physical cause was thus a heresy until the fifteenth century when the new science of anatomy began to challenge it.[5] Then, with great advances through the germ theory of disease in the second half of the nineteenth century and modern medicine's increased focus on finding specific microorganisms as causing specific diseases, the more holistic view of health and healing was soon forgotten.[6] Apparent progress took a step backwards.

Inevitably the modern, scientific world, with its focus on analysis, observation and technique, lost the full sense of personhood. Paul Tournier, the renowned Swiss medical doctor and psychologist, for one, believed firmly in the healing of the whole person, of deeply appreciating the spiritual, psychological physical dimensions of personhood. The thinking of the modern era has led to an inner conflict in modern man caused by "that separation between our spiritual and our technological life."[7] The true sense of self has therefore been lost, "Because man has closed his eyes to the world of the Spirit, he has become incomprehensible to himself. He no longer understands himself and lives in confusion."[8] As a result healing is often much less than it could be and *shalom* is not as frequently realized as it could be. Healing will often involve, essentially, overcoming the "repression of the spirit." Accordingly, technical methods will not solve today's problems because the problems are primarily spiritual.[9] The Cartesian thinking of the world has caused a "fundamental divorce between the spiritual and the material and this is the disease from which our modern world is suffering."[10] Most philosophers agree that Descartes, in the seventeenth century, with his focus on rational, visible proof for the scientific method, severed the link between emotions and health; this was due in part to religious wars that he observed throughout most of his life.[11] This divorce plus the resulting reductionism and materialism then led to less-than-satisfying solutions for the real and deep needs of man. As Tournier wrote:

> Cartesian thinking… constructs systems which are satisfying to reason but have nothing to say to the real anguish of man. They leave him to fight his inner battle alone and he is always defeated.[12]

Barrett, a philosopher, acknowledged the soul in Descartes as still being a Christian soul, but "it is a soul that has undergone another crucifixion: this time on the cross of mathematical physics."[13] That is a profound observation. In other words the reliance on rationalism ultimately reduces and denies one's true self, and one's soul is effectively dead (crucified) by the scientific and empirical world. Tragically, unlike being crucified with Christ, dead to the world and raised unto newness of life in Him, there is no resurrection from the Cartesian world. In contrast to the good news of the gospel, that is bad news.

Paul Tournier: A Medical Doctor's View

From his years as a Christian medical doctor, Tournier gave numerous examples of healing involving a person's relationships, attitudes, past experiences and crises and how those factors impacted his patient's health. A woman's asthma was caused by a childhood terror of her father.[14] Menstrual problems were often the physiological expression of moral anxiety.[15] A Boston medical doctor and specialist reported 270 cases of patients cured of arthritis by removing fear, worry and resentment. He concluded that about sixty percent of arthritis as seen in his medical practice was due to moral conflict.[16] Hypertension is often a physical expression of moral hypertension, so one must then uncover and release the spiritual tension.[17] Some skin problems are caused by moral issues, such as furunculosis caused by some secret worry.[18] A lady's tachycardia, or rapid heart beat, stemmed from the death of her cat.[19] A man with bronchial asthma greatly improved when he encountered Jesus and opened his heart in prayer to Him through Tournier, his physician.[20] Some physical illnesses actually symbolize an inner spiritual state like a girl who had such poor posture that she stooped, all caused by fear of her father.[21]

A woman who had dysmenorrhea (painful periods) was also very masculine in her voice and actions. Tournier encouraged her to pray and wait on God, and when she did, the Lord brought back a whole series of memories that showed her clearly how and why she hated her own gender. From her childhood she had a negative attitude to her femininity and had despised her mother. Upon receiving prayer she was healed and able to accept herself fully. As a result her voice became more feminine, her actions more gentle and the dysmenorrhea left completely. Laboratory tests revealed that she had clinical endocrine malfunctioning which in reality was caused by hatred of her gender. In her case, drugs did not help but prayer leading to reconciliation with herself brought a deep healing.[22]

Prayer for Before Birth

When Mary visited Elizabeth, the baby in Elizabeth's womb leapt for joy upon hearing Mary's voice and blessing (Luke 1:41-45). The baby had consciousness, could hear and even internalized the emotion of joy (Luke 1:44). The unborn child was six months old (Luke 1:36). Jacob and Esau "jostled" in the womb (Gen. 25:22), and Jacob had definite intentions in grasping Esau's heel (Gen. 25:26; Hos. 12:3). The Lord knows all about our development in the womb (Ps. 139:13-16), and from our mother's womb we are His (Ps. 22:10). The Lord brought us out of the womb and taught us the very first things about trust (Ps. 22:9-10; Ps. 71:6).

Prenatal psychology has shown that certainly by the second trimester, as in Luke 1:44, an unborn child experiences an emotional life.[23] The unborn child is a "feeling, remembering, aware being" affected (but not determined) by his mother's emotions and well-being.[24] A newborn child has been known to refuse her mother's breast because the mother had wanted an abortion but gave birth to the child on the father's insistence.[25] Since the mother had emotionally rejected the child, the child then rejects the mother. Based on over 1,200 subjects it has been shown that a fetus can feel and remember either acceptance or rejection from the mother when the mother first realizes the pregnancy.[26] A study of over 1300 children and their families has shown that a child born into a stormy marriage has about a 237 percent greater risk of being psychologically or physically negatively effected.[27] An adult can even remember and recall music that was heard previously only as an unborn child as happened to a philharmonic conductor.[28]

Prenatal psychology gives further details and understanding in praying for the effects on a person even before birth. The Lord has led me a number of times to pray for a person's womb experience since something had happened in that very early part of their life which had an effect on the present. Kraft[29] and the Sandfords,[30] among others, listed and categorized their observations in praying for *in utero* wounds. Pytches was led by the Spirit to pray with people through their womb experience, thereby connecting with strong feelings again.[31] Tapscott wrote how deeply imbedded feelings of rejection can come from the womb for people conceived out of wedlock and may even be felt by others on a prayer team.[32] Healing prayer from conception to birth is "one of the most powerful forms of emotional healing."[33] Dearing wrote how a lady received prayer for deep fears stemming from her *in utero* experience.[34] As Jesus was invited to enter that time of her life marked by pain and terror, the lady began to cry uncontrollably and after some wailing was overcome by great peace. That prayer brought a deep and lasting change in her life, completely overcoming the fear.

Prayer ministry might even be relevant for before conception. Spiritual or relational issues may at times cause infertility or barrenness, especially when medical tests reveal no physiological reason. A womb may be "closed" for various reasons, including a sinful attitude (1 Sam. 1:5-6), sexual sin (Lev. 20:20-21), a curse (Jer. 22:28-30) or potential sin (Gen. 20:17-18). In response to prayer God opened Leah's womb (Gen. 29:31), Rebekah's womb as Isaac interceded (Gen. 25:21), Rachel's womb (Gen. 30:22) and Hannah's womb (1 Sam. 1:5-6; 19-20), showing the spiritual dimension of conception. There are even times when infertility and miscarriages stem from the sins of a nation or community (Hos. 9:11, 14).[35]

The clear implication is the strategic relevance and importance of the ministry of healing prayer for infertility, miscarriages and pre-birth experiences. Lana's testimony below is but one small example of the healing which can come from allowing the Lord to minister to one's earliest stages in life.

Lana's Anger Toward Her Mother

I had asked Dieter and his prayer partner to pray with me before leaving Winnipeg. We gathered together on the Saturday evening. I had grown up not wanting my mother to touch me. I always felt very uncomfortable with her touching me even as an adult but never knew why. As we prayed the Lord took me back to my mother's womb. The Holy Spirit revealed that when I was in the womb, I developed anger towards my mother for smoking. I could actually connect with those feelings again and for a brief moment saw my mother lighting up a cigarette. The Lord showed me how the anger increased as I grew up and saw her continuing to smoke and the defilement of it on her—even the stains on her fingers. I became more and more disgusted with her and did not want her around me or to touch me. I actually hated the thoughts of it and when she did touch me I would freeze up. As the Holy Spirit shone His flashlight into the roots of this I went back to the womb where the smoking began. I forgave my mother and was cleansed of the defilement.

Dieter then prayed that the Holy Sprit would take me back through my life history and hold me and comfort me all those times when I could not allow my mother to do that. I wept and wept as the Lord took me back through the years and healed my heart. I was visiting my parents recently and I did not have any anxiety towards my mother and her touching me. My heart was much softer towards her, and there is a bond between us that had not been there.

After praying with Lana I came across a medical researcher's study results concerning smoking mothers:

> ...an unborn child grows emotionally agitated (as measured by the quickening of his heartbeat) each time his mother thinks of having a cigarette. She doesn't even have to put it to her lips or light a match; just the idea of having a cigarette is enough to upset him. Naturally, the fetus has no way of knowing his mother is smoking—or thinking about it—but he is intellectually sophisticated enough to associate the experience of her smoking with the unpleasant association it produces in him.[36]

Psychosomatics and PsychoNeuroImmunology: Catching Up with the Old Testament

The biblical view of man and health is finally being appreciated, at least in part, by the "mind-body" areas of scientific research like psychosomatic medicine or PsychoNeuroImmunology (PNI). As medical research affirms more and more, our attitudes and emotions can greatly impact our health and well being. Lewis and Lewis, in their book *Psychosomatics: How Your Emotions Can Damage Your Health*, compiled a considerable amount of medical research and case histories showing the connection between body and mind. The authors state the basic premise of psychosomatic medicine as such:

> Every emotion you feel is a physical event. When you have a strong emotional reaction, even one generated by watching a movie, hormones are secreted and your body chemistry is altered. When the feelings are particularly strong, the physical reactions are likely to be equally extreme. Emotion can alter your endocrine balance and your blood supply and pressure, inhibit your digestion change your breathing and the temperature of your skin. A sustained state of emotional upset may cause changes that lead to disease. Your psyche may trigger the overreaction of hormones, which may produce a disease process.[37]

An example from Ezekiel illustrates the basic premise of psychosomatic medicine where an emotion is translated into a physical event. The news of impending judgment upon Israel, with all the accompanying fear and trauma, meant that, *"Every heart will melt and every hand go limp; every spirit will become faint and every knee become as weak as water"* (Ezek. 21:7). Likewise Habakkuk's heart pounded, lips quivered, bones felt weak and his legs trembled upon hearing of God's impending judgment (Hab. 3:16). The wife of Phinehas, who was pregnant and near the time of delivery, immediately went into labor when she heard that her husband and father-in-law were dead and Philistines had captured the ark (1 Sam. 4:19-20). The terrible news caused strong emotions that in turn affected her body such that it induced labor pains and delivery. It seems the emotion of deep despair (1 Sam. 4:20) was so strong that she died during delivery. Similarly when King Belshazzar saw a human hand appear and write upon the wall, his face turned pale and he became so frightened that his knees knocked together and his legs gave way (Dan. 5:6). Later he became even more frightened, and his face grew yet more pale (Dan. 5:9).

Hyperthyroidism, when an overactive thyroid gland releases too much thyroxin, is usually due to an overactive pituitary gland which in turn is often caused by traumatic or strongly emotional and disturbing events or even relationships. One study identified 94 percent of 200 cases of hyperthyroidism as having "psychic trauma;" another clearly showed 85 percent of 3343 cases, 61 percent of which had long periods of continual emotional disturbances like worry, disappointment or grief.[39] Hyperthyroid victims often experience deep insecurity in early childhood; many lost their mothers early in life.[40] One Harvard surgeon concluded that psychotherapy is the most effective treatment for hyperthyroidism, better than surgery, radioactive iodine and antithyroid drugs that treat only the thyroid gland and not the real emotional causes which untreated can possibly "go on to produce... some other bodily disturbance."[41] Thus healing prayer as the "psychotherapy" could be profoundly effective for hyperthyroidism by releasing the person from the painful emotional effects that supercharge the pituitary gland.

The Scriptures admonish us not to harbor bitterness towards other people (Eph. 4:31; Heb. 12:15) but rather to be forgiving. Maybe it should not surprise us, then, that just having a bitter thought can actually change a person's blood chemistry.[42]

Stress can have a major impact on one's health. If stress is prolonged and uncontrolled such that the body continues to manufacture hormones and chemicals (which initially helped to mobilize you) from nerves and glands, those same hormones and chemicals in your body will debilitate you and typically impair your immune system.[43] An accumulation of cortisol such that there is an imbalance in one's body shuts down the immune cell response.[44] In fact "chronic stress can shut down the reproductive hormones in men and women."[45] Research has also shown that "a memory of a stressful event can turn on the stress response almost as much as the original event itself."[46] This means that painful recurring memories, for example, could impact one's health more than is often appreciated. Obviously the solution to the above health concerns could involve decisions and priorities in life as well as healing prayer to restore peace into one's soul. Medication to manage hormonal levels in one's body would not be the real solution.

Physical symptoms are not always constantly related to the same emotional or relational cause. Psychosomatic medicine has recognized "psychosomatic shifts" where symptoms can move from one body system to another, such as from migraines to peptic ulcer to a heart condition.[47] Beneath psychosomatic shifts are forgotten, rarely discerned, "unconscious" or perhaps repressed emotions. A person who believes that "good Christians never get angry" or even a hint of tears is "being weak" will have emotions and their unresolved issues plus pain stuck in their soul. While a person may try to forget pain or issues from the past, the body will not. While feelings may go underground they often surface later in physical effects.

Psychogenic pain is the pain of emotional origin sometimes experienced by emotionally troubled people with chronic illnesses.[48] Such "pain-prone" people typically experience more pain in the head and trunk continuously for long periods of time but not at night.[49] People with psychogenic pain often have conscious or unconscious guilt wherein the pain serves as a means of atonement—self-inflicted pain to alleviate the guilt.[50]

Hypochondriacs are people who are preoccupied with their supposed ill health and use it as a means to draw attention to themselves or perhaps even build their identity around the illness. Medication, symptoms, diagnoses and doctors are a big part of their life. But this typically stems from a deep need to be understood and loved. As one researcher concluded:

> …from such patients there is a lifelong cry to be taken care of. This is mixed with anger that there has never been enough love, protection, affection. Their symptoms arise evidently as a body language expressing their need to be cared for… while such patients are searching for something, it is not really medical care per se. It is to be *taken care of*.[51]

Psychosomatic medicine would support the theory that a personality profile might often be matched to a corresponding physical illness.[52] To prove this Dr. Ring had his colleagues refer 400 patients to him, all of whom suffered from any of "asthma, backache, coronary occlusion, degenerative arthritis, diabetes, dysmenorrhea, glaucoma, hypertension, hyperthyroidism, migraine, neurodermatitis, peptic ulcer, rheumatoid arthritis and ulcerative colitis."[53] Dr. Ring was only allowed to interview the patients for fifteen to twenty-five minutes solely to determine their personality; the patient's body was fully covered during the interview. Based on personality information alone, he detected 100 percent of the hyperthyroid cases, 83 percent of those with peptic ulcer and rheumatoid arthritis, 71 percent with coronary occlusion and from 60 to 67 percent for those with asthma, diabetes, hypertension and ulcerative colitis.[54]

While the mind, with its beliefs and emotions, can affect our body, sometimes the reverse is true and this must not be forgotten.

Depressive psychosis is sometimes caused by cancer of the pancreas.[55] Pellagra, caused by a lack of niacin, has been known to cause psychosis, hallucinations and delusions which disappear once niacin is added to the diet.[56] An abscess in the brain can cause depression, anxiety or vague headaches.[57] Cushing's disease, characterized by an enlarged pituitary gland which may have a tumor, causes an excess of adrencorticotrophic hormone (ACTH) which stimulates the adrenal glands and can cause clinical depression.[58]

Proverbs teaches that cheerfulness, laughter and mirth effect one's well-being and health. *"A cheerful look brings joy to the heart, and good news gives health to the bones"* (Prov. 15:30). *"A cheerful heart is good medicine, but a crushed spirit dries up the bones"* (Prov. 17:22). Scientific research concerning mirth and laughter brings a fuller appreciation for this apparently simple teaching from Proverbs. Hostetler summarized results from one research laboratory, confirmed by others:

> Plasma immunoglobulins IgM, IgG and IgA all increase in response to mirthful laughter. The elevation of immunoglobulins indicates the strengthening of the immune system in general. Additional positive findings include the rise in the percentage of natural killer cell activity and an increase in the body's level of T-cells in response to mirthful laughter. The increase in these cellular immune components indicates that the immune system is strengthened. In addition, the group's work indicates that laughter increases the production of enkephalins and betaendorhpins.[59]

Laughter is, in fact, good medicine, and that is no joke. While negative attitudes and situations can diminish health, we see here that positive attitudes and situations can bring healing and maintain health. For example people who experience deep appreciation or love for five minutes typically have IgA levels elevated by 40 percent or more for more than six hours.[60]

We can now appreciate how one's attitudes, past history and relational issues can often (but not always) directly impact one's health and physical well-being. Effectively underlining the need for healing prayer and spiritual direction, Tournier wrote, "…experience does nevertheless show how closely a person's physical and psychological state depends on victories which are won only in the realm of the Spirit."[61] This is vindicated by scientific research:

> Research indicates that some diseases may be reflections of the psyche. It appears that bereavement causes a depression in lymphocyte count and there is a depression in the quality of the immune system during marital disruption and that there is a relationship among immunity, emotions and stress.[62]

Researchers understand the pathway that affects our immune system as an image or recollection from a memory which affects our mood which in turn causes a hormonal response which then impacts the immune cells:

> …repeated, relentless mood shifts, the wearing sort that come from the constant stress of chronic care-giving, a long drawn out divorce, or painful relationships, are the kind of social stresses that wear us down and make us vulnerable to disease. And they do so, at least in part, through the activation of nerve chemicals and hormones that affect the immune cell function.[63]

Strong relationships can be the "strongest net to save us in our deepest time of need."[64] This is expected since, if painful relationships can cause the immune system to break down, then peace, harmony and loving relationships can restore the immune system. Other medical research has shown that a "lack of bonding can affect one's ability to recover from an entire range of physical illnesses, including cancer, heart attack and stroke."[65] Therefore, loving relationships and healing prayer would be a more exact and comprehensive solution to restoring health than medication. Upon reviewing the latest medical research on stress, Jacobson proposes God's exhortation to find rest for our souls by entering His rest (Heb. 3:7-11, 19; 4:9-11) as a major antidote for stress.[66] The spiritual effects of stress as too much adrenaline in the body include lessened spiritual energy as desire for God, more destructive spiritual energy as negative attitudes and relationships and the confusion of adrenaline arousal as true spirituality.[67] Expressions of spirituality can become linked to adrenaline arousal when there is an inordinate desire for "high impact experiences" of God or worship—in contrast to Psalm 46:10.[68] Essentially one becomes addicted to adrenaline which can lurk behind addiction even to ministry.[69]

The implications of the above from medical research and the Scriptures show that healing prayer has great relevance and strategic importance for one's health and well being. Neglecting Scriptures and the ministry of healing prayer could well mean more years spent in a nursing home later in life. While emotional and relational issues are not always involved in many of today's illnesses, especially the chronic ones, they often are. The late medical doctor and psychiatrist, Dr John White, concluded the following concerning our emotions, spirituality and health: "It is likely that there is not a bodily ailment which is not connected in some way with our hidden fears, our unexpressed grief and our inability to rejoice without restraint."[70]

Avoiding Therapeutic Tunnel Vision

With the above emphasis on healing of the whole person in the context of their whole life and all their relationships, one can see why different approaches to healing can be ineffective or insufficient. It is precisely because the issues of life and soul are so complex that our real need of Jesus is so great.

Considering the complexity of heart-mind-body issues, one must avoid simple solutions. People want to systematize life and reduce its complexity into manageable packages with steps or procedure or techniques. This temptation must be resisted to achieve true healing and wholeness. Healing prayer must minister to the whole person not just symptoms. One must avoid therapeutic "tunnel vision" or reductionism that focuses on any dimension of life to the exclusion of any other dimension. Some major forms of reductionism are considered here briefly.

Biological reductionism occurs when modern medicine looks only at the physical and biological dimension of life to the exclusion of all else. As we have seen, Psychosomatics and PsychoNeuroImmunology as well as the recent push for "holistic" medicine have arisen to counter this. Typically, relational and spiritual issues are overlooked.

Psychological reductionism occurs when the focus is on psychological issues only and spiritual issues of life are not addressed, or even when the idea of demonic oppression is portrayed as utter nonsense. Often there may not be a great appreciation of how one's emotions and relationships can impact health, especially if the focus is on counseling.

Spiritual reductionism is subtler and occurs in several forms. One is when there is a focus on deliverance ministry to the exclusion of other dimensions of life and healing. Thus deliverance is

160

seen as a "magic cure" and at times deliverance ministry can be insensitive or focused on a "quick fix" mentality.[71] I know of some people who were worse off after going to certain deliverance ministries. Jesus did both healing and deliverance and knew when to move between either type of ministry. Often there is a need for emotional or relational healing before or alongside any deliverance ministry. This is why some people will experience a "release" but not a great improvement after going through Neil Anderson's "Steps to Freedom," not to take away any of the good things accomplished by that ministry. The overall goal is wholeness and sanctification, not rebuking demons or breaking spiritual bondages as ends in themselves.

Another form of spiritual reductionism is praying that does not allow enough time for the Spirit to reveal the deep issues (when they are there) and that focuses on the spiritual gifts but does not fully operate in the presence of Jesus. It's like praying "at" someone instead of *with* someone in His presence. One must guard against simplifying the issues of the heart and soul and expecting a "more immediate" result. Restoration from depression, for example, often requires a deep understanding of the ways of the soul according to the wisdom of Jesus (Isa. 11:2). Some people approach inner healing as a "quick fix" and then, in issues of grief, the stages of mourning, for example, are bypassed or ignored.[72] One should not trivialize pain or short-circuit what Jesus might wish to accomplish.

A friend of mine knew a Christian lady who was ill with cancer. She went to a healing prayer service where the "faith healer" talked a lot about the power of Jesus and the anointing for healing. The lady went forward for prayer and was prayed over by the faith healer who basically commanded her to "receive her healing" and announced that as long as she had enough faith, she would be healed. My friend noticed that at the end of the meeting the lady appeared discouraged. It was obvious that she was now dealing with guilt, for if she did not get better it would be due to her lack of faith and thus she was responsible. How sad that one's faith in Jesus, no matter how little at times, can be turned into a liability by "ministry"! I was sad when I heard this story because it is another example of spiritual reductionism with little or no time for the Spirit to reveal or Jesus to come. It comes close to "faith in faith." A better closure to ministry to the seriously ill in particular is the assurance of God's love no matter the outcome.

Another form of spiritual reductionism is the use of New Age healing therapies like Reiki or Therapeutic Touch. Quite apart from the serious theological problems[73] [74] of monism, pantheism and reducing God to an impersonal force or "energy field," is the fact that relational issues are totally bypassed. If, for example, the Holy Spirit and the Scriptures and medical research all concur that a person has lower back pain due to a forgiveness issue, the person must forgive the past offender. One cannot ignore this relational issue. The whole idea that hands are simply waved over someone's body, as in Therapeutic Touch, to redistribute the energy balance in order to heal the person then becomes reductionism. That devalues the person and ultimately undercuts the cross of Christ.

One of the worst forms of spiritual reductionism is outright denial, wherein Christians are declared never depressed since they are called to "live victoriously." Some might claim that since it is all "under the blood" there should be no problem. As the Sandfords wrote, "All one had to do was to accept Christ as Lord and Savior. That falsely became the magic which was to have accomplished everything to fit us for life here and in heaven."[75] This is also a theological reductionism with almost no concept of appropriating the cross and Christ's resurrection power into one's entire life and being. Others say that if there is a problem, it is because of unconfessed sin. Yes, sins are forgiven such that one's name is in the book of life, but Christ is not yet completely formed in us, His healing has not yet been fully appropriated to the whole of one's life and we have not yet learned to fully practice His presence. Being born again means that we have to learn to live again.

How Then Shall We Pray?

The goal, then, is healing prayer that ministers to the whole person. One prays as led by the Spirit and in Jesus' presence through all the dimensions of one's life, all of one's past history and all of one's relationships. Divine healing seeks wholeness for the whole person and one's entire emotional being.[76] At conferences and healing prayer services I have found it not unusual to pray for healing and deliverance for one person, physical healing for the next, emotional healing for the next person, interpretation of dreams for the next person, only physical healing for the next person, perhaps only deliverance for the next person then emotional plus relational issues behind the next person's need for physical healing and so forth. This is only possible as we collaborate with Jesus and His Spirit fully, always drawing on His wisdom and never on our own or on methods or techniques. This is an example of praying all kinds of prayers in the Spirit (Eph. 6:18).

Kristin's story, as recounted at the beginning of this chapter, is an example of how relational, emotional and spiritual issues were connected to physical issues in order to bring more healing and wholeness. As I prayed with her during what seemed like a confusing maze of issues, Jesus soon "wrapped it all up" and in several dimensions of her life there was restoration. Just prayer for deliverance or cognitive understanding or techniques in behavior modification or establishing boundaries, among many other approaches, would not have helped.

The technical mindset has so deeply and subtly affected many in the Church such that many Christians are not fully aware of what has happened. The technical mindset has affected even our spirituality and approach to ministry. In order to more clearly articulate the dynamics of healing prayer rooted in the presence of Jesus and His Spirit, the next chapter deals with the technical mindset.

Endnotes ───────────

1 Dieter Mulitze, *The Great Omission: Resolving Critical Issues for the Ministry of Healing and Deliverance* (Belleville: Essence Publishers, 2001) pp. 79-82.

2 Esther M. Sternberg, *The Balance Within: The Science Connecting Health and Emotions* (New York: W.H. Freeman and Co., 2000) p. 8.

3 Howard R. and Martha E. Lewis, *Psychosomatics: How Your Emotions Can Damage Your Health* (New York: The Viking Press, 1972) p. 5.

4 Ibid.

5 Sternberg, 10.

6 Lewis, p. 6.

7 Paul Tournier, *The Whole Person in a Broken World* (New York: Harper & Row, 1964) p. 25.

8 Tournier, 1964, p. 37.

9 Tournier, 1964, p. 72.

10 Paul Tournier, *The Healing of Persons* (New York: Harper & Row, 1965) p. 226.

11 Sternberg, p. 5.

12 Tournier, 1964, p. 226.

13 William Barrett, *Death of the Soul: From Descartes to the Computer* (New York: Anchor Press/Doubleday, 1986) p. 20.

14 Tournier, 1965, p. 6.

15 Tournier, 1965, p. 7.

[16] Tournier, 1965, p. 27.

[17] Tournier, 1965, p. 30.

[18] Tournier, 1965, p. 36.

[19] Tournier, 1965, p. 39.

[20] Tournier, 1965, p. 43.

[21] Tournier, 1965, p. 64.

[22] Tournier, 1965, pp. 65-68.

[23] Thomas Verny, M.D. with John Kelly, *The Secret Life of the Unborn Child: How you can prepare your unborn baby for a happy, healthy life* (New York: Dell Publishing Co., 1981) p. 12.

[24] Verny, pp. 1-94.

[25] Verny, p. 78.

[26] Mary Pytches, *Yesterday's Child* (London: Hodder and Stoughton, 1990) pp. 34-36.

[27] Verny, p. 49.

[28] Verny, p. 22.

[29] Charles H. Kraft, *Deep Wounds, Deep Healing: Discovering the Vital Link Between Spiritual Warfare and Inner Healing* (Ann Arbor: Vine Books, 1993) pp. 138-144.

[30] John and Paula Sandford, *Healing the Wounded Spirit* (Tulsa: Victory House, 1985) pp. 27-52.

[31] Pytches, 1990, p. 35.

[32] Betty Tapscott, *Inner Healing Through Healing of Memories* (Houston: Betty Tapscott, 1975) p. 35.

[33] Norma Dearing, *The Healing Touch: A Guide to Healing Prayer for Yourself and Those You Love* (Grand Rapids: Chosen Books, 2002) p. 138.

[34] Dearing, p. 141.

[35] Paula Sandford, *Healing Women's Emotions* (Tulsa: Victory House, Inc., 1992) pp. 91-92.

[36] Verny, p. 20.

[37] Lewis, p. 6.

[38] Lewis, pp. 34-42.

[39] Lewis, p. 36.

[40] Lewis, p. 38.

[41] Lewis, p. 37.

[42] Henry Cloud, *Changes That Heal: How to Understand Your Past to Ensure a Healthier Future* (Grand Rapids: Zondervan Publishing House, 1992) p. 56.

[43] Sternberg, p. 111.

[44] Sternberg, p. 112.

[45] Sternberg, p. 118.

[46] Sternberg, p. 122.

[47] Lewis, p. 84.

[48] Lewis, pp. 96-97.

[49] Lewis, p. 96.

[50] Lewis, p. 97.

[51] Lewis, p. 125.

[52] Lewis, p. 70.

[53] Lewis, p. 71.

[54] Ibid.

[55] Lewis, p. 12.

[56] Ibid.

[57] Ibid.

[58] Sternberg, p. 57.

[59] Jep Hostetler, "Humor, Spirituality Well-Being," *Journal of the American Scientific Affiliation*, Vol. 54(2), 2002 p. 109.

[60] Michael D. Jacobson, *The Word on Health: A Biblical and Medical Overview of How to Care for Your Body and Mind* (Chicago: Moody Press, 2000) p. 190.

[61] Tournier, 1964, p. 43.

[62] Hostetler, p. 109.

[63] Sternberg, p. 152.

[64] Sternberg, p. 157.

[65] Cloud, p. 56.

[66] Jacobson, p. 183.

[67] Archibald Hart, *Adrenaline and Stress* (Dallas: Word Publishing, 1991) pp. 37-41.

[68] Hart, pp. 40-41.

[69] Hart, pp. 65-77.

[70] John White, *When the Spirit Comes With Power: Signs & Wonders Among God's People* (Downers Grove: InterVarsity Press, 1988) p. 50.

[71] Mary Pytches, *Dying to Change: An exposure of the self-protective strategies which prevent us becoming like Jesus* (London: Hodder & Stoughton, 1996) pp. 3-4.

[72] Pytches, p. 3.

[73] John Ankerberg and John Weldon, *Encyclopedia of New Age Beliefs* (Eugene: Harvest House Publishers, 1996) pp. 477-508.

[74] Paul C. Reisser, Dale Mabe and Robert Velarde, *Examining Alternative Medicine: An Inside Look at the Benefits & Risks* (Downers Grove: InterVarsity Press, 2001)

[75] John and Paula Sandford, *The Transformation of the Inner Man* (Tulsa: Victory House, 1982) p. 6.

[76] Anne S. White, *Healing Adventure* (Plainfield: Logos International, 1972) pp.19-20, 46-49.

 Chapter Six

The Technical Mindset and Spirituality

Do not conform any longer to the pattern of this world, but be transformed by the renewing of your mind. Then you will be able to test and approve what God's will is—his good, pleasing and perfect will (Rom. 12:2).

Some trust in chariots and some in horses, but we trust in the name of the Lord our God (Ps. 20:7).

Mark's Sleep Disorder

Mark was struggling with a sleep disorder and came for healing prayer. Although I had some ideas as to what may have been the source of His problem, the Spirit would have to reveal this exactly. The Spirit started a significant healing when a memory came back vividly. Within the context of the Lord's direction and continued healing, Mark was able to benefit from some cognitive behavioral and stress management techniques. Mark wrote:

> My problem began simply enough. I had just been diagnosed with a very mild case of obstructive and central

sleep apnea. Sleep Apnea (SA) is a disorder where a person stops breathing for short periods while they sleep. In severe cases these "stops" can be up to a few minutes in length and pose a significant health risk. Obstructive SA (OSA) is due to a collapsing of the soft tissue in the throat so that the airway becomes blocked, a very treatable condition. Central SA (CSA) is due to the brainstem not regulating breathing properly, a less treatable condition. In my case the symptoms due to both causes were considered so mild that no treatment was recommended. This was the type of diagnosis I had been expecting because at the time of the test I was not experiencing any symptoms of sleep apnea. In fact I had debated whether I should take the test at all. I had been referred to the sleep clinic three years previously by my family physician when I was being troubled by chronic fatigue. The state of Canadian Health Care being what it was circa late 1990s, it took three years before my turn came up at the sleep clinic. By this time my trouble with chronic fatigue was gone, but I was determined to get "my fair share" of healthcare, so I went anyway. The diagnosis of CSA was a bit troubling because it was completely unexpected due to its rarity and the difficulty in treating it. In my research I had stumbled into some newsgroups for CSA sufferers, and there were some very sad stories from people in very desperate situations.

I pursued help from all avenues available to me. I have never felt that my faith and conventional medicine were contradictory; in fact I have always seen them as complementary care, a holistic approach for treating both body and spirit. Unfortunately, due to the severe rationing of Canadian Healthcare, it was not possible to get much conventional medicine in a timely fashion. The sleep specialist did see me on short notice, and after I explained to him that I didn't have any problems at the time of my sleep evaluation, he concurred that my symptoms were more likely due to the anxiety of sleep apnea than to sleep apnea itself. All my family physician could offer was medication for an anxiety disorder which could take four to six weeks to alleviate the symptoms—an eternity when you're not sleeping. I was also registered for cognitive behavioral therapy, but that would be a multi-month wait.

The soothing words from the sleep specialist didn't help. I couldn't let go of my fear. As my condition continued I got to the point where I would have micro-sleeps while I was walking. I could sleep while walking but not in a bed. It struck me that there was something rather evil about that. I don't use the term lightly. Though I have been a Christian for many years, I have many secular friends with whom I can't even talk about God let alone evil. I continued to pray.

Comfort of the Holy Spirit eventually came and with His still gentle voice gave me the expectation that I would receive a healing at the altar call next Sunday. The confidence with which I expected the healing was astounding. It was like it was done already. I just had to go up to the front of the church as a formality, sort of like getting your high school diploma—the grades are in, you've passed and you just have to show up and receive it.

I was also given the expectation that my complete healing would take considerable time and a lot of effort on my part. The understanding I was given was that I needed to develop life skills through this trauma as valuable tools for the rest of my life. I also realized I didn't truly value things that I hadn't had to struggle for (ouch!).

On the altar call I went up for prayer. Dieter started by anointing me with oil and praying over me. And then, as he silently prayed, we waited on the Holy Spirit to reveal what was going on. The Holy Spirit gave me silent direction, one word: "drowning." It was completely out of the blue. I knew instantly the incident in question; it had occurred over thirty years ago, and I had practically never thought about it since.

It happened on a family outing to a provincial park that had a swimming hole with a diving board. I was twelve at the time and a reasonable swimmer for my age. I had done several dives, and on this particular occasion I was swimming back and was quite close to the shore when I tried to stand up. To my surprise the water was still over my head and I went under, taking in a huge gulp of the brackish water. I panicked. If my dad hadn't strode in to literally pull me out by the scruff of my neck, I would have drowned. It took just a few seconds from panic to sputtering safety on the shore. My dad insisted I dive again and I did and continued for the rest of the afternoon. By day's end the near drowning was all but forgotten.

So I hadn't thought much of the event, even then, or especially since. But here was the Holy Spirit drawing it to my attention as a seminal event. As Dieter directed me to remember the incident, I recall being surprised by how vividly I could remember that day. The sounds of the other kids running and playing, the heat of the sun on my shoulders, the smell of the water, the way my wet hair stuck to my head—I was there. As Dieter directed me to think about the actual moment of my panic, for a brief instant I experienced pure primal terror. It is impossible to relay how that felt unless perhaps you have had that sensation of going down for the third time. I'm not sure, but I believe I cried out when this occurred.

Immediately afterwards I felt some relief from my symptoms. My diaphragm, which had been doing the "hula," immediately calmed down. I had become so fixated on my breathing that it seemed my conscious thought and autonomic nervous system were both grappling for control. In time I began sleeping better, generally in small incremental improvements. My understanding now is that the sleep apnea diagnosis created an opportunity for demonic forces to capitalize on the foothold that they had gained from the near-drowning incident. The enemy was able to exploit the parallels between the two to paralyze me with fear. I believe the Holy Spirit has brought peace to the drowning incident and has provided me with a spiritual healing.

I did eventually take the cognitive behavior therapy and found it very helpful. The course provided a possible explanation for the symptoms I experienced on a trip; I was having a panic attack and the out-of-breath symptom was due to hyperventilating (panic attacks can occur while you sleep). It also provided me with life-long stress management techniques such as paced breathing and progressive muscle relaxation. I believe that many of these skills were what the Holy Spirit had alluded to.

I felt bad for many of the other participants in the course; because of their belief system they could not avail themselves to the healing power of God. The cognitive behavioral model only superficially touched on root cause issues and then just in generalities and never in specifics. The primary philosophy was that they would help us deal with our symptoms and the cause didn't really matter. In my opinion this unfortunately results in providing the participants with a treatment as opposed to a true cure.

Through additional sessions of healing prayer several other chronic issues were resolved, some of them quite subtle but all essential. I feel that the Spirit-led healing I have received has somehow made me whole. It's so hard to explain; it's like some of the gaps or damaged bits have been repaired. Different issues where I would keep getting stuck in my life, for example, like getting angry about the same things, I am now able to move on, freed to pursue God's purpose for my life.

Technical Thinking: An Occupational Hazard?

I (Dieter) have been immersed in the world of computer software, technology and analysis for almost thirty years. My introduction to the world of computers, which epitomizes our technological world, was in 1972 when I began my university studies in mathematics and computer science at the University of Waterloo. Those were the "Neanderthal" days of keypunch machines, card decks, the esoteric JCL (Job Control Language) and mainframe computers. During those years I learned seven computer languages, wrote thousands of lines of computer software code and developed three computer software applications—two for mainframe computers and one for desktop personal computers, and I also founded a computer software company. My doctoral dissertation involved the computer simulation of genetic models.

In all those years it never occurred to me that immersion in the technical, analytical world could change me. I didn't realize that the all-pervasive technical mindset could be an occupational hazard. I began to wonder if my preoccupation with the technical, analytical world was affecting my relationships. I finally realized that there was a connection, and its effects were greater and subtler than I had ever imagined.

Then the Lord unexpectedly led me into the ministry of healing prayer. It has been quite a journey beyond my normal comfort zone to understand this "new realm." I soon discovered that I had to undo the effects of a technical mindset in order to minister faithfully.

An understanding of the technical mindset helps to realize the consequences of substituting the presence of Jesus with methods and techniques. One can then more fully appreciate the effects on ministry in general and healing prayer in particular.

From Magic to Microchips

We are surrounded by technology. We readily think of computers with microchips, microwaves, fax machines, web sites, jumbo jets and cell phones, for example. But technology is much more subtle and pervasive than that. Technology and techniques are not restricted to objects or mechanics. There are also psychological and spiritual techniques to allegedly transform or empower the human mind and soul. Merton offered this definition of technique:

> …technique refers to any complex of standardized means for attaining a predetermined result. Thus it converts spontaneous and unreflective behavior into behavior that is deliberate and rationalized.[1]

The "complex of standardized means" could be a twelve-step program for recovery from an addiction, the sequence of steps for combustion in a diesel engine or the steps involved in hypnosis. Jacques Ellul, who has probably studied the technical mind more than anyone, defined technique as "the totality of methods rationally arrived at and having absolute efficiency (for a given stage of development) in every field of human activity."[2] Technique is more than a machine; it is a mindset that "transforms everything it touches into a machine."[3] The technical phenomenon "takes what was previously tentative, unconscious and spontaneous and brings it into the realm of clear, voluntary and reasoned concepts."[4] Analysis and rationalization are paramount for the technical mind. There are many psychological techniques that seek to adapt man to the modern world; therefore man himself becomes the *object* of technique.[5]

Techniques are not, strictly speaking, a development of our modern, scientific world. One might expect that the primitive tribes in the Amazon jungle or the Bushmen of the Kalahari Desert are totally exempt from the technical mindset. Not necessarily, since techniques have been around for centuries in primitive forms like magic:

> ...magic is a technique in the strictest sense of the word.... Magic developed along with other techniques as an expression of man's will to obtain certain results of a spiritual order. To attain them, man made use of an aggregate of rites, formulas and procedures which, once established, do not vary.[6]

> In the spiritual realm, magic displays all the characteristics of a technique. It is a mediator between man and the "higher powers," just as other techniques mediate between man and matter. It leads to efficiency because it subordinates the power of the gods to men and it secures a predetermined result. It affirms human power in that it seeks to

subordinate the gods to men, just as technique serves to cause nature to obey.[7]

Witchcraft is an example of contemporary spiritual technique. Through spells, hexes, curses and such standardized spiritual means, evil spiritual forces are utilized to bring about a predetermined result. Witchcraft is satanic power used to ultimately impose Satan's will on people and exert control over their emotions, behaviors or circumstances.[8] A series of steps are followed to yield a predetermined result. Hypnosis is a psychological technique used to bring people typically into an altered state of consciousness in order to recall memories, overcome certain emotional problems and cause other types of healing.[9] Even some Christians defend the use of hypnotism in certain situations.[10]

Kraft suggested that a biblical precedent for technique is the Lord's Prayer in response to the disciple's request to learn how to pray as well as Jesus' listening to the Father.[11] But such examples reflect spiritual direction, obedience and relationship with God and others instead of technique. The Lord's Prayer would only be a technique if reciting it would cause predetermined effects and put people in control of God. But the Lord's Prayer is all about God's will, forgiveness and our dependence upon Him, even for our daily bread. To turn the Lord's Prayer into a technique would violate its very essence. These examples do not fit the definition of technique as framed by Merton or Ellul. If the Lord's Prayer really is a technique, almost everything else in the Scriptures is a technique.

Technique transforms "means" into "ends," and the "how to" into ultimate value. That is why in this era there are so many "how-to" books in Christian bookstores: "how to evangelize," "how to grow a church," "how to enrich your marriage," "how to overcome anxiety," "how to be filled with the Spirit" and so forth. Perhaps we need a title like, "How to Get Close to God in Seven Easy Steps" to make us stop and wonder about the "how-to" mentality. Whether and how something "works" is the basis of pragmatism and utilitarianism. If one justifies the use of techniques by claiming that "it works," the preoccupation with whether it "works" or not is immediately an example of technical thinking which values efficiency and result. The technological society reinforces a type of thinking that is highly pragmatic and also deeply skeptical.[12] Bloesch, an evangelical theologian, noted the technological mindset's essence of pragmatic results, power to control and the inevitable shortsighted spiritual vision:

> The technocratic mentality values performance, not prayerful reflection. It admires and rewards the producer rather than the saint or the savant. The goal is to gain power over the world rather than the wisdom that teaches us how to live in the world as brothers and sisters with a common origin and destiny. A preoccupation with things and gadgetry crowds out a vision of spiritual reality that transcends the world of natural phenomena.[13]

The principle intellectual tragedy of the modern world, according to Ellul, is our obsession with technology which has "completely eclipsed our ability to reflect about *what* we are doing with technology and *why*."[14] We have become so focused on *how* that we do not think and reflect seriously enough about *what* and *why*. With the separation of means from goals and purposes due to the preoccupation with "how," values and ultimate ends are hard to assess and integrate. The result is much activity with tunnel vision. Hence "...the technological habit of mind is anti-teleological. It is largely uninterested and indeed incapable, of appreciating the notions of final causality or ultimate purpose."[15] It's almost like becoming efficient at not knowing why one is doing something.

Technology can be a blessing and is part of the cultural mandate (Gen. 1:26, 28; 2:15). The Holy Spirit is not only active in redemption and in the Church through spiritual gifts but also in creation with the exercise of creational skills and abilities. There are biblical references that support the Spirit's involvement in work.[16] The Lord chose Bezalel and *"filled him with the Spirit of God, with skill, ability and knowledge in all kinds of crafts... to engage in all kinds of artistic craftsmanship"* (Exod. 35:31, 33). The Holy Spirit actually put the architectural plans for the courts of the temple of the Lord in David's mind (1 Chron. 28:11-12). The Spirit instructs farmers in their preparing the soil, planting, harvesting and making flour—all of which *"comes from the Lord Almighty, wonderful in counsel and magnificent in wisdom"* (Isa. 28:29). The Holy Spirit makes all human work possible, and all work that has God's values and purposes is accomplished by the instruction and inspiration of the Holy Spirit.[17]

Given the Holy Spirit's involvement in work in general and also technical skill in particular, technology *per se* is not intrinsically evil. The challenge is to use techniques and technology only where intended and suitable, to never put our confidence and hope in them, to never use or develop them for evil or unethical purposes and to never access evil power through them. The Scriptures admonish us to have our faith and trust in God and not in man. There is a curse upon those who trust in man or depend on flesh for their strength (Jer. 17:5). Kings are not saved by the size of their army, and warriors do not escape by their great strength (Ps. 33:16). *"A horse is a vain hope for deliverance; despite all its strength it cannot save"* (Ps. 33:17). It is better to trust in the Lord than to put one's confidence in man or princes (Ps. 118:8-9; 146:3). Technical skill and competence do not guarantee success in life (Eccl. 9:11). Like anything else in creation, techniques or technology can be idolized. The technical mindset fosters *technicism*, its own ideology or religion with progress as a core doctrine.

Trademarks of the Technical Mindset

Given that techniques extend to every corner of our lives, how does this affect our personality and our relationships? Psychotherapist Craig Brod, for one, spent three years interviewing adults and children at various levels of computer involvement.[18] He was able to describe a number of effects the computer had on their interpersonal relationships. He summarized the following characteristics of people who over-identified with computers:

> …an unusually high degree of factual thinking, an inability to feel, an insistence on efficiency and speed, a lack of empathy for others, an intolerance for the ambiguities of human behavior and communication and a lessening of their ability to think intuitively and creatively.[19]

The above "trademarks" or characteristics of the technical mindset are among those discussed below. While these characteristics may have other origins for a given person, they are still typical of a technical mindset. The degrees to which they are evident in a person are influenced by that person's length and depth of involvement in the technical mindset and their individual personality.

Impatience. This comes from the almost obsessive insistence on efficiency and speed. Computers thrive on speed, and they must be ever more faster. If you're used to almost instantaneous results, an extra second or two becomes next to intolerable. This reinforces the impatience of our world with instant coffee, fast food, instant communication, instamatic cameras, instant gratification and more. Because something *can* be done quickly, it *must* be done quickly, and then since everyone else does it quickly you must also do it quickly.

Just when you've learned how to do it quickly, technology changes again and you have to learn how to do it even faster. Some people almost explode if they have to wait at a really slow checkout counter; others will actually fire a gun if they are blocked on a highway.

This impatience in our culture, heightened by the computer revolution, can easily impact our spirituality when we must learn to wait upon God, be still and know that He is God, grow in listening prayer and persevere in intercessory prayer. Can we so easily "switch gears" from this fast-paced world to times of contemplation and prolonged patience in the presence of God? Christian maturity does not come at "warp drive." James Houston, board of governor's professor of spiritual theology at Regent College, wrote:

> This temper of impatience, reinforced by the morality of the efficient, is hostile to the "waiting upon the Lord" that is essential for the maturity of Christian character. Patience is much more than the brake to the impatient spirit. It is also the exercise of docility, accepting the will of God in all areas of life, waiting upon the grace of God....[20]

An unusually high degree of factual thinking. Information processing is the "soul" of computer science. From the media and other sources we are bombarded with information, much more than we could ever hope to use or understand, almost like "drowning in trivia."[21] We become "information processors" like computers. Our conversations become more like "facting"—exchanging facts—instead of a meeting of hearts and minds. Informationism—a faith in information processing as a mean to personal happiness and social progress—preaches measurement over meaning, observation over intimacy and the "is over the ought."[22] Alarmingly the preoccupation with information technologies and informationism derails the quest for moral wisdom.[23]

181

But when it comes to biblical knowledge, it is not so much a matter of information as *transformation*. To hear the Word means to obey; to believe means to know and then to act and thus God will graciously reveal more of Himself as we follow Him in His ways. Sermons and Bible studies can become a mere forum for exchanging theological information. Instead of only interpreting the biblical text, we must let the biblical text interpret our life text. We do not read the Scriptures to master them, but rather, the Scriptures and the Living Word must master us. The truth of the Word must be incarnated in us so that the world cannot only hear truth but also see it lived. Biblical knowledge is correlated with obedience. It's as if the information processes us instead of us processing the information.

Inability or difficulty to feel. With a focus on fact, information, computation and algorithm, the already unfortunate split between heart and mind, referred to as "the terrible schism in the heart of man,"[24] becomes even more pronounced. Information overload can desensitize us to the issues of the heart. But we must know our hearts and be in touch with our emotions that are indicators of our soul. *We must know the language of our hearts.* Feelings are a part of our humanness; we were created with them. There is such a thing as emotional intelligence—where feelings and emotions communicate deeper issues—which shrivels up from an immersion in the technical mindset. The inability to feel could lead to difficulties in marriage or less effectiveness in healing prayer. It's like the mind suffers a miscarriage.

Lack of empathy for others. From an inability or difficulty in feeling comes a lessened ability to feel for others or empathize. Yet we are called to bear one another's burdens, to mourn with those who mourn and to rejoice with those who rejoice. We must understand other people's woundedness and at least try to understand the issues of other people's hearts.

An obsession for order and predictability. This is closely related to intolerance for the ambiguities of human behavior and communication. The computer's information processing, under the control of software with pre-defined algorithms, assures known results (most of the time!). Since technical or procedural thinking follows sequence and steps, impatience with anything that doesn't fit a procedure or pattern is a direct result. Order, sequence, steps and logical progression all require clear, rational and known events. Anything ambiguous does not fit and thus is devalued or rejected by the technical mind. Mystery or the unknown in God's presence becomes problematic.

But people are not always predictable, life is not always cut and dried and there must be character to cope with difficult situations. Some interruptions are divine appointments wherein we must be open to the leading of the Spirit. God at times will put us through trying, unpredictable situations to test us, help us grow and force us to realize our true character. With this characteristic one might be prone to embrace a simple, predictable theological system with "God in a box" and everything either black or white.

In the ministry of healing prayer, where Jesus and His Spirit lead, you do not know at the outset what will happen or the direction of the ministry time. Sometimes a person will receive healing from something totally different than the "presenting problem." This is all totally at odds with any therapeutic approach that has a series of predetermined steps.

Need to control. The technical mindset has the built-in idea of control since determinism is its core characteristic. Since a predetermined result is desired, the steps must occur to realize the result. But this all implies that one can then control the outcome by using the technique. The illusion is that one is in control, determining things. This is clearly seen in those who are "control freaks." Letting the

Holy Spirit do something different, seemingly unusual and unpredictable is not easy for those with a technical mindset. Any loss of control means entry to the unknown or unpredictable or ambiguous, all of which are anathema to the technical mind. Human determinism is totally at odds with the Holy Spirit. The spirit of modern technology is "fundamentally anthropocentric and manipulative."[25] Man wants to be at the center and in control.

Lessening of the ability to think intuitively and creatively. This is a progressive atrophy of one's creativity due to an over-emphasis on memorizing details and following procedures. The focus is on cognitive, step-wise, "linear" thinking. This partly explains why some people in healing prayer do not see images or pictures, or take a long time to see the creative or different way in which Jesus or the Spirit can accomplish healing or spiritual direction.

Focus on function and final results. The highest value comes from achieving results. We too readily view one another through our work or function in society instead of who we are in Christ. Identity is seen through performance; doing comes before being. Believers tend to see the work of the Holy Spirit as a performance, stressing the outward gifts such as speaking in tongues, preaching, prophesying or healing. "Since we live in a function-oriented culture, where our identity is associated with what we do, it is not surprising that so much emphasis is given to these activities."[26] But the Spirit gave the apostle Paul power to bear trials with humility and to live contentedly through times of hardship as well as times of success.[27] Perseverance is not often understood as an empowering of the Spirit in someone's life. There is a tendency to view God as "useful" because He answers prayer or takes us through certain spiritual experiences or phenomena. Do we value our relationship with Him by what He does for us rather than simply by being loved and in His presence? Are we tempted to value "success" over faithfulness?

Problem-solving, highly analytical mentality. The tendency here is to see everything as a problem to be solved. Just define the context, ascertain the inputs and work on a solution. But are all "problems" really problems? We so readily see people with a problem as people to be "fixed." Husbands who try to "fix" their wives soon find out this is not the greatest idea. What if we should be spending more time pursuing God instead of solving problems? Might we end up understanding God as primarily a problem solver? Should we not be concerned with the many Christian "how-to" books? Sometimes it's not a solution to a problem that's needed, but rather just being present for someone else in a great time of need, or accepting a situation. The book of Job is difficult to appreciate for incessant problem-solvers. Since God's ways are not our ways, our solutions are not always His solutions either. And what of mystery in our walk with God? Or what of taking risks in response to the Spirit's prompting? One runs the danger of ruthlessly analyzing oneself which can lead to introspection, the disease of our age.[28] The paralysis of analysis becomes its own tragedy. There are indeed problems to be solved, but that must never become the all-consuming preoccupation.

The Technical Mindset and Healing Prayer

The ministry of healing prayer is intensely relational and not at all technical. Even if there are "steps" one might follow, they are more like components or principles. Attempting to turn ministry into technique or approaching ministry with a technical mindset causes problems and typically quenches the Spirit.

This is a perennial temptation for people in ministry. The temptation with method or technique is that we rely on it rather than the Lord. Using a method or technique is easier than learning to follow and observe Jesus and His Spirit. It also conveniently lets us shift responsibility because when it "does not work," we can say that the method or technique failed.

Kraft discussed the role of technique in healing prayer, noting how it appears contradictory when the Holy Spirit leads this ministry.[29] Kraft points out that "techniques" in ministry are not foolproof, have no power in themselves and are always used under the guidance of the Spirit.[30] Anything that appears as technique, like retrieving memories, must be "…bathed in prayer and continual attention to the guidance of the Holy Spirit."[31] Tapscott emphasized the non-technical nature of inner healing: "We cannot box God in, we cannot limit Him! We cannot program the Holy Spirit like a computer."[32]

Some have argued that if Satan or the world uses a technique, we should not. Just because Satan or the world uses a given technique does not mean that believers cannot use it. Satan quoted Scripture (Luke 4:10-11); does it therefore follow that we cannot quote Scripture? Of course not!

One must consider the essence, determined end and hence nature of the technique. Here I disagree with Kraft in suggesting that the nature of a technique is not the issue apart from the power behind it.[33] It is not that simple. Techniques are not neutral. There is nothing neutral about a bullet piercing one's heart at hundreds of miles per second. The bullet and gun were specifically designed to kill and as efficiently and instantly as possible according to the criteria of technology. One would not ever use white witchcraft or a visualization technique that predetermines when and how "Jesus" will appear since, by their nature, they manipulate reality and are not totally submitted to the direction of the Spirit. What Kraft and many similar writers often describe are not techniques in the truest sense but rather steps or patterns of ministry that the Spirit often leads a person through in healing prayer that might "after the fact" appear like a technique.

Confession and forgiveness have also been referred to as clinical counseling techniques, and some would like to turn them into techniques.[34] True confession is the work of the Holy Spirit who convicts the world unto sin and righteousness (John 16:8-11; 1 John 1:9). Jesus commands forgiveness in the Lord's Prayer and elsewhere (Matt. 6:12,15; Mark 11:26; Eph. 4:32; Col. 3:13). If confession and forgiveness are techniques, why not use repentance and salvation as techniques? Confession and forgiveness are relational issues of the heart involving humility, obedience, love and grace. Classifying them as techniques is confusing; attempting to turn them into techniques is ill-advised and undermines their very essence.

In healing prayer, one does not know what the "steps" or "events" are at the outset and not always through the ministry session. They are determined by Jesus and His Spirit and ultimately follow the logic and reason of the Father (whose ways are not always our ways!) and not the rationalization of any technique.

In overcoming the technical mindset in healing prayer, we first realize the need for patience. There are times when we must wait on the Lord, when it seems as if there is no clear direction. The Lord might bring seemingly unrelated memories, pictures and feelings for even an hour, and then begin to "weave" things together to a moment of focused, deep healing. I have seen this frequently, and I marvel at Jesus' wisdom and the Spirit's role as counselor. This requires patience in His presence.

The ability to feel and the understanding of emotional intelligence should not remain underdeveloped or blocked by a strong focus on factual and analytical thinking. Some people in healing prayer ministry have such a heightened ability to feel that they can feel exactly what the person receiving ministry will feel and sometimes even before they do. This has happened to me a number of times when receiving prayer from people especially gifted in this ministry. The ability to truly feel makes compassion possible which is crucial for the ministry of healing prayer. When we can truly feel, we can more deeply identify with those to whom we minister.

Order and predictability is largely absent since there are no predetermined steps to follow. You do not always know what Jesus is going to do, nor where the Spirit will lead. The goal is *follow the steps of Jesus* for that specific prayer session for that specific person and not any set of predetermined steps. There are no "hard and fast rules" for how one is to minister each time, and the Spirit may lead a different way each time.[35] For example while often one or a series of memories will come and the Lord ministers to the lies or pain from each, sometimes Jesus will release the person from all the pain almost in one instance. I have seen this several times; I prayed for the presence of Jesus and the comfort of the Spirit into a woman's past sexual abuse and, after several minutes of complete silence, the woman would say she knows she has been totally healed. The person's life was changed from that day on. It's as if Jesus "broke His own rules." This calls for a huge paradigm shift, for you cannot come with a method or technique; rather you listen intently to Jesus and His Spirit and follow their lead. In total contradiction to the technical mind there is no need to control; rather you are under the control of Jesus and the Spirit. The most obvious time to "take control" is over evil spirits that might interfere or compromise ministry, but that is more like moving in the authority given by Jesus to His followers for His purposes.

You have to think intuitively and creatively since the Lord can be quite creative at times. I can remember once when a team member told me the Lord was telling her to ask if we could leave the door to our prayer room open just a crack but turn the light off. I had no idea why we should do this but asked the lady receiving prayer if that would be okay. She agreed, and about thirty seconds after we had done so a long-forgotten memory came back, triggered by light coming into a dark room through the doorway. Because of her unexplained fears the lady had often wondered about sexual abuse in the past. We did not probe in this area since we did not want to suggest anything and only wanted the Spirit's leading. The very memory that came back, involving her father, was one in which the Lord revealed clearly that there was no sexual abuse at all. Had we not obeyed the Lord, the prayer time would have been much less fruitful.

Healing prayer focuses on listening to Jesus and obeying Him. "Success" comes in bringing the person into Jesus' presence so they can hear His words and experience more of His peace and love where needed most. In contrast to the technical mindset, function and final result are second to obedience and faithfulness. Of course one would like to see every person experience deep and substantial healing. But sometimes very little happens in healing prayer. As Jesus followed the Father we only speak and do as led by Jesus and His Spirit.

There is some analysis in healing prayer, but this must be submitted to Jesus and redeemed for Him. This has been the hardest for me given my intensely analytical background. At times I have held back from analysis as things have unfolded in ministry. I am often hesitant to ask too many questions or "probe" too much, not wanting to slip into the role of an analyst or psychotherapist. I guard against taking time away from what Jesus will potentially be doing. I have seen numerous times how Jesus ministers quickly, gently and deeply such that I anticipate this for most people who come for prayer. But there are times for diagnostic questions, and the Lord does give words of wisdom, and He does want us to use the minds He has given us. Just as we use our hearts to feel for others, we use our minds to think in His presence with others. Reason is a gift from God to be used for His glory like anything else but not ever idolized. Jesus is never unreasonable, it is just that His ways can be beyond reason.

Long and Strickler emphasized the absence of technique in the ministry of healing prayer:

> We do not present a technique for doing healing. Instead, we describe the dynamics of a relationship between the prayer minister, the person being prayed for and the Holy Spirit who is mediating the presence and working of Jesus Christ. Offering a technique would be a lot easier! Our approach is more complicated, but we believe it is true to reality as revealed in the Bible and will lead to the extraordinary fruit of inner healing and deliverance.[36]

Wimber wrote much the same concerning the dynamics of healing prayer ministry:

> The most fundamental skill required for healing is openness to the Holy Spirit, emptying oneself and receiving His leading and power. Frequently I encounter people who want a method for healing, a formula they can follow that guarantees them automatic healings. But divine healing is neither automatic nor dependent on our right actions; it is rooted in a relationship with God and the power of His Spirit.[37]

Technique presumes that life is essentially rational, so through calculation and algorithm man will control his world. Technique substitutes *presence with procedure, mystery with mastery, faith with formula and compassion with calculation.* This is totally at odds with the relational ministry of the Spirit. Healing prayer ministry requires the virtues of patience, faith, hope, humility, obedience and love as from the Spirit. Those virtues are profoundly different from those of the technical spirit: efficiency, control, analysis, rationalization and predictability. As we are immersed in information technologies and breathing informationism, "we are sharpening our informational practices while dulling the habits of our hearts."[38]

Healing Prayer and Theophostic Ministry

Theophostic ministry has gained much attention lately and has brought true and lasting emotional healing to many people around the world. This is primarily because it presupposes the actual presence of Christ and His Spirit to do the healing. Smith, the founder of Theophostic Ministry, has reversed the Great Substitution in His ministry by relying on Jesus instead of methods and techniques. In this regard, which requires humility, God has blessed Smith's ministry.

As one would expect, Theophostic ministry is more effective than psychiatric medication, cognitive therapy, exposure therapy and EMDR (Eye Movement Desensitization and Reprocessing)[39] and certainly many other therapeutic techniques. This is also true of healing prayer that truly relies on the presence of Jesus and His Spirit and not on therapeutic or spiritual techniques. Many of the principles and insights of Theophostic ministry are not new; they have already been incorporated in healing prayer ministries for decades.[40] Payne, among others even before her, has already covered many of the principles of Theophostic ministry[41] but in a different writing style and presentation. The way that Smith has clarified his insights and principles of emotional healing, especially the importance of uncovering lies, has been helpful to many and has increased some people's effectiveness in prayer ministry. I have at times used Theophostic principles and can attest to their effectiveness when so led by the Spirit for a particular prayer session.

191

Theophostic ministry is a method[42] or a "systematized model or avenue"[43] and I believe that is part of its appeal although it certainly does rely on the Spirit and Jesus. Theophostic ministry has many similarities with research-supported psychotherapies[44] and thus is more readily accepted by professionals. Rational Emotive Therapy (RET), based on the idea that wrong or irrational beliefs cause emotional disturbances, has become widely accepted in a Christianized form by many Christian counselors and therapists.[45] Theophostic Ministry has the essential ministry components of finding lies embedded in memories that cause emotional pain in the present.[46] This appears quite similar to RET although the major difference is that Jesus exposes the lies and brings the truth instead of the therapist or counselor. This is not a criticism of Theophostic ministry; it is an observation. Those who are more rationally oriented more readily understand the central focus on finding lies, or cognitive distortions, and hearing the truth. Indeed RET has been easily grasped by many conservative Christians because of its "highly rational and didactic nature."[47]

Theophostic ministry is a valuable contribution to the ministry of healing prayer. But as Smith himself states, it is one form of ministry.[48] Alongside the strengths of Theophostic ministry, there are some limitations.

First, there is a built-in determinism or expectation in the method in finding a lie behind one's emotional pain. This is because Theophostic ministry is developed from a lie-based theology and lie-based thinking.[49] But that may not be Jesus' priority in a given prayer session, and it may not even be the real problem. I have all too often seen that to be the case. What of prenatal wounds, intergenerational sin, the prior interpretation of dreams for healing, prayer for mother love or father love, strengthening of a person's will, healing of the masculine or feminine, renewing the symbolism of one's heart to name just a very few? There are even times when people are completely healed from the pain of forgotten memories without ever recalling them.[50] Sometimes entire known memories are healed in an instant without ever going back to them. Of course Smith acknowledges that Jesus will and can do more than uncover lies and speak the truth.

Second, the apparent non-emphasis of the spiritual gifts, including words of knowledge or words of wisdom and the withholding of pictures or visions received by the person facilitating ministry[51] during the ministry time is unfortunate. While the use of the spiritual gifts has caused some confusion and even ministry abuse, they still are part of the ministry of Jesus and we should follow His example.[52] The incarnational presence of Jesus in us means that He might want to speak through us to the person being healed. I have seen many times how these gifts have brought deep healing much more effectively and quickly than Theophostic ministry. This is all part of ministering in the Holy Spirit. Could it be that making use of spiritual gifts a part of a ministry method would "slow down" its transferability and transportability, especially among professionals?

Third, there is little emphasis on the Spirit's anointing, although I do not believe Smith would argue against that at all. Again this is part of the example of Jesus (Luke 4:18; Acts 10:38) and the biblical pattern. I remember a healing prayer conference where the speaker had an obvious anointing for healing prayer. As the speaker, a lady, led in prayer for the healing of memories, several hundred people immediately experienced deep and lasting healing in the very real presence of Christ. We dare not miss all that God has for His people!

Adhering to the model and system of Theophostic Ministry, with its principles and guidelines,[53] does help to identify and

protect the ministry as well as making it more transferable, trans-
portable and repeatable. One can appreciate Smith's excellent
means of clarification, analysis and explanation. But this is a
double-edged sword since it involves standardization and rationalization with some reductionism and at times lessening of
effectiveness in ministry. This is especially true for those who are
more technically and procedurally oriented. I know of a number
of people whose effectiveness in healing prayer has actually
decreased the more they ministered Theophostically.

The Theophostic model can lead to an analytical mentality.
This is reinforced with searching for reasons or "troubleshooting"
as to why the method did not work for a given person. Since the
method is supposed to work for just about everyone, analysis
inevitably becomes important. This may be a symptom of not fully
using the gifts of the Spirit in the first place. One can appreciate
the need for understanding and discernment, but one should not
ever underestimate the potential technical, problem-solving mentality. The tragedy is that one may be less open to the wisdom of
Jesus which might utterly transcend or "violate" the Theophostic
ministry model or paradigm. This is a caution not a criticism.

A presence and love-based theology focused on experiencing the
grace and mercy of Jesus is much more comprehensive and integrative than a lie-based theology. One focuses on His presence to do
whatever He would do, whether it involves lies or not, rather than
requiring His presence to uncover lies in past memories. However,
you cannot "package the presence" like you can a method or technique. Understanding the presence is not easy for many believers—
a reflection of the mindset of our age. Thus forms of prayer which
are not conducive to a method are not easily understood or "trans-
ferred." Discussions about the relative "effectiveness" of types of
prayer ministry can become an illusion. A comparison of effective-

ness of methods is often made without the prior question of whether one's spirituality or mindset "is the problem." It is my experience that once the Presence is understood and experienced, one will never want to revert to former ways or rely on any other method or system.

Some years ago I learned Theophostic ministry. I approached the next number of sessions Theophostically. For the next two weeks every single prayer session was totally non-Theophostic and any attempt to follow a Theophostic approach would have ended in disappointment had I not quickly adjusted and prayed as before with no preconceived idea as to what would happen and without following any steps or method. I'm convinced the Lord arranged this to remind me that one must never follow a method or turn ministry into a method. It is best to minister Theophostically only if that is Christ's direction.

No method or system or set of guidelines can include all that Jesus and His Spirit might accomplish. Not all people will be completely helped by Theophostic ministry, but we can be thankful for those who are being healed and helped by it. Some people have actually come to me for healing prayer precisely because they do not want Theophostic ministry. Theophostic ministry is but part of the wider ministry of healing prayer in the Church and complements other types of healing prayer.

The Technical Mindset in the Church

Since technology is the very substance of our culture, a tendency of Christians is to all too easily employ *techne* (techniques and the technical mindset) in churches and relationships. Yet the dangers are many, as Houston warned:

> What many Christians do not realize is that *techne* is the Trojan horse in the city of God. Innocently, we introduce

techniques for counseling, tools for Bible study, organiza-
tion for church life, only to find that when they become
substitutes for the "fear of the Lord," technocratic religion
usurps the sphere of the Holy Ghost. The kingdom of
God cannot be extended by the technological society, for
it is not a kingdom of this world.[54]

If there is not much passion for evangelism, for example, there
is the temptation to use programs to manufacture it and methods
to measure it.

Techne can impact relationships among believers within the
Church and undermine sanctification. Therapeutic techniques are
now sought for relationships, self-esteem and victory over addictions, control over anxiety, managing anger and more. Essentially
the goal is to master life by technology with *techne* invading spirituality. But since the focus is on immediate relief, subjective well-
being and comfort, "the therapeutic orientation provides no serious
discipline for the soul."[55] Feeling good and with proper self-
esteem, as important as that is, is then given higher value than holiness and sanctification. The therapeutic approach to life and the
life of faith in God are mutually exclusive.

> The Christian religion, for example, draws the believer out
> of him or herself and into the obedience of faith, thus
> opening up the possibility of self-transcendence. The ther-
> apeutic disposition, on the other hand, tends to leave the
> individual in control of his or her own development.[56]

Therapy becomes an attempt to "manipulate a sense of well-
being" rather than seeking well-being in convictions about truth
and reality.[57] This is not surprising at all when you consider that a
major reason for the use of the scientific method in psychology was
a technical mentality in North America that valued "explanation,

prediction and control of phenomena."[58] If people were machines, this would not be a problem at all.

But all this is irreconcilable with the way of the cross, self-denial, humility and dependence on Jesus and His resurrection power (Phil. 3:10). Being blind to ultimate destiny and purpose and focused on well-being, "the modern therapeutic disposition mortgages eternal destiny for the sake of comfort."[59]

> The Christian faith is indeed a matter of healing and rehabilitation—indeed of resurrection—but it cannot be construed therapeutically, which is to say instrumentally. Faith in God through Jesus Christ and by the power of the Spirit is not a means, but is, along with hope and love, the end or purpose of human existence.[60]

The Mathematics of Emotions

Overcoming depression has been reduced by one author to a therapeutic formula. In his book, *How to Win Over Depression*, LaHaye wrote:

> Of one thing I am confident: you do not have to be depressed. If you or someone you love has this problem, you will welcome the good news of a means to gain victory over it. I am convinced that by using the formula in this book, you can avoid ever being depressed again.[61]

The basic premise in the book is that one's mental attitude is the cause of depression, excepting true physical or demonic causes.[62] Therefore, altering one's thinking patterns will overcome the depression.[63] LaHaye wrote that God's cure for anger is the following formula:[64] "(1) Admit that your anger is sin... (2) Confess your sin of anger to God... (3) Ask God to take away the habit pattern of anger... (4) Give thanks for God's mercy, grace and power...

(5) Repeat this formula every time you are angry." LaHaye stated that invoking this formula only once will probably not work since the ultimate victory comes with repetition—in one case 1000 times per day (or almost once every waking minute for 16 hours, if my math is correct!).[65] LaHaye claimed that victory comes by "conscious and repetitive attention, combined with the gradual exercise of new mental habit patterns."[66] Similarly he defined a five-step formula to gain victory over self-pity which also must be repeated many times.[67] In other words it is cognitive restructuring or positive thinking by one's efforts. LaHaye even presented a depression formula which he claimed is validated by experience: (Insult or Injury or Rejection) + Anger x Self-Pity = Depression.[68]

I have no problem with the biblical content in LaHaye's book and his helpful understanding of the causes of depression. I do not deny that his book may have helped some people, especially those more cognitively oriented in the first place. I am thankful for his encouragement that people have a personal relationship with Jesus. The problem is when a technical mindset is superimposed on scriptural principles and selected parts of Scripture are packaged into a formula (a standardized set of means) for a predetermined result. That very process reduces the complexity of the soul and brings control to a procedure that has a predetermined path and direction.

I am not excited about the mathematics of emotions or an algebra of the soul. LaHaye's formula falls apart for those with wounded hearts or crushed spirits (Ps. 34:18). What about those who are in bondage to undiscovered lies that make belief in God and His nearness next to impossible? What about those with so little hope and strength that they cannot follow his steps? I have met and prayed with believers who bought his book and tried his steps, but were never helped and thereby ended up even more depressed. That, unfortunately, is truly depressing. Job had a dim view of self-help and "guaranteed formulae:" *"What strength do I have, that I should still hope?"* (Job 6:11a). *"Do I have any power to help myself, now that success has been driven from me?"* (Job 6:13). LaHaye's book nowhere mentions the healing presence of Jesus. I have seen firsthand Jesus heal the deepest wounds of the soul which were behind depression and in the process some of LaHaye's steps were involved. The difference was the power of Jesus' healing presence corresponding to the Scriptures as opposed to one's own technical mastery and determination using scriptural principles.

Prayer as Faith Formula

The technical mindset can make major inroads into our prayer life which can then become increasingly technical and "useful." Houston wrote:

> Prayer is clearly more of a posture and attitude before God than a correct way of doing or saying things… our relationship with God does not depend on the good things we do, but on God's mercy towards us. So prayer can never be made to work automatically through pressing the right buttons and following the right techniques… when prayer is seen as just another technique for trouble-free living, it can never compete. All other technical solutions to the problems of everyday life will eventually kill prayer that is merely technical.[69]

Our walk with God then becomes more technical than relational. But the focus of prayer is not prayer, or problems, but God Himself.

The technical approach to prayer can easily turn faith into formula not unlike the "health and wealth" gospel. The Faith Movement has defined faith as a force that is behind all reality which

199

empowers the spiritual world. To get the spirit world to function for you, you then use faith formulae.[70] So you determine the result you want—wealth or health or something else—and then apply the faith formula which involves a series of steps (sometimes four) as taught by various faith movement teachers. This all implies impersonal laws of the universe with faith as a "power force" that can be put to use for one's own goals.[71] In other words it is a standardized set of means to attain a predetermined result.

How can one ever consider grace, submission to the will of God, confession, sacrifice, suffering and servanthood when, with such a spiritual technique, efficiency and function are all that really matter? God becomes the ultimate celestial computer wherein we insert the appropriate spiritual software and "press Return" for results. Houston's insights again are profoundly applicable here:

> This is the grave threat of the technical, that it appears to make readily, easily, universally and even instantly available what was once scarce and valued. Commitment then ceases to be an exercise of the soul. If, then, the spirit of the technical undermines the need for commitment, is it not likely that faith in *techne* tends to atrophy the spirit of man, so that the exercise of prayer, of personal discipline and of human relationships becomes increasingly difficult?[72]

Endnotes

[1] Jacques Ellul, *The Technological Society* (New York: Vintage Books, 1964) p. vi.

[2] Ellul, p. xxv.

[3] Ellul, p. 4.

[4] Ellul, p. 20.

[5] Ellul, p. 321.

[6] Ellul, p. 24.

[7] Ibid.

[8] Rick Godwin, *Exposing Witchcraft in the Church* (Santa Barbara: Creation House, 1997) p. 2.

[9] Martin and Deidre Bobgan, *Hypnosis: Medical, Scientific, or Occultic?* (Santa Barbara: EastGate Publishers, 2001) pp. 1-30.

[10] Bobgan, pp. 109-113.

[11] Charles H. Kraft, *Deep Wounds, Deep Healing: Discovering the Vital Link Between Spiritual Warfare and Inner Healing* (Ann Arbor: Vine Books, 1993) p. 111.

[12] Craig M. Gay, *The Way of the (Modern) World: Or, Why it's Tempting to Live as if God Doesn't Exist* (Grand Rapids: Eerdmans Publishing Company, 1998) p. 88.

[13] Donald G. Bloesch, *A Theology of Word & Spirit: Authority & Methodology in Theology* (Downers Grove: InterVarsity Press, 1992) p. 27.

[14] Gay, p. 90.

[15] Gay, p. 92.

[16] Miroslav Volf, *Work in the Spirit. Toward a Theology of Work* (New York: Oxford University Press, 1991) p. 113.

[17] Volf, p. 114.

[18] Craig Brod, *Technostress: The Human Cost of the Computer Revolution* (Reading: Addison-Wesley, 1984)

[19] Allen Emerson and Cheryl Forbes, *The Invasion of the Computer Culture* (Downers Grove: InterVaristy Press, 1989) p. 86.

[20] James Houston, *I Believe in the Creator* (Grand Rapids: Eerdmans Publishing Co., 1980) p. 181.

[21] Quentin J. Schultze, *Habits of the High-Tech Heart: Living Virtuously in the Information Age* (Grand Rapids: Baker Academie, 2002) p. 53.

[22] Schultze, p. 26.

[23] Schultze, p. 21.

[24] Leanne Payne, *The Healing Presence* (Wheaton: Crossway Books, 1984) p. 133.

[25] Gay, p. 99.

[26] James Houston, *The Transforming Friendship - A Guide To Prayer* (Batavia: Lion Publishing, 1989) p. 121.

[27] Houston, 1989, p. 120.

[28] Payne, 1984, p. 155.

[29] Kraft, pp. 109-132

[30] Kraft, p. 111.

[31] Kraft, p. 114.

[32] Betty Tapscott, *Ministering Inner Healing Biblically* (Houston: Tapscott Ministries, 1987) p. 14.

[33] Kraft, p. 118.

[34] Mark R. McMinn, *Psychology, Theology and Spirituality in Christian Counseling. AACC Counseling Library.* (Wheaton: Tyndale House Publisher, 1996) p. 204.

[35] Tapscott, p. 14.

[36] Brad Long and Cindy Strickler, *Let Jesus Heal Your Hidden Wounds: Cooperating With the Holy Spirit in Healing Ministry* (Grand Rapids: Chosen Books, 2001) p. 9.

[37] John Wimber and Kevin Springer, *Power Healing* (New York: HarperCollins, 1987) p. 180.

[38] Schultze, p. 20.

[39] Karl D. Lehman and Charlotte E.T. Lehman, "Theophostic Ministry: Assessment and Recommendations," revised 6/19/2002. www.kclehman.com, FAQS. pp. 1-2.

[40] Karl D. Lehman and Charlotte E.T. Lehman, "Theophostic: What Is Unique?" revised 5/10/2002. www.kclehman.com, FAQS. pp. 1-12.

[41] Leanne Payne, *Restoring the Christian Soul Through Healing Prayer: Overcoming the Three Great Barriers to Personal and Spiritual Completion in Christ* (Wheaton: Crossway Books, 1991).

[42] Ed M. Smith, *Beyond Tolerable Recovery* (Campbellsville: Alathia Publishing, 1996, 4th ed. 2000) pp. 6, 9, 114.

[43] Edward M. Smith, *Healing Life's Deepest Hurts: Let the Light of Christ*

Dispel the Darkness in Your Soul (Ann Arbor: Vine Books, 2002) p. 15.

[44] Lehman and Lehman, 6/19/2002, p. 3.

[45] Stanton L. Jones and Richard E. Butman, *Modern Psychotherapies: A Comprehensive Christian Appraisal* (Downers Grove: InterVarsity Press, 1991) pp. 177-179.

[46] Smith, 2000, pp. 39-57.

[47] Jones and Butman, p. 192.

[48] Smith, 2002, p. 15.

[49] Smith, 2000, pp. 52, 58-89, 221-236.

[50] Payne, 1991, p. 77.

[51] Smith, 2002, pp. 183-184.

[52] David Pytches, *Come Holy Spirit: Learning How to Minister in Power,* 2nd ed. (London: Hodder & Stoughton, 1995).

[53] Smith, 2002, pp. 183-184.

[54] Houston, 1980, p. 161.

[55] Gay, p. 186.

[56] Ibid.

[57] Herbert Schlossberg, *Idols for Destruction: Christian Faith and its Confrontation with American Society* (Nashville: Thomas Nelson Publishers, 1983) p. 20.

[58] Mary Stewart Van Leeuwen, *The Sorcerer's Apprentice: A Christian Looks at the Changing Face of Psychology* (Downers Grove: InterVarsity Press, 1982) p. 45.

[59] Gay, p. 187.

[60] Gay, p. 188.

[61] Tim LaHaye, *How to Win Over Depression* (Grand Rapids: Zondervan Publishing House, 1974) p. 12.

[62] LaHaye, pp. 20, 48, 110, 192.

[63] LaHaye, p. 55.

[64] LaHaye, pp. 93-95.

[65] LaHaye, p. 95.

66 Ibid.

67 LaHaye, p. 199.

68 LaHaye, p. 100.

69 Houston, 1989, p. 26.

70 Hank Hanegraaf, *Christianity in Crisis* (Eugene: Harvest House Publishers, 1993) p. 73.

71 D.R. McConnell, *A Different Gospel: Biblical and Historical Insights into the Word of Faith Movement* (Peabody: Hendrickson Publishers, 1995, updated edition) pp. 133-135.

72 Houston, 1980, p. 161.

Chapter Seven

Modern Psychotherapies: Built on Sand?

Since you died with Christ to the basic principles of this world, why, as though you still belonged to it, do you submit to its rules: "Do not handle! Do not taste! Do not touch!"? These are all destined to perish with use, because they are based on human commands and teachings (Col. 2:20-22).

Are you so foolish? After beginning with the Spirit, are you now trying to attain your goal by human effort? (Gal. 3:3).

Anna-Marie's Years of Pain

Years of therapy and support groups, years of suffering and pain and years of depression. That's how I would describe my life to anyone who would listen. I was tired of hurting, and I was tired of hurting others as well. I had unbelievable pain, and I had no idea what to attribute it to. I also realized that I had lived most of my life this way. I have been bitter and insecure, angry and ashamed. I thought it was abuse—which it probably was for the most part, or so I thought. But now I know where the pain originally came from.

Now it is gone. I had to do something, and I had been trying for years, but finally the day came. I want to share with you this very special day.

I knew that Deeper Love Ministries was coming to our town. Someone had told me, and I had marked my weekly planner. My plan was to attend, but my fear was very strong. I subconsciously knew that if I attended this conference, things would start churning inside me. I also knew it wasn't going to be easy. And it wasn't. I went in Saturday afternoon and was absolutely terrified not knowing what to expect. My pain and suffering were affecting my relationships, slowly destroying them and slowly destroying me. As I sat there, determined not to let "them" affect me, I hurt more and more and I still didn't know why. Suddenly I burst into tears with so much pain I had to leave. My heart was black from the hurt. I couldn't explain my feelings and make anyone else understand them because I didn't understand. So I ran to the ladies' washroom for a break.

Needless to say, I was a mess. I was definitely not going back. It hurt too much.

So when I got home from the afternoon session, I sat in the bathtub and cried. A friend of mine who had been at the afternoon session called me, and we talked about things. He told me I needed to go back, and I knew he was right. "He" wasn't telling me, Jesus was telling me. Jesus was telling me to go back. It was what I had to do. It was my last chance to be healed, one last hope of freedom from pain. So I went. It was the best thing I could have ever done for myself. As I walked in, I was afraid. I was hurting. I felt exactly how I had felt the first time I had gone in for the afternoon session. I entered the church at 7 p.m. in a mess, and my friend introduced me to Dieter who then proceeded to make an appointment for me for healing prayer after the teaching sessions. I was very emotional during the teaching, and I was dreading the end. Nearing the end I went to freshen up, and as I came back Dieter was waiting for me.

We entered the prayer healing room together with his prayer ministry assistant. We talked for a little bit about why I was coming for prayer, and then Jesus started working on me. Something happened to me in that room, something I never thought was possible. He spoke to me. He came to help me. I asked for help and He came. (Now I say this because I had been doubting for many years, wondering why God would allow such horrible things to happen to me). I went in for help dealing with an abusive relationship that had turned into a kidnapping. I ended up getting help for something totally unrelated—the root of all my problems, my mother.

I felt His presence, and I felt Him inside me. I heard Jesus speak to me. He wanted to help me and He did. All the hurt was torn up and addressed, and I cried and wailed like a baby. I was so embarrassed. The pain just came out, and more pain came out the more answers Jesus gave me. I had many questions and all of them were answered. For the first time in my life I knew why I was hurting. I asked Him to relieve me of my anger, my shame and my hate. I was able to forgive a cousin for having sexually molested me when I was four years old, the shame and anger of which I was still living with. A weight was lifted. We were able to get to the root of my pain through this healing prayer. I felt happy and joyful when I left the prayer room. I felt "reborn." I felt like a child again, you know, without the pain that an adult carries around (which I thought was normal). I left the room looking absolutely horrible but had never felt so amazing! People were telling me that I was glowing. Everyone knew. They knew Jesus had helped me that night. They knew I had been healed and freed. I can truly say, "Now I know. Now I know that Jesus loves me." I was afraid to go to sleep that night. I was afraid that I would wake up in the morning and the pain would be back, but it wasn't. What I experienced was real.

Techniques and Methods in Counseling and Therapy

Christian counselors, therapists and psychologists frequently debate the relative merits and effectiveness of various methods and techniques in counseling and therapy. But few scholars and writers stop to ask the question: Is it even fundamentally a question of method or technique? What if it isn't? Could it possibly be that mountains of ink have been spilled for the wrong reason? What if trying to integrate methods and techniques of psychotherapy with theology is like trying to fit a square peg into a round hole?

McMinn wrote about a hypothetical committed Christian (named Chris), truly desiring to serve Christ and others. He completes a graduate program in clinical psychology from a Christian institution and then graduates:

> Five years later, doctoral degree in hand, Chris is ready to begin his work as a Christian psychologist. He is armed with an arsenal of therapeutic concepts and techniques: systematic desensitization, progressive relaxation, cognitive restructuring, analysis of resistance, projective identification, unconditional positive regard, daily record of automatic thoughts and many more. *Here's the irony: Chris has never been taught and never stopped to question why he is using these techniques.* What is the goal of therapy? How do we define healing (emphasis mine)?[1]

This is precisely my point. Have we really asked the fundamental question whether helping people in their pain and woundedness is a matter of technique and method? What are all the consequences of such an approach? If, for Christians, the goal is sanctification and transformation of the human soul and becoming a child of God, how adequate are methods and techniques? The transformation of the human soul, more than anything else, requires a relational instead of a technical encounter. Furthermore it is centered on our relationship with Christ. If we are Christ's workmanship, is Jesus insufficient and in need of methods and techniques to realize this? There are many reasons that challenge the supposed sufficiency or validity of methods and techniques including a substantial body of secular research.

Character and Relationship Above Technique

The counselor or therapist's character counts more than any method or technique. The "value of counseling is found less in one's training and theoretical orientation than in one's character."[2] It has been shown many times that some core characteristics of the therapist are more crucial to effect any change than methods or techniques. In fact therapists can employ contradictory techniques and be equally effective as long as they are equally empathetic, understanding and truly compassionate.[3] Many studies have shown that "…different therapies seem to work equally well."[4] Many researchers have reported this and refer to it as the *equal outcomes phenomenon*.[5] Thus a person's presence and relationship are more critical than the methods and techniques. A strong therapeutic relationship "is one of the best indicators of success."[6] Dawes, professor at Carnegie-Mellon University and a recognized authority and researcher on psychological evaluation and decision making, pointed to substantial evidence that "good therapists tend to be empathetic, trustworthy and warm."[7]

This implies that methods and techniques are almost irrelevant given the importance of an authentic personal presence. A truly loving, caring and understanding person with a listening heart and common understanding of the issues of the soul could be as effective as a trained professional. So why place so much emphasis on the right method, theory or technique when it's not the critical factor?

Related to the character of the counselor or therapist is the idea that love itself is crucial and fundamental to people's healing and restoration. Hart, citing the renowned psychotherapist Karl Menninger, wrote:

> Karl Menninger, after decades of work in psychotherapy, lays aside all learned talk of psychic maladies and of therapeutic techniques and utters one simple overarching truth: **It is unlove that makes people unwell and it is love and love alone that can make them well again.** His contention is buttressed by more general studies and surveys, in which it has been shown that those therapists who are most successful in bringing health back to their clients are best able to convey love…. This explains in part why some psychotherapists seem to do so little for people even after years of appointments and some complete amateurs are able to make a significant difference in a short time (emphasis mine).[8]

Jesus emphasized love and demonstrated compassion in His ministry. Jesus commanded that we love one another as He has first loved us. Loving others is a core of Christian discipleship and spiritual formation. Therefore the complex and "scientific" world of psychotherapy is once again finally catching up to the clear, simple and immensely profound teachings of Jesus. The command and empowering of Jesus to love people, as well as experiencing His love for oneself, can be understood as intensely therapeutic and psychological although it is much more than that.

Professional Competence: Some Second Thoughts

Since methods and techniques are really not that effective, one would logically expect that training in them will not lead to greater effectiveness either. This is shown repeatedly by a great number of studies. Dawes considered carefully the claims of mental health professionals to alleviate emotional distress based on their effectiveness as therapists, their insight about people and the relationship between how well they perform and their degree of experience. There are over three hundred empirical studies and summaries proving that "these professionals' claims to superior intuitive insight, understanding and skill as therapists are simply invalid."[9]

In his chapter on psychotherapy, *The Myth of Expertise*, he wrote:

...the credentials and experience of the psychotherapists are unrelated to patient outcomes, based on well over five hundred scientific studies of psychotherapy outcome.[10]

Research results show that "the effectiveness of therapy is unrelated to the training or credentials of the therapist."[11] Regarding the results of analyses on effectiveness of therapy, he wrote:

...the credentials and experience of the therapist don't matter. This result is rather unpleasant for professionals who require years of postgraduate training and postdoctoral experience for licensing to perform therapy and would like to restrict practice to those who are licensed. In the years after the Smith and Glass article was published, many attempts were made to disprove their finding that the training, credentials and experience of therapists are irrelevant. These attempts failed.[12]

Hurding concluded the same after reviewing the literature and research results:

> Good or bad therapy hinges strongly on the personality of the counselor regardless of degrees and diplomas achieved, courses attended or positions held. This conclusion has been well supported by research carried out from the mid-1960s onwards.[13]

Crabb, a respected Christian psychotherapist for over twenty-five years, referred to recent research in psychotherapy to show that "the considerable good done by trained counselors could, in many cases, be done as well or better by mature, nonprofessionally qualified people who relate well."[14] He also wrote that evidence does not support the popular belief that only highly trained people can practice professional counseling:

> ...there is reason to suggest that caring, intelligent people, with much less training than is required to become a professional counselor, can achieve equal and sometimes better results when their efforts to helpfully talk are carried out as part of healthy community.[15]

While affirming that some counselors are successful and effective, Collins wrote how a former president of the American Psychological Association estimated that three quarters of all counselors are ineffective.[16] Collins cited research on counselors published in 1971 which concluded that "...we can be 'quite certain' that two out of three practitioners are ineffective or even harmful; involved in spending energy, commitment and care in a wasteful manner."[17]

Dawes wrote that "there is no *positive* evidence supporting the efficacy of professional psychology."[18] When therapy does work, it is not even always known why it worked. Many studies have, in fact, shown that:

> ...not only was the therapist's credentials and training unrelated to its effectiveness, but also even the type of therapy (except possibly for behavioral therapy for behavioral problems) and the length of therapy were unrelated to the success of a therapy.[19]

The next logical question is whether psychologists, counselors and psychotherapists are worth the credibility and status afforded them in the healing of people's deepest emotional needs. Dawes summarized many research findings and concluded:

> Emotional suffering is very real and the vast majority of people in these expanding professions sincerely wish to help those suffering. But are they really the experts they claim to be? Is our society justified in granting them special status and paying them from common funds? Are they better therapists than minimally trained people who may share their knowledge of behavioral techniques or empathetic understanding of others? Does possessing a license imply that they are using scientifically sound methods in treating people or providing an "expert opinion"? ...Psychologists themselves have studied these questions quite extensively, often. *There is by now an impressive body of research evidence indicating that the answer to these questions is no* (emphasis mine).[20]

Most people can complete years of study in theories, methods and techniques of therapy and counseling; that is not terribly difficult. But when faced with an actual person with years of life and pain in all its mysteries, the challenge is far greater. Generalizations about

213

people can be found in textbooks, but the required understanding of an individual in all of his or her complexities simply cannot.[21]

With everything considered thus far it is no wonder that in 1975 Crabb noted the "growing disillusionment" with professional efforts of psychologists and psychiatrists to solve the personal problems of people and therefore the search for other approaches.[22] Gay summarized the failure of therapeutic techniques as follows:

> The supreme irony of the contemporary "culture of narcissism," a culture obsessed with self-development and self-actualization, is thus that it fails, finally, to produce real human persons. Neither self-realization by means of therapeutic technique, nor by means of the sheer will-to-self-definition, is capable of bearing the full weight of human personality... the quasi-religious therapeutic regimens which have arisen to replace Christianity in the name of individual liberty and/or rational science are simply not up to the task.[23]

The Major Traditions of Psychotherapy

There are about 260 different schools of psychotherapy[24] developed from four major streams or traditions.[25] These major streams have different assumptions and philosophies about the nature of man, the world and God.

Psychoanalysis, developed by Freud, is an early tradition that focuses on the inner life with its instincts and unconscious drives, especially from the early stages of life.[26] Jung, a student of Freud, developed his analytic psychology with an emphasis on the "collective unconscious," a sort of storehouse of latent memories from past generations.[27]

Personalism, with the humanistic and existential therapies, extends the optimism of classical Freudian analysis.[28] The focus is on self, subjective experience, feelings, self-actualization or self-realization and includes Carl Roger's Person-Centered Therapy. The preoccupation with "self" leads to a cult of self-worship in the absence of a holy God.[29]

Transpersonalism assumes a reality beyond people such as a Higher Consciousness, for example, and involves eastern, New Age, mystical and related therapies.[30] People realize their full potential when they are transformed by their connection to the transpersonal realm.[31]

Behaviorism defines humanity in terms of what can be observed and recorded.[32] The focus is on behavior and thought such that people are basically machines that can be repro-grammed.[33] This tradition includes the Cognitive-Behavioral Therapies and Rational Emotive Therapy developed around the idea that beliefs influence our emotions.[34] This is the most "scien-tific" and reductionistic of all the traditions.

Family and Systems Therapy, developed since the 1950s from other therapies, focuses on relationships and attempts to under-stand and treat family dynamics as well as the individual.[35] The medical or biological view holds that people are more like physical machines with defects and must be fixed either physically or chem-ically.[36] That is certainly true of psychiatry with a fixation on drug therapies for "mental illnesses."

These therapies are more than just methods or techniques to make you feel better. They are, in fact, alternative spiritualities with disciplines for realizing their own idea of personhood.[37] Their sub-tleties and seductions must be fully acknowledged lest "our souls turn out Therapeutic rather than Christian."[38] Establishing one's identity in Christ and becoming a child of God in order to enter the kingdom of God, for example, is totally alien to these therapies yet totally central to Jesus.

Rats, People, Moss, Subatomic Particles and Chemicals

The weaknesses and limitations of methods and techniques in counseling and therapy, especially when developed from behaviorism, are largely a reflection of the flawed methodology in the research behind them. The more recent history of psychology as modern scientific psychology starts from 1879 when Wilhelm Wundt in Liepzig, Germany, opened the first psychology laboratory.[39] From his time onwards, most of psychology has been dominated by the scientific method of the increasingly impressive natural sciences.[40]

The scientific method requiring experiments, repeatable steps, empirical observations only, analysis, measurement and explanation of the natural sciences was applied directly to humans in psychological research. It was just simply assumed that you could study people and their "mental processes" just like you could study chemicals, rats, subatomic particles and moss, for example. There were those who objected and said that people are not passive subjects to be studied and that an entirely different methodology, suited to people, must be developed. Their objections were ignored and over time the obvious and predictable flaws in using the scientific method on people have become increasingly apparent. For a number of solid and core reasons, the promises of modern scientific psychology have not materialized due to the flawed methodology.[41] The "apprenticeship" of psychology to natural science is personally unsatisfying and simply does not work.[42] So after decades of debate and mountains of research papers and endless conferences, it was finally concluded that, after all, you could not study people and their "mental processes" just like you study chemicals, rats, subatomic particles and moss. An amazing discovery! Koestler criticized the dehumanizing tendency of behaviorism this way:

> Behaviorism is indeed a kind of flat-earth view of the mind. Or, to change the metaphor: it has replaced the anthropomorphic fallacy—ascribing to animals human faculties and sentiments—with the opposite fallacy: denying man faculties not found in lower animals; it has substituted for the erstwhile anthropomorphic view of the rat, a *ratomorphic view of man* (emphasis mine).[43]

In other words one studies rats and wonders why the results do not directly apply to people. There would be no problem in this whole discussion if one could examine the soul under a microscope.

Assumptions as Sinking Sand

Each of the major traditions of psychotherapy and the resulting over 260 schools rest on a number of critical assumptions. When those assumptions are unfulfilled or simply wrong, they rest on "sinking" sand (Matt. 7:26; Luke 6:49). A house is only as solid as the foundation on which it is built; therapies are only as good as the assumptions on which they are built. It is beyond the scope and intent of this book to discuss the limiting assumptions of each modern psychotherapy. Instead I will briefly discuss the assumptions behind these psychotherapies.

Reductionism rolls onto the scene when people are reduced to machines as in some behavioral therapies or personhood is reduced to "parts" for analysis. Behaviorism rummages around with a focus on people's external behavior and no concern about what goes on in their heads.[44] Determinism flares up when past events or present stimuli or the environment are said to largely determine a person's behavior. Empiricism rears its ugly head every time only observable or measurable phenomena are accepted as valid data. Scientism lurks around when only empirical data are analyzed and logical hypotheses are considered as the only means to arriving at truth. Rationalism ruminates all too often when the logic and thought of man pretend to explain and control everything. Naturalism, the first cousin to scientism, demands that only the natural, observable world is real and hence the supernatural does not exist. Pragmatism oozes out in all too many places, claiming that "if it works," that's what matters most. Functionalism, a sophisticated fig leaf for pragmatism, places ultimate value on a function, purpose and utility of a behavior. Relativism, a blood brother of empiricism which claims that there are no absolute truths, confuses almost everything. But then relativism is built on a false absolute ("there are no absolutes") and thus sinks itself.

In the Footsteps of Nebuchadnezzar

Humanism is the great grandfather of the above assumptions, wherein man is deemed the center of the universe and the measure of all things. Humanism holds that man is quite capable of solving his problems by himself without any need of God who is conveniently declared non-existent.[45] Humanism is not only opposed to God but also hostile to Christianity.[46] Nebuchadnezzar was a humanist when he declared that his kingdom was built by his power, for him and for his glory and majesty (Dan. 4:30; Isa. 10:13).[47] Humanism is not new since *there is nothing new under the sun* (Eccl. 1:9).

The one fatal flaw of much modern psychotherapy is therefore its exclusion of the personal God as revealed in the Scriptures.[48] Jesus is truly the one and only perfect example of personhood, yet He is ignored by psychology. Gayle put it well: "Today, the greatest irony within psychology, the science of human behavior, is that it ignores the only Person who can impart full personality."[49]

No wonder there are so many assumptions. They exist, of course, precisely because God is removed from the picture and something else must be erected in His place to make anything work. As Tournier astutely observed, "…man cannot dispense with the spirit, so he invents surrogates for it" like ideologies, philosophies and therapies.[50]

Everything then becomes incredibly complex as anyone who has studied the field can attest. So not getting along with Mom as a small child, for example, becomes a major discussion in "object relations theory." The wisdom of Ecclesiastes is self-evident here: *"The more words, the less the meaning, and how does that profit anyone?"* (Eccl. 6:11).

Smorgasbord for the Soul

Since there are so many therapies with so many assumptions, it is quite obvious that no therapy is completely adequate for anyone. The inadequacies and errors of all these therapies have been documented in detail.[51] No surprise, then, that many therapists and counselors realize this and are "eclectic." Not tied to any one method or theory, they switch and choose among methods and theories as clients come and go.[52] Eclecticism in counseling or therapy, like choosing from a smorgasbord for the issues of the soul, is then a symptom of the inadequacies of methods and techniques. A "responsible" eclecticism where one decides with much thought and ethics is advocated for Christian counselors and therapists.[53]

There are many Christian counselors who are cognitive or cognitive-behavioral therapists, focusing on having the right ideas or truth and also on changing behavior through many types of methods, techniques and effort. Other Christian counselors use techniques from transaction analysis or Gestalt therapy.[54]

The Integration of Psychology and Theology

Eclecticism implies some integration of psychology with Christian theology. But to what degree and how does one use the thinking of the world in the care of souls? Can one truly "integrate" as required by eclecticism?

Integrationists typically appeal to general revelation to support their position. Since all truth is God's truth, true insights even from the world can be adopted. The Lord even reveals to a farmer how to prepare soil, plant, harvest and thresh (Isa. 28:24-29). An ant can teach anyone about diligence (Prov. 6:6-8). God's law is written on the hearts of unbelieving Gentiles (Rom. 2:15). Mankind has some knowledge of God from creation (Rom. 1:20) and experiences His provision (Acts 14:17). Mankind is not totally unaware of God and issues of the heart. Paul quoted a pagan poet's view of Cretans and affirmed it as true (Tit. 1:12-13). While preaching in Athens he quoted the poets Epimenides and Aratus, acknowledging the value of their understanding of God (Acts 17:28).[55] Paul's statement to the Corinthians—*"Bad company corrupts good character"* (1 Cor. 15:33)—is actually from the Greek poet Menander and thus affirms an insight from the world.[56] Significantly Jesus Himself did not deny the wisdom of the world operating within its own categories (Matt. 11:25; Luke 10:21, 16:8). Barclay sums up the issue well:

> The Bible does not dismiss all human knowledge and understanding as nonsense. It consistently points out its fundamental inadequacy for the knowledge of God and of His will, but it does not despise its practical usefulness or those of its insights that are true.[57]

But there is also the depravity of man and error in the world's thinking. While mankind can think and conduct research, the results cannot be accepted uncritically. This is especially true of the human "sciences" which have their own philosophies on the nature of man.

True knowledge and wisdom come from the fear of the Lord (Ps. 111:10). To not fear the Lord from the outset means that one may well embark on foolishness. The Spirit of God is not received by the world nor known by the world (John 14:17), and without the Spirit one simply cannot know the things of the Spirit (1 Cor. 2:14). Since the Spirit lives in us and we are a new creation in Christ (2 Cor. 5:17), secular psychologists have a disadvantage from the beginning. No wonder most forms of cognitive therapy are silent on the spiritual life.[58] Since the goal in life is to become like Christ and seek after the kingdom of God, the whole direction of secular psychology will be suspect. Mankind cannot comprehend the ways of God (Eccl. 3:11, 8:17). The mind of fallen man can even be corrupted (Titus 1:15). The world tends to suppress truth (Romans 1:18-25) and avoids Jesus (John 1:5) and sin (John 3:19-21).

Psychologists are often hostile to Christianity because they tend to believe man can engineer his own fate and that man is basically good.[59] To admit anything else reveals pride and confesses the actual need for a saviour.[60] Then there is the disturbing fact that some of the prominent humanistic psychologists, including Carl Rogers, have contacted spirits.[61] Carl Jung's grandmother was actually a medium, his mother had psychic experiences, his medical thesis concentrated on occult phenomena and he himself had contact with evil spirits in his adult years.[62] The more recent trend of humanistic transpersonal psychology's adoption of Hinduism and Bhuddism is alarming.[63] Academic psychology in North America "attracts persons who see in it a socially and intellectually acceptable way of evading, if not actually attacking, their Judeo-Christian heritage."[64] Some psychologists hold that the Christian faith is a cause for neurosis or psychopathology, as if faith in Jesus will make you mentally ill.

Nevertheless some Christians are called into the disciplines of psychology and psychotherapy as difficult as that arena may be for Christians. But these disciplines have a great potential for serious, general error and even creating a rival psychotherapeutic religion since they deal with the very nature of man of which the Scriptures have much to say.[65]

Integration as Salvaging from the World

So can we integrate at all? Yes, but in a very limited way and more like "embellishment" or "addition" or *intersection*. We should avoid anti-intellectualism, exhibit humility in learning from the world and dialogue constructively with the world. Unless we are clear about the temptations of compromise and syncretism, integration can be dangerous. "We can bend Christian assumptions to conform to existing techniques, but at some point our belief system snaps and we are left only with theistic scraps saturated by atheistic definitions of mental health."[66] Integration is difficult and at times impossible precisely because Christian therapy should revolve around the person and presence of Jesus whereas secular therapy is diametrically opposed in revolving around the complete rejection and absence of Jesus.

The Christian faith, with its correct view of reality, must be the solid grid through which the world's thinking is accepted or rejected. The kingdom of God and the priorities of Jesus must be paramount at all times. Jesus and the written Word, not the wisdom of men, must set the agenda and determine the categories and frame of reference.

The modern therapies are not all totally wrong. Each has some truth but also error. Each therapy contradicts Christianity in at least one way or leaves out something essential.[67] To adopt these therapies uncritically could be like spending years climbing up a ladder only to find that the ladder was leaning against the wrong wall.

To conceptualize a "limited integration," imagine a several-hundred-year-old house with gleaming hardwood floors and great craftsmanship throughout. The foundation, walls and roof represent the general view of reality as set forth in the Scriptures. While there are some furnishings in the house, there is room for more furnishings as well as some decisions on painting a wall or mounting a picture. Those represent finer details regarding the nature of man and his behavior. Anything coming into the house (understanding, insight and such) must not violate or alter the structure of the house, nor can it be "out of character" with the house, nor can it bring anything else (hidden assumptions, for example) that would disturb the house in any way. Any understanding or insight from therapy or psychology can only serve to add some details or develop further what God has already revealed. This may mean that our understanding of the Scriptures and God may be challenged at times because our interpretations of Scripture are not perfect and theology is still man's construction and not the same as the written Word. One must avoid syncretism and compromise.

Given man's depravity, it often comes down to "salvaging" from the world's thinking to see what might be helpful. Crabb characterized careful integration as "spoiling the Egyptians" where the Israelites took silver, gold and clothing from the Egyptians upon their departure (Exod. 12:35-36).[68] Common grace makes the exercise worthwhile since something of redeemable value can be found in the world's thinking.

The Bible Only?

Other writers would oppose any integration since the "Scriptures are sufficient." Some see attempts at integration as psychoheresy[69] or myth.[70] This is typical of some of the biblical or spiritual counseling movement. For example Jay Adams and his nouthetic (Gk. *nouthesis* and *noutheteo*) counseling which focuses on confronting people with their sin in order to effect "personality and behavioral change."[71]

This exclusionist position is commendable in desiring to be true to the Christian faith and avoid syncretism. I do not doubt the sincerity and Christian commitment of those who hold this position. Nevertheless there are some shortcomings and problems.

First, the Scriptures *plus Jesus* are sufficient. "It is God, not the Bible itself, who is declared to be all-sufficient, to provide all that pertains to life."[72] Exclusionist authors typically lack a theology of the presence due to the focus on the Scriptures. This is a glaring and fundamental weakness. We need both the written Word and the Living Word. This is partly why memorizing Scripture and claiming Bible verses is rarely sufficient for healing the soul.

Second, the Bible does not give a direct answer for every problem or concept. We need to develop a Christian mind by applying biblical truth and principles to all of life. Basing arguments on whether a term or concept is found in the Bible is simplistic and untenable. Under such logic, writers and founders of "discernment ministries" have invalidated and disqualified themselves because, strictly speaking, the Scriptures only talk about elders, apostles or pastors in churches correcting doctrinal error. Then we may as well remove all organs from churches and refuse all discussion about the ethics of genome sequencing or molecular marker technology. The "Bible only" position is flawed from the outset.

Third, much of the exclusionist thinking tends to be developed in reaction to the world's erroneous thinking. Nouthetic counseling, for example, is focused on finding out one's sin. The exclusionist critique of secular psychology in denying sin and claiming it is *never* the problem is certainly correct. But that does not justify the opposite error of claiming that one's sin is always the problem. While in one sense all problems originate from sin, there is more than uncovering one's sin and awaiting confession in the healing of the soul. I find Adam's assertion that, "Nobody has an emotional problem; there is no such thing as an emotional problem"[73][74] quite alarming. Did not Jesus have an emotional problem in sweating blood in deep anguish (Luke 22:44) or Paul when his heart felt the sentence of death (2 Cor. 1:8-9), and does not God comfort the downcast (2 Cor. 7:6)? Further, just because Rogerian client-centered therapy shows little direction, one need not focus on confrontation. Christian counseling and therapy must be developed from the Scriptures and not in reaction to secular error. Such counseling can become quite doctrinaire and authority-focused in making the Bible the center.[75][76] One can easily make the Scriptures an "inquisitor's law book" and the pastoral counseling relationship a "moral inquisition."[77]

The Illusion of Non-Integration

Perhaps the main flaw of the "Bible only" exclusionist position is that in the final analysis, no one can avoid integration. Those in the "Bible only" camp have in fact already integrated even though it has not been fully recognized. Here are some examples.

Nouthetic counseling is a cognitive and behavioral approach with methods that use a "two-factored process of *dehabituation* and *rehabituation*."[78] While a cognitive and behavioral emphasis parallels some themes in Scripture, the real question is whether that is the major theme in Scripture.[79] This is implicit integration.

Nouthetic counselors have integrated the technical mindset with a focus on a system with pre-determined steps involving homework and assignments for the counselee.[80] The steps may help some, but will they help everyone with their built-in determinism? The focus is on solving a problem and working it out, a symptom

225

of the technical mindset. What if someone needed to simply expe-rience the love and healing presence of Jesus without any homework and hardly any questions? Any system will fall short of Jesus' pattern of ministry wherein Jesus did much more than confront or point to sin.[81] A system will never be as good as the presence of Jesus. I do not deny that nouthetic and other counselors acknowledge the role of the Holy Spirit. What happens in actual practice is what really counts. Clearly, integration has already occurred.

Some exclusionists have written against inner healing and the healing of memories, for example, by citing secular research from brain, memory and cognitive research along with their arguments from the Scriptures. But in so doing, they ascribe some measure of authority and legitimacy to secular research. This is even done when critiquing those who even appear to use secular research in their thinking. In short, they criticize integrationists *while using integrationist thinking.* The same authors will often cite the scien-tific invalidity of much of the secular research in psychology and related human "sciences." So science is valid when they want to use it and invalid when it does not serve their purposes.

Again I commend all my brothers and sisters in Christ on both sides of this debate. I merely wish to bring some more light where there tends to be too much heat. It is not a question of whether one integrates or not but how and how much and why. The goal, as always, is to remain faithful to Jesus and first seek His kingdom and His righteousness.

Aileen's Depression: Who Really Failed?

Aileen, a Christian woman in her late forties, came to my team for healing prayer. We could tell just by looking at her that she was liv-ing with discouragement and depression. With tears she slowly shared her story which included years of pain and disappointment.

In seeking help she had bought a number of popular self-help books written by Christian authors, tried everything that was suggested but with little improvement. She then saw several professional counselors that cost her time and money, and yet she was still not better at all. That was a huge disappointment, and she concluded that there was little hope for her and she was the reason for the failure. With more tears she said that she believed that she had failed her husband, her children, her church and ultimately God. The "wasted and lost" years and lack of fruitfulness seemed to haunt her.

After we had prayed for the Spirit to comfort Aileen still more, I said there was another interpretation for her situation. I told her that it was not that she had failed others and the Church but rather that the Church had failed her by using the methods and techniques of the world to attempt to transform her soul. The Church had not taught her how to pray and experience His presence. And that, I said, was truly depressing. I even went so far as to say that it was not all bad that the methods failed because if they had worked, she might have relied on them instead of the incomparable healing presence of Jesus. She replied that she had never thought of it that way, and she began to feel more hopeful.

After an hour of concentrated healing prayer, Jesus came and revealed some major causes of pain and deep shame, released her soul from all the pain and woundedness and in that short period of time her depression largely disappeared. Once again we see the power of Jesus' presence.

As was so true of Aileen and Anna-Marie in the beginning of this chapter, only Jesus can truly change people. Techniques cannot transform the human soul. When trying to overcome addictions, for example, attempts to change behavior and thinking patterns (cognitive behavior therapy, for example) really amount to sin-management techniques.[82] But this falls into the ancient heresy of

Pelagianism (sin is in the actions) and reduces Christian sanctification to controlling specific behaviors.[83] The techniques are further limited in practice because one's will and motives can be wounded or tainted by sin.[84] Our only hope is the cross of Christ, His blood, His precious presence and His work of inner transformation in us.

Modern man's self-absorption and preoccupation with the technical spirit in the end destroys personality. Man cannot engineer or transform himself. Even with all the psychological and therapeutic insights and techniques, man fails to truly understand himself.[85] As Gay wrote:

> ...real self-understanding appears further removed today than it was when the distinctively modern project of self-construction by means of rational technique began three hundred years ago... the contemporary quest for self-realization by means of psychological therapies of self-knowledge is, in other words, a cul-de-sac. By its very nature, the therapeutic quest for self-discovery must end in self-deception and, finally, in self-annihilation.[86]

That is the inevitable result when Jesus is excluded from the transformation of the human soul. We only come to truly know who we are when we encounter Jesus and His Father in the presence of the Spirit. Ultimately there is no substitute for Jesus. We only become true persons as we are connected to Jesus. Anna-Marie received a profound healing in the presence of Christ which years of therapy could not deliver. That healing was miraculous and permanent. Man cannot "figure himself out" or "fix himself" apart from God.

Endnotes

[1] Mark R. McMinn, *Psychology, Theology and Spirituality in Christian*

Counseling. AACC Counseling Library (Wheaton: Tyndale House Publisher, 1996) pp. 17-18.

[2] McMinn, p. xi.

[3] Roger F. Hurding, *Roots and Shoots: A Guide to Counselling and Psychotherapy* (London: Hodder and Stoughton, 1985) p. 28.

[4] Larry Crabb, *Connecting: Healing for Ourselves and Our Relationships, A Radical New Vision* (Nashville: Word Publishing, 1997) p. 195.

[5] Martin and Deidre Bobgan, *The End of "Christian Psychology"* (Santa Barbara: EastGate Publishers, 1997) pp. 68-71.

[6] McMinn, p. 13.

[7] Robyn M. Dawes, *House of Cards: Psychology and Psychotherapy Built on Myth* (New York: Free Press, 1994) p. 60.

[8] Thomas N. Hart, *The Art of Christian Listening* (New York: Paulist Press, 1980) p. 18.

[9] Dawes, p. 8.

[10] Dawes, p. 38.

[11] Dawes, pp. 5, 15.

[12] Dawes, p. 55.

[13] Hurding, p. 30.

[14] Crabb, pp. xvi-xvii, 191-207.

[15] Crabb, p. 192.

[16] Gary R. Collins, *Christian Counseling: A Comprehensive Guide* (Waco: Word Books Publisher, 1980) p. 22.

[17] Ibid.

[18] Dawes, p. 58.

[19] Dawes, p. 52.

[20] Dawes, p. 4.

[21] Dawes, p. 76.

[22] Lawrence J. Crabb Jr., *Basic Principles of Biblical Counseling* (Grand Rapids: Zondervan Publishing House, 1975) p. 15.

[23] Craig M. Gay, *The Way of the (Modern) World: Or, Why It's Tempt-*

ing to Live as if God Doesn't Exist (Grand Rapids: Eerdmans Publishing Company, 1998) p. 230.

[24] Stanton L. Jones and Richard E. Butman, *Modern Psychotherapies: A Comprehensive Christian Appraisal* (Downers Grove: InterVarsity Press, 1991) p. 11.

[25] Roger Hurding, *The Bible and Counselling* (London: Hodder and Stoughton, 1992) p. 47.

[26] Hurding, 1992, p. 49.

[27] Jones and Butman, p. 121.

[28] Hurding, 1992, p. 50.

[29] Paul C. Vitz, *Psychology as Religion: The Cult of Self-Worship* (Grand Rapids: Eerdmans Publishing Co., 1977) pp. 126-139.

[30] Hurding, 1992, pp. 50-51.

[31] Morton Kelsey, *Christianity as Psychology* (Minneapolis: Augsburg Publishing House, 1986) p. 23.

[32] Hurding, 1992, p. 48.

[33] Kelsey, p. 22.

[34] Jones and Butman, p. 31.

[35] Jones and Butman, pp. 349-351.

[36] Kelsey, p. 22.

[37] Robert C. Roberts, *Taking the Word to Heart: Self and Other in an Age of Therapies* (Grand Rapids: Eerdmans Publishing Co., 1993) p. 4.

[38] Ibid.

[39] Mary Stewart Van Leeuwen, *The Sorcerer's Apprentice: A Christian Looks at the Changing Face of Psychology* (Downers Grove: InterVarsity Press, 1982) p. 26.

[40] Van Leeuwen, pp. 26-48.

[41] Van Leeuwen, pp. 61-92.

[42] Van Leeuwen, p. 91.

[43] Hurding, 1985, p. 51.

[44] Van Leeuwen, p. 33.

[45] Nelson Hinman, *An Answer to Humanistic Psychology* (Irvine: Harvest House Publishers, 1980) p. 21.

[46] James Montgomery Boice, *Mind Renewal in a Mindless Age* (Grand Rapids: Baker Books, 1993) p. 77.

[47] Boice, p. 76.

[48] Hinman, p. 74.

[49] Grace M.H. Gayle, *The Growth of the Person: Psychology on Trial* (Belleville: Essence Publishers, 2001) p. 22.

[50] Paul Tournier, *The Whole Person in a Broken World* (New York: Harper & Row, 1964) p. 90.

[51] Jones and Butman, p. 382.

[52] Ibid.

[53] Jones and Butman, pp. 379-397.

[54] Hurding, 1985, p. 268.

[55] F.F. Bruce, *The Book of the Acts Revised: The New International Commentary on the New Testament* (Grand Rapids: Eerdmans Publishing Co., 1988) pp. 338-339.

[56] Gordon D. Fee, *The First Epistle to the Corinthians: The New International Commentary on the New Testament* (Grand Rapids: Eerdmans Publishing Co., 1987) p. 773.

[57] Oliver R. Barclay, *The Intellect and Beyond* (Grand Rapids: Academie Books, 1985) p. 74.

[58] McMinn, p. 33.

[59] Harry Piersma, "Christianity and Psychology: Some Reflections," *Journal of the American Scientific Affiliation*, Vol. 28(3), 1976, pp. 98-99.

[60] Piersma, p. 99.

[61] William Kirk Kilpatrick, *The Emporer's New Clothes: The Naked Truth About the New Psychology* (Westchester: Crossway Books, 1985) p. 42.

[62] Jones and Butman, p. 122.

[63] Kilpatrick, pp. 25-37.

[64] Van Leeuwen, p. 44.

[65] Paul C. Vitz, *Psychology as Religion. The Cult of Self-Worship* (Grand Rapids: Eerdmans Publishing Co., 1977)

[66] McMinn, p. 17.

[67] Roberts, p. 10.

[68] Lawrence J. Crabb Jr., *Effective Biblical Counseling* (Grand Rapids: Zondervan Publishing House, 1977) p. 47.

[69] Martin and Deidre Bobgan, *PsychoHeresy: The Psychological Seduction of Christianity* (Santa Barbara: EastGate Publishers, 1987).

[70] Richard Ganz, *PsychoBabble: The Failure of Modern Psychology—and the Biblical Alternative* (Wheaton: Crossway Books, 1993) pp. 61-72.

[71] Jay E. Adams, *Competent to Counsel* (Nutley: Presbyterian and Reformed Publishing Co., 1977) p. 45.

[72] Jones and Butman, p. 26.

[73] Hurding, 1985, p. 289.

[74] Adams, p. 53.

[75] Oates, p. 31.

[76] James A. Oakland and Gerald O. North, Rosemary Camilleri, Brent Stenberg, George Daniel Venable and Kenneth W. Bowers, "An Analysis and Critique of Jay Adams' Theory of Counseling," *Journal of the American Scientific Affiliation*, Vol. 28(3), 1976, pp. 108.

[77] Oates, p. 64.

[78] Hurding, 1985, p. 283.

[79] Jones and Butman, p. 219.

[80] Adams, pp. 193-203.

[81] Duncan Buchanan, *The Counselling of Jesus* (Downers Grove: InterVarsity Press, 1985) pp. 154-155.

[82] McMinn, p. 133.

[83] Ibid.

[84] McMinn, p. 136.

[85] Gay, p. 229.

[86] Ibid.

 Chapter Eight

Inner Healing: Avoiding Visualization and Mind Power

But I am afraid that just as Eve was deceived by the serpent's cunning, your minds may somehow be led astray from your sincere and pure devotion to Christ (2 Cor. 11:3).

Phyllis: Overcoming Fear, Self-Hatred and Extra Weight

Phyllis came for healing prayer for a number of reasons. The first one was for being somewhat overweight. She had followed all the recommendations of her nutritionist and dietitian who said there should be no reason for the extra weight since she was eating and exercising sensibly. On a deeper level, there were various fears. When I asked how long the fears had been with her, she replied that it had been basically lifelong. The major fear, she explained, was of being alone and also a fear of men.

I anointed her with oil, invoked the presence of Jesus and His Spirit and simply waited for a while before asking any more questions. When I asked her if she sensed or saw anything, she simply said she thought the Lord was reminding her about a memory from when she was two years old, but it was only a very vague memory. With no other direction at that point in the ministry session, I simply asked the Spirit to bring to remembrance anything that was important and to also further reveal this memory if that was where the healing was to come from. She explained that she only had a very faint memory of being under the wood frame of the house she lived in, near the front steps, at age two. The house was painted red and had a huge hedge all around it. I simply asked her to remain with the memory, allow her to be in touch with any of the feelings from that time and wait on the Lord.

Several minutes passed by in total silence, and I began to sense that the Lord would reveal more, but I had no idea what it was. She then said that she could remember the insects crawling around her and feeling afraid, and as a few more minutes went by, she could see a face. I asked if she could recognize the face and she said she could not, at least initially. My prayer partner and I simply waited a few more minutes in silence, asking the Spirit to reveal anything more that she needed to know. We did not give any "hints" as to what the event was about, nor in any way asked her to imagine or visualize anything.

She then said she sensed that before ending up underneath the house, she was given something to swallow and did not know what it was, but she did know that it was "not nice." We waited a few more minutes still and then she began to experience a sick, repulsive feeling in her stomach. She said that she almost wanted to throw up. At that moment I received a word of knowledge that she had been forced into oral sex, but I did not mention that to her or my prayer partner. I prayed for more of the peace of the Holy Spirit to come upon her and that the Lord would reveal everything needed for her healing that night.

After still a few more minutes she was struck by the sudden revelation that the face of the man was her own father. I asked her if she knew what she was forced to swallow, and she said that she knew, but she was obviously too embarrassed and ashamed to say what it was. There were a lot of tears. I then said that I could understand and told her what the Lord revealed to me and with still more tears she concurred.

After prayer for forgiveness towards her father, which she was ready to offer, I simply asked Jesus to heal her from the pain, shame, fear and disgust of this past event. As a small, two-year-old child, this was a devastating and deeply hurtful moment in her life. I did not know what Jesus would do, nor did I tell her to imagine or visualize anything. A few minutes passed again, and more peace came upon her. I asked her what had happened, and she said that Jesus actually came into that crawl space underneath the house, laid down beside her, put His arms around her and held her close. This was His way of relieving her of the fear and valuing her when she had been abandoned and devalued as a sex object. She said His presence was real, and she could feel it as she was sitting in our midst. All the pain of the memory, including the shame, had now disappeared from that past event and no longer affected her as an adult.

Phyllis then told us how this past event, not uncovered until now, explained so many other symptoms and problems in her sexuality and relationships with men as identified by counselors. I can see why Jesus did not bring back the entire memory at once. This event was very painful, involving sexual abuse by her own father, and would have been too much to bear all at once. Jesus knew how she would react, and He knew that it would be best to reveal things in stages, giving her enough time to accept each new revelation from the Spirit and adjust emotionally.

Some months later Phyllis wrote the following concerning an unexpected blessing from the prayer time:

> A week after you prayed with me I noticed that I wasn't biting my fingernails anymore. Since I was two I had bitten them until they bled. My nails are getting long, and I know it is because of what happened during our prayer time. I know God still has some work to do, and I am looking forward to being made whole.

The Presence of Jesus: Authentic or Visualization?

The ministry of healing prayer necessarily involves the presence of Jesus and His Spirit and the use of the spiritual gifts. For example in the prayer session with Phyllis as recounted above, Jesus brought healing into the pain of the past by bringing peace and comfort to her memories of a deeply painful time as a two-year-old girl.

But some would argue that this is not "biblical" at all and in fact has more to do with visualization techniques or New Age and occult practices. How does one discern the true presence of Jesus and avoid error and confusion in the ministry of healing prayer? Since inner healing is part of the wider scope of healing prayer, this is an important question.

Blazer, in assessing Seamand's examples of healing from damaged emotions which involves the presence of Christ in a memory, wrote that Seamands derived his approach from "behavioral therapies developed during the 1950s by psychiatrist Joseph Wolpe."[1] Basically, if a patient has a problem with fear, for example, they visualize the object of fear while relaxed and induce relaxation by relaxing muscles through imagining a peaceful experience like being at the beach.[2] Blazer then maintains that "Seamands therefore has put a spiritual spin on the behavioral therapy technique of reciprocal inhibition."[3] Thus walking through memories and experiencing Jesus' healing presence becomes just a psychological technique since the visualized presence of Jesus is the "induced relaxation."

Gumprecht, in critiquing Agnes Sanford's theology of healing, defined inner healing as:

> ...healing of the unconscious or subconscious through healing—counseling sessions which incorporate some of the mechanisms used for physical healing, such as meditation-visualization.[4]

Hunt and McMahon claim that visualization is the "major technique used for inner healing of the memories and even for healing at a distance."[5] They claim that any appearance of Jesus in healing prayer or the healing of memories is not only biblically unsound but also an occult or New Age practice involving visualization.[6] They consider the presence of Jesus in this context as nothing different from a New Age spirit guide.[7]

The ministry of healing prayer has been linked to Jungian techniques involving active imagination or visualization in order to enter the unconscious mind.[8] Matzat wrote:

> Those who promote the technique of visualization in inner healing and in Jungian mysticism claim that through visualization the real person of Jesus Christ is able to be encountered. The problem is: *The same technique of visualization used to allegedly encounter Jesus is used in occultism for the purpose of contacting spirit guides.*[9]

The Bobgans maintain that inner healing involves guided imagery and visualization.[10] They characterize inner healing as involving the recreation of memories wherein "Jesus" is brought into the memory by the inner healer in a way that the inner healer expects will bring some healing.[11] They conclude that inner healing is based on "faulty memory, guided imagery, fantasy, visualization and hypnotic-like suggestibility."[12] The Bobgans claim that Smith's Theophostic Counseling uses guided imagery, visualization and even hypnosis, thereby confusing the real Jesus with an imagined one.[13] This is in spite of the fact that Smith clearly disclaims such practices in his training manual and appeals to an authentic presence of Jesus.[14]

Is healing prayer or inner healing involving the appearance of Jesus really based on visualization techniques? Can we ever consider visualization a neutral technique and thus justify it because, after all, we seek Jesus?

The ministry of healing prayer involves the intentional and real presence of Jesus and His Spirit. One must decide if Jesus is always totally invisible and totally silent yet present (Matt. 18:20, 28:20b) or not always totally invisible and totally silent. This depends on one's theology of the Presence and one's being open, in practice, to His supernatural presence. Much confusion abounds in the books and articles written on inner healing, "healing of memories" and healing prayer because the authors rarely discuss the implicit assumption on the presence—or presumed functional absence—of Jesus. When the assumption is addressed, it is often dealt with simplistically.

Reports of an appearance of Jesus anywhere at all in this world before the second coming, including in memory, have been criticized by not a few writers. Matzat, for one, quoting Titus 2:13 where Paul wrote about waiting for the appearance of the glory of *"our great God and Saviour, Jesus Christ"* wrote that there will be no appearance or manifestation of the Lord Jesus until the end of this age.[15] Gumprecht, while affirming that Jesus is divine and not bound by time or space, nevertheless argued from passages like Mark 16:19 that Jesus is not traveling through our "personal time" and is "not appearing or disappearing now."[16] Jesus has ascended into heaven to be seated at the right hand of the Father and continues there (Ps. 110:1; Heb. 10:12).[17] Yet as shown in the chapter, "Understanding the Presence of Jesus," after the ascension this was not true and therefore such an interpretation of Titus 2:13 or Hebrews 10:12 is not biblically possible. Acts 23:11 alone, where Jesus appeared in resurrected bodily form to Paul, immediately demolishes such a view. Paul had in mind in Titus 2:13 the same thing he thought of in 2 Thessalonians 1:7—the second coming when Jesus is revealed in heaven in blazing fire with His powerful angels. This also holds true for 1 Peter 1:8 where Peter wrote to Christians who had not seen Jesus in the direct physical sense like the apostles had.

Clearly we must distinguish between the future public and worldwide appearance of Jesus and the personal, private, supernatural appearances of Jesus to any of His saints (John 14:21) at any time He chooses until the second coming. Considering the pre-incarnate and post-resurrection appearances of Christ, the Scriptures record that Jesus appeared in dreams, visions, a burning bush, a blazing fire and a flashing light, among others, as shown in the chapter, "Understanding the Presence of Jesus." Given the ways in which Jesus has appeared and that He is co-creator of the universe and the Lord of time and thus eternally present to all of time, it is no surprise at all that He *may* appear in someone's memory in a moment of healing prayer.

Healing Prayer and the Real Presence: Avoiding Counterfeits

Since Jesus can have a localized presence today as a person of the Trinity, we need to adjust our theology to allow for this. Jesus is divine and the Lord of time. There is nothing in the Scriptures that prohibits His presence in a memory in healing prayer, for example. Jesus sees all of time before Him, and He can be contemporaneous to all of time. The book of Revelation itself is an example of someone in the present able to see into and experience the future, being in the Spirit (Rev. 1:10, 4:2) and in the presence of Jesus (Rev. 1:12-18). But please note very clearly: Jesus is Lord and He reveals His presence how and when He will and never ever in response to any attempt on our part to conjure His presence or manipulate reality by any type of visualization. Any such notion is evil since it attempts to put a person at the center of the universe with the Lord as an object under one's control.

It is entirely possible that there are some who use visualization techniques to "help" Jesus appear as in the ministry of healing prayer. That is an unbiblical and dangerous practice. While it may "look good" on the surface, it borders on control and manipulation of reality and may well open one up to powers of the mind and occult seduction. If one attempts to visualize Jesus, one must then decide how "Jesus" will appear and what He will do. Effectively this puts the visualizer in control of his or her own healing with a spiritual technique instead of submission to the presence and will of Jesus.

Wright advocated imagery exercises to help overcome the pain of the past.[18] Maybe you have confessed past sins to the Lord but never felt His forgiveness. Apparently you can experience freedom from guilt through the following exercise.[19] First, you relax with your eyes closed and visualize a large blackboard with words and phrases concerning those past sins written on it. Then you visualize Jesus beside the blackboard erasing the words and asking you to come to Him and put your hand in His to feel His hand erasing the words. Thus you experience His forgiveness. Then you visualize Jesus placing His hand on your shoulder and directly speaking forgiveness to you. Wright concluded that, "You may need to run this picture and sequence through your mind again and again until, through imaging, you experience the acceptance and forgiveness that are yours."[20] Wright outlined other imaging exercises such as "role-rehearsal runs" to overcome anxiety [21] or picturing oneself as a child and then visualizing Jesus speaking His loving acceptance so that one can re-parent oneself to overcome rejection.[22]

While Wright affirms the presence of Christ and the Spirit [23] in the believer's life, and some people may have been helped by the above exercises, the approach to healing is not centered in the true presence of Jesus. The very fact that one often has to repeat the exercises reveals its lack of power and reality. Since such techniques are used to improve success in sports,[24] how could they ever be adequate to transform the human soul? This is another example of spiritual technique that puts man at the center and Jesus in a lesser role as subject to technical determinism. Why not let Jesus actually and directly speak and touch one's being in whatever way He chooses, as shown by the examples in this book? What if one's pain is so deep nothing but the love and actual presence of Jesus can heal and restore? What if a person is so depressed they cannot even get past the second step? Why not let Jesus determine what will happen and when?

In the ministry the Lord has given me and many others that I know, I *never* suggest to a person that they visualize Jesus. I typically ask Jesus to come and minister to the person as He wills and chooses and after some time ask the person receiving prayer what is happening—what they might see, hear or feel. If the person sees Jesus with their spiritual eyes, it is up to that person to tell me what Jesus is doing. There is no pre-conceived expectation of what Jesus will do or say or how and even if He will appear. Jesus is Lord of one's healing just as He is the Lord of all. To visualize in such a context is not wise; it is an attempt to manipulate His presence and thus reality. The scriptural model is for Jesus to show up how and when He chooses and sometimes in ways that truly surprise us. A number of times, quite unexpectedly in my presence, the person receiving prayer actually felt Jesus' hand on his shoulder or even felt Jesus hugging him. These are among the ways that He might manifest His presence (Matt. 28:20).

We can use our imagination in godly ways, like reflecting on Scripture and meditating, but never to control or manipulate. One only "imagines" in healing prayer as one looks up to Jesus, asking for His revelation and words to one's heart and mind. Sometimes false images come from one's unhealed or confused inner being and heart, past trauma, the world or the enemy of our souls. Some people have nightmares and dreams with vivid scenes—images—so one cannot avoid dealing with images and the imagination. Imaging and visualization can lead to subjectivism, man-centeredness, an unhealthy reliance to the exclusion of sound biblical teaching and a mixture with Neo-Gnosticism and materialism.[25] The challenge is to have the right understanding of Jesus, the Father and oneself not only in thought, but also in pictures and images as one truly comprehends reality. Our imagination must be used as God intended lest it become an idol of the mind.

Healing prayer and "inner healing" do not involve hypnosis, sorcery, visualization, magic, psychoanalysis or psychological technique. It does not involve leading questions and suggestion until "the patient finally dredged up some hurt from the past" as some allege.[26] It has everything to do with experiencing more of Jesus and His love. Since the Holy Spirit is the counselor and Jesus leads us into all truth, it is not an issue of false or fabricated memories. Phyllis' memory, as recounted above, came back slowly under the direction of the Spirit, and it was real.

John and Mark Sandford noted the misuse of the imagination by another author of inner healing with an example of a person with a brutal father. The person would be led in prayer to imagine or picture Jesus coming to him as the hurt child and to also imagine and picture the father as kind and gentle.[27] However, this avoids repentance for any judgments against the father or the need to forgive, continues a lie and is an example of "mind games."[28] The pictures or images and any vision of Christ must all be initiated by Christ Himself and His Spirit and are thus in accord with the written Word, never bypassing sin, the cross and truth. Virkler wrote that in prayer ministry we must never "control or guide Jesus" or "paint scenes of our choosing" but rather fix our eyes on Jesus, follow His lead and rely on the revelation of the Spirit.[29] Dearing voices a similar caution when praying for healing from pain of the past:

> When praying for another person, it is important not to dictate what the Lord does in this memory. Dictating the Lord's involvement is called "guided imagery" and is the reason inner healing has been criticized by some as being New Age. The Lord taught me long ago that my job as a prayer minister is only to invite Him into the memory. He does all the rest.[30]

On several occasions I have encountered a false Jesus not unlike Smith reported.[31] A Jesus "came" and did something in a memory that is uncharacteristic of the true Jesus of Nazareth. This occurred because the person had either engaged in past visualizations, had been led down this path by such a prayer ministry or had received a spirit guide thereby opening a door to the occult. We know that Satan himself can masquerade as an angel of light and deceive people (2 Cor. 11:14). When this happened, I just rebuked the evil presence and asked the true Jesus to be in complete control whether He "appeared" or not. From that moment there was a complete turn-around in the ministry session.

In my experience, in perhaps two-thirds of healing prayer sessions the person receiving prayer has a very strong sense of the presence of Jesus, typically seeing Him in a memory. This was true of Cindy when Jesus released her from all the pain of her abortion as recounted in the beginning of the chapter, "Understanding the Presence of Jesus."

His more direct presence is not strictly always necessary for healing. For the other prayer ministry sessions, there is usually a sense of release or greater well-being. It is a fundamental error, therefore, to minister healing prayer by asking anyone to visualize Jesus since He does not always manifest His presence to heal His people. It could well be that the presence of His Spirit is all that is necessary for that prayer session. Sometimes it is just not the appointed time; the *kairos* (God-ordained special event time) moment is not yet. When there is no noticeable effect or feeling, it does not mean nothing has happened or that some healing has not begun. The person coming for prayer might harbor unforgiveness, disbelief, a secret sin or disobedience in an area of their life, any of which can hinder ministry. In any case Jesus is always present (Matt. 18:20), and He always does love us. We must never become more excited about the sense of His presence than His actual presence. Whether one sees Jesus or not, or has an expected manifestation or not, that is not what counts. It has all to do with fruit in one's life, becoming more like Jesus, discipleship, sanctification and experiencing more of the love of Jesus—in short, living by grace. The appearances of Jesus discussed in this book and experienced in healing prayer happen as Jesus Himself decides and initiates and never in response to any visualization or imagination technique.

Jill: Healing from Sexual Abuse

Dr. David Lewis, a cultural anthropologist at the University of Cambridge, wrote about the true story of Jill, a seventeen-year old girl, who directly received healing from Jesus for deep trauma and emotional pain when she was four years old.[32] While this girl lived with her pastor's family, the Lord appeared to her in visions and led her back to those memories. Jesus personally ministered to her, bringing deep healing from prolonged horrific sexual and other forms of abuse. This was all initiated by Jesus, not by any healing prayer with her and did not involve suggestion of any kind. After a few months of His appearances, Jesus assured her that she was healed and then the visions ceased. Her healing has been complete such that she has trained as a psychiatric nurse and is especially able to work with sexually abused children.

Darrin: Healing for the True Masculine

The following is the testimony of a pastor who has been personally experiencing more of the healing presence of Jesus, often apart from healing prayer time with another person. Since no one was leading him in inner healing and the visions were unexpected, it has nothing to do with guided imagery or visualization. These healing encounters occurred after healing prayer sessions many months earlier, some of which I had the joy and privilege of being a part of. Darrin wrote:

> Dieter, here is what Jesus showed me during the worship times at the recent Deeper Love Ministries conference. It took me a little while to understand the full significance of these visions. God was "reprogramming" how I saw Him as a Father. My earthly father was a good man but also very negative, and He didn't take the time to play with me. So

245

up until even a few months ago I could not fully receive God's blessings and promises because I felt He was unpleased with me and "negative" toward me most of the time. Actually, I should back up. As I said, a few months ago God began giving my wife and me many wonderful promises, but I could not fully believe in them, so I asked Jesus to show me why. Immediately He said that I viewed Him as negative, just like my dad. This in itself was an amazing revelation because I was praying alone.

A few weeks later Jesus gave me the first vision, again while I was alone in prayer. I saw Jesus and me—in the vision I was about four to six years old—sitting on a beautiful riverbank, dangling our feet into the water. He was laughing and holding me affectionately close to His side. I wept for a while because it totally reframed how Jesus was—not negative, not displeased with me, not scolding but the polar opposite. Then, a few weeks later at the conference, He gave me two more visions of His character. In the first, during the Friday worship, Jesus and I were playing tag—again I was four to six years old—in a beautiful green meadow with bits of flower petals flowing in the breeze as we would run after each other. It was very vivid. He would run a few feet ahead of me and look back laughing and smiling as I would try to tag Him. Then on Saturday, again during worship at the conference, I saw a vision of Jesus and I playing soccer in the yard of the home in which I grew up. As a kid I knew my dad would not be interested in playing soccer, so I don't think I even asked him to play very often. Much later in life my dad told me how harsh, negative and un-affirming his own father was and how that affected his fathering. Jesus was a good soccer player, but the fun He was having being with me was such powerful healing because this is the true picture of the Father.

About a week ago, while praying in my office, Jesus showed me a rapid series of pictures of Him doing four main things that I enjoyed doing when I was a bit older. Around eight to ten years old, I saw myself playing with my slingshot, playing with the bow and arrows, riding my little dirt-bike (motorcycle) and snowmobile. Jesus was with me in every one of those activities. He then told me that when an earthly father intentionally spends time and plays with his son, that is how the true masculine is built into a boy. So now Jesus is specifically healing me in this area—the true masculine. It is humbling, deeply moving and extremely exciting to describe what Jesus is doing... I could go on and on.

Powers of the Human Mind for Healing?

The ministry of healing prayer relies totally and absolutely on the grace and love of Jesus and not at all on anyone's power to imagine or skill or mastery at visualization. Jill's encounter with Jesus directly challenges the allegation that inner healing involves suggestion or visualization techniques since it only involved Jesus and herself. Similarly Roberta experienced Jesus' healing presence quite unexpectedly one Saturday night, as recounted in the chapter, "Healing and Restoring the Soul." No one was there to lead Roberta in healing prayer, nor did she know of or use any visualization or imaging technique whatsoever. Jesus, with His Spirit, simply decided to minister to her. Darrin was not expecting any such visions from Jesus; they were completely and spontaneously initiated by Jesus. Given the compassion of Jesus and how He joyfully and gently received children in His arms and blessed them (Mark 10:13-16), it is not hard to believe in His appearances to Darrin.

Now instead of unwisely visualizing Jesus to bring healing, some writers have advocated the visualization or imaging of a person healed or a healing process to bring healing. The shift is now from an imagined presence of Jesus to the power of the human mind to effect a healing.

Agnes Sanford, an early writer in the ministry of healing prayer, advocated the method of creative imagination for healing, especially physical healing. She outlined four steps in her method: (1) Choose one symptom or weakness to pray about; (2) Form the prayer to suggest the healed condition; (3) Make a picture in the imagination of the objective of prayer and recall the picture or image whenever or if the symptom recurs; (4) Give thanks that God's healing power is entering to bring wholeness.[33] She explained the third step's power of the mind where we:

> ...create in our minds the picture of that person well. Thus we set in motion our powers of spiritual creativity. Those things that we see in our minds tend to become so. This is a law as certain as the law of gravity and to this law we shall return again and again. Let us draw the image in our minds. Let us make the blueprint. Let us dwell at the time of prayer and at all other times, whenever the person comes to mind, on the picture of that one well.[34]

Sanford believed in the power of imagination to bring healing.[35] [36] [37] [38] She acknowledged this is really the power of positive thinking which was taught by Jesus, but He simply called it faith.[39] Positive thinking apparently has an actual power as does negative thinking. Apparently Jesus taught about faith as positive thinking, like in moving mountains (Mark 11:23-24), or negative thinking, like evil thoughts (Matt. 15:19) causing evil behavior. She wrote, "we create by thought, whether we want to do so or not"[40] and stated that she taught this in all her books.[41] She understood faith as the use of visual imagination to "construct in the mind carefully the picture of the thing that one desires and to train the mind to dwell upon that picture"[42] and advocated "mental training."[43] When interceding for others, she believed that by seeing or remembering them as ill one actually "fastens sickness" upon them and therefore they will not get well.[44] She wrote how a minister was healed from painful memories solely by her imagining him as a boy meeting Jesus and then visioning Jesus entering his subconscious.[45]

Other writers besides Sanford have advocated the power of the mind. Peale promoted mental imaging as a technique to solve many of life's problems and needs, including healing. His basic premise is that "there is a powerful and mysterious force in human nature that is capable of bringing about dramatic improvement in our lives. It is a kind of mental engineering…."[46] He defined it as follows:

> Imaging is positive thinking carried one step further. In imaging, one does not merely think about a hoped-for goal; one "sees" or visualizes it with a tremendous intensity, reinforced by prayer. Imaging is a kind of laser beam of the imagination, a shaft of mental energy in which the desired goal or outcome is pictured so vividly by the conscious mind that the unconscious mind accepts it and is activated by it. This releases powerful internal forces that can bring about astonishing changes in the life of the person who is doing the imaging.[47]

Peale wrote that the promise of Jesus concerning believing prayer (Mark 11:24) stands behind mental imaging.[48] Imaging, in addition to hope, faith and truth, can help one recover from illness or prevent illness.[49] Apparently a man was healed of cancer by, in addition to prayer and faith, imaging or visualizing his white blood cells attacking the cancerous cells.[50] Peale referred to Kimmell's imaging technique to overcome tension wherein one visualizes all unhealthy thoughts causing the tension to leave the body and then visualizes good thoughts taking their place.[51] Imaging can be positive thus bringing victory, or negative with resulting defeat.[52] The technique of "mind drainage" involves imaging negative emotions like fear and anxiety literally being drained from one's mind.[53] A woman apparently restored her marriage from her husband's adulterous affair by repeatedly picturing the new relationship, his better qualities and harmony in the home.[54] Christ must be the "silent partner" in all imaging to ensure the right goal or aim.[55] Peale applied the method of positive imaging to everyday problems like loneliness, financial worries, one's self-image, anxiety and more, with a final admonition to stay close to Jesus.[56] Peale was aware of Sanford's book, *The Healing Light*.[57]

Many psychological techniques have been developed from the basic idea of mental imaging. Wright, for example, presented techniques of mental imaging in order to overcome fears.[58]

But do we really need mental imaging in healing prayer? How theologically sound is mental imaging or the power of creative thinking? We certainly must believe in prayer and the power of the Holy Spirit,[59] grow in faith, nurture hope, think positively (Phil. 4:8), avoid pessimism and negativity, experience the power of God and exercise a vital and living faith. Images are part of everyday life and certainly true for artists, sculptors, inventors, scientists, architects and others. One can appreciate the appeal to positive thinking and hope in the midst of the Depression with its gloom in everyday life.[60] But one cannot so easily support the idea of the powers of the human mind with the Scriptures. In fact it raises more problems.

The *object* of one's faith is as important—indeed even more important—as having faith in the first place. The object of faith must always be Jesus, the Father (Mark 11:22), His promises, grace, mercy, love and faithfulness, not the powers of one's mind or imagination. This is a subtle but significant point.

Jesus did not teach about negative thoughts to underline the power of the human mind but rather to highlight the nature of sin and the absolute need to live by His grace, forgiveness and mercy in order to surpass the righteousness of the Pharisees. Jesus taught on what truly makes a person "unclean" (Matt. 15:19-20, cf. Gal. 5:19-21, Titus 2:11-12), the deep issues of the heart and the power of sin and not on the power of the human mind. The Sermon on the Mount shows how impossible it is to live by our own will power and resources and thus our utter need for Jesus and our personal relationship with the Father.

The apparent power of negative thoughts can be challenged since negative thoughts do not always bring about negative consequences. For example Elijah, Jonah and others wanted to die (1 Kings 19:4; Jonah 4:3), but that did not happen.[61] Even though David prayed when deeply depressed, his prayer was soon answered (2 Sam. 15:30-32; 17:1-23).[62] Fortunately the grace of God prevailed in these situations.

A focus on mind power is flawed since the mind is not just simply free to "create reality." The mind is not free from the power of sin (Rom. 7:23-25), can even be corrupt (1 Tim. 6:5), its thoughts must be taken captive (2 Cor. 10:5) and must be renewed (Rom. 12:2). One's will can be in bondage to sin which impacts the mind's resolve and direction. Anyone struggling with pornography or lustful thoughts and the typical lurid images in the mind recognizes the need for liberation and wholeness, not the supposed reality of mind power. Given the reality of sin and temptation and its effect on the mind, we need Jesus and His grace far more than techniques in mind power.

Sanford, like other writers, quoted Proverbs 23:7 from the King James Version—*"as he thinketh in his heart, so is he"* (KJV)—in support of man's power to "create by thought."[63] But such an interpretation wrenches the verse totally out of context. The verse is a warning about eating with a stingy man and craving his delicacies. No matter how generous he pretends to be and invites you to eat and feast, it is not reality because, despite appearances, *"his heart is not with you."* In other words, as he thinks in his heart, so is he in reality. It is about consistency, not power to create one's being. The implication is that there is no real fellowship during the meal because he might ask for favors later; the meal involves manipulation since his heart never truly was with you but for himself all along. Furthermore the oft-quoted phrase is a questionable King James translation. The NIV more reliably renders it, *"...for he is the kind of man who is always thinking about the cost. 'Eat and drink,' he says to you, but his heart is not with you."* Proverbs 23:7 simply does not support the power of positive thinking.

The sovereignty and purposes of God directly challenge the power of positive thinking and imaging. The Lord's purposes prevail over the plans in one's hearts coming from one's thoughts (Prov. 19:21), and the Lord even determines one's steps (Prov. 16:9, 20:24). Control over life's circumstances, whether by the power of the mind or intelligence or strength, is pure illusion since: *"The race is not to the swift or the battle to the strong, nor does food come to the wise or wealth to the brilliant or favor to the learned; but time and chance happen to them all"* (Eccl. 9:11).

God maintains the universe according to His will and purposes and no mental power will change this:

> *Consider what God has done: Who can straighten what he has made crooked? When times are good, be happy; but when*

times are bad, consider; God has made the one as well as the other. Therefore, a man cannot discover anything about his future (Eccl. 7:13-14).

We do not even know about tomorrow since it all depends on God's will (Jas. 4:13-16). Technique implies control, and mental technique puts man in control as God is expected to work in response. Thus "…mental processes are or can become omnipotent: they can become 'as God' which takes us back to the Garden of Eden."[64]

Righteous living is more important than mental technique. We influence the future positively, not by the power of our minds but by trusting in the Lord (Jer. 17:7), living righteously (Jer. 17:10; Ps. 1:1-2) and hoping in God's unfailing love as we fear Him (Ps. 147:5-11). At times healing comes directly from obedience (Isa. 58:6-8). Blessing and prosperity come from fearing the Lord (Ps. 128:1-2). Joseph (Gen. 39:3) and David (1 Sam. 18:14) were successful in all they did, not fundamentally because they practiced the power of positive thinking or mental imaging but because the Lord was with them. The power of the Lord's presence was more important than the powers of the mind. Hezekiah (1 Kings 18:5-7) and Jehoshaphat (2 Chr. 20:20) believed that trusting in the Lord was the key to success. We live by God's grace and blessings, not by mental technique.

Trusting in the powers of one's mind amounts to trusting in man which is strongly admonished in the Scriptures (Jer. 17:5; Isa. 2:22; Ps. 147:10). The apostle Paul experienced severe hardship so that he would not rely on himself, or any powers within himself, but only on God (2 Cor. 1:8-10). We are "jars of clay" to show that any power is not from us but from God (2 Cor. 4:7). Strength, success and victory come from God and not from within ourselves (Judg. 7:2; Deut. 8:17, 8:18; Ps. 44:3; Isa. 10:13-14; Jer. 9:23-24) lest we be tempted into pride.

Mind power and positive thinking use techniques with steps leading to a pre-determined result. How can one be so sure the "image" is what God intends? What if a secret sin, or a deep-rooted lie, or a need for obedience or discipleship in the sick person is blocking the healing? What if an evil spirit of infirmity is causing the illness? No amount of positive thinking or mind power will ever help. Reliance on spiritual technique inevitably leads to reductionism and determinism.

The focus on mind power and its spiritual or psychological techniques typically comes from a mechanistic view of the universe. For example while Peale emphasized the importance of a true faith in Jesus and His Spirit,[65] he also wrote that prayer releases spiritual energy through its own scientific procedures, techniques and formulae.[66] Apparently Christianity is somewhat scientific since the Bible contains "a system of techniques and formulas designed for the understanding and treatment of human nature."[67] Peale wrote that prayer sends out vibrations into the universe which itself is vibrating, thereby using forces "inherent in a spiritual universe" to realize one's objectives.[68] Apparently power from the "Higher Power" is always available and can be accessed by anyone in any situation.[69] But that overlooks the fact that, apart from the atoning work of Christ upon the cross, a person is not reconciled to God or in relationship with God (Rom. 5:10; 2 Cor. 5:18; Col. 1:22) and thus cannot draw upon this power at will. Further, a technical view of the universe is completely at odds with living by grace in a personal relationship with Jesus and the Father.

The reliance on the supposed powers of the mind tends to put man at the center instead of God. *The focus must be on the power of the risen Christ in our midst, not the power of our minds.* Receiving images from the Holy Spirit for understanding and direction in healing is totally different from creating an image in one's mind in order to "make a person well." One of Peale's examples in support of imaging is most likely an example of personal prophecy. Mary Crowe, the young daughter of a miner and from a poor family during the Depression, one day received a vivid image of her graduating from a college.[70] By God's amazing provision she received the money to attend a college she had never seen before, and incredibly the campus was exactly as she had seen in the image.

Peale, Sanford and others point to many testimonials and stories of people who found the techniques successful. But might there have been other reasons that contributed to a positive outcome, or did it sometimes happen in spite of the mental technique? What of the times when the mental technique did not work? What about the thousands of other stories where people were healed or were "successful" without mental imaging or the power of creative imagination or the power of positive thinking? What about those who cannot follow the steps of these mental techniques due to deep wounds of the soul from the past, or depression or a spiritual blockage in believing in the love and goodness of a heavenly Father?

The whole thrust of the power of positive thinking or mental imaging is to achieve a certain result in healing or "success" in some area in life. Although authors like Sanford and Peale also write about a personal relationship with Jesus, the promotion of any mental technique is at the expense of a relationship with Jesus. Consider 1 John 5:14-15:

> *This is the assurance we have in approaching God: that if we ask anything according to his will, he hears us. And if we know that he hears us—whatever we ask—we know that we have what we asked of him.*

Strictly speaking, where is the need for mental imaging or the power of positive thinking or the power of creative imagination in

1 John 5:14-15? Why do we now need to insert mental techniques between asking and receiving? This passage and many others like it (Matt. 7:7-11, 18:19, 21:22; John 14:13-14, 15:7, 15:16) reveal that the way to realize any goal or imagined result in life is relational, not technical. It rests on the depth of our relationship with God, our confidence in His presence, knowing His will and finally His character and faithfulness. It does not rest on our ability to focus repeatedly on a mental image until it seeps into our consciousness and then releases power. That is entirely different from fervent, persistent prayer to our heavenly Father. Mental techniques may actually be a handicap since God already wants to do in our lives much *"more than all we ask or **imagine**, according to his power that is at work within us"* (Eph. 3:20). Such techniques begin to take us away from a sincere and pure devotion to Christ (2 Cor. 11:3) and entangle us with basic principles and human traditions of the world (Col. 2:8). Studying and using these techniques can draw one away from loving God and one's neighbor to focusing on one's self and self-empowerment.[71] In fact involvement with that type of literature can even alienate a person from God.[72]

These techniques, however well intentioned, have more to do with the human potential movement and the North American preoccupation with "success" than the Scriptures. Self-help and positive thinking have their roots in William Jame's American philosophy of pragmatism which has greatly influenced evangelical thinking and practice to this day.[73] Religion becomes spiritual technology and a "power to which we are adjusted for the sake of gaining our own power."[74]

Phyllis did not need the power of positive thinking or mental imaging to overcome her fears. She did not need to learn mental exercises to "image herself" as without fear or anxiety. But she did need the power of His positive presence led by a simple devotion to Jesus and a faith in a loving, heavenly Father. She experienced the healing presence of Jesus under the direction of the Holy Spirit. *There is simply no real substitute for His authentic presence.*

Endnotes ——————

1 Dan Blazer, *Freud vs. God: How Psychiatry Lost Its Soul & Christianity Lost Its Mind* (Downers Grove: InterVarsity Press, 1998) p. 160.

2 Ibid.

3 Ibid.

4 Jane Gumprecht, *Abusing Memory: The Healing Theology of Agnes Sanford* (Moscow: Canon Press, 1997) p. 97.

5 Dave Hunt and T.A. McMahon, *The Seduction of Christianity* (Eugene: Harvest House Publishers, 1985) p. 114.

6 Hunt and McMahon, pp. 172-173.

7 Ibid.

8 Don Matzat, *Inner Healing: Deliverance or Deception?* (Eugene: Harvest House Publishers, 1987) p. 67.

9 Matzat, p. 80.

10 Martin and Deidre Bobgan, *Competent to Minister: The Biblical Care of Souls* (Santa Barbara: EastGate Publishers, 1996) p. 202.

11 Ibid.

12 Bobgan, p. 204.

13 Martin and Deidre Bobgan, *Theophostic Counseling: Divine Revelation or PsychoHeresy?* (Santa Barbara: EastGate Publishers, 1999) pp. 69-94.

14 Ed M. Smith, *Beyond Tolerable Recovery* (Campbellsville: Alathia Publishing, 1996, 4th ed. 2000) p. 15.

15 Matzat, p. 65.

16 Gumprecht, p. 103.

17 Ibid.

18 H. Norman Wright, *Making Peace with Your Past* (Old Tappan:

Fleming H. Revell Co., 1985) p. 50.

[19] Wright, 1985, p. 51.

[20] Ibid.

[21] Wright, 1985, p. 57.

[22] Wright, 1985, pp. 98-99.

[23] Wright, 1985, pp. 10-12.

[24] Wright, 1985, p. 55.

[25] Leanne Payne, *The Healing Presence: How God's Grace Can Work in You to Bring Healing in Your Broken Places and the Joy of Living in His Love* (Wheaton: Crossway Books, 1989) pp. 152-154.

[26] Gumprecht, p. 106.

[27] John and Mark Sandford, *Deliverance and Inner Healing: A Comprehensive Guide* (Grand Rapids: Chosen Books, 1992) p. 80.

[28] Ibid.

[29] Mark and Patti Virkler, *Prayers that Heal the Heart* (Gainesville: Bridge-Logos Publishers, 2001) pp. 152-153.

[30] Norma Dearing, *The Healing Touch: A Guide to Healing Prayer for Yourself and Those You Love* (Grand Rapids: Chosen Books, 2002) p. 134.

[31] Smith, 139.

[32] David C. Lewis, "A Social Anthropologist's Analysis of Contemporary Healing," pp. 329-331, in Gary S. Greig and Kevin N. Springer, ed., *The Kingdom and the Power: Are Healing and the Spiritual Gifts Used by Jesus and the Early Church Meant for the Church Today?* (Ventura: Regal Books, 1993) pp. 329-331.

[33] Agnes Sanford, *The Healing Gifts of the Spirit* (Philadelphia: Trumpet Books, A.J. Holman Co., 1976) pp. 49-50.

[34] Agnes Sanford, *The Healing Touch of God* (New York: Ballantine Books, 5th printing, 1987. First published in 1958 by Macalester Publishing Co. as *Behold Your God*) p. 37.

[35] Sanford, 1976, p. 55.

[36] Agnes Sanford, *The Healing Light* (Plainfield: Logos International, 1976, originally published in 1947 by Macalester Park Publishing Co.) p. 26.

[37] Sanford, 1987, p. 72.

[38] Agnes Sanford, *Creation Waits* (Plainfield: Logos International, 1977) p. 118.

[39] Sanford, 1987, p. 38.

[40] Ibid.

[41] Sanford, 1977, pp. 122, 126.

[42] Sanford, 1987, p. 42.

[43] Sanford, 1947, p. 161.

[44] Agnes Sanford, *Sealed Orders* (Plainfield: Logos International, 1972) p. 149.

[45] Sanford, 1987, pp. 74-75.

[46] Norman Vincent Peale, *Positive Imaging: The Powerful Way to Change Your Life* (New York: Fawcett Crest, 1982, formerly published as *Dynamic Imaging*) p. 1.

[47] Peale, 1982, pp. 1-2.

[48] Peale, 1982, p. 1.

[49] Peale, 1982, pp. 86-100.

[50] Peale, 1982, pp. 6-7.

[51] Peale, 1982, p. 135.

[52] Peale, 1982, p. 17.

[53] Norman Vincent Peale, *The Power of Positive Thinking* (Englewood Cliffs: Prentice-hall, Inc., 1956) pp. 22, 145.

[54] Peale, 1956, pp. 57-58.

[55] Peale, 1982, p. 31.

[56] Peale, 1982, pp. 189-190.

[57] Peale, 1982, p. 186.

[58] H. Norman Wright, *The Healing of Fears* (Eugene: Harvest House Publishers, 1982) pp. 93-144.

[59] Sanford, 1976, p. 56.

[60] Peale, 1982, p. 18.

[61] John Weldon and Zola Levitt, *Psychic Healing* (Chicago: Moody Press, 1982) p. 214.

[62] Ibid.

[63] Sanford, 1987, 38.

[64] Weldon and Levitt, p. 214.

[65] Norman Vincent Peale, *The Positive Power of Jesus Christ* (Wheaton: Tyndale Publishers, Inc., 1980) pp. 37, 99.

[66] Peale, 1956, pp. 52-55.

[67] Peale, 1956, p. 220.

[68] Peale, 1956, p. 61.

[69] Peale, 1956, p. 267.

[70] Peale, 1982, p. 4.

[71] Nelson E. Hinman, *An Answer to Humanistic Psychology* (Irvine: Harvest House Publishers, 1980) p. 38.

[72] Ibid.

[73] Os Guiness, *Fit Bodies Fat Minds: Why Evangelicals Don't Think and What to Do About It* (Grand Rapids: Baker Books, 1994) pp. 55-59.

[74] Guiness, pp. 57-58.

 Chapter Nine

Early Influences on Healing Prayer: The Need for Discernment

Dear friends, do not believe every spirit, but test the spirits to see whether they are from God, because many false prophets have gone out into the world (1 John 4:1).

Agnes Sanford: Pioneer of Healing Prayer

Agnes Sanford has been acknowledged by many as a pioneer in healing prayer, especially since her book, *The Healing Light*, first published in 1947. Bennett, writing in 1982, acknowledged that many involved in the healing movement "owe their start to Agnes Sanford's inspiration and teaching."[1] Payne referred to Agnes Sanford as a "magnificent trailblazer in the art of healing prayer."[2] Pearson acknowledged Sanford as a pioneer of spiritual healing in the mainline churches.[3] The Sandfords wrote that Agnes Sanford was known worldwide as the pioneer for healing among mainline churches and a forerunner on the healing of the inner man.[4] Wise, who knew Sanford, described her as authentic, orthodox, having an "acute sense of the transcendence and mystery of God" with a mystical bent and having a strong desire and compassion for healing, among other qualities.[5] Her Schools of Pastoral Care have influenced thousands of Christians, and her teaching has impacted many Christians, including those in the charismatic movement.

Understandably writers often equate Sanford's teachings and books as the foundational or definitive statement and description of inner healing or the healing of memories. While Wise and many others would vouch for the strong orthodox and Christian foundation in her teaching and books, others describe her as basically New Age or New Thought.[6] Some writers even labeled her as a champion of the occult.[7] Ganz wrote that Sanford popularized receptive visualization techniques with their ancient roots in Tantric yoga as well as some of Jung's teaching—most notably the "collective unconscious" and individuation.[8] Ganz maintained that Jungian teaching, as advocated by Sanford, is behind the current practice of "receptive visualization" in the Church and "particularly in healing ministries."[9]

Where does the truth lie? What accounts for such a divergence of opinion? If her teaching and theology is not completely Christian and is in fact even somewhat New Age and she is the pioneer of inner healing and the "healing of memories," are such practices also in error and maybe even dangerous? Is it true that everyone, or even mostly everyone, involved in inner healing today bases their theology and practice on Agnes Sanford's works and the alleged Jungian influences? These are important questions for the theology of healing prayer today. To begin, one must take a close look at her writings.

I have never met Agnes Sanford personally, nor did I ever have the opportunity to attend any of her Schools. My analysis below is therefore based only on what she wrote in her books. I am thankful for Sanford's desire to see the Church exercise a healing ministry, to seek God's power to achieve His purposes and see people touched by God's love. I do not wish in any way to detract from all the good things she accomplished for the Church nor from the lives of people she touched for God's glory. However, as I read her books and understand her theology, I am disturbed. What follows is a consideration of the "disturbing things" in her writings and in no way pretends to assess her entire theology. I trust my assessment will not appear unduly critical given the many good things one can affirm in her books.

God, Energy and Healing

A pivotal concept in Sanford's theology of healing prayer is power, or energy and its effective channeling by the healer for the one being healed.[10] Sanford frequently emphasized the concept of God's creative energy which is everywhere in the universe[11] and is actually His life as well[12] and can flow through people and into those in need of healing. God's life "was a kind of light."[13] One must learn certain laws that allow God to more fully work through people who pray for healing.[14] God works "through the application of powers that He has created" which requires persistent prayer "to keep the door open for the power that heals."[15] The crux of faith is to believe that God's power is real, pervades the universe and one's faith can connect to God to effect a healing.[16] God's healing power is available; our role is to adjust to it and remain open to it by faith and a proper attitude which includes thankfulness.[17] The Holy Spirit is "a power, an energy, the water of life" which should circulate in the Church.[18] Those who pray for healing are channels of God's healing power, a "transmitting center" for the power of God,[19] and should concentrate on "the spiritual energies of God."[20] In praying for a baby girl ill with pneumonia, Sanford noticed the girl's hands and feet vibrated as the "new life" from God was coming into her.[21]

263

She could feel power, with her hands shaking and quivering, entering a girl suffering from a heart condition.[22] Sanford was not ambiguous when it came to the laying on of hands:

> …when we pray for another with the laying on of hands, a power passes through us; a real energy; an actual radiation of a kind of light that cannot usually be seen by the eyes. This may cause our hands to quiver slightly as though a current of electricity were flowing through them which in a way it is.[23]

Sanford attempted to find biblical support for her focus on God's healing energy in Ephesians when she wrote:

> St. Paul advised the new Christians in Ephesus to "walk as children of light": to live, that is as if they were made of a living, moving energy like light. A few centuries ago we would have thought this just a fanciful idea. Now, thanks to scientists, we know that it is really true. For scientists have discovered that the body is not hard, solid matter, but is made up of specks of energy.[24]

Although she gave no scriptural reference, Sanford implicitly quoted Ephesians 5:8: *"For you were once darkness, but now you are light in the Lord. Live as children of light…."* Such an interpretation of Scripture, however, is problematic if not impossible.

First, Sanford's interpretation violates the context of the passage and Paul's entire epistle. Paul immediately qualifies this "living as children of light" by defining the fruits of light as goodness, righteousness and truth (Eph. 5:9). Did he really mean that photons generate righteousness? Living as children of the light means pleasing the Lord (Eph. 5:10) in contrast to doing the deeds of darkness (Eph. 5:11). Would darkness then mean an absence of photons?

Paul refers to darkness as a spiritual darkness, living and walking in sin and blind to the truth (Eph. 4:18, 5:11-13; cf. 1 Thess. 5:5-8). We were rescued from the kingdom of darkness (Col. 1:13), called out of darkness into God's light (1 Pet. 2:9) and, as light, have no fellowship with darkness (2 Cor. 6:14). Walking in the light means loving others, reflecting God's character and having true fellowship with God as opposed to hating others which is walking in darkness (1 John 1:6-7, 2:9-11). Walking in the light is a matter of holiness, righteousness, love and truth and not ever a matter of quantum mechanics. The light-darkness vocabulary in the New Testament consistently has a "thoroughly ethical content" concerned with doing the will of God.[25] Light and darkness are therefore simple, common biblical metaphors that readily convey spiritual realities and must not be taken literally in this and many other passages. The context of a passage will clearly determine if a literal light is meant (for example, Gen. 1:3, 15, 18; Matt. 24:29; Acts 9:3, 12:7, 22:6; Rev. 8:12).

Second, the original readers would never have had this notion which is only now discussed in the modern scientific era. If quantum physics is required to really understand Paul's verse, his original readers did not really know what he meant and God's people have been waiting for centuries to understand the basic idea of this verse. The attempt to relate modern science to this passage is therefore an anachronism and reading something into it. If this really was Paul's understanding (given Sanford's notion that *all* people are made of energy), it defeats Paul's imperative to walk as children of light. It is like commanding a person to have two arms and two legs.

Third, there is a misunderstanding about quantum mechanics. Sanford wrote that we are made "not of solid and impenetrable matter, but of energy."[26] But we do have matter, and we are made up of matter, and that matters. In fact even light with its photons have mass and are observed either as waves or particles according to the Wave-Particle Dualism.[27] Einstein's equation, $E=mc^2$, does not mean that we are made up of light or energy but rather if even a small part of matter were converted to energy, it would result in the release of a huge amount of energy. Hence Sanford's application of physics to Scripture is technically incorrect from the beginning.

Sanford quoted, I believe, Matthew 5:14 in further support of her concept of healing energy:

> "Ye are the light of the world," said that amazing carpenter whose light still shines down through the centuries. This is literally true. We are the electric light bulbs through whom the light of God reaches the world. Thus we are "part God".... Knowing then that we are part of God, that his life within us is an active energy and that he works through the laws of our bodies, let us study to adjust and conform ourselves to those laws.[28]

Sanford violates the context of Scripture since Jesus Himself clearly defines the "light" as a metaphor for good deeds in Matthew 5:16, as fits with Matthew 5-7 where He teaches about life in the kingdom, its righteousness and its ethics. If one takes "light" in Matthew 5:14 literally, why not take "you are the salt of the earth" literally as well and argue that the human body has a certain percentage of salt in it? The context is abundantly clear: "light" is a metaphor just as "salt" is a metaphor.

If "light" is understood in a literal sense in Matthew 5:14, why not declare Jesus to be literal energy since He is the light of the world (John 8:12, 9:5), His life is the light of men (John 1:4), He is a light for revelation to the Gentiles (Luke 2:32) or light for the Gentiles (Isa. 42:6, 49:6) and the Lord Himself as energy since He is one's light (Micah 7:8, Ps. 27:1) or a lamp (2 Sam. 22:29)? This is actually not too far-fetched in Sanford's theology since either her wording was too loose and reflects mysticism, or she believed in pantheism—that God is in His creation and it is a part of Him.[29] She wrote that God is "primal energy, the original force that we call God,"[30] "...He's in nature and He is nature"[31] and has "made everything out of Himself and somehow He put a part of Himself into everything."[32] She wrote that the life of the Creator, the very essence of His being, is in creation and can flow into a person[33] and the very cells of our bodies "are filled with God."[34]

But we are not "part God" but rather, as Christians reconciled to the Father by the Son, indwelt by the Holy Spirit and adopted into God's family. We are still finite, created beings, but now indwelt by God because of the finished work of Christ upon the cross through whom only we are reconciled to the Father. God is both transcendent and immanent yet separate from His creation (Gen. 1:1).

God is never a force or energy; He is always a person, a member of the Trinity. The Scriptures declare that God is love because that reflects His character and is one of His personal attributes. The Scriptures *never* say that God is energy since that is an impersonal attribute. Worse still, if God really was energy and people can channel and manipulate this energy, then people can channel and manipulate God!

Energy and power may *manifest* His presence and can express His will, but that is not His essence. I have felt energy or heat in a few cases in healing prayer, and a few people receiving prayer have sensed heat or energy, but I feel no need to develop a theology around it. The New Testament records examples of power coming from Jesus when He healed people (Mark 5:30; Luke 6:19, 8:46), but it does not focus on people being a channel of power *per se*. Such experiences are a manifestation of God's presence and action, an expression of His love to bring healing. I suspect Sanford was

267

attempting to use a natural category, from physics, to explain her experiences in healing prayer. Her autobiography showed her sense of God's transcendence, mystery and awe, but I fear that her attempts to describe such things readily suggest pantheism.

Sanford often referred to God as three persons of the Trinity but at times apparently slipped into the Trinitarian heresy of modalism with one God appearing in three different ways or modes.[35] She wrote that the three persons of the Trinity are "one God, manifesting Himself in three different ways, each of those manifestations able to assume what we for want of a better name call personality."[36] She referred to Jesus as the second manifestation of God.[37]

Sanctification by Mind Power?

With a focus on power and energy, healing becomes "mechanical" with the spiritual virtues subservient to the technique. Sanford confused love with energy, writing that God's love is "an energy rather than an emotion,"[38] an overwhelming energy[39] or still an emotion but powerful, radiant, life-giving and charged with healing power.[40] Following Sanford's logic, love as a virtue and fruit of the Holy Spirit is re-defined to be more like energy to manage and manipulate.

A focus on channeling and directing power all too easily lends itself to manipulation. Apparently the love of God can be projected into an animal, like a bull, to prevent it from hurting someone.[41] Sanford gave the example of a burglar breaking into one's house and suggested the following course of action:

> One would project into the burglar's mind the love of God, by seeing him as a child of God and asking God to bless him. And if one were strong enough in faith and love, the burglar's mind would change. He would leave the family unharmed and go away.[42]

Sanford used her mind to change people by creating an image in her mind of the person at their best or at peace and so forth and then, as she strongly held onto this image in prayer, the person would eventually change. She started this with her children:

> If I heard angry voices anywhere in the house, I had only to make in my mind the image of a child at peace and project it into reality by the word of faith. And after a time this work was accomplished and there was no more need to think about it, for my children lived in peace together from day's end to day's end.... The creation of peace in someone else, by projecting into that one the love of God, is true forgiveness, the remission of sins, the changing of the other person, so that the quality in him that has annoyed us will not be there anymore.[43]

Sanford advocated something similar within the Church wherein, before a service, one should pray for anyone who one disapproved of or felt uncomfortable with, not denying their faults and thereby "redeeming them" through prayer:

> We asked the love of Christ to come into us and go through us into the person, healing the memories and bringing forth all that was good and lovely in his nature. Then we gave thanks as one does with the prayer of faith and with inspired imagination we made in the mind a picture of that person transformed into the image of his real Christ-self and we rejoiced that this was so. Inevitably our feeling about this person changed. Through our prayer we gave birth to his spirit....[44]

This was all without their conscious awareness, for in the church "they are quiet and attentive with their minds more or less open to God—and so you can sneak into the back door of the unconscious and they cannot keep you out!"[45]

She wrote that since God is Creator and we are too, we can actually "re-create" people by forgiving them, changing our attitudes to them and then projecting virtues into reality in the person's life as part of their transformation according to our imagination.[46] Intercession involved "projecting the power of God into man."[47] She advocated that this method be applied to any person in need.[48]

Sanford wrote that the healing of the world can be furthered by praying for leaders of nations.[49] One would bless the leaders and "hold them up into the light of God's love and send the love of Christ into their minds," which then calls forth the potential goodness which is found in all men.[50] To overcome minds closed to the Spirit and sinful "thought-vibrations" in the world, intercessors must atone for their sin and the sins of the world and take the leader to the cross of Christ so the leader receives the forgiveness of Jesus.[51] This is all without the leader himself ever repenting of his own sin directly and coming to the cross of Christ. When enough intercessors have so prayed, the "pent-up current of the redemption of Jesus Christ will rush upon the minds of men and heal the soul-sickness...."[52] But what about conviction of the Holy Spirit and people's direct call to repentance and sanctification and the utter holiness of God the Father? That is blurred and missing in Sanford's model of world healing. Her focus is on the love of Christ being projected into people by the efforts of others and likewise the redemption of Christ channeled into people.

I can appreciate "imagining" another person in terms of thinking the best of that person as an aid to build an atmosphere of faith in intercession. But we are Christ's workmanship (Eph. 2:10; Phil. 1:6; Heb. 13:21; Ps. 51:10), not another believer's workmanship however well-intentioned. Christ is transforming us. Sanctification cannot bypass the cross, our wills, our need of self-denial and our growing in the knowledge of Christ firsthand. Since the other person is passively involved, there is no remission of sins. What about concrete acts of love towards others? If a burglar is breaking into your house, what about the conviction of the Holy Spirit or asking Jesus to protect the family, or the burglar possibly coming to repentance and faith in order to, by his will, receive God's grace and love? Projecting God's love into people, as noble as it sounds, actually devalues people by bypassing their will and treating them as objects and foreclosing the possibility of repentance. Sanford's thought projection has too much in common with mental telepathy and psychic technique. Sanford calls this a new "love-power" sufficient to "change hearts here and there."[53] Why didn't Jesus use this "love-power" to change the Pharisees, Sadducees or the rich young ruler? Was John the Baptist in error by calling people to repentance instead of projecting love into them? The peace of Christ cannot be projected into anyone; everyone must receive it directly from Jesus as He gives to each person (John 14:27).

I cannot agree with Sanford that this "is forgiveness—real forgiveness; giving the love of Christ to one who needs it."[54] This is a misleading application of biblical forgiveness, effectively redefining and undermining the biblical doctrine of forgiveness because it does not involve sin and repentance on the part of the one "receiving" the love. Neither is this redemption. Redemption is only by the blood of Christ (Rom. 5:9; Eph. 1:7; Heb. 9:12; 1 Pet. 1:18; Rev. 1:5).

Love is always and only personal, and there can be no confusion here. The Father bestowed love on the Son (Matt. 3:17; 17:5); we must love our neighbor (Matt. 5:43) and God with all our heart (Matt. 22:37). Love is expressed by obedience (John 14:15, 15:9)—not *energy management*. Love is the fulfillment of the law

271

(Rom. 13:9) and defined in relational, personal, emotional attributes (1 Cor. 13:1-13). You simply cannot project love into people like a commodity or an impersonal force.

New Thought and the Fox Connection

To truly understand Sanford's theology one must appreciate some of the other writers who influenced her as well as the predominant thinking at the time. The Mind-Cure movement was well known in her day, as was New Thought.

P.P. Quimby (1802-1866) was the father of mental healing—the metaphysical idea that healing lies in the mind[55]—and much of Christian Science.[56] Mary Baker Eddy (1821-1910), founder of Christian Science, plagiarized a considerable amount of material from Quimby and also from a manuscript of Dr. Francis Lieber, a known authority on the philosophy of Hegel.[57] Hegel was an Idealist and taught, among many other things, that ultimately there is only Mind, God is not really a person and thoughts cause reality.[58] For healing, the Christian Science healer would perform several mental exercises: "…name the disease, convince himself of its unreality and maintain a mental picture of the patient as perfectly well."[59] This is strikingly similar to Sanford's use of the creative imagination in healing.

New Thought is directly from Quimby's system of mental healing and thus is quite similar theologically to Christian Science.[60] The key to salvation then becomes being open to the divine inflow of higher forces and powers.[61] The New Thought movement, from the 1880s, was so called because it did away with "old thought" like sin, darkness and misery in the world and focused on life and light and using thought and the power of the mind to overcome sorrow and suffering.[62]

From New Thought came the Unity School of Christianity founded in 1891 by Myrtle and Charles Fillmore (1854-1948)[63] which has become the largest Gnostic cult in Christendom.[64] Along with New Thought, Unity teaches pantheism as made clear by Fillmore: "each rock, tree, animal, everything visible, is a manifestation of the one spirit—god—differing only in degree of manifestation...."[65] Atonement means reconciliation between man and God or Divine Mind by a reuniting of one's consciousness with God consciousness.[66] If God is then everywhere and in everything, salvation is everywhere.

This reliance on the power of the mind is typical of the New Thought movement with its Mind-cures. Not surprisingly Sanford taught that we must overcome negative thought-vibrations with new thought-habits.[67]

Emmet Fox, in *The Sermon on the Mount*, declared that original sin, substitutionary atonement and the "Plan of Salvation" are not taught by the Bible at all.[68] All people, no matter how sinful, always have "direct access to an all-loving" God who will forgive and strengthen people.[69] The great spiritual key to understanding Jesus' teaching is that the whole outer world, including the physical body, everyday life and creation, are amenable to a man's thoughts.[70] Fox wrote that "*all causation is mental* and that your body and all your affairs—your home, your business, all your experiences—are but the manifestation of your mental states."[71] Was Paul a spiritual failure because he was stoned, lashed several times, shipwrecked three times, naked, cold, often hungry and in much danger (2 Cor. 11:25)? Fox wrote that Jesus taught only about mental states, and the Bible is actually a textbook on metaphysics.[72] God is Divine Mind and people reverse the Fall and overcome limitations by changing their thoughts and mental states.[73] Man is essentially divine, and by his own choice can change his consciousness via certain spiritual laws, rising into the realm of the Spirit beyond material limitations, all of which constitutes "the Gospel."[74] Essentially you think your way to salvation and into heaven. Concerning Christ, Fox wrote:

> In the Bible the term "Christ" is not identical with Jesus, the individual. It is a technical term that may be briefly defined as the Absolute Spiritual truth about anything. Now, to know this truth about any person, or condition, or circumstance, immediately heals that person, or condition, or circumstance, to the extent that such Truth is realized by the thinker. This is the essence of spiritual healing.... Whenever the Christ (that is the True Idea concerning anything) is raised up in thought by anyone, healing follows....[75]

Sanford was influenced by Fox's book which she described as "based strongly and squarely on the words that Jesus actually said."[76] Sanford considered Fox's book as a "standard" for the purpose of teaching on the prayer of faith.[77] Eventually Sanford began to wonder "...if the power of right thinking could establish in us the thing we affirm, then why was the Cross necessary?"[78] For an answer she turned to Fox's book, *The Sermon on the Mount*, and, while not accepting everything he wrote, she did regard him as a "teacher of the truth."[79] In attending one of his lectures she learned how forgiveness of sins and the Cross meant today that Jesus lowered His thought-vibrations to the thought-vibrations of humanity. In other words, Jesus entered into the subconscious of people.[80] It then appears that, in applying forgiveness, the thoughts of Christ are projected into people and their potential and consciousness of God rises accordingly. For the practical application of this idea of forgiveness Sanford looked to a book by H. B. Jeffrey who she identified as a "student of truth."[81] Jeffrey, however, was a "famous speaker at Unity conventions"[82] and thus can hardly be identified as a student of truth.

Fox's theology is not based "strongly and squarely" on the words of Jesus. While there is some truth in Fox's *The Sermon on the Mount*, there is much error plus outright denial of essential doctrines of the Christian faith (sin, redemption, Christology, personhood of God, sanctification and more). Fox claimed to present the gospel which is actually another gospel[83] for which the apostle Paul had some serious words (Gal. 1:8-9; cf. 1 John 4:6). Equally serious is Fox's direct denial of Jesus as the Christ (1 John 2:22-23) and hence the Scripture's admonition to avoid such teachers (2 John 1:10) and never commend them. Jesus is the Christ who came in the flesh and cannot ever be construed as an Idea or a Cosmic Principle or Cosmic Consciousness as advocated by New Age writers. Fox's Unitarian theology, directly derived from New Thought, exalts the mind, diminishes any need for repentance and disregards the effect of sin on one's mind and will. Positive thoughts are expected in the Christian life, but the power of positive thinking is not the source of our salvation and sanctification. This is only achieved by the life of the Spirit, the presence of Christ in us and living by grace. New Thought is actually "Wrong Thought" and not even new (Eccl. 1:9-10).

Thoughts Floating in the Air

Sanford believed that the thoughts of deceased people actually exist in the air: "…thoughts of past generations still exist among the intricate thought-patterns of the air."[84] She linked this to the idea of the "mass subconscious" of the human race which involves a connection in man's inner being from the past with the present.[85] She based this on her experience of hearing singing from another world, the angels singing to shepherds (Luke 2:13), the magi seeing a star (Matt. 2:1-11), the mystery of the universe and God being outside of time.[86] She referred to mystics who speak of

275

"Akashic" records that "may be tapped and read by those with spiritual vision."[87] This whole belief was relevant to her idea of Christ's redemptive work wherein He entered into the mass subconscious of mankind. The idea is behind her notion of "gathered thought currents of humanity" from all ages.[88] It was also relevant to her belief that one could actually "pick up" thoughts from the memories of the human race.[89]

But the whole idea of disembodied thoughts is alien to the Scriptures where thoughts are in people's hearts and minds (Ps. 13:2, 55:2, 139:2; Prov. 1:23; Matt. 9:4; Luke 2:35; Heb. 4:12). Typically there is no remembrance of people in the past (Eccl. 1:11, 2:16, 9:5). The Lord will cut off any memory of evil people from the face of the earth or under heaven (Ps. 9:6, 34:16b, 109:15b). Their thoughts do not float around in the air so that people in the future may connect with them. God knows our thoughts and we can receive His thoughts, but that is different from thoughts just floating around in the air for centuries.

When I lived in Aleppo, Syria, I worked at an international agricultural research center some twenty kilometers south of the city. It just so happened that Tel Mardikh was about twenty kilometers further south on the highway to Damascus. Tel Mardikh has the ruins of Ebla dating to 2300 or 2500 BC.[90] I visited this amazing archeological site many times after work and observed the archaeologists' progress. Except for the over 17,000 clay tablets unearthed and any other historical records, there is no other trace of those people. Do we really believe that their thoughts are floating in the air above Syria?

Furthermore, the Akashic records are associated with occultists and New Agers and not just mystics:

> Occultists believe the physical earth is surrounded by an
> immense spiritual field known as Akasha, in which is

impressed every impulse of human thought, will and emotion. It is therefore believed to constitute a complete record of human history.[91]

Edgar Cayce, among many, accessed the Akashic records many times while in a trance and learned from these "records" that Jesus had twenty-nine previous incarnations.[92] The idea of Akashic records, with past-life memories and "race memories," is used to defend reincarnation and the work of psychics and mediums.[93] The whole idea is not only unbiblical but also illogical, irrational and fictional—people's thoughts are not suspended in a "spiritual ether."[94] In the final analysis Sanford's idea about thoughts or "thought-currents" in the atmosphere is impossible and untrue, and her positive reference to occultic Akashic records is misleading and unfortunate. Her biblical references from the Gospels do not support this idea, and she appears to have been guided by mystical experience instead of by the Scriptures.

The Healing of Memories: Borrowing from C.G. Jung

In trying to explain the healing of memories Sanford advocated Jung's idea of the "collective unconscious." She held that when God incarnated Himself into man, in Jesus He thereby entered into the "collective unconscious of the race: into the deep mind of every person; there being available for healing and help."[95] Sanford looked to modern psychological thought to begin to explain how Jesus could miraculously heal the pain and sorrow from past memories.[96] Not only do we have an unconscious mind, it is connected with the unconscious of others in the human race, or the "collective unconscious," which Jesus entered into and lived in during Passion Week.[97] Sanford wrote:

Our Lord, when He took our sins and sorrows into Himself,

277

made the connection with all of us. He became forever a part of the mass mind of the race, so that even though His living being is now in heaven at the right hand of the Father, a part of His consciousness is forever bound up with the deep mind of man. He has no tomb upon earth, for His body rose again, transformed into a different kind of body—one both flesh and Spirit. Yet in another sense a part of Him is forever buried with the hearts of men.[98]

...He became man, mankind; one with the mass mind of the human race. Therefore, since He became a very part of the collective unconscious of the human race, when He died upon the cross a part of humanity died with Him.[99]

The redemption of the human race required that Jesus "...sink deeper into humanity: to become part of the subconscious mind of every man" and submerged Himself deeply into man.[100] Similarly she wrote how the redemptive love of Jesus entered into the "gathered thought currents of humanity from the beginning to the end of time" and thus the "mass-mind of humanity was pierced to the very depths."[101] Furthermore a part of us, and also the *entire human race*, has apparently already ascended into heaven.[102]

This whole concept and teaching is fraught with numerous theological problems. If a "part of humanity" died with Jesus on the cross, is humanity involved in effecting salvation? Only "us who believe," those in Christ, are joint-heirs with Him and are seated in the heavenly realms (Eph. 1:19, 2:6). No part of Jesus' consciousness is in all mankind since many in the world reject Jesus (John 1:10-11; 1 John 3:1b) and would rather live in the dark (John 1:5). Those who have not accepted Jesus as Saviour and Lord upon repentance of their sin are objects of God's wrath (Eph. 2:4), not reconciled towards God, have not the mind of God (Rom. 8:5-8) and will perish (John 3:16). Those who do not have eternal life in Christ by repenting of their sins (John 3:15, 3:36, 4:14, 5:24, 6:27, 40, 10:28, 17:2,3; Acts 4:12) are alienated from God and are actually enemies of God in their minds (Col. 1:21) which are corrupted by sin (1 Tim. 6:5). Can Christ really enter into a consciousness that is His own enemy? Since those whose name is not written in the book of life will perish in a lake of fire (Rev. 20:11-15), and if Jesus' consciousness is "bound up forever with the deep mind of man," does that mean that a part of Jesus' consciousness will perish? Clearly the whole Jungian concept must be summarily and absolutely rejected. Jesus' taking up the sins of the world onto Himself is different from entering into the minds of sinful people.

There really is no need for any notion of the "collective unconscious" to explain the presence of Jesus in inner healing. A theology of the presence, relying on the supernatural presence of Jesus, will suffice. Jungian thinking leads to universalism and avoids sin and the cross. Jungian thinking is a redevelopment of Gnostic spirituality.[103] Not surprisingly Gnostics today are like the early Gnostics: "...people who refused to accept that salvation required substitutionary, atoning sacrifice, the central message of both Old and New Testament."[104]

Strictly speaking it is not true that inner healing or the healing of memories is derived from Jungian thinking or techniques. Rather, Jungian thinking was used by Sanford to explain after the fact what happened in such healings. Given Jung's association with the occult and much of his unscriptural thinking, one must be extremely cautious of adopting any of his ideas. Payne relates Jung's thinking to Gnosticism and uncovers some serious problems with his system of thought.[105]

A teaching of the New Age movement is that the "Christ consciousness" or "Christ principle" is found in *all* people. This is utterly different from the historical Jesus Christ of Nazareth, born of the Virgin Mary, who suffered under Pontius Pilate, rose from the dead on the third day and is known only to those who repent of their sins and confess Him as Lord and Saviour (Acts 4:12). New Agers would rather bypass the need for sin and repentance, thus undercutting the cross of Christ and denying Christ in the flesh (1 John 4:2).

Sanford also had a rather novel way of linking the blood of Jesus to the healing of memories. She wrote that the blood of Christ dried after the crucifixion, turned to dust and was disseminated into the wind and mingled with all of life.[106] That dried blood, now breathed by everyone in the world, is an "invisible current of a heavenly energy, an actual energy, a perceptible energy, an effective energy."[107] This invisible energy now supplies to people what the universal love of God is too impersonal and diffuse to achieve, namely, healing of memories, freeing of the subconscious mind, integration of one's personality which people seek.[108] Effectively all people can then simply breathe in the redemption of Christ and bypass their own decisions for repentance, denying self and taking up their own cross.

Teilhard de Chardin: Panpsychism and Cosmic Evolution

Sanford thought highly of Pierre Teilhard de Chardin,[109] a Jesuit paleontologist and theologian who believed in a material and spiritual evolution of the universe, the basis of what is known today as process theology.[110] In it God and creation are one evolving essence with panpsychism wherein everything in the world has psychic energy and a latent consciousness.[111] Sanford affirmed Teilhard as a great scholar and effectively upheld his panpsychism.[112]

Embracing pantheism, Teilhard believed in a cosmic Christ and said little about the incarnate Christ of Nazareth.[113] He sometimes referred to a personal God but more often wrote of God as an impersonal energy or force and Christ as the "whole inner energy of the universe."[114] His writings can be summarized as a "hybridized mystical Christianity that met Eastern pantheism more than halfway."[115] Such views fit perfectly with New Thought and New Age. His beliefs were profoundly shaped by many mystical experiences wherein he experienced a mystical unity with the universe not unlike Sanford's mystical experiences.[116] Some of Sanford's writing reflects Teilhard's thinking, and Teilhard has also influenced many New Age leaders.[117]

Following Teilhard, Sanford believed that the Creator could evolve people, birds and trees "out of nothing at all except His own Being."[118] She wrote that God is more than pure energy,[119] and God has created the world from His own being.[120] She believed that people evolved from the Godhead and existed before coming to earth.[121] This is consistent with her apparent pantheism wherein God "is not only in us or the sun or the rocks or the trees."[122]

Her view of creation is in error. God is completely distinct from His creation which cannot be "even remotely considered an emanation from God."[123] Creation is *not* part of God's being; it is fully sustained by and dependent upon God (Neh. 9:6; Acts 17:25, 28).[124] In contrast to Sanford's views God created the universe *ex nihilo* (out of nothing) and *per verbum* according to His personal will.[125] He gives life and energy to the universe through His creativity, glory and power which are evident in the universe that He sustains continually. Christ sustains the universe by His power (Heb. 1:3). All things were created by Christ and for Him (Col. 1:16; John 1:3).

Agnes Sanford: A Conclusion

All things considered, what might one think of Sanford's theology and writing? Let us first remember that pioneers often make mistakes[126] and that is usually inevitable with those blazing new trails. She wrote her books and practiced healing prayer when the Church was hardly exercising this ministry, and in much of the Church dispensationalist and cessationist thinking essentially justified disbelief and disobedience in terms of Jesus' healing ministry today. She noticed a great contradiction between what Jesus taught and commanded and what the Church in her day actually practiced. It was as if the idea of Jesus healing and doing miracles in the 1900s was itself a heresy. She wrote that the "real heresy had taken place centuries ago when people made up the idea that the age of miracles was past: that this is a new dispensation and God no longer does miracles among His people."[127] For many years she was not openly received by the Church which basically thought her idea of Jesus being alive and healing today was a heresy[128] and thus hardly anyone taught or practiced healing in the Church in her time.[129] One can be thankful for her desire to see the ministry of healing restored to the Church which had lost much of its power due to cessationist thinking. Many should be thankful to Sanford for her valid and groundbreaking contribution to the healing of memories or forgiveness of sins. This is truly all to her credit.

Sanford developed her practice and theology of healing from the desire to experience and channel God's power[130] and asking questions like, "How can I get this power?"[131] This is understandable given the relative powerlessness for healing in the Church of her day and the few examples she saw firsthand. But before one answers a question, one should make sure it is the right question. If she would have asked, "How does Jesus heal?" or, "How can I bring someone into the presence of Jesus to experience His healing?" she would have written her books quite differently. The preoccupation with power and being a channel makes healing too man-centered and less Christ-centered. It is not even always necessary since people can experience healing directly from Jesus without anyone being a channel for them. I see this repeatedly in healing prayer when people hear, see and experience Jesus directly as He decides. The preoccupation with power in general is not without temptation; it has unfortunately led many people into witchcraft.

Regrettably Sanford borrowed some of the thinking and terminology from New Thought and the Unity School of Christianity, both cults with major and serious doctrinal error. But why did those cults appear? Those cults rose partly because the Church failed to follow Jesus in the ministry of healing due to its theological rigidity.[132] The mainline churches, locked into cessationism, rationalism and exhibiting Phariseeism, rejected and squelched the healing revivals of the 1800s.[133] This in turn gave rise to the metaphysical and Mind-Cure movement which spawned Christian Science and then New Thought.[134] Mary Eddy Baker experienced healing while reading the New Testament and then tried to bring healing to the churches in Boston, but unfortunately she was ridiculed.[135] There were few writers and theologians in the Church who wrote and mentored in the area of healing, so it is no surprise that Sanford conversed with those movements that emphasized healing which the Church largely argued against or was not the least bit interested in. While this does not excuse any erroneous thinking or theology that has entered her works from those sources, including that from Emmett Fox, it reminds us that those sources existed in part because of the disobedience of the Church. It is unfortunate that some of her writing and theology can mislead people, but the Church as a whole is partly responsible. Thus, before looking at the proverbial speck in her eye, one must check for a plank in one's own eye (Matt. 7:3-5; Luke 6:41-42). This teaching is especially relevant for those who would criticize her while holding on to their cessationist thinking. One error does not excuse or justify another error.

283

Sanford's use of Carl Jung's thinking and terminology is unfortunate and unnecessary for a theology of healing prayer. Reference to Jung, one of the major psychologists at the time, was her attempt to explain Jesus' presence in memories, but that has brought a whole host of problems. She also referred to Jung's "autonomous complex" in writing on deliverance issues.[136]

It is unfortunate that Sanford developed some of her thinking from unreliable sources like Emmet Fox, C.G. Jung and Teilhard de Chardin. Citing such sources is not necessarily in itself a problem since even cults and heresies often contain some truth. The critical point is that Sanford incorporated some of the erroneous ideas and theology from those sources as is readily evident from carefully reading her books.

It would be unfair to suggest that she was into the occult which she herself argued against.[137] In giving much good counsel on the ministry of deliverance, she denounced spiritualism as disobedience and the danger of séances.[138]

Was Sanford New Age? This is strictly not possible since she wrote at a time when the New Age movement was not as it is today. However, New Thought was a pre-cursor to New Age, and some of Sanford's writings appeal to New Agers today. Thus, after the fact, we see a concordance between New Age thinking and some of Sanford's writing. By her own admission in *Sealed Orders*, she has borrowed from New Thought. Sanford was among those especially important to the "biblical filtration of New Thought theology and its introduction into the mainstream of Christendom."[139] Brooks Alexander traced how Sanford introduced visualization into mainline churches with her New Thought theology.[140]

Her mystical experiences of merging with God in a valley,[141] being "one with the universe" on a ship,[142] her out-of-body experience during an operation,[143] her experience of infilling of God's life by a lake,[144] and a mystical experience that led her back in time to Sparta[145] have effected her writing and terminology. One cannot fault Sanford for simply having such experiences. After all, Ezekiel was "lifted up" by the Spirit "between heaven and earth" and "in visions of God" was transported to Jerusalem (Ezek. 8:3). That almost sounds like an out-of-body experience and a type of "soul travel." It is more a question of discerning the true source and the correct interpretation of those experiences. I fear that too much of her theology was driven by her experiences and not firmly rooted in the Scriptures. Spiritual experiences and human theology are both imperfect and at times will challenge one another, but in the final analysis they must still both come under the authority of the Written Word which is opened to us by the Living Word.

All things considered, and in full appreciation for all that God accomplished through her including numerous healings, I do not see how one can commend her books and writings as being fully Christian and orthodox. Her writings in many places lack precision, are sometimes contradictory, open to misinterpretation, display syncretism, sometimes refer to the Scriptures inappropriately and at least suggest pantheism. She may well have changed her views and theology on some things in her later years as have some well-known evangelical theologians. I fear that many Christians have read Sanford's books and affirmed her thinking while almost totally oblivious to the ideas and implications of New Thought, Mind-Cure, Emmet Fox, Christian Science, Jung and Teilhard de Chardin among others.

It appears God used Sanford in spite of her theological errors. Even so, the great things God accomplished through her do not justify an uncritical acceptance of her theology.

The theology of healing prayer which she espoused is quite different from that practiced by many today. The focus on healing prayer should not be on power or energy and channeling. We do pray for God's anointing and increased faith and the true power of the Holy Spirit. As in the Gospels, the focus must be on the healing presence of Jesus. Sanford's model of prayer does not do justice to the fact that people often receive healing and wholeness directly from Jesus and not through anyone as a "channel." Sanford focused too much on spiritual technique (steps in meditation, centering, imaging, visualization, thought training, channeling energy, etc.) at the expense of a relational presence with Jesus in healing prayer. Under such a model of healing prayer, the channeling and management of energy may well substitute the presence of Jesus. That is a core doctrine of New Age energy healing today, along with the idea that we are ultimately energy, and God is energy as well.

Endnotes ———————

[1] Rita Bennett, *Emotionally Free* (Old Tappan: Fleming H. Revell Co., 1982) p. 149.

[2] Leanne Payne, *The Broken Image: Restoring Personal Wholeness Through Healing Prayer* (Wheaton: Crossway Books, 1981) p. 13.

[3] Mark A. Pearson, *Christian Healing: A Practical and Comprehensive Guide* (Grand Rapids: Chosen Books, 1995) p. 11.

[4] John and Paula Sandford, *Healing the Wounded Spirit* (Tulsa: Victory House, 1985) p. 181.

[5] Robert Wise et al., *The Church Divided* (South Plainfield: Bridge Publishing, Inc., 1986) pp. 185-193.

[6] Jane Gumprecht, *Abusing Memory: The Healing Theology of Agnes Sanford* (Moscow: Canon Press, 1997).

[7] John and Mark Sandford, *Deliverance and Inner Healing: A Comprehensive Guide* (Grand Rapids: Chosen Books, 1992) p. 84.

[8] Richard Ganz, *PsychoBabble: The Failure of Modern Psychology— and the Biblical Alternative* (Wheaton: Crossway Books, 1993) p. 35.

[9] Ganz, pp. 35-36.

[10] Agnes Sanford, *Sealed Orders* (Plainfield: Logos International, 1972) p. 48.

[11] Agnes Sanford, *The Healing Light* (Plainfield: Logos International, 1976, originally published in 1947 by Macalester Park Publishing Co.) p. 2.

[12] Sanford, 1947, p. 3.

[13] Sanford, 1947, p. 20.

[14] Sanford, 1947, pp. 4-5.

[15] Agnes Sanford, *The Healing Gifts of the Spirit* (Philadelphia: Trumpet Books, A.J. Holman Co., 1976) p. 49.

[16] Sanford, 1976, p. 48.

[17] Sanford, 1947, pp. 14-15.

[18] Sanford, 1976, p. 58.

[19] Sanford, 1947, pp. 89-94.

[20] Sanford, 1947, p. 26.

[21] Sanford, 1947, p. 22.

[22] Sanford, 1972, p. 140.

[23] Sanford, 1976, p. 70.

[24] Sanford, 1947, p. 18.

[25] F.F. Bruce, *The Epistle to the Colossians, to Philemon and to the Ephesians: The New International Commentary on the New Testament* (Grand Rapids: Eerdmans Publishing Co., 1984) p. 373.

[26] Sanford, 1947, p. 19.

[27] Peter Zoeller-Greer, "Genesis, Quantum Physics and Reality. How the Bible agrees with Quantum Physics—An Anthropic Principle of Another Kind: The Divine Anthropic Principle," *Journal of the American Scientific Affiliation*, 52(1):8-17, 2000 p. 9.

[28] Sanford, 1947, pp. 22-23.

[29] Gumprecht, pp. 38-40.

[30] Sanford, 1947, p. 19.

[31] Sanford, 1947, p. 24.

[32] Sanford, 1976, p. 27.

[33] Sanford, 1972, p. 30.

[34] Sanford, 1976, p. 69.

[35] Alister E. McGrath, *Christian Theology: An Introduction* (Oxford: Blackwell Publishers, 1994) pp. 256-257.

[36] Agnes Sanford, *The Healing Touch of God* (New York: Ballantine Books, 5th printing, 1987, first published in 1958 by Macalester Publishing Co. as *Behold Your God*) p. 82, 107.

[37] Sanford, 1987, pp. 64, 107.

[38] Sanford, 1972, p. 112.

[39] Sanford, 1947, p. 57.

[40] Ibid.

[41] Sanford, 1947, p. 54.

[42] Sanford, 1947, pp. 54-55.

[43] Sanford, 1947, p. 62.

[44] Sanford, 1976, p. 60.

[45] Sanford, 1976, p. 61.

[46] Sanford, 1947, pp. 61-64.

[47] Sanford, 1947, p. 159.

[48] Sanford, 1947, p. 64.

[49] Sanford, 1947, pp. 180-194.

[50] Sanford, 1947, p. 184.

[51] Sanford, 1947, pp. 185-186.

[52] Sanford, 1947, p. 191.

[53] Sanford, 1947, p. 55.

[54] Sanford, 1976, p. 61.

[55] Ron Rhodes, *The Counterfeit Christ of the New Age Movement* (Grand Rapids: Baker Book House, 1990) p. 148.

[56] Walter R. Martin, *The Kingdom of the Cults* (Minneapolis: Bethany Fellowship, Inc., 1965, revised edition 1977) p. 112.

[57] Martin, pp. 112-114.

[58] Martin, pp. 113-114.

[59] William DeArteaga, *Quenching the Spirit: Discover the REAL Spirit Behind the Charismatic Controversy* (Orlando: Creation House, 1992) p. 169.

[60] Martin, p.144.

[61] Martin, p.146.

[62] Rhodes, pp. 148-149.

[63] Rhodes, p. 151.

[64] Martin, p. 275.

[65] Rhodes, p. 152.

[66] Martin, p. 280.

[67] Sanford, 1947, pp. 35-37.

[68] Emmet Fox, *The Sermon on the Mount* (New York: Harper and Brothers Publishers, 1934) pp. 4-5.

[69] Fox, p. 5.

[70] Fox, p. 13.

[71] Fox, p. 29.

[72] Fox, pp. 19-21.

[73] Fox, p. 40.

[74] Fox, pp. 125-126.

[75] Fox, p. 124.

[76] Sanford, 1972, p. 103.

[77] Sanford, 1987, p. 81.

[78] Sanford, 1972, p. 189.

[79] Ibid.

[80] Sanford, 1972, p. 190.

[81] Ibid.

[82] Gumprecht, p. 36.

[83] Fox, p. 126.

[84] Sanford, 1987, pp. 79-80.

[85] Sanford, 1987, p. 80.

[86] Sanford, 1987, p. 79.

[87] Sanford, 1987, pp. 79-80.

[88] Sanford, 1987, p. 110.

[89] Sanford, 1976, p. 118.

[90] Clifford Wilson, *The Impact of Ebla on Bible Records* (Melbourne: Word of Truth Productions, 1977) pp. 1-93.

[91] Rhodes, p. 37.

[92] Rhodes, p. 40.

[93] Brad Scott, *Embraced by the Darkness: Exposing New Age Theology from the Inside Out* (Wheaton: Crossway Books, 1996) pp. 140-142.

[94] Ibid.

[95] Sanford, 1976, p. 101.

[96] Sanford, 1976, p. 118.

[97] Ibid.

[98] Sanford, 1976, p. 119.

[99] Sanford, 1976, p. 140.

[100] Sanford, 1987, p. 99.

[101] Sanford, 1987, p. 110.

[102] Sanford, 1976, pp. 140-141.

[103] Jeffrey Satinover, *The Empty Self: C.G. Jung and the Gnostic Transformation of Modern Identity* (Westport: Hamewith Books, 1996) p. 47.

[104] Satinover, p. 46.

[105] Leanne Payne, *The Healing Presence* (Wheaton: Crossway Books, 1989) pp. 200-219.

[106] Sanford, 1987, pp. 113, 128.

[107] Sanford, 1987, p. 113.

[108] Ibid.

[109] Agnes Sanford, *The Healing Power of the Bible* (Philadelphia:

Trumpet Books, 1969) pp. 50, 65, 154.

110 James Houston, *I Believe in the Creator* (Grand Rapids: Eerdmans Publishing Co., 1980) pp. 169-170.

111 Ibid.

112 Sanford, 1969, p. 38.

113 Houston, p. 170.

114 Rhodes, p. 227.

115 Tal Brooke, ed., *The Conspiracy to Silence the Son of God* (Eugene: Harvest House Publishers, 1998) pp. 40-41.

116 Brooke, p. 39.

117 Dave Hunt and T.A. McMahon, *The Seduction of Christianity* (Eugene: Harvest House Publishers, 1985) p. 78.

118 Sanford, 1987, p. 82.

119 Agnes Sanford, *Creation Waits* (Plainfield: Logos International, 1977) p. 7.

120 Sanford, 1987, pp. 26, 30.

121 Sanford, 1987, p. 79.

122 Sanford, 1987, p. 15.

123 Bruce K. Waltke with Cathi J. Fredricks, *Genesis: A Commentary* (Grand Rapids: Zondervan, 2001) p. 60.

124 Ibid.

125 Houston, p. 51.

126 Sandford, John and Mark, p. 85.

127 Sanford, 1972, pp. 49, 149.

128 Sanford, 1972, p. 143.

129 Sanford, 1972, p. 165.

130 Sanford, 1987, p. 2.

131 Sanford, 1972, p. 106.

132 Morton Kelsey, *Healing and Christianity* (Minneapolis: Augsburg Publishing, 1995) p. 190.

[133] DeArteaga, pp. 108-142.

[134] DeArteaga, pp. 165-176.

[135] Kelsey, p. 189.

[136] Sanford, 1976, p. 168.

[137] Sanford, 1972, pp. 151-155.

[138] Sanford, 1976, pp. 167-181.

[139] DeArteaga, p. 175.

[140] DeArteaga, p. 210.

[141] Sanford, 1976, p. 29.

[142] Sanford, 1976, p. 36.

[143] Sanford, 1976, p. 40.

[144] Sanford, 1976, p. 135.

[145] Sanford, 1976, pp. 218-282.

 Chapter Ten

The Power of Christ's Healing Presence

And I pray that you, being rooted and established in love, may have power, together with all the saints, to grasp how wide and long and high and deep is the love of Christ, and to know this love that surpasses knowledge—that you may be filled to the measure of all the fullness of God (Eph. 3:17b-19).

Georgette's Final Acceptance of Her Mentally Disabled Child

One of the more significant healings in my life took place several years ago. I have a child who is mentally disabled, and he was ten years old when this healing occurred in my life. For several months I was always folding my arms across my chest, holding them very closely to my body. It got to the point that several people were noticing this about me. I began asking the Lord why I was doing this and if there was something I was trying to hold in. I began feeling like I needed someone to hold me, and if they could hold me long enough and hard enough, something was going to come out of me. One evening as I was reading the Word of God the Holy Spirit quickened Isaiah 54:11 to me: *"O afflicted city, lashed by storms and not comforted."* I began to weep and weep and wondered, "From what have I never been comforted?"

A few weeks later I was at a special meeting with a guest speaker from out of town. Earlier that morning I had completely come to the end of myself with holding in this problem. I cried out to the Lord, saying, " Lord I have no one here who can hold me so that this can come out. Lord you are going to have to be the one to hold me." I never said a word to anyone about this, and that evening as I went forward for prayer all this man said as he came over to pray for me was, "Father, hold your daughter tonight." The Holy Spirit came over me, and I felt myself relax and gently fall to the floor. As the Holy Spirit began doing His work I went back to the day my son was born; I was in the delivery room and the doctor was telling me that my son had microcephaly, an abnormally small head, and they did not know the outcome. As I lay on the floor with my Father in heaven holding me the pain began coming out of me from hearing the truth about my newly born son. What came out of me was a deep wailing of, " No... no..." and I sobbed uncontrollably and loudly as the Lord healed me. The denial left me in those wails of "no" that night. When I finally got up off the floor and the Holy Spirit was finished, my arms were no longer around myself trying to hold all of that in. After ten years I was finally free, and my arms were wide open. Thank you so much, Jesus.

Learning from Christ's Presence

There is always a temptation to look upon the rather "simple and unsophisticated" accounts of Jesus encountering "everyday common people" as recorded in the Gospels as not totally relevant or rigorous enough for our modern, scientific world. After all, there is no mention of neurolinguistic programming, existentialism, Gestalt therapy, logical positivism, selective serotonin reuptake inhibitors (SSRI), obsessive-compulsive disorder (OCD), cognitive-behavior techniques, rational-emotive therapy (RET), 12-step programs, Hamilton Depression Rating Scale and so forth in the Gospels. True, they were all developed centuries later. Nevertheless the teaching and healing ministry of Jesus is much more profound than often appreciated. The depth of Jesus' teaching and healing cuts to the core of much more than we realize. To think otherwise is a serious mistake and great loss to our souls.

Since the ministry of healing prayer is rooted and centered in the actual and real presence of Jesus and His Spirit, one can learn certain "principles" from the presence. These are a number of basic, foundational principles that also cut to the heart of much of psychology and psychotherapy and show the weaknesses of their methods and techniques. I have seen the following principles, which are also rooted in the Scriptures, demonstrated repeatedly in the ministry of healing prayer. In other words knowledge also comes by *participation* which evangelical theology is only now beginning to appreciate.[1]

The intellectual tradition has so greatly impacted evangelical theology that much of it is abstract and descriptive.[2] As Williams wrote: "Pick up almost any evangelical theology book and you will notice the way theological knowledge takes the form of description."[3] But what good is truth if you cannot live it or do not have enough power to realize it? Truth should not remain abstract. True theology is experienced. In the ministry of healing prayer we learn by being immersed in the written Word and also by actively participating with the Living Word as He ministers to His people. This is also why I have included true stories of many people's actual healings in this book.

The Kingdom of God: Truth and Reality 101

Nicodemus was a Pharisee and prominent religious teacher who came to see Jesus at night (John 3:1-15). With some flattery and probably condescension from what he claimed he and others knew, he acknowledged Jesus as a teacher from God. Jesus wasted no time, directly declaring via "I tell you the truth" that no one can see the kingdom of God unless they are born again. Jesus directly challenged Nicodemus' way of knowing and the presumption that Nicodemus could know about miracles and hence the kingdom of God. He assumed this came by study, tradition, observation and rational analysis. Jesus knew that if this basic presupposition was not addressed, the whole discussion that night would be a waste of time.

Nicodemus was surprised and taken aback to the point that he almost mocked Jesus' statement with a reply about a man entering into his mother's womb again (John 3:4). He was on the verge of telling Jesus He was talking nonsense. Jesus replied directly again via "I tell you the truth" and declared that being born again involves purity and a work of the Holy Spirit which is beyond the control and direction of man (John 3:5-8). The work of the Spirit, like "wind," is not subject to man's analysis, spiritual technique or psychological manipulation. Nicodemus again stated that he could not understand. Jesus replied that this involved His work on the cross so that everyone who believes in Him will have eternal life (John 3:9-14).

This dialogue of Jesus with Nicodemus has profound implications for modern psychology and therapy. The most basic need of people is salvation—a total rebirth, a complete regeneration of their whole being (John 3:16; Jer. 24:7; Ezek. 36:26). Sin is so deep and serious that nothing less than a total renovation of one's being is required. It's like things got so bad you may as well start all over again. The emotions, will and intellect have all been warped by sin such that people are alienated from God and are under His righteous judgment (Rom. 1:18-32). People are not fundamentally "okay." The most basic healing of the soul comes from being united with God and having eternal life. This is in direct contradiction to the idea that people are evolving or improving, that man can transform himself by psychological technique or that surface or behavioral techniques are an answer for the human condition. Union with Jesus and the Father is different from the world's band-aid solutions of self-realization, self-fulfillment or self-empowerment.

In order to truly understand oneself and reality as well as the more advanced things (John 3:12)—those of heaven—one must be indwelt by the Spirit. True comprehension of knowledge, or "epistemology" as the philosophers and other pundits call it, comes from union with God and being His child (John 1:12-13; 1 Cor. 2:10-14). This idea "drove the Greeks crazy" (1 Cor. 1:23). This is beyond intellectual brilliance, religion or philosophy and is readily seen in Nicodemus who, with all his knowledge and learning, simply could not grasp what Jesus taught. True wholeness and healing require an understanding of how things really are; hence union with Jesus and His Spirit is fundamentally and absolutely required. Encountering a person (John 14:6) is not the same as mastering abstractions of reality. Ultimate knowledge comes through God's grace, mercy and love, not ever anyone's mental ability or rising to a "higher consciousness." Trying to understand reality without the Spirit and Jesus is far worse than trying to drive across Europe with only a map of Africa.

Jesus set His priority and agenda with His reference to the kingdom of God (John 3:3,5). Living in and under the rule and reign of God brings freedom, power, healing, truth, peace, joy and life (Rom. 14:6; 1 Cor. 4:20). God's kingdom is radically different from the kingdom of men and the kingdom of this world from which we must be rescued (Col. 1:13). Where your heart and soul are anchored and where you ultimately live affects your whole life. Meaning, purpose, significance and hope for the future are linked to being in the kingdom of God (Jas. 2:5; Heb. 12:28; 2 Pet. 1:11). Unfortunately modern psychology and psychotherapy are not all interested in the kingdom of God that was so crucial to Jesus (Matt. 4:23, 5:19, 13:1-58; Luke 11:2; Acts 1:3) and a spiritual priority for His followers (Matt. 6:33). Therefore people live and suffer under the ethics, techniques, theories, philosophies and ideologies of the kingdom of men in their search for wholeness and healing. Knowing to which kingdom you belong and are operating in is critical to everything else, which is why it was on Jesus' agenda with Nicodemus. For psychology and psychotherapy to ever have any deeper meaning they must reflect the worldview and priorities of the Son of Man. Otherwise they will suffer from a "meaning disorder" and general anxiety over their identity.

There is no Substitute for a Presence

There is no substitute for the presence of Jesus. Imagine a mother, Ann, going to a huge and very busy department store with her five year-old daughter, Susie, just before Christmas. After an hour or so in the store, in the midst of many people and bustling activity, Susie is separated from her mother. Understandably Susie panics and begins to cry. Fortunately a store clerk comes by and makes an announcement over the intercom for her mother to come to a certain checkout counter and be reunited with her daughter. Of course everyone knows the most obvious—there is nothing like the presence and embrace of the child's mother to overcome the anxiety, sadness and insecurity. The mother does not even need to analyze the situation nor does the child analyze anything upon seeing her mother. Healing from the emotional distress comes solely from the presence of one who loves. What if the store clerk referred the child to a mental health professional who decided that the child needed an explanation of separation anxiety or general anxiety disorder and techniques in modifying the behavior? Or what if the child was given 20 mg of Paxil? When I share this story at conferences, the audience always immediately laughs at the very idea of the last two solutions.

But as adults, why do we so quickly accept techniques or medication? Why is it so different now? We are still people, are we not? Would not experiencing the presence of Jesus, who has redeemed us and is the lover of our soul, be the logical progression for a personal presence? Just as a child coming into the presence of a mother brings healing, why cannot our coming into the presence of Jesus bring our healing? Since even secular research has shown that the character of a counselor or therapist is crucial to any healing, we see the ultimate realization in Christ who has all the fruits of the Spirit (Gal. 5:22-23), is full of compassion and love, is the Wonderful Counselor (Isa. 9:6) and who was the most genuine of all human beings.[4]

We need to cultivate a simple, but not simplistic, faith in Jesus. Jesus invites all His followers to come directly to Him to unload their burdens (worries, addictions, compulsions, anxieties, fears, stress and more) and experience His rest directly from Him (Matt. 11:28-29). The Lord Himself will restore our souls (Ps. 23:3), create a pure heart in us and renew our spirits (Ps. 51:10). God's unfailing love will comfort us (Ps. 119:76) just as we should desire His compassion (Ps. 119:77). The Lord saves those who are crushed in spirit (Ps. 34:18) and heals the brokenhearted (Ps. 147:3). The Lord can turn our hearts around (Ps. 119:36).

The transformation of our inner being thus comes out of our union, or connection, with Jesus and the Father and His Spirit.

This logically requires our experiencing their presence instead of relying on any intervening mental, behavioral or spiritual techniques to heal and transform our souls. Especially in the issues of heart and soul we must continue to live in Jesus as we first received Him (Col. 2:6-7), rooted and built up in Him.

We must become as children in order to enter the kingdom of God in the first place, so why must the healing of our souls be so complex? Things become much simpler and clearer when we learn to live out of our union with Jesus, the hope of glory who is in us.

Love is the Greatest Power

Acknowledging the fundamental need for a relational presence, we appreciate that Jesus was so incredibly effective because He was so compassionate and fully exhibited the love of the Father. How much you love is more pivotal than how much you know. He had compassion on the multitudes, touched the "untouchable" and rejected lepers, stopped for the blind and lame and more. His love healed. The secular world is just finally beginning to appreciate the importance of love for health and healing. Medical science is beginning to appreciate the fact that love is the greatest stimulus to the immune system.

Many times in healing prayer I have seen how Jesus shows His love and compassion especially to the deeply wounded. A deep need for love can be behind rejection, lack of self-acceptance, some addictions or even gender confusion. That may be due to a lack of love from a mother or father early in life. In such cases Jesus can "supernaturally fill" that empty place in a person's heart.

Mark was trying for years to overcome smoking. He disclosed that when he smoked, he was longing for feelings of comfort. As we prayed, the Lord revealed that he had never received comfort from his mother. When I asked Mark if he could remember being held by his mother, he replied that he could not remember even once being held by her. Mark was quite willing to confess the addiction and for-give his mother, and he desired Jesus to touch his heart. The Lord then healed and "filled" his heart with the comfort he had missed as a child. He was completely delivered from smoking. This is not always the case for everyone who smokes, and it did not involve any evil spirit. But it was the case for Mark.

Some people on prayer teams have a special anointing for min-istering mother or father love. I remember one conference in partic-ular where a young lady had much pain from the past as well as a deep love deficit. As my female prayer partner put her arm around her, we prayed that Jesus' love would fill those empty places, and He did. It was very obvious from the look on her face and how she felt that something undeniably real had happened in her spirit. Some-times a person will feel warmth all over their being; other times they actually feel like Jesus is holding them and often they "just know" that the aching part of their heart has been filled supernaturally. This is an example of experiencing the love of Jesus—which surpasses knowledge (Eph. 3:19)—and comfort from His love (Phil. 2:1).

I received such a prayer once for healing from a "separation anxiety" event from my mother when I was very small. The whole next day I felt so calm and relaxed I could hardly work—a miracle in itself for how intense and task-oriented I was at the time. The effect was real.

Love will often come from genuine and caring relationships which is also another means by which the incarnational presence of Jesus can touch our spirits.

Healing Must Touch the Whole Person

A person hurt by a traumatic event such as sexual abuse or incest is hurt in their emotions, heart, soul, spirit and mind and maybe body as well. The event impacts the whole person not just the mind. Therefore it is often true that the reversal—the true and lasting healing—comes when the whole person is impacted and touched in the healing process. This typically happens when Jesus comes to heal and touch the emotions, heart, soul, spirit, body and mind in the ways described in this book by people who have experienced more of Jesus. People are more than just "logic boxes" who need right information or advice. I often hear people say that they know lots of biblical truth in their head, but they cannot connect it to their heart. In effect they are saying that they want healing for their whole person. This happens when we enter into a relational presence with the One who can, indeed, touch our whole being. Biblical truth is important, but it must be appropriated and experienced and there must be power to realize it to the depth of one's being. In healing prayer for sexual abuse, for example, I often see a deep and complete healing that removes shame, guilt, hatred and all the pain of the memories from the event. Lies and pain are typically imbedded in our memories, in our inner being, through an experience. Conversely an experiential encounter with Jesus will replace the lies with truth and the pain with healing. The biblical truth we know in our heads, through the presence of Jesus goes right into our hearts and our memories. Jesus and His Spirit then minister to the whole person, not just one's intellect and behavior patterns as addressed by any number of cognitive-behavioral or other techniques.

When an emotional wound is truly the issue, an intellectual answer will not help because the real problem lies elsewhere.[5] Just like you can only deal with an intellectual argument when you are thinking and discussing it, you "can only deal with a feeling when you are feeling it."[6] Only then can you connect to the hurt or pain and give God access to it.[7] A physical issue for the body might only be overcome by exercise and good nutrition, and an issue of the will is remedied by decision and choices. Likewise an emotional issue must engage the emotions and healing appropriate for the emotions and what is behind them.

Jesus taught that we understand not only with our minds but also with our hearts (Matt. 13:15; John 12:40). When hearts are hard, understanding is almost impossible (Mark 6:52, 8:17). It is through the eyes of our hearts that we understand much about Christ (Eph. 1:18). Thus, to truly understand, we understand with our whole being; to truly experience, we experience with our whole being. Instead of Descartes' "I think, therefore I am," it is more like "I am loved, therefore I understand." True understanding involves feelings and facts. The world is finally beginning to catch up to the biblical understanding of knowledge with research into "emotional intelligence." Truly, "...our emotions are an important source of information necessary for a full comprehension of things."[8]

Truth is Powerful When Spoken by Jesus

Perhaps we have believed lies, or in spite of what the Scriptures tell us we are not sure about what Jesus thinks of us given what we have done or has happened to us. As an analogy, think of a son searching for approval from his father who tends to be uncommunicative and somewhat distant. Others may well tell him that of course his dad approves of him. His mother may say, "Of course your dad approves of you, he has just not yet told you." His schoolteacher may well affirm him and suggest that since he is a fine young boy, his dad must approve of him. But his dad never says so. From whose lips would the issue be settled once and for all? Only from his dad's lips, hearing his own father affirm him directly. Likewise there are times when we need to hear directly from Jesus.

In praying with Walter, a man recovering from decades of depression, I learned that he still believed he was a failure in God's eyes. This was understandable given the outward perception of many lost years in his life. I did not at first present Scripture verses to impress or convince him otherwise. I strongly sensed that Jesus wanted to tell him directly, so I simply said that he should listen should Jesus tell him directly what He thinks of him. Some time later, as we were in prayer, he was silent for several minutes and wept silently for a short while. After he had wiped away the tears, I asked him what happened. He said that he clearly heard Jesus say, "You are my son, and I am pleased with you." When he heard that, it was an incredibly moving and powerful moment that brought deep healing and release. I then remarked that he heard this from the very throne of Father God, and there is no higher authority on earth or in heaven. For Walter, the issue was settled. While some might argue that Walter just needed more faith to believe what the Scriptures teach, I would argue that God's mercy and grace is such that the Lord knew Walter needed to hear it directly from the Living Word. Did not Jesus say that His sheep will hear His voice (John 10:3, 27)? Since Jesus spoke directly to the apostle Paul about his thorn in the flesh after Paul asked Jesus three times (2 Cor. 12:9), might He not speak to any of us as well should He so decide? Are we not loved as much in the kingdom as the apostle was? Might there not be other times when Jesus speaks to us to bring us back into closer fellowship with Himself (Rev. 3:20)?

Juanita came from a very dysfunctional family which consistently denied all the sexual abuse she received from them as a little child. As is often the case in such families, Juanita was blamed for any problems in the family and labeled the "sick one." She received considerable healing through several prayer sessions but was struggling with recurring anger towards her brother, one of her abusers. She had forgiven him entirely and could not understand why she was still angry. I could think of a number of reasons why this might be the case but chose to wait on Jesus to hear what He would say. After about two minutes Juanita was overcome with the sudden realization of the root of her anger when Jesus very clearly spoke to her and said, "You are angry because I love your brother as much as I love you." This word from Jesus, which at other times can come as a word of knowledge or wisdom, led to further deep healing and release for Juanita.

Ultimately truth is relational, an impossible concept for the Greeks. Jesus is the way and the truth and the life (John 14:6). As Baker puts it:

> Jesus knew that people using their intellect alone could never come to a complete understanding of the truth about life. He didn't say, "Let me teach you about truth"; he said, "I am the truth." He knew that the highest form of knowledge comes from trusting relationships rather than greater amounts of information.[8]

Jesus Can Forgive Your Sin: The Power of the Cross

Sin is experienced by all people in this world and is part of the human condition. Guilt is the emotion attached to it. Guilt is not an invention of the Bible or of the Church; it is "universally present in the human soul."[10] The function of guilt is to bring us to God where we can experience His grace and restoration to wholeness and not be "found out" or embarrassed or condemned. True guilt is a ministry of the Holy Spirit (John 16:8-10; 2 Cor. 7:10) as opposed to false guilt from the world. Think of guilt as a smoke alarm sending a signal that something is wrong in the house in order to give a chance to escape to safety.[11] When there is a problem in one's soul due to a "smoldering issue," the rising smoke—

guilt—signals a need for healing and restoration. Similarly "repentance is the door to grace."[12]

Unfortunately much of psychology and therapy have neglected the reality of personal sin and guilt.[13] Psychology and psychotherapy have all but forgotten sin, denying its reality and suppressing the truth with ideas like we are all basically okay or the very idea of sin will cause a neurosis. Christian counseling training programs have little or no emphasis on confession in most curricula.[14] This is in contrast to Jesus who warned about the seriousness of sin (Matt. 5:29, 18:8; Mark 9:45) and came to take away the sin of the world (John 1:29). In healing prayer Jesus can forgive even the worst sins and begin to restore a person to wholeness.

Paulette came for prayer and reluctantly shared how she had become very promiscuous for several years. She was truly embarrassed about her past, including numerous occasions of oral sex. She said that she felt quite "filthy" and defiled. As we prayed and she confessed her sin and also forgave the many sins of others against her, the Lord began to restore her. The Lord also removed all the defilement from her soul and even went to the root where it all started, giving her freedom. For a while it was hard for her to really believe the Lord could forgive her, but the Lord was enabling her to receive His love. I explained that God's intent was not to embarrass or expose her but to bring her sins to light so that she could be restored and cleansed. I reassured her that it is all about learning to live by grace. As we were concluding our time of prayer, the Lord gave her a picture of herself in a pure, white gown. This symbolized, of course, her purity in His sight. There is no substitute for the power of Christ's forgiveness of one's sins. As Long and Strickler wrote:

> True, life-transforming forgiveness comes from Jesus alone. This is why Christian healing prayer can go far beyond anything that secular therapy and counseling can offer.[15]

The tragedy is that thousands of people have been denied this experience due to the darkened thinking of men (John 1:5). This shuts the door to grace.

Jesus Prevails Over Spiritual Forces

In Christ we have victory over Satan (1 John 4:4) and all manner of spiritual forces that seek to keep us in bondage. We are commanded to be strong in the Lord and also in His mighty power (Eph. 6:10). Deliverance ministry, as a part of the larger ministry of restoration and wholeness, is a reality for the Christian life and must be taken seriously. For the development of the biblical and practical foundations for this ministry, as well as some correctives, I refer the reader to chapter eight, "Deliverance Ministry: Myth or Mandate?" in my book, *The Great Omission: Resolving Critical Issues for the Ministry of Healing and Deliverance.*

Henrietta, a Christian woman and mother, recently began to recall some early childhood memories. These memories were coming spontaneously and not as a result of seeing any counselor or from suggestions from anyone. But she did know that the memories were quite disturbing and had decided to come for prayer. As she started to share the memories, it was clear to me that she had been forced as a child into some traumatic rituals. One memory did not make much sense to her. She remembered being in a dark church basement with many witnesses. Worse still, she had an uncomfortable feeling that she had been sexually violated as part of some ceremony. As she shared more details, she began to realize that as a child she had been married to Satan through a ritual. I then explained that Jesus had the power to set her free and begin to deal with all the pain and shame of that hideous event. I then simply stated, in a very calm voice, that she was a child of the living God and a member of the bride of Christ (Rev. 19:7; Eph. 5:25-

30). In that very instant she began to manifest the presence of evil spirits. As I had expected, with the truth of the Word of God spoken in a direct and specific way against the kingdom of darkness, there would be an immediate reaction. Jesus, by His Spirit, began to bring freedom and healing.

Martha had suffered for years from fear and rejection which occasionally brought on depression. Martha was in a graduate program in counseling at a seminary and came for prayer seeking release. As we talked and listened to the Spirit, I discerned a strong "soul tie" with her mother who had been excessively dominating and verbally abusive throughout her whole childhood. Martha had forgiven her mother for many things, including the domination and verbal abuse, and did not harbor any anger and resentment. She simply wanted to be healed. For some years I had been skeptical about soul ties (1 Cor. 6:16), thinking that it was some "charismatic presumption," but I have learned from the Scriptures and experience that there are at times very real spiritual connections at work in soul ties. I explained the concept of soul ties to her and suggested that we should include this in our prayer time. As soon as I prayed to ask the Lord by His Spirit to break this ungodly soul tie between mother and daughter, she experienced a deep and almost unbearable pain in her stomach. Both she and I were caught off guard. I took authority over the pain and commanded all spirits to immediately stop causing the pain. In a few seconds her pain disappeared as fast as it had come. I then broke the soul tie by the sword of the Spirit, and she felt an immediate release and freedom. For a half hour she felt waves of joy and peace flood her being as the Lord continued directly to minister to her. She actually broke out in laughter for a while which was a release from years of bottled up pain. For the rest of the healing prayer service she sat in a pew with an unmistakable glow on her face. She was changed by the power of the Lord's presence.

Elinor had lived with a man who was involved in some occult and New Age practices, including yoga. Years later she became a Christian and soon confessed all her past involvements and truly sought the Lord's forgiveness. Nevertheless she still felt connected in some strange way to this man. She told me that whenever he would come to the city, which had over half a million people, and even though she had not met with him since the relationship had been severed years ago, she somehow knew he was there. She could "sense" when he arrived and exactly when he would leave. She said that she even wondered if she was "going psychic." I explained there was still a spiritual connection with him because of the sexual and emotional involvement. We prayed with her and in Jesus' name and by His Spirit asked the soul tie to be completely severed. Since that moment of specific prayer she had no knowledge of his comings and goings as later informed by some old friends who told her after the fact that he had been in the city. No drug or psychotherapy could ever overcome this spiritual connection.

Patricia was suffering from sleep deprivation. For almost twenty years she had found it difficult to get a good night's sleep, and for the last year she had to resort to sleeping pills. A few days earlier she almost killed herself by walking across an intersection against the lights. She was so tired, almost like a zombie, and was startled by the sound of cars braking and honking at her. Understandably she was desperate for help. As we prayed and waited in Jesus' presence I asked how long this had been a problem. She replied that it had been twenty years now. From an earlier prayer session I remembered that she had been molested at a supposed spiritual retreat weekend. I sensed from the Lord that this was the origin, but I did not know exactly what the connection was. As we waited Jesus suddenly spoke directly to her and revealed that she firmly believed from that traumatic experience she had to stay awake to survive. She had been drugged during the evening meal soon after arriving at this supposed spiritual retreat center. She soon fell asleep and was then sexually molested. When she began to regain consciousness she sensed what was happening and tried to stay awake at all costs but was not always able to. The belief was that "it is not safe to fall asleep." The Lord then brought up other memories over the years of waking up and being oppressed by evil spirits and with the same idea that she had to stay awake since it was not safe to fall asleep. I helped her to confess and proclaim that Jesus is the sovereign Lord, that she can always rest in His presence, that He will prevail over all forces of evil and that she is safe in Him. Then in Jesus' name I banished all evil spirits that tormented her from that time onwards and asked Jesus to replace all the fear from those memories with His peace and security. Jesus did exactly that, and immediately she felt a release from all the fear and trauma. Since that prayer time she has been sleeping extremely well, in fact, on average eleven hours a night. Her strength is coming back from a normal sleeping pattern. She said it was almost like "getting her life back." All it took was the Spirit's revelation and the presence of Jesus, not any imaging technique where she repeatedly imagined herself sleeping or completing exercise sheets on fear or any of the seemingly endless "self-help" strategies.

I share the above true stories not to add sensationalism to this book. This is about lasting fruit, freedom and experiencing more of Jesus. There are many very real spiritual forces at work which, when present, must be discerned and dealt with for the healing and wholeness of those coming for ministry. Such forces cannot be dealt with by cognitive restructuring, Prozac, depth psychology, transactional analysis, object relations theory, visualization, etc. Those methods are totally and woefully inadequate. Henrietta had actually spent several months in a psychiatric ward and several years on psychiatric medication due to the after effects of the rituals behind suppressed memories and denial from her family. The only solution is the power of Jesus' presence, His name, His blood and His Spirit. Almost no counseling literature even discusses such things, which is a reflection, I believe, of the preoccupation with the modern empirical mind that cannot fathom unseen spiritual realities (2 Cor. 4:18).

I fully realize that there are some who might laugh at the above examples. However, I have ministered to those who have wept and agonized sometimes for years over the influence of such spiritual forces in their lives. It was never a laughing matter for them.

The Wisdom of Jesus is Supreme

Jesus is the Wonderful Counselor (Isa. 9:6) in whom are hidden all treasures of wisdom and knowledge (Col. 2:3). Jesus Himself is the wisdom and power of God (1 Cor. 1:24). While He does give wisdom to counselors and those who lead in healing prayer, Jesus at times will also show His wisdom more directly to those receiving healing prayer. This again is part of learning to minister in the real presence of Jesus and His Spirit. The following examples are but a few of the sorts of things that are experienced in healing prayer. An entire book could be written on this topic alone.

Freda was never close to her father who was a man of few words. He cared for his family and was a good provider. But Freda has this "ache" in her heart. She did not come to this awareness by introspection or narcissism. It was holding her back in her Christian walk and making it hard, among other things, to receive love from her heavenly Father. Halfway through the prayer time I asked the Lord to take her to whatever painful memory was yet to be dealt with by His healing presence because we were not sure at that juncture what He would do next. There was silence for a while and then there was a stream of tears. I knew better than to ask what was happening; I did not want to interrupt Jesus in His work as the "ultimate psychotherapist." When she opened her eyes, I asked what had happened. With an almost childlike joy she said that she had just gone fishing with Jesus. I asked her to explain. She said that her father's favorite pastime was fishing, and as a little girl she had always wanted to go fishing with him. But he never once took her along. So she had many memories of standing on the dock watching her father go off onto the lake by himself. Progressively there was sadness in her heart that she could never be with her father. This was a main source of the "ache" in her heart, for the memories were strongest there. But now Jesus took her right back to the memory when she was standing on the dock. He came in a boat to her, asked her to join Him and together they went fishing. This was a profoundly healing event, for Jesus' love was such that He would do that with her. As a result the void from the relationship with her father was filled and healed.

This healing was not any form of visualization or guided imagery since I did not even know what was happening and she was not prepared for what Jesus was about to do. Jesus, in His wisdom, knew exactly what would touch her heart. Hours of therapy might not ever uncover this, and if it did, one is left with the question of how to possibly heal that part of her life. This story might seem trivial and simple, but to a small child it is not. From what I know of Jesus in the Gospels, where He showed deep compassion and gentleness and joyously received little children into His lap (Matt. 19:13), I can easily imagine Him taking a little girl fishing. Can you?

Francine came for prayer and for a while there seemed to be no direction. She wasn't quite sure about healing prayer and what her deepest needs were, but she did come out of obedience to the Lord. My prayer partner had a picture of an apple pie coming repeatedly to his mind for some time. Initially he thought it was his imagination or maybe some hidden craving for food. Finally, with some hesitation, he mentioned this to Francine. Immediately she said that was her favorite pie, and when she was a child her grandmother baked many such pies which she always enjoyed. This soon led to a flood of memories, all of which were good and revolved around many happy times with her grandmother. This encouraged her heart to realize that the Lord was truly at work and gave her confidence to go deeper in healing prayer. Jesus, in His wisdom, used her enjoyment of apple pie to open wide the door to healing. Not what you usually expect!

Cynthia was unable to sleep peacefully through the night, typically bothered by all sorts of fears. This had been going on for years and was depriving her of energy and joy in her Christian life. As we talked for a few moments when she began to share her heart, I discerned that she was unsure of God's love for her and that she was tormented by some deep fears. After waiting upon the Lord in silence for His direction, two childhood memories came back, both involving a coffin and one with a deceased person in a coffin. The other memory was more vivid, stronger, with more fear and involved a closed coffin that was covered in dust. Cynthia said that in those two past events, now relived and felt by her memories, she sensed a fear of death and some sort of evil. The Lord prompted me to gently declare His love for Cynthia from her childhood and also His glory, majesty and power over death and evil. I prayed that Jesus would eradicate the fears from her heart and mind. From that point I wasn't sure what Jesus would do, so my prayer partner and I simply waited again in silence. After several minutes Cynthia silently wept and then burst out in joy with laughter. I asked what had happened, and she told us that first Jesus spoke to her directly to reassure her of His love for her and that she belonged to Him.

Then He took her back to the strongest and most vivid memory, the one with the closed coffin. Although she did not see Jesus, she knew that it was He who blew off the dust, opened the coffin and then—incredibly—made hundreds of pure white doves fly out from the coffin. That immediately broke the power of fear in her heart such that she started to laugh. I had anticipated that we would help her walk through some past memories wherein Jesus may well expose lies, speak the truth to her and possibly rebuke some evil spirits, but Jesus knew better! Once again the ingenuity and wisdom of Jesus accomplished in an instant what imaging or cognitive techniques could not. Since that prayer time Cynthia has been sleeping extremely well and without any fear at all. She wrote as follows regarding the moment when Jesus spoke to her:

> Today I feel great. Since I got up I cannot stop thinking about God's words last night, "I love you and you are mine." This is the most direct message from Him I have ever had. I always thought some of the pictures and dreams were just my "fruitful" imagination. Now I know it was Him. But to hear "I" love you and you are "mine." It was a complete sentence and in first person. I could not have said that in my head. It was definitely Him.

Olivia was suffering from increased confusion, anxiety and fear. The confusion was especially strong, consistently undermining her ability to think clearly. Her past was filled with pain and psychiatric drugs even as a young teenager. Through healing prayer on a number of occasions, as well as loving relationships in her faith community, she was able to reduce the number of drugs from over twenty to about seventeen. Under the care of her psychiatrist she was able to lower the dosage of some of the remaining drugs, including the antipsychotic drugs.

As we began in healing prayer she felt the fear and confusion very strongly, so I asked for more of the presence of the Spirit to comfort her. In a few minutes her mind was more at peace. I knew of many things I could pray with her as well as the types of things that Jesus could do in a situation like this. But I just waited to see how He would direct since the wisdom of Jesus is what really counts.

After a short while in prayer Olivia said that she could see herself screaming many times as a child in a series of situations. But then she said that she never once screamed. I said that the Lord was telling her that in her family she was not allowed to express her emotions or communicate her thoughts and feelings. Thus, though she didn't scream, she certainly felt like it. Then the Lord suddenly brought back one memory where this was very clear and from that time onwards she was drugged in order to "resolve" the problem. I led her in a prayer of specific forgiveness for that devaluing dynamic in her family. She expressed the fact that there was very little love from her family, and I just laid my hands on her and asked the Lord to supernaturally fill her heart in those empty places. In those moments she said that she could feel a solid sense of peace and warmth come over and into her.

Next, as we waited in prayer, the Lord gave her a vision of a door which was partially open with light streaming out. She was in the dark and looking towards the door. She knew Jesus was on the other side, and He was inviting her to walk through the door. Olivia was not sure what the vision meant, but the Lord revealed to me that it symbolized her making a transition in life from dependency on drugs and others and identity with her illnesses over the years to new responsibilities and a new future now that she had experienced a greater measure of healing. I encouraged her to open the door further and step into the light with Jesus. That took a few minutes; there was some hesitation because of the unknown. After she had finally walked through the door, Jesus told her to turn around and shut the door. When she told me that, I replied that Jesus wanted her to decide that she would not go back and live in the past and this would be a real transition, a "clean break" with the past. Suddenly a bridge appeared and Jesus was asking her to walk across the bridge to the other side. This took more time on her part, but with Jesus walking beside her she was able to cross the bridge. That part of the vision symbolized her first major challenge in walking out her healing and growing in new responsibilities.

The Lord directed me to lay hands on her and pray for the healing of her brain to overcome the effects of the psychiatric drugs. She received that prayer and reported that she could feel warmth in her head and a "newness" in her mind.

When the prayer time was done she said that the confusion was completely gone, her mind was clear and even her natural vision was much sharper and clearer. She also had a profound sense of peace in her whole being. That all came from the presence of Jesus. Notice how this prayer time was not the typical "healing of memories;" it was focused on the spiritual direction of Jesus who did something different. This experience with Jesus has been a real turning point in her life, and she has been able to constructively make steps to reorder her life.

Learning from Ezekiel

Olivia's healing experience might seem "weird" or "different" to some Christians. How do we even begin to understand this theologically? Olivia experienced a vision from the Lord, and it is not hard to understand theologically when you consider the spiritual experiences of Ezekiel.

While among the exiles by the Kebar River, "the heavens opened" and Ezekiel first saw the glory of the Lord and experienced his call from God all in "visions of God" (Ezek. 1:1-3:15). The Hebrew text indicates that it was not so much a vision of God but "divine visions" by an opening of the heavens so that he might observe supernatural realities.[16] Of necessity his supernatural eyes were opened so that he could see into the spiritual realm.

While he was sitting in is house and the elders of Judah were sitting before him, the "hand of the sovereign Lord" came upon him—that is, he experienced the presence (Ezek. 8:1) as God's overwhelming intervention in his own consciousness.[17] He looked into the spiritual realm and saw a figure like that of a man who stretched out what looked like a hand and took him by the hair of his head (Ezek. 8:2-3). The Spirit lifted him up between heaven and earth and, "in visions of God," he was taken from Babylon to Jerusalem some hundreds of miles away. This was not an actual physical transport; it was entirely through supernatural visions.[18]

The Spirit first took him, in this vision, to the entrance of the north gate in the inner court (Ezek. 8:3-4) where he saw the glory of the Lord as in the plain before (Ezek. 1:4-28). The Lord commanded him to look north and asked him a question (Ezek. 8:5-6). Then the Lord "brought him" via the vision to the entrance of the court where, again in a visionary state, Ezekiel was commanded to dig a hole in a wall (Ezek. 8:7-8). Then, in the vision, he was to walk into the court and observe the wicked things being done there (Ezek. 8:9-14). Then he was taken to the north gate and the inner court to see more evil practices and idolatry (Ezek. 8:14-18). Ezekiel then saw the future judgment upon Jerusalem for its wickedness as well as the departure of the glory of the Lord (Ezek. 9:1-10:22). The Spirit then "lifted up" Ezekiel, again in the vision experience, to the gate that faces east to observe evil men and prophesy against the house of Israel as led by the Spirit (Ezek. 11:1-21). The Spirit then "lifted up" Ezekiel and brought him back to the exiles in Babylonia "in the vision given by the Spirit of God" and then the vision he had seen "went up" from him (Ezek. 11:24-25). In contrast to the first vision (Ezek. 1:4-2:8a) where Ezekiel was a spectator, here he was an active participant.[19]

The presence of the Lord came when "the hand of the Lord" was upon Ezekiel and the Spirit transported him to a valley full of dry bones (Ezek. 37:1). Again this was an entirely visionary experience; he was not actually in a valley of dry bones.[20] The Hebrew text clearly indicates "trancelike prophetic experiences and there is no need to suppose a literal physical journey in any of these instances."[21] The Lord asked Ezekiel if those bones could live, and he was then told to prophesy upon which the bones startled to rattle and people eventually appeared (Ezek. 37:3-10). This is probably the most "interactive" of all Ezekiel's visionary experiences since his prophetic words actually influenced the vision.[22] This whole visionary experience was symbolic in that the dry bones symbolized the house of Israel's loss of hope and thus the Lord's desire for new life and hope in the future (Ezek. 37:11).

The "hand of the Lord" again came upon Ezekiel and, "in visions of God," he was taken to the land of Israel up on a very high mountain (Ezek. 40:1-2). The Lord then took him by vision to see all parts of the future new temple (Ezek. 40-48).

The above visionary experiences were initiated and directed by the Holy Spirit. They were real and involved observing, hearing the Lord's voice, sometimes interacting like digging a hole in a wall (all in the supernatural realm) or prophesying, symbolism and being "transported" to different places. The book of Ezekiel thus describes a "category of experience" when one is in the supernatural or visionary realm. This is all part of a theology of the presence since it starts with "the hand of Lord was upon him" in the presence of the Spirit. But how is this relevant for Christians today?

Since the Spirit is now in all Christians and these are the latter days, there will be some Christians who will see visions or dream or prophesy (Joel 2:28). The Lord spoke to Peter in a vision involving a large sheet with animals (Acts 10:9-16) and to Paul in a vision (Acts 18:9). Those are examples of what Jesus and His Spirit are still doing today among His people. It happens at times in the ministry of healing prayer even today.

Ezekiel did not use the power of his mind or mental imaging or any spiritual technique to bring about these visions. They just happened; the Spirit initiated them. Likewise in healing prayer, when we invoke the presence of Jesus and His Spirit and wait in His presence, at times the Lord brings visions not unlike what Olivia above experienced. Jesus spoke to her, used symbolism and directed her in the midst of a very real and powerful vision for her healing and wholeness. In a visionary experience Ezekiel was told to dig a hole in a wall; the Lord told Olivia to walk through a doorway, close a door, turn a knob and cross a bridge. Dry bones symbolized the nation of Israel (Ezek. 37:11); Olivia's vision symbolized her transition to a new life. Such experiences do, at times, happen in healing prayer. Neither Olivia nor I used any spiritual technique or imaging—it just happened. We both believe in the reality of Christ's presence and His Spirit. This all requires discernment and fully comprehending the wisdom of Jesus.

Olivia's spiritual experience was not "weird" or "strange" when you consider Ezekiel, Peter and Paul's experiences. It is only "weird" or "strange" when one does not fully appreciate or understand the categories of experience that the Scriptures describe. Perhaps the "healing of memories" or "inner healing" could at times be called "healing through visions from the Lord"?

Endnotes

[1] David Alan Williams, "Knowing as Participation: Toward an Intersection Between Psychology & Postcritical Epistemology," in Mark R. McMinn and Timothy R. Phillips, *Care for the Soul: Exploring the Intersection of Psychology & Theology* (Downers Grove: InterVarsity Press, 2001) pp. 332-345.

[2] Williams, p. 336.

[3] Ibid.

[4] Roger F. Hurding, *Roots and Shoots: A Guide to Counselling and Psychotherapy* (London: Hodder and Stoughton, 1985) pp. 35-36.

[5] Tom Marshall, *Free Indeed!* (Kent: Sovereign World Ltd, 1975) p. 50.

[6] Marshall, p. 51.

[7] Ibid.

[8] Mark W. Baker, *The Greatest Psychologist Who Ever Lived: Jesus and the Wisdom of the Soul* (New York: HarperCollins Publishers, 2001) p. 187.

[9] Baker, p. 8.

[10] Paul Tournier, *Guilt and Grace: A Psychological Study* (London: Hodder and Stoughton, 1974, new edition) p. 135.

[11] Lynda D. Elliott, *An Invitation to Healing* (Grand Rapids: Chosen Books, 2001) p. 23.

[12] Tournier, pp. 66, 122.

[13] Philip G. Monroe, "Exploring Client's Personal Sin in the Therapeutic Context: Theological Perspectives on a Case Study of Self-Deceit," in Mark R. McMinn and Timothy R. Phillips, *Care for the Soul: Exploring the Intersection of Psychology & Theology* (Downers Grove: InterVarsity Press, 2001) pp. 202-217.

[14] Mark R. McMinn, *Psychology, Theology and Spirituality in Christian Counseling. AACC Counseling Library* (Wheaton: Tyndale House Publisher, 1996) p. 194.

[15] Brad Long and Cindy Strickler, *Let Jesus Heal Your Hidden Wounds: Cooperating With the Holy Spirit in Healing Ministry* (Grand Rapids: Chosen Books: 2001) p. 48.

[16] Daniel I. Block, *The Book of Ezekiel, Chapters 1-24: The New International Commentary on the Old Testament* (Grand Rapids: Eerdmans Publishing Co., 1997) p. 85.

[17] Block, 1997, p. 279.

[18] Block, 1997, p. 280.

[19] Ibid.

[20] Daniel I. Block, *The Book of Ezekiel, Chapters 25-48: The New International Commentary on the Old Testament* (Grand Rapids: Eerdmans Publishing Co., 1998) p. 372.

[21] Block, 1998, p. 373.

[22] Block, 1998, p. 372.

Chapter Eleven

Conclusion

What is highly valued among men is detestable in God's sight (Luke 16:15b).

This is love for God: to obey his commands. And his commands are not burdensome, for everyone born of God overcomes the world (1 John 5:3-4a).

Let us fix our eyes on Jesus, the author and perfecter of our faith... (Heb. 12:2a).

The Great Substitution: Why Did it Happen?

Why did much of the Church substitute the real presence of Jesus with the methods and techniques of the world for the healing and wholeness of its own people? Because the Church gradually moved away from living out of the incarnational presence of Jesus and His Spirit. A theology of the presence began to fade in much of the Church. With the "modern" era and the rise of secularism, the Church came under increasing pressure to conform to the world. The "pressure points" include the following.

The idolatry of reason. Rationalism appears whenever the Church tiptoes in the footsteps of Enlightenment thinkers. Evangelical Christianity, victimized by "Enlightenment" thinking which exalts reason and information processing, has adopted "human technique-centered methods for solving problems" and been rendered powerless.[1] Evangelicals commonly "believe that God has stopped talking and doing the incredible things we read about in the Scriptures."[2] This is partly why some Christians do not easily grasp belief in the supernatural presence of Jesus and understand a theology of the presence.

Scientific credibility. There is the perennial pressure to "validate" Christian counseling and therapy in the world's scientific context and language.[3] Christian psychologists have actually been among the strongest *defenders* of positivism (the use of empirical science and logic to study people) in spite of its many flaws and holes.[4] Not surprisingly the effectiveness of the use of Scripture, the spiritual gifts and the power of the Holy Spirit in counseling even for Christians have not even been seriously considered and apparently await further scientific research "to determine the empirical validity."[5] Can the presence and work of Jesus and His Spirit ever be subject to the scrutiny and empiricism of men? You cannot empirically verify or control or test the work of the Spirit (John 3:8) nor can you put Jesus into a therapeutic technique or formula.

The lure of technique. As Tournier astutely observed in reference to his difficulty in teaching his approach to therapy which did not easily lend itself to a method, "… Americans like a clearly formulated doctrine and a technique that can be taught."[6] Tournier understood the technical mindset. The modern mind readily has a fascination with "what works"—pragmatism: results before truth, technique before theology.

Cessationism. The belief that some of the gifts of the Spirit ceased as of the early Church era was—and is still in some places—taught by seminaries and Bible schools as gospel truth.[7] Cessationism is an unbiblical teaching that has robbed the Church of much of its power.[8] Thus the critical "tools" to realize healing prayer were not even acknowledged and of course not practiced. Cessationism is part of a larger tragedy in the Church:

> One of the greatest tragedies in Christian churches today, especially in the Reformed family of churches, is the rejection of the gift-giving, empowering work of the Holy Spirit. The result is churches full of Christians who are saved, who truly believe the Bible, who are working hard at doing the right things, but who are not experiencing the healing, life-transforming work of Jesus in their lives.[9]

Money. Insurance companies and government agencies do not normally recognize healing prayer as a billable therapeutic intervention and do not recognize it as legitimate counseling.[10] This presents a quandary for counselors who make their living from counseling fees: in order to make money they must use methods and techniques approved by the world.[11] Client assessment and proposed treatment plans are expected to use approved methods, practices and techniques recognized by managed care organizations.[12]

Seminaries and Bible schools offer counseling programs that are accredited and acknowledged by the world in order to attract students. Graduates who want to become professional counselors must be able to generate revenue according to the world's criteria and standards. This is not all wrong since Christians should have a presence in the world as counselors and therapists—being in the world but "not of it." A faithful Christian presence in academic institutions should challenge and critique the assumptions of those disciplines since Christ is ultimately the Lord of all disciplines, research and knowledge.

But the context is different for the healing and restoration of God's people. When the Church adopts the world's methods, it reminds me of Jesus' second temptation when Satan offered Him the "authority and splendor" of the world (Luke 4:5). At times one must decide whether one serves God or money (Matt. 6:24). Van Leeuwen has argued that the desire for power and wealth is behind the Christian psychologists' support of positivism: "To put it bluntly, it is easy to convince oneself that a given mode of investigation is above reproach as long as it is being handsomely financed."[13] The words of Jesus—"...*what is highly valued among men is detestable in God's sight*" (Luke 16:15)—can be quite unsettling at times.

The temptations of academic recognition, scientific credibility, professional status and wealth cannot be taken lightly. In becoming accredited by the world Christian institutions of higher learning should not lose their accreditation from Jesus. If Jesus was not concerned about His reputation, why should we be (Phil. 2:7)? Like Paul we are exhorted to imitate the humility of Jesus (Phil. 3:7-14). In any desire for intellectual respectability one should never be ashamed of Jesus or His words (Luke 9:26) or risk friendship with the world (Jas. 4:4).

Professionalism. There is a tendency to devalue the "common layperson" involved in healing prayer. After all, they are not "professionals" and healing prayer does appear as a very "professional" endeavor. Some believers even hesitate to enter this ministry because they feel inadequate and inferior when compared to clinical psychologists or therapists with years of professional experience. But such an understanding is flawed. The modern healing professions, along with most other professions, are a recent development from the late nineteenth century and thus an artifact of the modern world.[14]

The professionalization of occupations in the modern era was driven by capitalism, specialization, careerism, money, prestige, status, recognition, the marketing of knowledge and the control of one's place in the marketplace.[15] The low esteem and "sinking fortunes" of the clergy led to their professionalization so they would appear as "serious professionals in the modern world."[16] Unfortunately the culture of professionalization has actually disabled and weakened the Church.[17]

Before being a professional, one should have a true sense of calling, anointing and spiritual gifting given the priesthood of all believers (1 Pet. 2:5). With those prior spiritual requirements, those in the healing ministry need not feel inferior to professionals. One can, of course, be called, anointed, spiritually gifted and also professional, and God can certainly bless those in the healing professions.

A Tale of Two Tragedies

Due to the Great Omission, the Church has not taken seriously the healing and restoring of souls. When it does so, the Church by and large uses the theories, methods and techniques of the world. As one would predict, Christians are referred to professionals and experts when the needs of the human soul are "difficult." Of course there should be referrals for legal, financial, medical, career and other such issues. I question referral for believers with deep emotional disturbances, for example.[18] Seminaries routinely stress, for partly legitimate reasons, that pastors should refer their parishioners when a situation is beyond their expertise or training. It would appear that the Church has become a large referral agency that readily provides clients and wealth to the healing professions. Smith wrote about a lady who came to him for healing after having spent $50,000 U.S.

327

of her own money over fifteen years for healing from deep emotional pain.[19] Spending large sums of money for emotional healing with little result is more common than one would think.

There are at least two tragedies here. First, some of those who are referred are not helped as much as hoped for, or at times not at all. Second, this is a counter witness to the world since it declares that while Jesus may well save a soul, the Church does not really have the spiritual resources to heal and transform the soul. But this is all backwards. Why could it not be the other way around? Should not the world be coming to the Church, having heard about the presence of the Living God to truly and powerfully touch the human soul in the deepest and most painful places? What would happen if the Church lived out of that which was humanly impossible and allowed Jesus to do everything He wants to do in its midst?

When the Church refers its most hurting people because their emotional and psychological needs are beyond the expertise or training of pastors or clergy, the implicit assumption is that it all depends upon human ability. Strictly speaking, that is humanism. Are not such people actually in the *greatest* need of the healing presence of Jesus?

Needed: A Theology of Healing Prayer

The Church should fully reclaim its original mandate and joyful responsibility for the care of souls. The Church needs a robust theology of healing prayer for the care of souls far more than more techniques, or more methods, or more integration, or more theories or more systems of counseling or therapy. With a theology of healing prayer and ministering in the presence of Jesus and His Spirit, more can often be accomplished in a few hours than months or years of counseling or therapy. The healing of the soul is typically permanent, no longer requiring "maintenance" or continued effort. But that never negates or minimizes the need for obedience, discipleship, forsaking sin, conscious decisions to foster unity and love, works of mercy and so forth.

The basic foundation of healing prayer is a thorough understanding of the real and authentic presence of Jesus and His Spirit. This excludes all forms of visualization, mind power and anything that is even remotely New Age. This is more comprehensive and integrative than focusing on sin, lies, methods, the power of human analysis, theories, psychoanalytic technique and more. A presence and grace-based theology focused on experiencing the love of Jesus is much more comprehensive and integrative since it involves collaborating with Him and His Spirit first-hand to see what should be done in each situation with each person. One then prays for physical, relational, emotional, psychological and related issues for the whole person and their entire past. One learns to listen and collaborate with Jesus and His Spirit and understand the language of the Holy Spirit. One must also understand Jesus' ways of knowing—"His epistemology." This is all fundamental and basic and will determine everything else in the ministry of healing prayer.

The gifts of the Holy Spirit are crucial in the ministry of healing prayer. Jesus used all the gifts of the Spirit and the Church is expected to do the same today. A true theology of healing prayer will fully embrace all the spiritual gifts that the Father desires to bestow on His people.

A complete theology of healing prayer will have the worldview of Jesus and therefore take seriously the reality of demonic oppression and the need for deliverance, just as Jesus did.[20] Many counseling books and seminaries avoid or deny this topic. Fortunately writers like Friesen,[21] Smith,[22] MacNutt[23] and Horrobin[24] among others are willing to address this issue seriously in the professional arena and in ministry.

The indispensable personal requirements then include growth in the spiritual gifts, understanding and knowing His presence, experience in collaborating with Jesus and His Spirit and steadily growing in the wisdom and character of God and the mind of Christ. Those have been the requirements for centuries in the Church and are prior to any professional criteria.

Needed: Healing Prayer Teams in Every Church

I thoroughly enjoy training people in the ministry of healing prayer. It is wonderful to watch the gifts of the Spirit begin to appear among God's people and see that sense of joy as God's people learn about the ways of God and the issues of the soul.

But will God's people have the energy and make the time for this ministry? Yes! We must first remember that it is not ever a question of competence or professionalism. In fact one's knowledge and supposed competence can easily get in the way of letting Jesus do the healing and taking a secondary role. A true feeling of inadequacy is a prior qualification for this ministry. Payne, in a chapter entitled, "Celebrating Our Smallness," reflected on a prayer time with Charles:

> ...I still do the same simple thing: invoke the presence of Jesus and trust in Him. I am still as inadequate in the face of any one of the needs I see today as I was in the face of Charles' need so long ago. I now have more experience and more knowledge of the faithfulness of God. But I could celebrate my inadequacy, my smallness then and I can now. To stop celebrating it would gravely threaten the ministry of prayer for healing. "When I am weak (in

human strength), then am I (truly) strong—able, powerful in divine strength" (2 Cor. 12:10b, Amplified).[25]

Smith came to a similar understanding after years of feeling burnout and defeat from using traditional counseling:

> I spent many years seeking to help people with emotional pain by giving them my truth. I prayed with them, quoted Scripture to them, counseled them, encouraged them and yet they still remained in pain. It wasn't until I admitted my inadequacy and depended on Christ alone to free people that I began to see consistent miracles occur.[26]

When Gideon was preparing to battle the Midianites, the Lord told him that he had too many men (Judg. 7:2). God did not want Israel to boast that her own strength saved her, so the Lord reduced the numbers from 32,000 to just 300 fighting men (Judg. 7:8). With such impossible odds, the victory could only be due to God's strength and power, and He alone should receive all the glory. Likewise God alone should be glorified in the healing of the human soul and not therapeutic technique or the wisdom of man.

For a number of reasons the nation of Israel eventually wanted a king. One reason was that they could have a visible leader who would go ahead of them in battle like all the other nations (1 Sam. 8:19). They would rather rely on a visible king to develop strategy, give orders and so forth. Relying on a presence which might come at the "last moment" or in ways not ever anticipated was uncomfortable at times. There is a similar application in healing prayer when there is a desire for methods, procedures or techniques, like all the other therapies of the world, instead of the presence.

In healing prayer centered in the presence, Jesus does much of the work and we collaborate with Him in what He is doing. Thus burn out is rare. Instead it is refreshing and amazing to watch Jesus

331

heal His people. This is a paradigm shift! I remember one conference where I was steadily praying with people until 2:00 in the morning. When I left, people were still waiting for prayer from the other teams. Even so, I was not tired at all because it was truly the Lord's work and not mine. I was filled and sustained with His joy as I saw people deeply touched by Jesus and His Spirit. I have found over the years that the ministry of healing prayer actually energizes me instead of causing burnout and depleting energy.

The ministry of healing prayer can make a major contribution towards the healing and strengthening of marriages. Much of marital conflict and unhappiness comes from the woundedness and past issues of one or both of the marriage partners. It's almost like each partner is "bumping into" manifestations of past pain, sin or woundedness in the other partner. As each partner seeks healing prayer for their own issues apart from the current marriage dynamic, the marriage often begins to improve. Previously complex issues in the marriage become simpler and often begin to disappear as each or ideally both partners seek more healing and wholeness from Jesus through healing prayer. Traditional marriage counseling will also help to understand marriage communication, expectations, roles, commitment and so forth. This all helps to lessen the demands upon clergy and strengthens the body of Christ.

The Church needs thousands more healing prayer teams—the need is just too great! Pastors and clergy who mentor and maintain healing prayer teams will find that most people are excited about this ministry and are truly energized by the joy of the Lord. This is part of "liberating the laity" and lessening the load from pastors who often become burdened and wearied with the work of counseling along with their other responsibilities. For additional reasons clergy burnout is so common that the pastor has been called an "endangered species."[27]

The formation of healing prayer teams in churches is part of the fulfillment of the Great Commission.[28] Since each church is more like a military barracks with Jesus as the commanding officer, healing prayer helps to strengthen the soldiers of the cross in the service of the King of Kings (Eph. 6:10). This is also an expression of our love for Jesus as we obey His commands (1 John 5:3-4a) and fix our eyes solely on Him (Heb. 12:2).

Jesus as the True Enlightenment

I have always been bothered by the term "Enlightenment era" in world history. As I see it, that era has brought darkness upon the world. The Enlightenment embodies idolatries of the mind and will that demand the allegiance of people and contribute to the disintegration of Western society.[29] As Hosea wrote "...*they make idols for themselves to their own destruction*" (Hos. 8:4c).

Enlightenment belongs to Jesus alone. Jesus is the light of men that shines in the darkness (John 1:4-5) and gives light to all people (John 1:9). Jesus is the light of the world (John 8:12, 9:5) and a light to all nations (Isa. 42:6, 49:6). Jesus is the True Enlightenment, and His wisdom surpasses anything in the world. Jesus is also the greatest intellect who ever walked the face of the earth. Willard referred to Jesus as the Master of Intellect:

> ...you can be very sure that nothing fundamental has changed in our knowledge of ultimate reality and the human self since the time of Jesus.... The multitudes of theories, facts and techniques that have emerged in recent centuries have not the least logical bearing upon the ultimate issues of existence and life. In this respect they only serve to distract and confuse a people already harassed witless by their slogans, scientific advances.... [30]

Jesus is the only one competent enough to tell us the truth about life, existence, meaning and ultimate reality. We become enlightened when we live in union and connection with Him and His people and learn to live in His kingdom. In contrast to the words of theorists and philosophers, the words of Jesus are spirit and life (John 6:63).

From Healing Souls to Fixing Brains

In this book I have referred to psychiatry in a number of places. As is well known, the Church has become quite accepting of psychiatry. Dan Blazer makes this clear:

> Many committed Christians with no serious mental disorders have sought my services specifically for a prescription of Prozac. Christian counselors and pastors have quickly deferred to me when emotional pain persists and Christian patients referred to me have willingly accepted almost every drug prescribed. Though some Christians continue to resist medications, the trend is clearly toward acceptance.[31]

What is not well known in the Church is that there is a huge debate concerning the validity of some of the major assumptions in psychiatry. For example many prominent Christian authors and much of the Church accepts the notion that a chemical imbalance of neurotransmitters in the brain causes clinical depression and other "mental illnesses." I used to believe that also without question. After all, "all truth is God's truth." I was somewhat shocked to discover that this is not true.

That belief is thoroughly contested by eminent scientists and authorities and for solid reasons. For example Joseph Glenmullen, a clinical instructor in psychiatry at the Harvard Medical School, concluded the following concerning Prozac and the serotonin-dopamine connection after an extensive compilation of medical research: "The unfortunate irony is that drugs heavily promoted as correcting unproven biochemical imbalances may, in fact, be causing imbalances and brain damage."[32]

Elliot Valenstein, Professor Emeritus of Psychology and Neuroscience at the University of Michigan, after years of research concluded:

> The chemical theories of mental disorders are particularly seductive because they suggest that a relatively simple explanation and solution exist for a problem that has been regarded as complex and often stubbornly resistant to treatment. We are living in an age that has little tolerance for uncertainty and ambiguity... not only has it not been established that chemical imbalances are the major cause of mental disorders, but the theory from which these ideas emanate may well be wrong.[33]

This all means that many Christians are unnecessarily on psychiatric drugs. Not only is there a considerable amount of scientific evidence to show that psychiatric drugs actually cause a chemical imbalance in the brain rather than correcting an imbalance as a supposed cause of "mental illness," the hazards and long-term negative effects of such drugs are actually worse than commonly believed.[34]

Due to the Great Substitution, many believers did not experience the healing presence of Jesus and were by default offered a chemical solution for their very real and deep emotional pain. This has led to more chemistry instead of more of Christ, more Prozac instead of more prayer and more lithium instead of more love. The care of souls is steadily reduced to fixing brains.

I sympathize with believers who "never had a good feeling" about psychiatric drugs but never knew why. That is only part of a huge and complex story which deserves a book in itself. Accordingly it will be explored in depth along with a biblical analysis of psychiatry in a forthcoming book, *The Great Reduction: From Healing Souls to Fixing Brains*.

I have had the immense privilege of ministering healing prayer to Jodine as part of her healing journey. Jodine knows the world of psychiatry well, having lived in it for many years. Jodine has also experienced the power of Jesus' presence and looks forward to what Jesus has yet in store for her.

Jodine's Depression and Psychiatric Drugs

I entered the world of psychiatry at thirteen years of age. I have had seventeen sets of shock treatments ending in 1995. It only "cured" me for six weeks. I have attempted suicide more than two hundred times. Yes, some attempts were cries for help since I was in so much pain and did not know how to communicate even though I was an adult physically. But I was a child inside, a child who needed love and acceptance to grow. When I first became a Christian, the psychiatrists thought I was crazy. But this is not true, since the Word and the healing power of God are more real and alive than any antidepressant or antipsychotic medication.

When I was nineteen years old, I had still not remembered my childhood sexual abuse. I was in a psychiatric ward, diagnosed as psychotic. If I was truly psychotic, I would not remember the following so clearly. The mental health system was filling me up with Haldol and it was early in the evening one day. I was with the other patients as they were having their supper. A nurse happened to walk by, and I screamed, "There is blood all over your pants." She was wearing a bright red very blood-like color pair of pants. Twenty years later, now with so much healing and knowing the truth of my past, I know that I was seeing the blood that was there when my father raped me and cut my vagina. At around twenty-four years of age I would always say, "I hear blood dripping." The psychiatrists simply stated that I was once again going psychotic. But the "dripping" was a memory of the time I was first raped and cut with a sharp object—a kitchen knife. Before long I had total memory recall through healing prayer ministry and by seeing a Christian therapist where the therapy was Christ-centered. Before the memory was totally recalled, I acted out of the hidden memory numerous times which sometimes involved cutting the inside of my own vagina. I thank the Lord I never cut it badly.

In the world of psychiatry they look for fast solutions—labels and medication. When I went under the care of a Christian therapist and experienced Christ-centered therapy after years of "normal" psychiatric therapy, things "started to move." I was diagnosed with MPD (Multiple Personality Disorder) or the new term DID (Dissociative Identity Disorder). I had seven different personalities of different ages. I found out through a doctor friend in our city and another doctor that my problem for over twelve years was due to being denied proper care. In the bigger picture I was coming to the point where God would clearly reveal Himself to me with healing from both prayer and Christ-centered therapy. I keep repeating "Christ-centered" since that is the key to such therapy—Christ Himself. My Christian psychiatrist and I would give the Lord control. It took three seemingly short years after being in psychiatric care for twenty-five years.

For two years I knew the Lord had said that He would use Dieter powerfully in finally setting me free. That does not take away from the prayer ministry of others or their walking alongside with me. God was telling me these things to strengthen me. I was not even aware that I was being patient for His time of healing. I always said and believed that I would be healed on God's timetable and not man's.

In May 2000 the Lord told me that I would be coming to a more complete healing sooner. For me that meant letting go of the need to be constantly in crisis and thus get attention from others. But it was the Lord speaking to me. I cried from May to October 2000 daily, once for twelve hours straight. Healing came through the tears which helped release grief, pain and sadness. On top of all this, my beloved grandmother took five weeks to pass on in the summer months. I cried even more. She gave me more gifts in her last five weeks than I could ever explain, but I did not even see her.

The more that depression, sadness, grief and anger are masked by powerful psychiatric medications, the longer it takes to heal. Yes, I am still on two antidepressants. No, these meds did not heal me, but they are there to help the rest of the healing happen. Then and only then will I know without the shadow of a doubt that the Lord has set me free of that need entirely.

Now back to the five months from May to October. In 2000 I hit the area of pain and despair, but at the same time my spirit knew that something big was happening... all those boxes of Kleenex. On October 11, 2001, I was in a suicidal haze I'll call it, or better yet, an attack of the devil. At other times in this state I could almost feel the battle of evil against me and the Lord who was with me. I could almost see the spiritual battle, and then I was on my way to my church. It turns out that a sister in Christ was in the healing prayer meeting, and during the worship time the Lord kept putting me on her heart. She was obedient, phoned me and came to my apartment. The police had also arrived and wanted to take me to the hospital. But I resisted, saying it would not make me better but worse.

We arrived at the church and eventually, when I was receiving prayer ministry, there were five people praying around me. Dieter came later and took the lead in the healing prayer. Dieter asked the Holy Spirit to come upon me with His peace, and then He asked Jesus to come right into the deepest of my pain and trauma. After some moments He asked Jesus to re-integrate me, to make me one person in Him. I finally screamed, "I am not Jennifer"—the integration had happened. The insight here is that this was so important because I even went by the name "Jennifer" from age thirteen to fourteen. At that time in my life I told the psychiatrist I was more than one person. From that time I was "hushed" with medication—Haldol, Stelazine and Mellaril. At times I was given combinations of these drugs, other times just one of them. It has been eight months today since I was integrated. The Lord knew when I would be healed and free of MPD. In the end, three years of intense Christ-centered therapy and prayer ministry is a short time considering the truth of the severity of my trauma.

In the mental health system people are labeled and crippled with various perceptions, attitudes, stigmas and pronouncements. This has been my experience. For example I was told, "You are unstable," or, "You are ill." Mental victimization then starts in a spiral from being labeled "mentally ill." I was first diagnosed with schizophrenia because I heard voices. Years later I recognized those voices as coming from my past and from me crying out in different stages of pain. The psychiatrist's action of doping me up with Haldol and other meds only stifled the feelings. The feelings then came out over the following many years as suicide or harming myself as in burning myself or cutting myself and then in intense rages. In psychiatry this fits into the awful label of "borderline personality disorder." But during that time, as a young teenager, I had lost seven close family members in five years. I was not psychotic but depressed and the grieving was suppressed, thus I developed this "disorder." It took years for the stifled grief to be processed and finally released. Today I know that the grief is for the losses I had experienced.

The world's view of depression is that an individual cannot snap out of it. The pronouncement is something like, "Oh my, you are mentally ill." In my experience depression is—and this will sound weird—actually a good sign. It means that you are feeling, that you are not in denial of life as if you would rather believe that all is going well. Depression is a symptom just as sneezing and a runny nose are symptoms that you have a cold from a virus. Colds are accepted as everyday occurrences in North America, and so is depression. For a cold you take a pill, and for depression now you take a pill. I am presently taking two different antidepressants, Wellbutrin and Manirix, but they are not doing much. They are not doing much because my depression is an extension of my depth of pain. I'm sad about my poor physical health due partly to the effects of antipsychotic drugs over many years. In common with many others who experience depression, I suffer from loneliness, isolation, financial difficulty or losses of any kind, low sense of worthiness and more. Christians also feel these things.

For me the greatest pain is from abandonment which is deep in the mind and spirit. Bringing Christ into the picture is the beginning of healing. I believe medicating people against anxiety should stop. Anxiety is really the clue of pain deep within the center of us. In that center only Christ can heal; no pill will ever do it, neither will money, gambling, drugs or food—the list is miles long. We can get our "fixes" from almost anything, but it will only be a temporary anesthetic for depression and inner pain. I think the greatest inner pain for all mankind comes from the need to be loved and accepted.

To start to heal from the depression, one must go to God and oneself deep within. Yes, going into one's center and letting oneself feel is scary. But once this journey begins and you truly start to heal, there is no turning back. Oh, you may want to turn back, but deep within you your spirit has felt the love of Christ and the pain of whatever your issues have been. Those issues may be sexual, emotional, physical, from abuse or even neglect. Neglect is just as painful as any abuse, it is just different in nature. I feel that inner pain and it does hurt, but it also frees up the spirit, mind and body. I am in the process of this journey. I do not know if it will ever end, for it never totally does for anyone. Through our lives and journeys we will encounter pain and loss and more. But the key is Christ, to first let yourself feel deep within and know that at that place the Lord will meet you, for the inner being is the deepest level of ourselves where the pain is buried.

My antidepressants are only like a rope to hang onto in this painful but healing journey. Like I have, you will cry when you feel again, and it may seem unbearable, but He will not give us more than we can handle. Allow yourself to feel the inner pain, and in that moment, you will get back the largest gift—the very love of Christ as He meets you there in the midst of it.

In the final analysis, it's all about Jesus!

Endnotes ———————

[1] Charles H. Kraft, *Christianity With Power: Your Worldview and Your Experience of the Supernatural* (Ann Arbor: Servant Books, 1989) pp. 37-50.

[2] Kraft, p. 41.

[3] Mark R. McMinn, *Psychology, Theology and Spirituality in Christian Counseling. AACC Counseling Library* (Wheaton: Tyndale House Publisher, 1996) pp. 21, 79.

4 Mary Stewart Van Leeuwen, *The Sorcerer's Apprentice: A Christian Looks at the Changing Face of Psychology* (Downers Grove: InterVarsity Press, 1982) p. 99.

5 McMinn, p. 121.

6 Roger F. Hurding, *Roots And Shoots: A Guide to Counselling And Psychotherapy* (London: Hodder and Stoughton, 1985) p. 332.

7 Kraft, p. 72.

8 Dieter Mulitze, *The Great Omission: Resolving Critical Issues for the Ministry of Healing and Deliverance* (Belleville: Essence Publishers, 2001) pp. 115-185.

9 Brad Long and Cindy Strickler, *Let Jesus Heal Your Hidden Wounds: Cooperating With the Holy Spirit in Healing Ministry* (Grand Rapids: Chosen Books, 2001) p. 53.

10 McMinn, p. 90.

11 McMinn, p. 91.

12 Neil T. Anderson, Terry E. Zuehlke and Julianne S. Zuehlke, *Christ Centered Therapy: The Practical Integration of Theology and Psychology* (Grand Rapids: Zondervan Publishing House, 2000) pp. 164-168.

13 Van Leeuwen, pp. 111-113.

14 David F. Wells, *No Place for Truth or Whatever Happened to Evangelical Theology?* (Grand Rapids: Eerdmans Publishing Co., 1993) p. 225.

15 Wells, pp. 218-257.

16 Wells, p. 221.

17 Wells, pp. 219, 222.

18 Gary R. Collins, *Christian Counseling: A Comprehensive Guide* (Waco: Word Books Publisher, 1980) p. 54.

19 Edward M. Smith, *Healing Life's Deepest Hurts: Let the Light of Christ Dispel the Darkness in Your Soul* (Ann Arbor: Vine Books, 2002) p. 26.

20 Mulitze, pp. 229-275.

21 James G. Friesen, *Uncovering the Mystery of MPD* (Eugene: Wipf and Stock Publishers, 1991).

22 Ed M. Smith, *Beyond Tolerable Recovery* (Campbellsville: Alathia

Publishing, 1996, 4th ed. 2000) pp. 286-293.

23 Peter J. Horrobin, *Healing Through Deliverance: The Practical Ministry* (Kent: Sovereign World Ltd., 1995).

24 Francis MacNutt, *Deliverance from Evil Spirits: A Practical Manual* (Grand Rapids: Chosen Books, 1995).

25 Leanne Payne, *The Healing Presence: How God's Grace Can Work in You to Bring Healing in Your Broken Places and the Joy of Living in His Love* (Wheaton: Crossway Books, 1989) p. 20.

26 Smith, 2002, pp. 14, 16.

27 R.A. Swenson, *The Overload Syndrome: Learning to Live Within Your Limits* (Colorado Springs: NavPress, 1998) p. 181.

28 Mulitze, pp. 55-76.

29 Herbert Schlossberg, *Idols for Destruction* (Nashville: Thomas Nelson Publishers, 1983) pp. 262-263.

30 Dallas Willard, *The Divine Conspiracy: Rediscovering Our Hidden Life in God* (San Francisco: Harper Collins, 1998) p. 93.

31 Dan Blazer, *Freud vs. God: How Psychiatry Lost Its Soul & Christianity Lost Its Mind* (Downers Grove: InterVarsity Press, 1998) p. 112.

32 Joseph Glenmullen, *Prozac Backlash: Overcoming the Dangers of Prozac, Zoloft, Paxil and Other Antidepressants with Safe, Effective Alternatives* (New York: Simon & Schuster, 2000) p. 50.

33 Elliot S. Valenstein, *Blaming the Brain: The Truth About Drugs and Mental Health* (New York: The Free Press, 1998) pp. 234-2

34 Peter R. Breggin and David Cohen, *Your Drug May Be Your Problem: How and Why to Stop Taking Psychiatric Drugs* (Cambridge: Perseus Publishing, 1999) pp. 33-110.

 Bibliography

Adams, Jay E. *Competent to Counsel.* Nutley: Presbyterian and Reformed Publishing Co., 1977.

Almy, Gary. *How Christian is Christian Counseling?* Wheaton: Crossway Books, 2000.

Anderson, Neil T., Zuehlke, Terry E., and Julianne S. Zuehlke. *Christ Centered Therapy: The Practical Integration of Theology and Psychology.* Grand Rapids: Zondervan Publishing House, 2000.

Ankerberg, John, and John Weldon. *Encyclopedia of New Age Beliefs.* Eugene: Harvest House Publishers, 1996.

Armstrong, John. H., ed. *The Coming Evangelical Crisis: Current Challenges to the Authority of Scripture and the Gospel.* Chicago: Moody Press, 1996.

Baker, Mark W. *The Greatest Psychologist Who Ever Lived: Jesus and the Wisdom of the Soul.* New York: HarperCollins Publishers, 2001.

Barclay, Oliver R. *The Intellect and Beyond.* Grand Rapids: Academie Books, 1985.

Barrett, William. *Death of the Soul: From Descartes to the Computer.* New York: Anchor Press/Doubleday, 1986.

Benner, David G. *Care of Souls: Revisioning Christian Nurture and Counsel.* Grand Rapids: Baker Books, 1998.

Bennett, Rita. *Emotionally Free.* Old Tappan: Fleming H. Revell Co., 1982.

Bergner, Mario. *Setting Love in Order: Hope and Healing for the Homosexual.* Grand Rapids: Hamewith Books, 1995.

Blazer, Dan. *Freud vs. God: How Psychiatry Lost Its Soul & Christianity Lost Its Mind.* Downers Grove: InterVarsity Press, 1998.

Block, Daniel I. *The Book of Ezekiel, Chapters 1-24: The New International Commentary on the Old Testament.* Grand Rapids: Eerdmans Publishing Co., 1997.

Block, Daniel I. *The Book of Ezekiel, Chapters 25-48: The New International Commentary on the Old Testament.* Grand Rapids: Eerdmans Publishing Co., 1998.

Bloesch, Donald G. *A Theology of Word & Spirit: Authority & Methodology in Theology.* Downers Grove: InterVarsity Press, 1992.

Bobgan, Martin and Deidre. *PsychoHeresy: The Psychological Seduction of Christianity.* Santa Barbara: EastGate Publishers, 1987.

Bobgan, Martin and Deidre. *Competent to Minister: The Biblical Care of Souls.* Santa Barbara: EastGate Publishers, 1996.

Bobgan, Martin and Deidre. *The End of "Christian Psychology."* Santa Barbara: EastGate Publishers, 1997.

Bobgan, Martin and Deidre. *Theophostic Counseling: Divine Revelation or PsychoHeresy?* Santa Barbara: EastGate Publishers, 1999.

Bobgan, Martin and Deidre. *Hypnosis: Medical, Scientific, or Occultic?* Santa Barbara: EastGate Publishers, 2001.

Boice, James Montgomery. *Mind Renewal in a Mindless Age.* Grand Rapids: Baker Books, 1993.

Breggin, Peter R. and David Cohen. *Your Drug May Be Your Problem: How and Why to Stop Taking Psychiatric Drugs.* Cambridge: Perseus Publishing, 1999.

Brod, Craig. *Technostress: The Human Cost of the Computer Revolution.* Reading: Addison-Wesley, 1984.

Brooke, Tal, ed. *The Conspiracy to Silence the Son of God.* Eugene: Harvest House Publishers, 1998.

Brown, Colin, ed. *Dictionary of New Testament Theology,* Vol. 2. Grand

Rapids: Zondervan Publishing House, 1976.

Bruce, F.F. *The Epistle to the Colossians, to Philemon, and to the Ephesians: The New International Commentary on the New Testament.* Grand Rapids: Eerdmans Publishing Co., 1984.

Bruce, F.F. *The Book of the Acts Revised: The New International Commentary on the New Testament.* Grand Rapids: Eerdmans Publishing Co., 1988.

Buchanan, Duncan. *The Counselling of Jesus.* Downers Grove: InterVarsity Press, 1985.

Busen, Karl M. "Eternity and the Personal God," *Journal of the American Scientific Affiliation,* 49(1): 40-49, 1997.

Cloud, Henry. *Changes that Heal: How to Understand Your Past to Ensure a Healthier Future.* Grand Rapids: Zondervan Publishing House, 1992.

Collins, Gary. *The Rebuilding of Psychology: An Integration of Psychology and Christianity.* Wheaton: Tyndale House Publishers, 1977.

Collins, Gary R. *Christian Counseling: A Comprehensive Guide.* Waco: Word Books Publisher, 1980.

Crabb, Lawrence J., Jr. *Basic Principles of Biblical Counseling.* Grand Rapids: Zondervan Publishing House, 1975.

Crabb, Lawrence J., Jr. *Effective Biblical Counseling.* Grand Rapids: Zondervan Publishing House, 1977.

Crabb, Larry. *Connecting: Healing for Ourselves and Our Relationships, A Radical New Vision.* Nashville: Word Publishing, 1997.

Dawes, Robyn M. *House of Cards: Psychology and Psychotherapy Built on Myth.* New York: Free Press, 1994.

Dearing, Norma. *The Healing Touch: A Guide to Healing Prayer for Yourself and Those You Love.* Grand Rapids: Chosen Books, 2002.

DeArteaga, William. *Quenching the Spirit: Discover the REAL Spirit Behind the Charismatic Controversy.* Orlando: Creation House, 1992.

Deere, Jack. *Surprised by the Voice of God: How God Speaks Today Through Prophecies, Dreams, and Visions.* Grand Rapids: Zondervan Publishing House, 1996.

Deinhardt, Carol, ed. *Foundational Issues in Christian Counselling*. Otterburne: ProvPress, 1997.

DeMar, Gary and Peter J. Leithart, *The Reduction of Christianity: A Biblical Response to Dave Hunt*. Fort Worth: Dominion Press, 1988.

Elliott, Lynda D. *An Invitation to Healing*. Grand Rapids: Chosen Books, 2001.

Ellul, Jacques. *The Technological Society*. New York: Vintage Books, 1964.

Emerson, Allen, and Cheryl Forbes. *The Invasion of the Computer Culture*. Downers Grove: InterVaristy Press, 1989.

Fee, Gordon D. *The First Epistle to the Corinthians: The New International Commentary on the New Testament*. Grand Rapids: Eerdmans Publishing Co., 1987.

Fee, Gordon D. *God's Empowering Presence: The Holy Spirit in the Letters of Paul*. Peabody: Hendrickson Publishers, Inc., 1994.

Flynn, Mike, and Doug Gregg. *Inner Healing: A Handbook for Helping Yourself & Others*. Downers Grove: InterVarsity Press, 1993.

Fox, Emmet. *The Sermon on the Mount*. New York: Harper and Brothers Publishers, 1934.

Friesen, James G. *Uncovering the Mystery of MPD*. Eugene: Wipf and Stock Publishers, 1991.

Ganz, Richard. *PsychoBabble: The Failure of Modern Psychology—and the Biblical Alternative*. Wheaton: Crossway Books, 1993.

Gay, Craig M. *The Way of the (Modern) World. Or, Why It's Tempting to Live as if God Doesn't Exist*. Grand Rapids: Eerdmans Publishing Company, 1998.

Gayle, Grace M.H. *The Growth of the Person: Psychology on Trial*. Belleville: Essence Publishers, 2001.

Geldenhuys, Norval. *The Gospel of Luke: The New International Commentary on the New Testament*. Grand Rapids: Eerdmans Publishing Co., 1951.

Glenmullen, Joseph. *Prozac Backlash: Overcoming the Dangers of Prozac, Zoloft, Paxil and Other Antidepressants with Safe, Effective Alternatives*. New York: Simon & Schuster, 2000.

Godwin, Rick. *Exposing Witchcraft in the Church.* Santa Barbara: Creation House, 1997.

Greig, Gary S., and Kevin N. Springer, eds. *The Kingdom and the Power: Are Healing and the Spiritual Gifts Used by Jesus and the Early Church Meant for the Church Today?* Ventura: Regal Books, 1993.

Guiness, Os. *Fit Bodies Fat Minds: Why Evangelicals Don't Think and What to Do About It.* Grand Rapids: Baker Books, 1994.

Gumprecht, Jane. *Abusing Memory: The Healing Theology of Agnes Sanford.* Moscow: Canon Press, 1997.

Hamilton, Victor. *The Book of Genesis, Chapters 18-50: The New International Commentary on the Old Testament.* Grand Rapids: Eerdmans,1995.

Hart, Archibald. *Adrenaline and Stress.* Dallas: Word Publishing, 1991.

Hart, Thomas N. *The Art of Christian Listening.* New York: Paulist Press, 1980.

Hanegraaf, Hank. *Christianity in Crisis.* Eugene: Harvest House Publishers, 1993.

Hinman, Nelson. *An Answer to Humanistic Psychology.* Irvine: Harvest House Publishers, 1980.

Horrobin, Peter J. *Healing Through Deliverance: The Practical Ministry.* Kent: Sovereign World Ltd., 1995.

Hostetler, Jep. "Humor, Spirituality, Well-Being," *Journal of the American Scientific Affiliation*, Vol. 54(2), 2002

Houston, James. *I Believe in the Creator.* Grand Rapids: Eerdmans Publishing Co., 1980.

Houston, James. *The Transforming Friendship - A Guide to Prayer.* Batavia: Lion Publishing, 1989.

Hunt, Dave, and T.A. McMahon. *The Seduction of Christianity.* Eugene: Harvest House Publishers, 1985.

Hurding, Roger F. *Roots And Shoots: A Guide to Counselling and Psychotherapy.* London: Hodder and Stoughton, 1985.

Hurding, Roger. *The Bible and Counselling*. London: Hodder and Stoughton, 1992.

Jacobson, Michael D. *The Word on Health: A Biblical and Medical Overview of How to Care for Your Body and Mind*. Chicago: Moody Press, 2000.

Jones, Stanton L., and Richard E. Butman. *Modern Psychotherapies: A Comprehensive Christian Appraisal*. Downers Grove: InterVarsity Press, 1991.

Kelsey, Morton. *Christianity as Psychology*. Minneapolis: Augsburg Publishing House, 1986.

Kelsey, Morton. *Healing and Christianity*. Minneapolis: Augsburg Publishing, 1995.

Kilpatrick, William Kirk. *The Emporer's New Clothes: The Naked Truth About the New Psychology*. Westchester: Crossway Books, 1985.

Kraft, Charles H. *Christianity With Power: Your Worldview and Your Experience of the Supernatural*. Ann Arbor: Servant Books, 1989.

Kraft, Charles H. *Deep Wounds, Deep Healing: Discovering the Vital Link between Spiritual Warfare and Inner Healing*. Ann Arbor: Servant Publications, 1993.

Kydd, Ronald A.N. *Healing Through the Centuries: Models for Understanding*. Peabody: Hendrickson Publishers, Inc., 1998.

LaHaye, Tim. *How to Win Over Depression*. Grand Rapids: Zondervan Publishing House, 1974.

Lewis, Howard R. and Martha E. *Psychosomatics: How Your Emotions Can Damage Your Health*. New York: The Viking Press, 1972.

Linn, Dennis and Matthew. *Healing of Memories*. Ramsey: Paulist Press, 1974.

Long, Brad, and Cindy Strickler. *Let Jesus Heal Your Hidden Wounds: Cooperating With the Holy Spirit in Healing Ministry*. Grand Rapids: Chosen Books, 2001.

MacArthur, John F., Jr. *Charismatic Chaos*. Grand Rapids: Zondervan, 1992.

MacNutt, Francis. *Deliverance from Evil Spirits: A Practical Manual.* Grand Rapids: Chosen Books, 1995.

Marshall, Tom. *Free Indeed!* Kent: Sovereign World Ltd, 1975.

Martin, Walter R. *The Kingdom of the Cults.* Minneapolis: Bethany Fellowship, Inc., 1965, revised edition 1977.

Matzat, Don. *Inner Healing: Deliverance or Deception?* Eugene: Harvest House Publishers, 1987.

McConnell, D.R. *A Different Gospel: Biblical and Historical Insights into the Word of Faith Movement.* Peabody: Hendrickson Publishers, 1995.

McGrath, Alister E. *Christian Theology: An Introduction.* Oxford: Blackwell Publishers, 1994.

McMinn, Mark R. *Psychology, Theology, and Spirituality in Christian Counseling. AACC Counseling Library.* Wheaton: Tyndale House Publisher, 1996.

McMinn, Mark R., and Timothy R. Phillips. *Care for the Soul: Exploring the Intersection of Psychology & Theology.* Downers Grove: InterVarsity Press, 2001.

Morris, Leon. *The Gospel According to John Revised: The New International Commentary on the New Testament.* Grand Rapids: Eerdmans Publishing Co., 1995.

Mulitze, Dieter. *The Great Omission: Resolving Critical Issues for the Ministry of Healing and Deliverance.* Belleville: Essence Publishers, 2001.

Narramore, Clyde M. *The Psychology of Counseling.* Grand Rapids: Zondervan Publishing House, 1960.

Newbigin, Lesslie. *Foolishness to the Greeks: The Gospel and Western Culture.* Grand Rapids: Eerdmans Publishing Co., 1986.

Oakland, James A., North, Gerald O., Camilleri, Rosemary, Stenberg, Brent, Venable, George Daniel, and Kenneth W. Bowers. "An Analysis and Critique of Jay Adams' Theory of Counseling," *Journal of the American Scientific Affiliation,* Vol. 28(3), 1976, pp. 101-109.

Oates, Wayne E. *The Presence of God in Pastoral Counseling.* Waco: Word Books, 1986.

Payne, Leanne. *The Broken Image: Restoring Personal Wholeness Through Healing Prayer.* Wheaton: Crossway Books, 1981.

Payne, Leanne. *Crisis in Masculinity.* Wheaton: Crossway Books, 1985.

Payne, Leanne. *Real Presence: The Christian Worldview of C.S. Lewis as Incarnational Reality.* Wheaton: Crossway Books, 1988.

Payne, Leanne. *The Healing Presence: How God's Grace Can Work in You to Bring Healing in Your Broken Places and the Joy of Living in His Love.* Wheaton, Crossway Books, 1989.

Payne, Leanne. *Restoring the Christian Soul Through Healing Prayer: Overcoming the Three Great Barriers to Personal and Spiritual Completion in Christ.* Wheaton: Crossway Books, 1991.

Payne, Leanne. *Listening Prayer.* Grand Rapids: Hamewith Books, 1994.

Peale, Norman Vincent. *Positive Imaging: The Powerful Way to Change Your Life.* New York: Fawcett Crest, 1982, formerly published as *Dynamic Imaging.*

Peale, Norman Vincent. *The Power of Positive Thinking.* Englewood Cliffs: Prentice-hall, Inc., 1956.

Peale, Norman Vincent. *The Positive Power of Jesus Christ.* Wheaton: Tyndale Publishers, Inc., 1980.

Pearson, Mark A. *Christian Healing: A Practical and Comprehensive Guide.* Grand Rapids: Chosen Books, 1995.

Piersma, Harry. "Christianity and Psychology: Some Reflections," *Journal of the American Scientific Affiliation*, Vol. 28(3), 1976

Pytches, David. *Come Holy Spirit: Learning How to Minister in Power,* 2nd ed. London: Hodder & Stoughton, 1995.

Pytches, Mary. *Yesterday's Child.* London: Hodder and Stoughton, 1990.

Pytches, Mary. *Dying to Change: An exposure of the self-protective strategies which prevent us becoming like Jesus.* London: Hodder & Stoughton, 1996.

Reisser, Paul C., Mabe, Dale, and Robert Velarde. *Examining Alternative Medicine: An Inside Look at the Benefits & Risks.* Downers Grove: InterVarsity Press, 2001.

Rhodes, Ron. *The Counterfeit Christ of the New Age Movement.* Grand Rapids: Baker Book House, 1990.

Rhodes, Ron. *Christ Before the Manger: The Life and Times of the Preincarnate Christ.* Grand Rapids: Baker Books, 1993.

Roberts, Robert C. *Taking the Word to Heart: Self and Other in an Age of Therapies.* Grand Rapids: Eerdmans Publishing Co., 1993.

Sandford, John and Paula. *The Transformation of the Inner Man.* Tulsa: Victory House, 1982.

Sandford, John and Mark. *Deliverance and Inner Healing: A Comprehensive Guide.* Grand Rapids: Chosen Books, 1992.

Sandford, John and Paula. *Healing the Wounded Spirit.* Tulsa: Victory House, 1985.

Sandford, Paula. *Healing Women's Emotions.* Tulsa: Victory House, 1992.

Sanford, Agnes. *The Healing Light.* Plainfield: Logos International, 1976, originally published in 1947 by Macalester Park Publishing Co.

Sanford, Agnes. *The Healing Touch of God.* New York: Ballantine Books, 5th printing, 1987, first published in 1958 by Macalester Publishing Co. as *Behold Your God.*

Sanford, Agnes. *The Healing Power of the Bible.* Philadelphia: Trumpet Books, 1969.

Sanford, Agnes. *Sealed Orders.* Plainfield: Logos International, 1972.

Sanford, Agnes. *The Healing Gifts of the Spirit.* Philadelphia: Trumpet Books, A.J. Holman Co., 1976.

Sanford, Agnes. *Creation Waits.* Plainfield: Logos International, 1977.

Satinover, Jeffrey. *The Empty Self: C.G. Jung and the Gnostic Transformation of Modern Identity.* Westport: Hamewith Books, 1996.

Scanlan, Michael. *Inner Healing: Ministering to the Human Spirit Through the Power of Prayer.* New York: Paulist Press, 1974.

Schlossberg, Herbert. *Idols for Destruction: Christian Faith and Its Confrontation with American Society.* Nashville: Thomas Nelson Publishers, 1983.

Schultze, Quentin J. *Habits of the High-Tech Heart: Living Virtuously in the Information Age.* Grand Rapids: Baker Academie, 2002.

Scott, Brad. *Embraced by the Darkness: Exposing New Age Theology from the Inside Out.* Wheaton: Crossway Books, 1996.

Scott, Steve, and Brooks Alexander, "Inner Healing," *SCP Journal,* Vol. 4/1, April 1980, Spiritual Counterfeits Project, Berkeley, California.

Seamands, David A. *Healing for Damaged Emotions: Recovering from the Memories That Cause Our Pain.* Wheaton: Victor Books, 1981.

Seamands, David A. *Healing of Memories.* Wheaton: Victor Books, 1985.

Smith, Ed M. *Beyond Tolerable Recovery.* Campbellsville: Alathia Publishing, 1996, 4th ed. 2000.

Smith, Edward M. *Healing Life's Hurts: Let the Light of Christ Dispel the Darkness in Your Soul.* Ann Arbor: Vine Books, 2002.

Sternberg, Esther M. *The Balance Within: The Science Connecting Health and Emotions.* New York: W.H. Freeman and Co., 2000.

Storkey, Elaine. *The Search for Intimacy.* London: Hodder and Stoughton, 1995.

Swenson, R.A. *The Overload Syndrome: Learning to Live Within Your Limits.* Colorado Springs: NavPress, 1998.

Tapscott, Betty. *Inner Healing Through Healing of Memories.* Kingwood: Hunter Publishing, 1975.

Tapscott, Betty. *Ministering Inner Healing Biblically.* Houston: Tapscott Ministries, 1987.

Thomas, Leo, O.P., with Jan Alkire. *Healing Ministry: A Practical Guide.* Kansas, Sheed & Ward, 1994.

Tournier, Paul. *The Whole Person in a Broken World.* New York: Harper & Row, 1964.

Tournier, Paul. *The Healing of Persons.* New York: Harper & Row, 1965.

Valenstein, Elliot S. *Blaming the Brain: The Truth About Drugs and Mental Health.* New York: The Free Press, 1998.

VanGemeren, Willem A., ed. *New International Dictionary of Old Testa-*

ment Theology & Exegesis, Vol. 4. Grand Rapids, Zondervan. 1997.

Van Leeuwen, Mary Stewart. *The Sorcerer's Apprentice: A Christian Looks at the Changing Face of Psychology.* Downers Grove: InterVarsity Press, 1982.

Verny, Thomas, M.D., with John Kelly. *The Secret Life of the Unborn Child: How you can prepare your unborn baby for a happy, healthy life.* New York: Dell Publishing Co., 1981.

Virkler, Mark and Patti. *Prayers that Heal the Heart.* Gainesville: Bridge-Logos Publishers, 2001.

Vitz, Paul C. *Psychology as Religion: The Cult of Self-Worship.* Grand Rapids: Eerdmans Publishing Co., 1977.

Volf, Miroslav. *Work in the Spirit: Toward a Theology of Work.* New York: Oxford University Press, 1991.

Waltke, Bruce K., with Cathi J. Fredricks. *Genesis: A Commentary.* Grand Rapids: Zondervan, 2001.

Weldon, John, and Zola Levitt. *Psychic Healing.* Chicago: Moody Press, 1982.

Wells, David F. *No Place for Truth or Whatever Happened to Evangelical Theology?* Grand Rapids: Eerdmans Publishing Co., 1993.

Wenham, Gordon. *The Book of Leviticus: The New International Commentary on the Old Testament.* Grand Rapids: Eerdmans Publishing Co., 1979.

White, Anne S. *Healing Adventure.* Plainfield: Logos International, 1972.

White, John. *When the Spirit Comes With Power: Signs & Wonders Among God's People.* Downers Grove, InterVarsity Press, 1988.

Willard, Dallas. *The Spirit of the Disciplines.* New York: HarperCollins, 1991.

Willard, Dallas. *The Divine Conspiracy: Rediscovering Our Hidden Life in God.* San Francisco: Harper Collins, 1998.

Willard, Dallas. *Hearing God: Developing a Conversational Relationship with God.* Downers Grove: InterVarsity Press, 1999.

Willard, Dallas. *Renovation of the Heart: Putting on the Character of Christ.*

Colorado Springs: NavPress, 2002.

Wilson, Clifford. *The Impact of Ebla on Bible Records.* Melbourne: Word of Truth Productions, 1977.

Wise, Robert, et al. *The Church Divided.* South Plainfield: Bridge Publishing, Inc., 1986.

Wimber, John, and Kevin Springer. *Power Healing.* New York: HarperCollins, 1987.

Wright, H. Norman. *The Healing of Fears.* Eugene: Harvest House Publishers, 1982.

Wright, H. Norman. *Making Peace With Your Past.* Old Tappan: Fleming H. Revell Co., 1985.

Zoeller-Greer, Peter. "Genesis, Quantum Physics and Reality. How the Bible Agrees With Quantum Physics—An Anthropic Principle of Another Kind: The Divine Anthropic Principle," *Journal of the American Scientific Affiliation*, 52(1):8-17, 2000.

Index

Printed in the United States
72121LV00002B/205